GRIM GAMBIT

Joseph McRae Palmer

GRIM GAMBIT

www.josephmcraepalmer.com

This book is a work of fiction. The characters, incidents, and dialog are drawn from the author's imagination and are not to be construed as real. Any resemblance to actual events or persons, living or dead, is fictionalized or coincidental.

ISBN (paperback) 978-1-961782-30-3
ISBN (ebook) 978-1-961782-29-7

Cover design: Donna Cunningham@BeauxArts.design

Prologue

You know, the funny thing about telling war stories when you're as old as I am—the lines between heroism and sheer dumb luck start to blur. My aide keeps telling me I should record these "for posterity," whatever the hell that means. So here I am, Admiral Kory Drake (retired), with joints that creak louder than an old starship hull and memories that sometimes feel like they happened to someone else entirely. But I promised you another chapter of this ridiculous odyssey I call my life, and if there's one thing decades of military service taught me, it's that you follow through on your promises—even the ill-advised ones.

Pour yourself something strong. You'll need it. I certainly do, especially for this part of the story. The whiskey helps with the arthritis, you see. At least that's what I tell the doctors.

Where did we leave off? Ah yes—Virelia. The glimmering jewel of the Collective Dominion, where I was supposed to stand trial for sydereal assault. Sounds impressive, doesn't it? Like I knew what the hell I was doing when I wounded Ban'ach during our fight in the Syderealium. The truth is, I was just a street kid from San Jose who somehow found himself captaining an insurgent starship called *Thunder,* then managed to piss off a female marac Soul Ravager. If you're detecting a pattern of me stumbling into situations beyond my understanding, congratulations—you're keeping up.

While awaiting trial on Virelia, the powers that be decided that instead of letting me pace around a cell, they'd send me to Officer Training School. Someone must have thought it was hilarious to take a former street orphan and teach him which fork to use at diplomatic dinners. I remember thinking they were trying to rehabilitate me—polish this rough human gem into something presentable to the Dominion courts. In reality, I suspect they were preparing me for what was to come, though I doubt anyone predicted exactly how sideways things would go.

The Space Warfare School followed. Let me tell you, there's nothing quite like learning tactical theory while simultaneously wondering if you'll be executed for crimes you barely understand. I was like a student cramming for finals while also preparing for his own funeral. Multi-tasking at its finest.

But then came Sofia Kohl.

Even now, with decades of marriage behind us, I still get a flutter when I say her name. Sofia. Chief Warrant Officer Kohl of the UHC military police. Tall, blonde, precise in everything she did. She had this German accent that made even her reprimands sound like poetry. I didn't know it at the time, but she'd been assigned to my protective detail. Yes, laugh all you want—the man who needed protection falling for his protector. The universe has a sick sense of humor.

I suppose I should have been suspicious when this gorgeous supposed civilian started showing interest in a scruffy human criminal like me. But in my defense, I was twenty-one and an idiot. Not that I'm claiming to be much smarter now, mind you, just older and with better stories.

She had this way of cutting through my nonsense with a single look. Blue eyes that could freeze you mid-sentence. A tactical mind that could outplan ten of me. And yet, somehow, we fit together like pieces of a puzzle neither of us knew we were trying to solve.

Of course, professional boundaries melted away rather quickly. They tend to do that when you're both facing the prospect of imminent death. Nothing accelerates a romance quite like the apocalypse breathing down your neck.

And speaking of the apocalypse—enter Arctis.

Now, every good story needs a villain, and Arctis, that backstabbing Dominion Glyphspeaker, fit the bill perfectly. While I was busy learning how to salute properly and stealing kisses with Sofia between classes, Arctis was planning a coup that would shake the Collective Dominion to its core.

I remember it vividly—alarms blaring across Astrithon, the capital city. Reports coming in of Dominion fleet movements that made no sense. Until they did. Arctis had turned part of the fleet against the queen, executing a power grab so bold it made even my criminal history look like child's play.

The queen was killed. Just like that. A ruler who had governed for centuries, snuffed out by ambition. And suddenly, Zeta—remember her? The igna who'd first approached me back on Earth, offering me command of *Thunder*—found herself thrust into the role of queen-in-exile.

I still see her sometimes, in my dreams. Not as the powerful ruler she became, but as she was that day—plasma form fluctuating with emotion within her octahedral capsule, her formal third-person speech faltering as she processed her mother's death. "Zeta must leave," she told us. "And you must come with her."

And so we fled. Sofia, Zeta, and I, escaping the Ignisara system with the remnants of loyalty to the true crown. No time to grab personal effects, no chance to say goodbye to the few friends I'd made. Just a desperate flight from a power-mad usurper who'd shown he had no qualms about killing anyone who stood in his way.

But our escape wasn't clean. When are they ever?

This brings me to the heart of the story I want to tell you now. During our hasty departure from Virelia, Sofia sustained a head injury. At the time, it seemed like just another complication in a day full of them—something we'd deal with once we reached safety.

I was wrong. So very wrong.

That injury would become the driving force behind every decision I made for weeks afterward. What initially presented as persistent headaches and occasional disorientation evolved into something far more concerning. The woman who could recite entire tactical manuals from memory began forgetting conversations we'd had hours earlier. The steady hand that could disassemble and reassemble a flechette rifle in seconds started to tremble.

We were headed back to Earth—or what was left of it after the Kergan Empire had torn through human civilization like tissue paper. Not exactly the ideal place to seek advanced medical care for a traumatic brain injury. The Kergans had methodically destroyed our medical infrastructure, either converting facilities for their own use or reducing them to rubble.

There's a special kind of helplessness that comes with watching someone you love suffer and knowing the best medical minds who could help them are either dead or serving the enemy. Sofia never complained—that wasn't her style. Instead, she pushed herself harder, insisted she was fine, and continued to perform her duties until she literally collapsed in the mess of Zeta's ship.

What I didn't understand then—what none of us could have predicted—was how Sofia's injury would connect to the larger events unfolding around us. What seemed like a personal tragedy, a cruel twist of fate affecting just the two of us, would prove to be a thread in a much larger tapestry.

No, scratch that. Not a tapestry. I hate that word. It's one of those flowery terms people use when they're trying to sound profound. Let's call it what it was—a complicated mess of cause and effect, with Sofia's injured brain somehow at the center of it all.

I realize I'm being cagey about the details. Old habits die hard, especially for someone who spent decades cramming classified military intelligence into his head about the events I'm describing. Some information is *still* classified, believe it or not. But more importantly, I don't want to spoil the discovery process for you. The way we unraveled the mystery of Sofia's condition, and how it tied back to the Kergan Empire, the Dominion, and even to Zeta's future as queen—that's a journey worth experiencing step by step.

What I can tell you is this: when Sofia finally received treatment, it came in the form of a Kergan brain implant installed by Dr. Chen, a brilliant brain surgeon who we managed to contact. The implant saved her life. It also changed it in ways none of us could have anticipated.

Have you ever seen someone remember things they never experienced? Watched the person you love most in the world suddenly speak in a language they never learned? Heard classified military information spill from the lips of someone who never had clearance to know it?

That's what the implant did to Sofia. It gave her back her

life while simultaneously filling her head with shadows of other lives—Kergan secrets, information that powerful people would kill to keep buried.

But I'm getting ahead of myself. Old men do that, you know. The timeline gets fuzzy when you've lived as long as I have. The beginning, middle, and end start to blend together until it's all just one continuous story without clear chapter breaks.

So let me reset. This next part of our adventure begins with Sofia showing early symptoms of her head injury, me holding her hand and making desperate promises I had no idea how to keep, and Queen Zeta coordinating our approach to a Earth that was both home and foreign territory. Three displaced individuals, each carrying our own scars, heading toward a wounded planet that might not have the resources to save any of us.

The story I'm about to tell you spans just a few months, but they were months that determined the course of the next several years—not just for Sofia and me, but for human-Kergan relations, for the future of the Collective Dominion, and for the gradual, painful process of reclaiming Earth.

And it all hinged on what was happening inside Sofia's injured brain.

Now, strap yourself in. Pour another drink if you need one. The ride gets bumpy from here, but I promise you this—it's one hell of a story. Not because I'm such a great storyteller—my aide is constantly editing my "colorful language" and tangential ramblings—but because sometimes truth really is stranger than fiction.

And this truth? It changed everything.

1

I sat on the bridge of the *Luminara* watching two balls of stellar plasma debate the finer points of tractor pod gravitational wave emissions, and I had never felt more useless in my life. Captain Borlo's white cube housing pulsed with each emphatic point while Zeta's more elegant vessel drifted in what I recognized as royal contemplation. Meanwhile, Sofia slumped beside me, her usual alertness dimmed to a worrying pallor that twisted my gut more than our recent brush with death.

The bridge of the *Luminara* wasn't built for human comfort. The circular room featured stations designed for kavreni crew members—all spindly limbs and reversed knees—with displays positioned for their oversized eyes and elongated fingers. The lighting favored the violet and ultraviolet spectrum, giving everything an eerie purple glow that made my eyes ache after a few hours. In the center, a depression in the floor served as the command area where Zeta and Borlo now hovered, their plasma forms shifting and swirling within their containment vessels.

Zeta's capsule was a marvel of engineering—an octahedron of polished metal that captured and reflected light in hypnotic patterns. When she spoke, the plasma inside pulsed and rippled like a miniature sun having a seizure. Borlo's cube was utilitarian by comparison, the igna equivalent of sensible shoes.

"The tertiary manifold coupling has experienced catastrophic desynchronization with the primary helix flow regulator," Borlo announced, his plasma form turning a deeper orange within his cube. "Borlo estimates three standard days of breathable atmosphere remaining at the current crew complement."

"Zeta finds this concerning," the queen-in-exile replied, her own plasma form shifting from yellow to a pale blue. "What of the damaged tractor pods?"

"Functional but compromised," Borlo's cube rotated slightly, producing a holographic display between them. "The gravitational wave emissions exceed acceptable parameters by 340%. Our stealth capabilities are effectively neutralized."

"The quantum field inhibitors cannot compensate?"

"Negative. The damage to the dorsal synchronization array prevents proper harmonic field generation."

I leaned toward Sofia. "Did you catch any of that?"

She just grunted, which wasn't reassuring.

The technical jargon continued to fly back and forth, each term more incomprehensible than the last. I was a starship captain—at least I had been, before I left *Thunder* to travel to Astrithon to answer criminal charges—but my expertise ended where igna technology began. The *Luminara* was generations ahead of anything in the UHC fleet, and I felt like a caveman watching rocket scientists.

"The probability matrix suggests implementing a

bypass through the secondary Hawking radiation buffers," Zeta suggested.

Borlo's cube tilted in what I'd learned was the igna equivalent of a skeptical head shake. "Borlo must advise against such a course. The buffers were not designed for continuous operation. Catastrophic failure would result."

"Zeta acknowledges the risk, but sees few alternatives."

I rubbed my temples. One year as captain of *Thunder*, then a year in two different military schools, and here I was, reduced to a glorified passenger with nothing to contribute. Technical discussions like this one had always been in Sofia's department. She had the mind for it—systematic, logical, capable of holding multiple variables in her head at once. On a normal day, she'd be right in the thick of it, offering suggestions that somehow bridged human and alien technology.

Today was not a normal day.

I glanced at Sofia beside me. Her honey blonde hair was uncharacteristically disheveled, strands falling across her forehead. Her normally sharp blue eyes seemed unfocused, staring at some middle distance between us and the igna. Her posture—always ramrod straight, a holdover from her military police days—had collapsed into a slouch that set off alarm bells in my head.

"Hey," I whispered. "How's the head?"

She turned slowly toward me, too slowly. "It hurts," she mumbled, the words slurring together slightly. "Bright in here."

The bump she'd taken during our escape from the *Inferis* had left a purple bruise along her hairline. The Luminara's medical bay had patched up her broken leg in a matter of hours—alien tech that should have had me geeking out like a kid in a candy store—but head injuries were different. The medical officer, a kavreni with particularly enormous eyes even for his species, had seemed uncertain about human brain physiology.

I reached over and gently massaged her scalp, careful to avoid the bruised area. "Better?"

"Mmm," she sighed, leaning into my touch. "Little bit."

The fact that she admitted to pain at all was concerning. This was a woman who'd once reset her own dislocated shoulder without so much as a whimper.

"We should get you back to medical," I suggested.

"No." That came out clearer. "Just... need rest."

As my fingers worked through her hair, I couldn't help thinking back to how we'd ended up here. The battle over Virelia had gone spectacularly wrong. The royalist forces loyal to Zeta had been outmaneuvered by Arctis's rebel fleet. The *Inferis*—the massive flagship where we'd been stationed—had taken heavy damage.

I still saw it when I closed my eyes: the command center collapsing around us, the ceiling support crashing down toward Sofia. I'd lunged for her, but not quickly enough. She'd pushed a kavreni technician clear but couldn't save herself. The metallic groan of the support giving way, the sickening crack as it struck her leg—these sounds had joined my personal collection of nightmares.

Somehow, we'd made it to an escape pod. I half-carried, half-dragged her through corridors filled with smoke and the cries of the wounded. Her face had been gray with pain, and unresponsive.

The escape pod had barely cleared the *Inferis* when the flagship's reactor went critical. The shockwave sent us tumbling, systems failing one by one. We'd had maybe an hour of air left when the *Luminara* found us.

Zeta had risked everything coming back for us. Her

royal yacht wasn't built for combat, but she'd insisted. "Zeta does not abandon her allies," she'd told me later, her plasma form glowing with what I'd learned to recognize as fierce determination.

We'd made a run for it, heading for a Lagrange point near one of the system's gas giants—a stable spot where we could safely jump to veilspace. But Arctis had expected this move. A rebel patrol ship was waiting, sleek and predatory.

"Energy signature detected," the kavreni tactical officer had announced, his stinger tail twitching nervously. "Rebel gunship *Fang of Virpa*."

"Evasive maneuvers," Borlo had ordered, his cube pulsing urgently.

Too late. The missile had struck just as the veilspace drive was spooling up. The ship had bucked and screamed, alarms blaring as system after system reported damage. But we'd made the jump, leaving our pursuers behind in a flash of twisted space-time.

And now here we were, limping through veilspace—a domain of the Syderealium—toward Earth, the ship damaged, life support compromised, and stealth capabilities shot. Earth was our only hope—the human insurgents might be able to offer safe haven, at least temporarily.

"Zeta proposes a six percent reduction in ambient temperature to extend life support duration," Zeta was saying now.

"Acceptable," Borlo agreed. "Borlo will also recommend rationing power to non-essential systems."

I tuned them out again, focusing on Sofia. Her skin felt clammy under my fingers, and the circles under her eyes had darkened to a bruise-like purple. When she'd first emerged from the medical bay, I'd been so relieved to see her walking that I'd missed the other signs—the slight hesitation in her movements, the way she squinted in normal lighting.

"I've got a solution to the broken life support system," I muttered to her with forced cheerfulness. "We could just hook it up to the hot air these two are generating."

That should have earned me at least an eye roll, maybe a gentle elbow to the ribs. Instead, Sofia just blinked slowly.

"What?" she asked, the word mushy around the edges.

My stomach dropped. Sofia never missed a beat, never failed to catch even my lamest jokes. Something was very wrong.

"Come on," I said, standing up and offering my hand. "We're going to medical. Right now."

She looked at my hand as if trying to figure out what it was for. Then, with agonizing slowness, she reached up and took it.

"Borlo believes the humans are departing," the captain's voice cut through my worry.

"We need to check something in medical," I called back over my shoulder, already guiding Sofia toward the exit. "We'll be back."

As the door to the bridge slid open, I heard Zeta add one final, cryptic comment: "Zeta wonders if they realize what awaits them on Earth."

I didn't have time to worry about whatever that meant. Sofia's fingers were stiff in mine, and her steps were uneven. One problem at a time, and right now, the woman leaning heavily against my side was the only problem that mattered.

2

The medical bay doors slid open with a pneumatic hiss that sounded too much like a death rattle for my comfort. Sofia stumbled against me, her weight shifting suddenly as if the floor had tilted beneath her feet. My hands steadied her shoulders, but nothing could steady the fear churning in my gut. A year commanding a starship through hostile territory, and I'd never felt as helpless as I did watching the sharpest person I knew struggle to walk in a straight line.

"I'm fine," Sofia mumbled, the words slurring together like ice cream on a hot day. "Just tired."

"You're not fine," I said, guiding her through the doorway. "And you're not going to sleep until we know what's going on inside that brain of yours."

The *Luminara*'s medical bay looked like what might happen if you gave a medical textbook to someone who'd only ever heard humans described by a drunk poet. The room was circular, like most spaces on the ship, with lighting that pulsed in ultraviolet waves across the ceiling. Three oval platforms that I assumed were examination tables dominated the center, surrounded by equipment that resembled anything from elegant sculptures to medieval torture devices.

A kavreni stood with his back to us, his elongated fingers manipulating what looked like a constellation trapped in a glass box. He turned at our entrance, massive eyes blinking in rapid succession. His ears—each the size of dinner plates—twitched and rotated toward us like radar dishes seeking a signal.

"Humans require assistance?" he asked, his voice clicking on the consonants. His stinger tail swished behind him. A habit I'd learned indicated curiosity rather than aggression.

"Yes," I said, helping Sofia onto the nearest examination platform. "She has a head injury. From the *Inferis*. When the ceiling collapsed on her."

Sofia tried to slide back off the platform. "I just need sleep. Please, Kory."

I caught her by the shoulders. "No. No sleep." I turned to the kavreni physician. "That's bad for head injuries in humans, right? Sleeping?"

The physician tilted his head, his oversized eyes blinking asynchronously. "Uncertain. Kavreni medical database contains minimal human physiology. Primarily reproductive and digestive systems."

Perfect. The aliens knew how humans crapped and copulated, but not how our brains worked. Seemed about right for my luck.

"Well, on Earth, they say not to let someone with a concussion sleep," I insisted, though I couldn't actually remember where I'd heard that. Some vid drama, probably. "Can you scan her head? See if there's bleeding or... I don't know, brain stuff?"

The physician approached, his reversed knees giving his gait an unsettling bounce. He leaned over Sofia, those dinner-plate ears swiveling toward her skull as if listening for something.

"Possible to attempt neural imaging," he said, "but interpretation problematic. Baseline comparative data for human neural patterns unavailable."

Sofia's eyes had drifted closed. I gently shook her shoulder.

"Hey, stay with me."

She blinked sluggishly. "I am with you. Always with you."

The sentiment would have warmed my heart if her eyes hadn't been so unfocused, like she was looking through me rather than at me. Her skin had taken on a waxy pallor that reminded me of the time she'd had an allergic reaction to something in the food on Astrithon.

"We'll try the scan," I told the physician. "Even if we can't interpret it perfectly, it's better than nothing."

The kavreni made a clicking sound with his tongue against the roof of his mouth—the equivalent of a human sigh. "Will prepare neural imager." He glided to a cabinet and began removing equipment that resembled delicate glass wind chimes.

Sofia tugged at my sleeve, her movements clumsy. "Don't need this. Just let me sleep, Kory. So tired."

My heart squeezed. Sofia had never been one to complain.

"No sleep yet," I said, trying to keep my voice light. "Doctor's orders."

"He's not even a proper doctor," she grumbled, a flash of her usual sharpness breaking through. "Not for humans."

"He's the best we've got right now."

The memory of the *Inferis* collapse replayed in my mind: the groaning of metal under stress, warning klaxons screaming, the sickening crack as the ceiling support gave way.

By some miracle, her head had been mostly spared—or so we'd thought. The bruise along her hairline seemed minor compared to her shattered tibia. The *Luminara*'s medical bay had fixed her leg in hours, bones knitting together under the influence of alien technology I couldn't begin to understand. But head injuries were sneaky bastards.

The physician returned with an arrangement of crystalline components that he began assembling above the examination platform. The pieces connected without touching, hanging in mid-air like a chandelier designed by a theoretical physicist.

"Please recline," he instructed Sofia.

She looked at me, uncertainty clouding her features. I nodded encouragingly, and she slowly leaned back until she was lying flat. The physician adjusted the floating components until they formed a halo around her head, then stepped back and manipulated something on his wrist that might have been a control interface or might have been jewelry.

The crystalline components began to emit a soft humming sound, gradually increasing in pitch until it passed beyond my range of hearing. Sofia winced, her hand instinctively rising toward her ear before falling back to her side.

"Discomfort normal," the physician assured us. "Neural mapping creates perception of sound that is not sound."

That made absolutely no sense to me, but I nodded as if it did.

"How long will this take?" I asked.

"Neural mapping complete in approximately seven minutes."

Seven minutes. I could handle seven minutes. I took Sofia's hand in mine, her fingers cold and unresponsive.

"Hang in there," I murmured. "Almost done."

Her blue eyes fixed on me, struggling to focus. "You worry too much."

"One of us has to."

A ghost of a smile touched her lips. "My job. I'm the worrier."

"You're taking a day off."

The humor faded from her face. "Something's wrong, isn't it? I can feel it. My thoughts... they're slipping away like..." She frowned, searching for a comparison. "Like... I don't know. Can't think of it."

My stomach dropped. Sofia was precise with language, always finding the exact right word for any situation. Her vocabulary made mine look like a child's picture book. For her to struggle with a simile was like a truck driver forgetting how to use a steering wheel.

"We're going to figure it out," I promised, squeezing her hand.

The minutes crawled by as the humming crystals orbited her head. I watched the subtle changes in her facial expression—confusion, discomfort, momentary clarity followed by foggy disorientation. My mind raced through our options, none of them good. The *Luminara* was damaged, limping through veilspace toward Earth. We couldn't divert to a closer system without risking detection by Arctis's forces. Human medical facilities were days away at best.

Finally, the crystalline components ceased their movement and drifted upward, assembling themselves into what looked like an abstract sculpture above the examination table.

"Neural mapping complete," the physician announced. "Will display results."

He made a complex gesture with his elongated fingers, and a three-dimensional image materialized in the air beside the table. It resembled a translucent human brain crisscrossed with veins of light in various colors.

I stared at it, hoping for some flash of insight. "What am I looking at?"

The physician tilted his head, ears twitching. "Neural activity patterns. Red indicates blood flow. Blue indicates electrical conductivity. Yellow represents axonal stress points."

That meant absolutely nothing to me. I studied the image, noting a large patch of red on one side and several blue streaks radiating outward from it.

"Is that bad?" I pointed at the red area.

"Unknown," the physician admitted. "Without comparative healthy human neural baselines, difficult to determine abnormality."

"But you're a doctor," I said, frustration edging into my voice. "Make an educated guess."

The kavreni blinked his massive eyes. "Based on general neurological principles across species, increased blood flow often indicates inflammation or hemorrhage. If human brains function similarly to kavreni brains in this respect, this pattern suggests intercranial pressure."

"That sounds bad."

"It would be considered concerning in kavreni physiology. But she is not kavreni."

Sofia had gone quiet beside me, her eyes fluttering closed again. I gently patted her cheek. "Stay awake, Sofia."

She opened her eyes with visible effort. "Tired of people talking about me like I'm not here."

"Sorry," I said. "What are you feeling right now? Besides tired."

She considered this, brow furrowing in concentration. "Pressure. Like my head's too small for my brain. And sounds are... wrong. Too loud or too soft. No in-between." She paused, struggling. "And I can't... I can't remember things. Simple things."

"Like what?"

"Like..." She swallowed. "Like your middle name."

My heart sank. We'd been together for nearly a year. She knew everything about me, including the embarrassing middle name I'd given myself at thirteen when I'd added it to my name after escaping the orphanage.

"It's Orion," I reminded her softly.

"Orion," she repeated. "Kory Orion Drake." She nodded, then winced at the movement. "I knew that. It's just... hiding from me."

I looked back at the physician. "What can we do for her?"

He made a gesture I recognized as the kavreni equivalent of a shrug. "Anti-inflammatory compounds might reduce pressure. Have limited human-compatible medications. Success uncertain."

"Better than nothing," I said.

The physician retrieved a small canister from a storage unit and attached it to a device that looked like a silver tuning fork. "Respiratory delivery. Most efficient for rapid absorption."

He held the device near Sofia's face. "Inhale deeply when ready."

Sofia looked at me, a question in her eyes. I nodded

encouragingly, though my confidence was pure theater. She took a deep breath as the device emitted a fine mist that she inhaled.

"Effects begin within minutes," the physician explained. "Duration approximately six hours."

"And will it help?" I asked.

"Unknown. But unlikely to cause harm."

Great. The medical equivalent of "this probably won't make things worse." Still, it was better than nothing.

"Can I sleep now?" Sofia asked, her voice small.

I looked at the physician, who made another kavreni shrug. "No clear consensus on sleep prohibition for human head injuries in our database. Some references suggest rest beneficial. Others advise monitoring consciousness."

"So helpful," I muttered.

The physician's ears flattened slightly—embarrassment, I thought. "Apologize for limitations. Ship's medical facilities not designed for human patients."

I sighed. It wasn't his fault. "I know. Thank you for trying."

I helped Sofia sit up. She swayed slightly, and I steadied her with a hand on her shoulder.

"We'll head back to the bridge," I decided. "I want to keep an eye on you."

"I should help with repairs," she said, her professional instincts fighting through the fog.

"Not a chance. Your job right now is to sit still and tell me if anything changes. Better or worse."

She didn't argue, which scared me more than anything else. Sofia lived to work, especially when it came to her duties.

"Ready to go?" I asked her.

She nodded carefully. I helped her off the examination

platform, supporting her with an arm around her waist. As we made our way toward the door, her legs moved as if she was walking through knee-deep mud, each step deliberate and uncertain.

The corridors of the *Luminara* seemed longer on the return journey. Sofia leaned heavily against me, her breathing shallow.

"Sorry," she mumbled as we paused for her to catch her breath. "Being weak."

"You've got a head injury," I reminded her. "You're allowed."

"You'd be... charging ahead. If it was you."

"I'd be whining like a baby and demanding sympathy back rubs," I corrected her. "You know me better than that."

That earned me a weak smile. "True. Big baby."

We resumed our slow progress. I watched her face, noting the flatness of her expression, the slight drooping at the corner of her mouth. Her normally precise movements had become clumsy, her posture listing to one side despite my support.

By the time we reached the bridge, my worry had crystalized into ice-cold fear. Sofia wasn't just concussed—something was seriously wrong, something the alien medical equipment couldn't identify or fix. And we were days away from proper human medical facilities, limping through veilspace in a damaged ship with compromised life support.

As the bridge doors slid open, I made a silent promise to the woman leaning against me: I would get her to Earth and proper medical care if I had to drag the *Luminara* through veilspace with my bare hands.

3

I slouched in my chair on Luminara's bridge, trying to look relaxed while my stomach pulled off Olympic-level somersaults. The tension in the air was thick enough to slice with a butter knife—if someone could be bothered to try—while Borlo and his crew quietly calculated just how doomed we were.

After escaping the Ignisara System, we'd landed in an uninhabited star system orbiting a dim red dwarf. It had a couple of gas giants and one rocky world hot enough to cook a meal on. Borlo was hoping to patch up our damage and maybe scavenge the materials we needed to keep the life support system from giving up entirely.

"Borlo estimates damage to secondary hull at seventeen percent," the captain announced to no one in particular, his voice resonating from the audio emitter on his capsule. "Primary propulsion intact, but emissions masking compromised."

I watched as his kavreni crew scurried across the bridge. Their reversed knees made their movements look like some kind of alien dance as they worked.

Next to me, Zeta sat regally in her octahedral capsule. Unlike Borlo's utilitarian cube, Zeta's housing was elegant—faceted crystal that refracted the light from her plasma body in mesmerizing patterns across the bridge. She was secured with a safety harness that looked too delicate for the job, but was probably stronger than anything Earth engineers could design. Igna technology never ceased to amaze me.

On my other side, Sofia occupied her seat with the stiff posture of someone who refused to acknowledge pain. Her honey blonde hair was pulled back in a severe bun that emphasized her heart-shaped face, currently set in a mask of concentration. I could tell from the tightness around her blue eyes that she was still in pain.

Borlo's capsule drifted toward us, the plasma inside shifting to a more intense yellow—anxiety, I'd learned, in igna body language.

"Your Majesty," he addressed Zeta. "Borlo regrets to inform the Queen that our life support systems continue to degrade."

Zeta's plasma flickered in what I recognized as concern, though her voice remained steady when she spoke. "The Queen would like a detailed assessment, Captain."

"Our CO_2 scrubbers are destroyed," Borlo reported. "Oxygen generation compromised. Emergency systems operational but limited."

I felt my heart sink. In space, air isn't just a convenience—it's the countdown timer on your life. The two igna could survive without it, but the rest of us humans and kavreni would soon be in trouble.

"How long do we have?" Zeta asked the question all of us were thinking.

"Three days at current consumption rates," Borlo replied, his plasma dimming slightly. "Perhaps four or maybe even five if some crew enter torpor."

Sofia muttered something in German that sounded distinctly unprintable.

"What about repairs?" I asked, leaning forward. "Surely we can patch something together?"

Borlo's capsule rotated slightly toward me. "Repairs require materials we do not possess, Commander Drake. The missile strike eliminated our supply of Xenon-129."

"That's the stuff for the scrubbers, right?" I clarified, trying to remember the crash course on igna ship systems I'd received when boarding.

"Correct. Without it, CO_2 will accumulate to toxic levels."

Sofia spoke up, her German accent more pronounced than usual. "Can we extract more from the gas giant? It must have trace amounts."

Borlo's plasma flickered in the igna equivalent of a head shake. "Our chromatic battery charge is sufficient only for the jump to the Sol System and transit to Earth. We lack power for a deep gravity well extraction operation."

Most Dominion starships ran on chromatic batteries—ultra energy-dense storage systems that stored power in the gluon fields binding quarks, rather than relying on traditional nuclear reactors. This design choice simplified ship construction and significantly reduced mass and volume, but came with a trade-off: when energy ran low, the ship had to be recharged, not refueled. Only the largest vessels, or those built for deep-space missions, were equipped with fusion reactors for sustained, long-range power generation. *Luminara* was neither type. It was a royal yacht.

"So we're down to two options," I summarized. "Either we find a source of Xenon-129 quickly, or we get to Earth before we suffocate."

"Succinct as always, Commander Drake," Zeta commented. Since taking up the mantle of Queen of the Collective Dominion, her speech had taken on a distinctly regal tone. In private, she still called me by my first name, but in public, she stuck to titles—part ceremony, part performance.

I took a hard look at our situation. We were damaged, low on air, and our stealth systems were unreliable at best. Stopping in this empty star system had cost us precious time and power with nothing to show for it. Thankfully, we still had just enough charge left for a single jump to Earth—our last shot at reaching my friends in the resistance and getting help for *Luminara* before everything fell apart.

"Zeta," I began, "I think we should make the jump to Earth. Once we're in the Sol System, we'll have more options and more data to work with."

Zeta's plasma swirled thoughtfully in her capsule. "The Queen concurs. Captain Borlo, set course for the Sol System."

"As the Queen commands," Borlo replied, his capsule bobbing in what passed for a bow before drifting back to the command console.

The bridge erupted into activity as the kavreni crew prepared for the veil space jump. I glanced at Sofia and was startled by how pale she looked. Before I could say anything, she let out a low groan that seemed to rise from somewhere deep in her chest.

"You okay?" I asked, keeping my voice down.

She turned to me, and I was shocked by the flash of irritation in her eyes. "I'm fine."

"You don't look fine," I persisted, reaching for her hand.

She pulled away. "I said I'm fine, Kory."

I blinked, taken aback by her tone. Sofia was typically reserved, but never snappish. Not with me, anyway. "Are you sure? You seem—"

"What part of 'I'm fine' do you not understand?" she cut me off, her voice sharper than the edge of a combat knife.

This wasn't the level-headed Sofia I knew, the woman who could calmly disarm a panicked civilian while explaining regulations in three languages. Something was definitely off.

"Can I get you anything?" I offered, trying a different approach. "Water? Something to eat?"

Sofia closed her eyes and pinched the bridge of her nose. "Unless you can produce some ibuprofen or aspirin, just leave me alone. I have a splitting headache."

I felt a twinge of embarrassment at her anger, coupled with genuine concern. Sofia wasn't just irritable—she was in pain. My concern for her health swelled. The image of that red shadow on her brain we'd seen in the med bay haunted me.

"Maybe the med bay has something," I offered, already rising from my seat.

"Don't bother," she sighed. "They don't stock human medications. I already asked."

I settled back, feeling useless. On the console, the jump sequence was ticking down, screens filled with equations complicated enough to kill us if even one went wrong.

Sofia leaned her head back and closed her eyes, the harsh bridge lighting deepening the shadows beneath them. I wondered if the stress of the past few days was hitting her harder than the head injury. Being fugitives on a failing alien ship with a dethroned queen wasn't exactly restorative.

As the countdown neared zero, I reached for Sofia's hand. This time, she didn't pull away—her fingers limp but there. It wasn't much, but I'd take it.

The displays flashed amber. My stomach dropped as the veilspace engines spun up. One mess behind us, another ahead in the Sol System. I squeezed Sofia's hand and braced for the jump.

Whatever came next, we'd face it together—like it or not.

4

I sat across from Sofia in the mess hall, poking at what the ship's synthesizer claimed was food. The gray paste had the consistency of wet cement and all the flavor of cardboard soaked in dishwater. I scooped a bit onto my spoon and watched it drip back to the plate with a wet plop. Maybe the CO_2 scrubbers weren't our biggest problem—we might die of culinary disappointment first.

We had been eight hours in veilspace since jumping out of the uninhabited system. Life support continued to be a problem, though Captain Borlo had put a third of the kavreni crew into torpor—a kind of kavreni mild hibernation—to conserve air, which would buy us an additional day or two.

Sofia considered the mush on her plate. "It's not that bad," she muttered, though she hadn't taken more than two bites of her own portion.

"It's protein paste and vitamin water," I replied, forcing down a spoonful and trying not to grimace. "I've had emergency rations with more personality."

The mess hall was barely that—just a small room with four tables bolted to the deck, designed primarily for the kavreni crew. The chairs were uncomfortable for human anatomy, with cutouts for tails we didn't possess. The lighting was too bright, casting harsh shadows across Sofia's face that made her look gaunt and tired.

My fingers drummed nervously against the table as I stared at my food, contemplating our situation. We were still six hours from reaching Sol System, the veil space jump having consumed most of our remaining power. The air was already feeling thinner, though that might have been my imagination.

"Stop that goddamned noise," Sofia snapped suddenly.

I froze mid-drum, looking up to find her glaring at me with an intensity that seemed disproportionate to my minor offense.

"Sorry," I said, deliberately placing my hands flat on the table. "Nervous habit."

"Well, it's annoying," she replied, rubbing her temple with two fingers. The dark circles under her eyes had deepened since our escape from the Ignisara System, and her skin had taken on a waxy pallor that worried me.

I leaned back and folded my arms, studying her. "Are you sure you're not getting worse? You've been... off since we left."

Sofia frowned, squinting slightly as if the light bothered her more than usual. "I told you, I'm fine. Just tired."

"You've been 'just tired' for two days," I pointed out. "And that headache hasn't gone away."

"Don't mother me, Kory," she said, her tone softening slightly. "I've handled worse."

I wanted to push the issue, but arguing with Sofia when she was in this mood was like trying to reason with a stubborn missile lock—futile and potentially explosive. Instead, I watched as she stood, grabbing her water cup.

"I'm getting a refill," she announced, taking a step toward the synthesizer unit.

What happened next seemed to unfold in slow motion. Sofia took a second step, then suddenly faltered. Her body swayed as if caught in an invisible current, her expression shifting from irritation to confusion. The cup slipped from her fingers, clattering against the deck with a hollow ping that echoed in the small space.

Then she crumpled, collapsing sideways onto the hard metal floor.

"Sofia!" I was out of my seat before I fully registered what was happening, lunging across the space between us.

A strange, keening noise erupted from her throat—not quite a moan, not quite a cry, but something animal and instinctive that sent ice through my veins. I dropped to my knees beside her, hands hovering uncertainly over her body.

"Sofia? What's wrong? Talk to me!"

Her eyes were open but unfocused, staring at something beyond the confines of the ship. Her left arm had gone rigid, sticking out at an unnatural angle, and her fingers were curled into a claw. As I watched, a tremor started in her hand, spreading up her arm in rhythmic shakes.

"Sofia?" My voice cracked with panic. "Can you hear me?"

Her lips began to smack together, a rapid, repetitive motion like she was tasting something unpleasant. Drool escaped from the corner of her mouth, running down her chin in a thin stream. Her right hand moved to her left side, patting at it weakly.

"What should I do?" I asked, the calm I was trying to project evaporating like water on a hot plate. "Should I call for help? Are you in pain?"

She mumbled something, the words slurred and barely coherent. I leaned closer, straining to understand.

"...can't feel... left side..." The words were garbled, coming from only the right side of her mouth, while the left remained slack.

A cold weight settled in my stomach. "Did you say left side? You can't feel your left side?"

Sofia gave a jerky nod, but her lips continued their strange smacking motion, and more drool escaped. Her eyes rolled slightly, focusing on me for a moment before sliding away again. The left leg began to shake in time with her arm, an uncoordinated dance of misfiring neurons.

I'd seen combat injuries, treated wounded soldiers under fire, but this was different. This was an enemy I couldn't see or fight. I did not know what was happening or how to help, and the helplessness was suffocating.

I looked up, suddenly aware of several kavreni crew members who had stopped to watch, their large ears twitching with what might have been concern or curiosity. None moved to help, perhaps as unsure about human physiology as I was about what was happening to Sofia.

"I need a medic!" I called out, though I knew it was futile. The ship's doctor was a kavreni specializing in igna and their own species' ailments. What would they know about human seizures—if that's what this was?

One of the kavreni chittered something in their native language, their bat-like face expressing what I took to be confusion.

I turned back to Sofia just as the rigid trembling in her limbs subsided. Her body went suddenly limp, collapsing fully against the deck like a marionette with cut strings. Her breathing came in shallow gasps, and a sheen of sweat covered her forehead.

"Sofia?" I gently brushed her hair back from her face. "Can you hear me?"

She blinked slowly, awareness returning to her eyes in stages. "Kory?" Her voice was thick, as if speaking through a mouthful of cotton.

"I'm here," I assured her, taking her hand. "You... something happened. You collapsed."

"Did I?" She sounded genuinely confused. "I don't remember..."

"You had some kind of... I don't know. Seizure, maybe?" I described what I'd seen—the rigid limbs, the trembling, the facial movements.

Sofia's expression remained blank for a moment before morphing into embarrassment. "That's not... that can't be right."

"I know what I saw," I insisted, helping her to sit up slowly. "This isn't normal, Sofia. Whatever's going on, it's serious."

"It's just a headache," she protested weakly, though the slur in her words undermined her assertion.

"A headache doesn't make you collapse and convulse," I countered, trying to keep the fear from my voice. "This is something else."

I noticed several kavreni still watching us, shifting nervously from foot to foot, their large eyes blinking in rapid succession. Their presence reminded me of our isolation—two humans on an alien ship, far from proper medical care.

"This isn't normal," I muttered, more to myself than to Sofia. "Something's wrong."

Sofia grimaced, raising a hand to her head. "My head feels like it's trying to split in half," she admitted. There was something almost sardonic in her tone, as if she were making a joke only she understood.

"Didn't you just have a seizure?" I asked directly, needing her to acknowledge the severity.

She shrugged, the motion lopsided and uncoordinated. "I don't know. Never had one before."

"You need to see a doctor," I insisted. "A human doctor, someone who understands our physiology."

"The doc here checked me out," she said, waving a hand dismissively. "Said I was fine."

"No, he didn't. Regardless, the doctor here is a kavreni," I reminded her, frustration seeping into my voice. "He's about as qualified to assess human neurological damage as I am to perform igna plasma surgery."

Sofia struggled to her feet, refusing my offer of help with a stubborn shake of her head. She swayed slightly, but managed to stay upright.

"I need to get to the bridge," I told her. "I'm going to talk to Zeta about getting you medical attention as soon as possible."

"Don't make a fuss," Sofia protested, but her objection lacked its usual conviction.

"This isn't a fuss, it's a medical emergency," I replied firmly. "Stay here and rest. I'll be right back."

I left Sofia leaning against the table, her normally perfect posture compromised by whatever was happening in her brain. The sight of her—strong, capable Sofia—reduced to this vulnerable state, twisted something painful in my chest.

The corridors of the *Luminara* seemed longer than usual as I made my way to the bridge, my mind racing through possibilities, none of them good. Seizure, stroke, brain hemorrhage—I wasn't a doctor, but I knew enough to recognize that neurological symptoms following a head injury were serious business.

I found Zeta on the bridge, her octahedral capsule hovering near the main display where Borlo was monitoring *Luminara*'s progress through veilspace. The plasma of her body shifted in slow, pensive patterns as she reviewed damage reports.

"Your Majesty," I said, approaching with more formality than I usually bothered with. "I need to speak with you."

Zeta's capsule rotated toward me, the facets catching the light in dazzling patterns. "Yes, Kory."

"It's Sofia," I explained, struggling to keep my voice steady. "She just had what I think was a seizure in the mess hall. She's confused, having trouble speaking, and says she can't feel her left side."

The plasma in Zeta's capsule flared briefly in what I recognized as alarm. "These are concerning symptoms in a human."

"Very concerning," I agreed. "I think it might be related to the head injury she sustained on *Inferis*. She needs proper medical attention—human medical attention—as soon as possible."

"Zeta understands," she replied. Her plasma swirled in complex patterns as she considered the situation. "Captain Borlo, what is our status?"

Borlo's capsule drifted closer. "Repairs to the secondary systems continue. We will reach the Sol System in approximately six hours."

"That may be too long," I interjected. "I know little about brain injuries, but I know that time can be critical."

Zeta's plasma pulsed with what seemed like determination. "The Queen agrees. Captain Borlo, direct all available personnel to focus on completing the necessary repairs. We must reach Earth with all possible speed."

"As the Queen commands," Borlo replied, his capsule bobbing in acknowledgment.

I felt a slight easing of the tension that had been building in my chest. It wasn't a solution, but it was action—and right now, that was all I could hope for.

"Thank you, Zeta," I said.

"The Queen values all who serve her cause," Zeta responded, her plasma forming a pattern that conveyed what I interpreted as genuine concern. "Warrant Officer Kohl's well-being is important to us."

I nodded, grateful for the sentiment, but still worried sick about Sofia. As I turned to leave the bridge, I couldn't shake the image of her collapsed on the deck, that strange keening sound escaping her lips.

Whatever was happening to Sofia, it was serious—and we were still hours away from any help that might save her. All I could do was return to her side and hope that we reached Earth before it was too late.

5

I left the bridge with my heart lodged somewhere in my throat, a persistent ache that wouldn't subside no matter how many times I swallowed. The corridors of the *Luminara* seemed to stretch and contract around me as I searched for Sofia, checking the mess hall first, then the small recreation area. I finally found her in our shared cabin, a glorified closet with barely enough room for the bed and our few belongings. She lay curled on her side in the darkness, the only illumination coming from the faint status lights of the environmental controls.

"Sofia?" I called softly, hovering at the threshold.

A muffled groan was my only answer. I took that as permission to enter and stepped inside, my hand automatically reaching for the light panel on the wall.

The cabin flooded with harsh fluorescent light, and Sofia recoiled instantly, pulling a pillow over her head.

"Turn it off," she begged, her voice muffled but unmistakably pained. "Please, Kory. My head is killing me."

I quickly flicked the switch, plunging us back into

merciful darkness. "Sorry," I murmured, using the faint glow from the corridor to navigate to the bed.

The mattress dipped as I sat on its edge, careful not to jostle her. My eyes adjusted slowly to the dim light, revealing the outline of Sofia's body curled into a protective ball. I reached out hesitantly, then gently ran my hand along her arm, feeling goosebumps rise beneath my fingertips.

"How are you feeling?" I asked, knowing it was a stupid question even as the words left my mouth.

Sofia shifted slightly, emerging from beneath the pillow. In the low light, her face was all shadows and angles, her usually bright eyes dulled with pain.

"Like someone's taken a dull spoon and is trying to scoop out my brain through my eye socket," she replied, attempting a wry smile that faltered halfway.

I continued stroking her arm, a rhythmic, soothing motion that seemed to calm us both. "Zeta's ordered the crew to expedite repairs. We'll get you to a doctor as soon as we can."

"You told her?" Sofia's voice wavered between accusation and relief.

"Of course I did," I replied. "You had a seizure, Sofia. That's not something to ignore."

She was quiet for a moment, then whispered, "I feel weak. Numb on my left." Her speech had a slight slur to it, as if her tongue was too thick for her mouth. "It's not just the headache anymore."

The admission hung in the air between us, weighted with everything it implied. Sofia Kohl didn't admit weakness. Not ever. That she was doing so now terrified me more than the seizure had.

"We'll be jumping into the Sol System soon," I assured

her, trying to inject confidence I didn't feel into my voice. "Earth has the doctors you need. They'll fix you up."

"Always the optimist," she murmured, but there was fondness beneath the sarcasm.

"One of us has to be," I replied, smiling in the darkness. "Otherwise, we'd both be cynical German ex-cops with trust issues."

That earned a small, genuine laugh that quickly transformed into a wince. "Don't make me laugh. It hurts."

"Sorry," I apologized, shifting to sit more comfortably on the bed.

We sat in silence for a few moments, the hum of the ship's systems providing a gentle backdrop to our breathing. I kept my hand on her arm, anchoring her with my touch, reassuring myself that she was still here, still with me, despite whatever was happening in her brain.

"I was thinking about my mother," Sofia said suddenly, her voice so soft I had to lean closer to hear her.

"Your mother?" I repeated, surprised by the non sequitur.

Sofia nodded slightly. "She died in Berlin. During the evacuation after the Kergan invasion."

I knew the bare facts of this—that Sofia had lost her mother during the chaotic days following the alien attack on Earth. But she rarely spoke of it, keeping her grief private as she did with so many things.

"What about her?" I prompted gently when Sofia didn't continue.

"She played the piano," Sofia said, a distant note entering her voice. "Professionally. In fancy restaurants, at social events. She was very good."

I tried to picture it—a woman with Sofia's features but older, honey blonde hair perhaps streaked with silver, long fingers dancing across ivory keys. "That sounds lovely."

"It was," Sofia agreed. "She could make the piano sound like it was speaking. Like it had a soul."

I squeezed her hand gently. "Did you ever learn to play?"

A ghost of a smile flickered across her face. "Yes," she admitted, with a modesty that seemed incongruous with her usual confident demeanor. "I haven't seen a piano in years, though."

"I didn't know that about you," I said, genuinely surprised. In all our time together, Sofia had never mentioned any musical talent.

"I started lessons with her when I was three," she continued, as if drawing strength from the memory. "I was good enough that I got accepted to the Hanns Eisler School of Music in Berlin after high school."

"You were going to be a professional pianist?" I couldn't keep the astonishment from my voice. Sofia Kohl, with her military precision and no-nonsense approach to life, had once been on track for a life of music and art.

She nodded, wincing slightly at the movement. "Life had other plans. My mother got sick. I had to join the German Army to support her. The military police seemed like a good fit for my... particular personality traits."

The way she said it, with a touch of self-deprecating humor, made my heart ache. I tried to imagine a younger Sofia, dreams of music replaced by the practical necessity of a military paycheck and healthcare benefits. How different her life might have been.

"I'd love to hear you play sometime," I breathed.

"That would be nice," she agreed. "If we can find a working piano somewhere in this war-torn galaxy."

"I'll make it happen," I promised, already making mental notes to check the town of Wolf Jaw for a piano when we returned. "Maybe you could teach me a few basics."

Sofia's laugh was weaker this time, but no less genuine. "You, playing the piano? With those soldier hands that can field-strip a flechette rifle in twelve seconds?"

"Hey, these hands are multi-talented," I protested with mock indignation.

"That they are," she conceded with a hint of suggestiveness that reassured me—whatever was happening in her brain hadn't entirely dampened her spirit.

We lapsed into a comfortable silence again. Sofia's breathing seemed to even out, and I hoped the pain was temporarily subsiding.

"I remember this one recital," she blurted, her voice taking on an animated quality that I hadn't heard since before her collapse. "I was eleven or twelve. There was this boy playing before me, a real prodigy type who everyone fawned over."

"Let me guess—you showed him up?" I ventured, already smiling at the image of a young, fiercely competitive Sofia.

"Not exactly," she replied with a snort. "He finished his piece—Chopin, I think—and got this standing ovation. I was so nervous following him I threw up in a potted plant backstage."

I chuckled, trying to imagine my collected, composed Sofia in such a state. "Did you still perform?"

"Oh yes," she continued, and I could hear the smile in her voice despite the darkness. "My mother wiped my mouth, gave me a mint, and pushed me onto the stage. I was halfway through my piece when I realized I was wearing my dress backward from when I'd changed after the vomiting incident."

A laugh escaped me, both at the image and at the rare

glimpse into a softer, more vulnerable version of Sofia. "What did you do?"

"Finished the piece, of course," she replied, as if it were the most obvious thing in the world. "Then took my bow with all the dignity an eleven-year-old with a backward dress and mint breath could muster."

"That's my girl," I said fondly, leaning down to press a kiss to her forehead.

Her skin felt clammy beneath my lips, a reminder of the situation we were trying so hard to momentarily forget. Reality crashed back, the brief respite of shared laughter giving way to the cold knowledge that something serious was happening inside Sofia's brain.

"I should let you rest," I murmured, making to stand.

"Stay," she said, her hand finding mine in the darkness. "Just for a little while. Until I fall asleep."

I settled back onto the bed, this time stretching out beside her, careful not to crowd her but close enough that she could feel my presence. "As long as you need."

We lay there in the dim cabin, listening to the subtle creaks and hums of the ship around us. I focused on Sofia's breathing, counting the seconds between each inhale and exhale, as if I could somehow regulate her body through sheer force of will.

Gradually, her breathing deepened and slowed. The tension in her body eased, and her hand in mine went limp. I waited a few more minutes, making sure she was truly asleep before carefully extracting myself from the bed.

Standing over her in the near-darkness, I was struck by how young she looked in sleep, the usual lines of concentration erased from her face. Her hair had escaped its tight bun and spread across the pillow in a fan, catching what little light filtered through the doorway.

I leaned down and pressed one more soft kiss to her cheek, inhaling the familiar scent of her—military-issue soap with faint traces of the jasmine perfume she allowed herself as a rare indulgence.

"Hang in there," I whispered, though I knew she couldn't hear me. "Just a few more hours."

As I stepped back into the corridor, gently closing the door behind me, I felt a complicated mix of emotions churning in my chest. Worry, of course—that was the dominant note in the symphony. But also tenderness, for this unexpected glimpse into Sofia's past. And determination, steely and unyielding, to get her the help she needed.

The *Luminara* continued its journey toward the Sol System, carrying its precious cargo of a deposed alien queen, a damaged life support system, and the woman I loved—whose mind was under siege from an enemy I couldn't fight with any weapon in my arsenal.

All I could do was wait, and hope, and prepare for whatever came next.

6

I slouched in the observer's chair on *Luminara*'s bridge, trying not to fidget as the royal yacht dropped out of veilspace. The familiar stomach-churning sensation washed over me—like being turned inside out and then right-side in again, only to find yourself slightly askew. Captain Borlo's white cubic capsule bobbed at the command station, the stellar plasma of his igna body swirling inside like an angry miniature sun. We'd made it to the Venus-Sol L5 point without being blown to atoms by a Kergan patrol, which I counted as a win. My standards for victory had become embarrassingly low lately.

"Translation complete," announced one of the kavreni crew, their head bobbing with each word. "Positional confirmation: Venus-Sol L5 Lagrange point. Earth distance: approximately forty-five million kilometers."

Borlo's cube rotated to face the main viewscreen. "Borlo is pleased by the accuracy of the jump. Navigator, commence acceleration toward Earth orbit at two-thirds standard thrust."

I squinted at the viewscreen. Earth was just a bright blue dot from here, indistinguishable from the thousands of other points of light that speckled the darkness. Somewhere on that dot was home—or rather, what used to be home before I got packed off to Astrithon and my life got exponentially more complicated.

The bridge of *Luminara* was nothing like *Thunder*'s utilitarian command center. This was a royal yacht, and it showed in every glossy surface and ergonomic contour. The command stations were arranged in a perfect semi-circle, each manned by a kavreni whose eyes hovered a few inches away from holographic displays. The lighting was blue-tinted, designed for kavreni eyesight.

"Kory." Zeta's voice pulled me from my thoughts. Her octahedral capsule drifted toward my observer's chair, the stellar plasma inside shifting in hypnotic patterns of gold and crimson. "Zeta trusts the journey was not too taxing for you or Warrant Officer Kohl?"

I straightened in my seat, trying to look less like a schlub in the presence of exiled royalty. "We're managing. Sofia's resting in our quarters."

I didn't mention that "resting" was a polite euphemism for "unconscious after another seizure." It had happened thirty minutes ago, and I was feeling increasingly alarmed because of Sofia's worsening condition. But Zeta had enough problems to worry about at the moment. There was no need to burden her even more.

"Borlo must report that our translation pods are still emitting gravitational waves at concerning levels," the captain said, his cube pulsing with agitation. "The damage sustained during our escape from Ignisara has not self-corrected."

I frowned. "How concerning are we talking? Enough to alert Kergan sensors?"

"Not at this distance," Borlo replied. "The waves dissipate exponentially. We would need to pass within approximately one million kilometers of a Kergan sensor array to register as more than background noise."

Translation pods were the heart of any interstellar ship—specialized quantum devices that pushed against space-time and allowed travel across a star system in days rather than years. They weren't supposed to leak gravitational waves like a sieve, but *Luminara* hadn't exactly had time for proper repairs since fleeing from the coup.

A hissing sound filled the bridge as vents along the ceiling opened. I felt a slight pressure change in my ears.

"Atmospheric scrubbers at maximum capacity," reported another igna from the environmental station. "Carbon dioxide levels exceeding comfortable parameters. Commencing controlled cabin purge and replenishment."

Borlo's cube bobbed in acknowledgment. "Proceed. Use reserve nitrogen and oxygen tanks sparingly."

I raised an eyebrow. "Couldn't you just run the excess CO2 through the nanoforge? Convert it back to carbon and oxygen?"

"*Luminara* must conserve power," the captain replied, his plasma swirling faster within his cube. "The nanoforge requires significant energy that we cannot spare with damaged translation pods drawing excess power."

Zeta's octahedron shifted colors, darkening slightly at the edges. "Zeta no longer possesses a personal nanoforge. Such technology is reserved for Heliacal consorts."

An awkward silence followed. I felt a warmth in my chest, an uncomfortable heat that I recognized as embarrassment. My brief stint as Zeta's consort wasn't something we discussed often. It had been a military arrangement—one that ended when she was recalled to

Astrithon after my criminal charges for sydereal assault forced me to leave *Thunder.*

"I should check on Sofia," I said, rising from my seat. "I'll be back shortly."

Zeta's capsule bobbed, which I took as royal permission to leave. I navigated the curved corridors of *Luminara,* nodding to the kavreni crew members I passed. Most of the ship's functions were handled by them.

Our quarters were one deck down from the bridge—modest by royal yacht standards but luxurious compared to the cramped cabins and berths on *Thunder.* I keyed the entry pad and slipped inside quietly.

Sofia lay on the bed exactly as I'd left her, blonde hair fanned across the pillow, her face pale and drawn. The seizure monitoring patch on her temple blinked green, showing her brain activity had stabilized. Small mercies.

"Hey," I whispered, sitting on the edge of the bed. "We've arrived at the jump point. Everything went smoothly."

Sofia's eyelids fluttered but didn't open. "Water," she murmured, her voice raw and cracked.

I grabbed the hydration bottle from the bedside table and held it to her lips. She took two small sips before turning her head away.

"You need to drink more than that," I said, trying to keep the worry from my voice.

"Can't," she whispered. "Nauseous."

"The anti-nausea meds should be working by now. When was your last dose?"

Sofia didn't answer, her breathing already evening out as she drifted back to sleep. I checked the medication log on my tablet. The last dose had been administered four hours ago. She was due for another.

I prepared the hypospray with shaking hands. *Thunder*'s

medical bay might have been able to help her, if we could reach it.

"This will help with the nausea," I said, pressing the hypospray against her neck even though I wasn't sure she could hear me. The device hissed as it delivered the medication.

I tried once more with the water bottle. This time, she took three sips before turning away. Progress, I supposed, but not enough to keep her hydrated. If the seizures continued and she couldn't keep fluids down, we'd need to consider more drastic measures.

I sat with her for nearly thirty minutes, watching the slight rise and fall of her chest, before reluctantly returning to the bridge. The main viewscreen now showed a magnified image of Earth, though we were still tens of millions of kilometers away.

"Status?" I asked, settling back into the observer's chair.

Borlo's cube rotated toward me. "Acceleration proceeding as planned. We will reach Earth proximity in thirty-four hours."

Zeta hovered near the tactical station, her octahedron glowing a steady amber. "Zeta has been discussing our options with Captain Borlo. We dare not enter Earth's atmosphere or even establish orbit with damaged translation pods."

"Agreed," I said. "*Luminara* needs somewhere to hide while we call for help."

Borlo's plasma flickered. "Borlo must ask how Commander Drake proposes to call for help. Our communications array is functional but limited in range."

I leaned forward, elbows on my knees. "We need to contact Wolf Jaw Base and request that *Thunder* rendezvous with *Luminara*. My crew can evacuate your yacht and get

Sofia to our medical bay."

"Borlo regrets to inform Commander Drake that our chromatic batteries have insufficient charge to send a syderealdyne message."

Syderealdyne communications were the standard for interstellar messages—sydereal signals sent through the Syderealium that allowed near-instantaneous communication across light-years. But they required enormous power, which *Luminara* apparently couldn't spare.

"Then we use old-fashioned radio," I suggested. "High-frequency tight beam aimed at Wolf Jaw Base."

Borlo's cube tilted at an angle that suggested skepticism. "HF is difficult to synthesize into a tight beam signal because of the low frequency. Borlo could rig a crude antenna array using the ship's drones, but power consumption would still be substantial."

I snapped my fingers as a better idea struck me. "What about sending a single drone into Earth orbit? It could transmit when it passes over Wolf Jaw Base. That would use much less power and be less likely to attract Kergan attention."

The plasma inside Borlo's cube swirled in what I recognized as the igna version of consideration. "Borlo finds this solution elegant and efficient. One drone could carry sufficient power for multiple transmission attempts."

Zeta drifted closer. "Zeta approves this plan for communication. However, we still require a location to conceal *Luminara*. Remaining in open space means detection by Kergan sensors is inevitable."

"What about nearby asteroids?" I asked. "Something within a few million kilometers of Earth that we could tuck behind?"

Borlo turned to the navigation station. "Navigator,

analyze system survey data for suitable asteroids within specified parameters."

We waited in silence for several minutes while the navigator consulted their displays. Finally, the kavreni's head bobbed and turned toward us.

"Three potential candidates identified," the navigator reported. "Most promising option: asteroid approximately 300 meters in diameter, currently 3 million kilometers from Earth, on an approaching trajectory. Closest approach will be 400 thousand kilometers in approximately four Earth days."

"Perfect," I said. "A 300-meter rock should easily hide *Luminara*'s 100-meter hull from casual scans."

"Does this asteroid have a designation?" Zeta asked.

The navigator's capsule dimmed slightly. "No formal designation in registry."

I grinned. "Then I'm naming it HideyRock. Because that's what we're going to do with it—hide."

Borlo's cube vibrated slightly—the igna equivalent of a chuckle. "Borlo finds Captain Drake's nomenclature unorthodox but fitting."

"It's settled, then," I said. "We send a drone to contact *Thunder*, and meanwhile, we tuck *Luminara* behind HideyRock and power down as much as possible to minimize our signature."

Zeta's octahedron glowed with approval. "Zeta is pleased with this strategy. Captain Borlo, set course for the asteroid immediately."

"Navigational course adjusted," Borlo announced, his cube bobbing toward the helm station. "Estimated arrival at... HideyRock... in twenty-nine hours, seventeen minutes. Borlo is putting Second and Third Watches into torpor. This will give us an additional day with the life support system."

I settled back in my observer's chair, allowing myself a small smile despite the circumstances. In my experience, having a plan—even a desperate one—was better than having no plan at all. All we needed to do was reach the asteroid, hide behind it, and send our message to *Thunder.* Then Sofia would get the medical attention she needed, and Zeta would be one step closer to safety.

Of course, plans had a nasty habit of falling apart the moment they contacted reality, but I decided to worry about that when it happened. For now, I watched as Earth grew larger on the viewscreen, a blue-white beacon of hope in the vast darkness of space.

7

I slipped into our quarters, the door hissing closed behind me with a pneumatic sigh that seemed designed to announce my presence. Sofia was propped up against a stack of pillows, her hair spilling over her shoulders as she squinted at her tablet screen. The soft blue glow illuminated her face, casting shadows across the hollows of her cheeks—hollows that hadn't been there a month ago. My heart did its usual stutter-step at the sight of her, followed by the now-familiar twist of worry. But she looked better today.

"Hey," I said, suddenly aware of how heavy my boots sounded against the metal floor. The *Luminara* wasn't built for stealth, at least not on the inside.

Sofia looked up, her blue eyes finding mine, and a smile—a real one this time, not the thin-lipped grimace she'd been wearing since the attack—spread across her face. "Hey yourself, Commander."

"How's the head?" I perched on the edge of the bed, resisting the urge to press my palm against her forehead like some ancient mother checking for fever. Sofia had made it clear after the third time that she wasn't a child with the sniffles.

"Better." She set the tablet aside. "That yellow goop the doctor gave me tastes like fermented socks, but it's working. The pounding's down to a dull roar instead of a full-blown metal concert."

I nodded, relief washing through me like a cool breeze. "Good. That's... that's good." The kavreni physician had warned us that human biology was only partially compatible with their medications. That it was helping at all felt like winning the cosmic lottery.

Sofia tilted her head, her long hair shifting like a curtain. "You've got that look."

"What look?"

"The 'I need something, but I'm afraid to ask because you're injured' look." She smirked. "It's a very specific look."

I laughed, caught. My shoulders relaxed a notch. "I've got orbital parameters in Dominion notation for HideyRock that I need to convert into Keplerian notation. I was hoping you could help."

"HideyRock?" Sofia chuckled, the sound warming me from the inside out. It had been too long since I'd heard her laugh. "What in the hell is HideyRock?"

I grinned, pleased with myself. "It's an asteroid. We're transiting there to hide and wait for *Thunder* to rendezvous." I reached for my tablet, pulling up the complex figures Borlo had provided. "I need to send a message to Wolf Jaw Base with these parameters so *Thunder* can find us."

Sofia's expression softened. "And you think I can help convert... whatever the hell that is?" She gestured at the screen full of Dominion mathematical symbols—all sharp angles and overlapping ovals that made Earthen calculus look like kindergarten arithmetic.

"Honestly? No." I nudged her shoulder gently with mine. "But I thought maybe you could dictate for me while I do the conversion. Two heads are better than one, even if one of them is slightly damaged."

She punched my arm, not exactly gently. "Ass."

"Guilty as charged." I settled more comfortably beside her, our shoulders touching. My tablet rested on my knees as I began the complex process of conversion.

I'd spent months at the Space Warfare School on Astrithon learning this crap. At the time, I'd complained to Sofia that I was wasting my time with mathematical minutiae when I should have been learning practical battle tactics. Now, with our lives literally depending on these calculations, I silently thanked whatever sadistic instructor had drilled orbital mechanics into my reluctant brain.

"Hand me my tablet?" Sofia asked, and I passed it over. "I'll take notes while you mutter and swear."

"I don't mutter and swear," I muttered, then swore as I misplaced a decimal point and had to start a calculation over.

Sofia snorted but didn't comment further.

The familiar formulas flowed through my mind as I worked, transforming the alien notation into something Earth's systems could understand. The basic physics was the same—objects in space followed the same laws regardless of who was measuring them—but the expression of those laws varied wildly between civilizations.

The Dominion notation emphasized the relationship between the star and neighboring celestial bodies, while Keplerian elements focused on the orbit itself. Converting between them required a series of transformations that made my brain hurt, but I pressed on, aware that Sofia was watching me with a mixture of amusement and something else—pride, maybe?

"You're actually good at this," she observed after fifteen minutes of silence, broken only by my occasional requests for her to note down intermediate values.

"Don't sound so surprised," I said, not looking up from a particularly tricky vector calculation. "I contain multitudes."

"So I see." Her voice was soft, almost tender, and I felt my cheeks warm slightly.

After about twenty minutes of mental gymnastics, I finally had what I needed. "Okay, write these numbers down." I straightened my back, feeling vertebrae pop after being hunched over the tablet. "Semi-major axis: 1.0723972 AU; eccentricity: 0.360987; inclination: 8.368182 degrees; perihelion: 0.714932 AU; aphelion: 1.484206 AU; mean motion: 0.61927462."

Sofia's fingers danced across her tablet as she recorded each value. "Got it," she said when I finished. "Not that I understand any of that gobbledygook."

"Let me see," I said, reaching for her tablet. Our fingers brushed, and I felt a spark—static from the dry recycled air of the *Luminara*, but it jolted me nonetheless. I checked her numbers against my own, nodding as I confirmed they matched. "That's good. Perfect, actually."

I leaned over and kissed her on the cheek, lingering for a moment to breathe in the faint lavender scent of her hair. It was a minor miracle that she'd packed her own shampoo before our hasty evacuation. "How are you really doing? And don't say 'better' again unless you mean it."

Sofia sighed, leaning her head against my shoulder. "I do feel better. My head still hurts, but not as bad as it did. Maybe it's not so serious after all. I just need a few days to get over it."

I smiled at her, but inside, memories of her seizures—her body rigid, eyes rolled back, the terrifying sound of her teeth grinding together—clamped anxiety around my chest like a vise. The kavreni doctor had used words like "intracranial pressure" and "possible neural damage."

But worrying about it wouldn't save her any faster. So instead of voicing my fears, I squeezed her hand and turned back to my tablet to draft the message that would accompany the coordinates.

"Short and sweet," I murmured as I typed. "Requesting *Thunder* rendezvous ASAP. Damaged spaceship. Injured human requiring medical attention."

Sofia read over my shoulder. "You think they'll come for us?"

"Destiny will come." Of that, I had absolute certainty. Whatever else happened in this chaotic universe, Destiny Austin would move heaven, earth, and several star systems to reach us if she knew we were in trouble. "I just need to make sure she gets the message."

I pulled up the encryption program and input the onetime pad that Destiny and I had agreed upon during our last meeting. It was a ridiculously old-school method—practically ancient by Dominion standards—but sometimes the simplest solutions were the most secure. The program churned through the algorithm, converting my straightforward message into a seemingly random string of alphanumeric characters that would be meaningless to anyone without the key.

"There," I said, saving the encrypted file. "Now we just need to get it to Wolf Jaw."

Sofia nodded, then winced slightly at the movement. "Go. I'm fine here with my tablet and this godawful yellow medicine."

I kissed her again, this time on the lips, gentle and brief. "Get some rest. I'll be back soon."

The corridors of the *Luminara* were eerily quiet as I made my way to the small hangar bay. Zeta's royal yacht wasn't designed for combat or even extended deep-space missions. It was meant for diplomatic functions and short interplanetary jaunts—the alien equivalent of a luxury cruise. That we were using it as an emergency escape vessel spoke volumes about how spectacularly our situation at Virelia and Astrithon had gone sideways.

The hangar bay doors slid open with a soft whoosh, revealing a space about the size of *Thunder*'s mess hall. Captain Borlo floated near the center, his white cube capsule hovering at chest height to the kavreni technicians that scurried around him. The igna's mechanical body always reminded me of a high-tech sugar cube with delusions of grandeur.

"Drake has arrived," Borlo announced. His synthesized voice carried a hint of relief. "Borlo was concerned about delays."

"No delays," I assured him, approaching the object of their attention—a matte black cylinder about the size of a large trash can. Clusters of sensors and antennas protruded from its exterior like metallic growths, giving it an almost cancerous appearance. "Is this our messenger?"

"Affirmative," one of the kavreni technicians replied, his bat-like face serious as he adjusted something on the drone's flank. "Modified communications probe. Short-range FTL capability, then conversion to conventional propulsion for solar system approach."

I held up my tablet. "The message is ready."

Two of the kavreni techs immediately detached themselves from the group and came to my side. Their long, thin limbs moved with a grace that belied their awkward appearance, and their reversed knees still gave me a moment of cognitive dissonance every time I watched them walk.

"We will assist with upload," the taller one said, his enormous ears twitching slightly as he spoke. "Fortunately, we have documentation for converting our communication system protocols into something your Wolf Jaw Base ham radio can understand."

I nodded, watching as they connected my tablet to their equipment. The conversion process took only minutes, though the technical jargon they exchanged made about as much sense to me as Sofia's German curses.

"Message loaded," the shorter kavreni finally announced. "Launch sequence initiated."

I watched as the drone was moved into the small launch tube at the far end of the hangar. A countdown appeared on a nearby screen—ten minutes until deployment.

"Anyone listening will hear what sounds like randomized garbage," I said, more to myself than to the others. "Unless they have the onetime pad."

"The message will reach your base?" Borlo asked, his cube rotating slightly—the igna equivalent of a head tilt.

"If the drone makes it through, yes." I hoped it would be understood by Destiny and that she'd come with *Thunder*. The alternative didn't bear thinking about. If *Thunder* couldn't—or wouldn't—come, *Luminara* would have to take its chances and descend to Earth before our air ran out.

Maybe the Kergans wouldn't destroy us outright. Maybe they'd just capture us, interrogate us, use us as bargaining chips. I'd survived worse odds.

But Sofia hadn't. And that thought—the image of her pale and in pain, subjected to Kergan "hospitality"—made my hands clench into fists at my sides.

"Drake is troubled," Borlo observed, his sensor array focusing on my face.

"Drake is fine," I replied, mimicking his speech pattern without thinking. "Just eager to get our people home."

The countdown continued its steady decrease. Eight minutes now. Seven. Six.

The drone in its launch tube seemed impossibly small and fragile for the burden it carried—our location, our message, our hope. But then again, hope had always traveled in unlikely vessels. Seven years ago, hope had been a skinny girl with curly black hair who'd shared her stolen sandwich with a starving orphan on the streets of San Jose. Two years ago, hope had been an alien octahedron offering command of a starship to a homeless kid with no future.

Today, hope was a trash-can-shaped drone with the course for HideyRock and a plea for rescue.

I watched as the final seconds ticked away and the launch sequence completed. There was a soft pneumatic hiss, barely audible, and then the drone was gone—shot into the void, carrying our coordinates and my encrypted message toward Earth, toward Wolf Jaw Base, toward Destiny.

"Godspeed, little messenger," I murmured. "Find her."

8

Space has a way of making you feel both insignificant and terrifyingly important all at once. As *Luminara* sliced through the void toward HideyRock—and our messenger probe took a course toward Earth orbit—I couldn't shake the feeling that we were simultaneously lost in an endless nothing and yet precisely where the universe needed us to be. Not that the universe cared much about my opinion on the matter. The tiny asteroid grew from a speck to a hulking mass outside our viewport, while beside me, Sofia's breathing grew more labored with each passing hour.

The next couple of days aboard the Luminara passed in a blur of anxiety and forced patience. I spent most of my time alternating between the bridge with Queen Zeta and the medical bay with Sofia, neither location offering much comfort. HideyRock emerged out of the black void like a burned potato someone had forgotten in the oven for a month—an unappetizing lump that nevertheless represented our best hope for survival.

The life support situation kept getting worse. We were

maintaining air quality by regularly venting the atmosphere and replacing it with fresh reserves—but that was just a temporary fix. Once the reserves ran out, so did our options.

"There it is," I said unnecessarily, as the asteroid bloomed larger in our forward screens. "Home sweet temporary hiding place."

Captain Borlo, ensconced in his pristine white cube capsule, hovered near the navigation console. "Borlo notes that HideyRock's albedo makes it difficult to detect at range. Most fortuitous for our circumstances."

"Most fortuitous indeed," I muttered, watching as the tiny rock grew in the viewport.

It was almost comical how something so small could become our salvation. Yet as we approached, HideyRock transformed from an insignificant speck to a looming mountain of space debris. Its surface was a testament to the violence of space—pockmarked by craters that resembled acne scars on the face of a celestial teenager. Boulders and gravel in varying shades of gray and dark brown littered its surface like discarded building blocks. Some areas shimmered with metallic glints, confirming what our scans had already told us—the asteroid was rich in iron oxides.

HideyRock rotated lazily, making one full turn about every five hours. I watched a particularly distinctive crater slowly disappear from view, only to reappear on the other side like a patient spinning in a doctor's chair. The asteroid stretched roughly 300 meters in length and 200 in width—not exactly spacious real estate, but large enough to conceal our vessel if we played our cards right.

"Her Majesty would like to know if Commander Drake approves of our selected hiding place," Borlo intoned, his cube pulsing slightly with each word.

I glanced over to where Zeta hovered in her octahedral capsule. Even contained within her vessel, there was something majestic about her plasma form, shifting and swirling in patterns that reminded me of solar flares in miniature.

"Tell Her Majesty that this potato rock looks perfect," I replied. "That crevasse on the side—can we fit in there?"

"Borlo assures you that *Luminara* was designed for precisely such maneuvers."

I raised an eyebrow. "Designed specifically for hiding in random asteroid crevasses? That's oddly specific engineering."

Borlo's cube vibrated in what I recognized as the igna equivalent of a huff. "Borlo meant that *Luminara* is designed for precision navigation in confined spaces."

"Just pulling your leg, Captain." I leaned forward as we approached the deep fissure that ran down the center of HideyRock along one side. "That's one hell of a canyon."

"A result of impact stress and subsequent cooling," Borlo explained. "Quite common in asteroids of this composition."

The captain guided *Luminara* toward the narrow slit with the delicate touch of a surgeon. The royal yacht responded beautifully, slipping into the canyon-like gap that nearly concealed us completely from external observation. The secondary tractor pods fired in careful bursts, adjusting our position until we were nestled snugly within the rocky embrace of HideyRock. The ship's exterior lights illuminated the rough, striated walls of our new home—layers of compressed minerals that told the asteroid's billion-year story in bands of black, brown, and rusty red.

With *Luminara* secured, I returned to our quarters, where Sofia lay sleeping. In the middle of our sleep cycle, I was jolted awake by Sofia's body going rigid beside me. Her back arched unnaturally, her limbs stiffening as a seizure took hold.

"Sofia!" I scrambled to her side, my heart hammering against my ribs like it was trying to break free.

There was little to be done except wait it out. I cradled Sofia's head in my lap, keeping her from banging against the bed frame, murmuring useless reassurances that she couldn't hear.

"It's okay, Sof. I'm here. You're going to be fine."

The seizure seemed to last forever, though the medical readout told me it was just under five minutes. Five minutes of helpless watching. Five minutes of being utterly useless. Five minutes of praying to a god I didn't know to please, please let her be okay.

When it finally subsided, Sofia collapsed back against the mattress, exhausted and disoriented. Her eyes fluttered open, unfocused and confused.

"What... happened?" Her voice was a rasp, her German accent thicker than usual.

"Just a little dance party," I said, trying to keep my voice light despite the fear choking me. "You've got some moves, Kohl."

She tried to smile but instead turned suddenly pale. I grabbed a basin just in time as she emptied what little was in her stomach. I held her hair back, remembering doing the same for a drunk Destiny a handful of times. This was infinitely worse.

I administered another dose of medication with the hypospray. "This should help with the nausea," I said. "But I'm concerned about the increasing frequency of these seizures."

I lay beside Sofia, careful not to disturb the various monitors attached to her. She'd drifted back to sleep, her breathing shallow but steady. I, however, remained wide awake, my mind racing with worry and fear and a thousand what-ifs.

The drone had been gone for two days now. Two days of silence. By my calculations, it should have reached Earth orbit by now and, if everything had gone according to plan, transmitted at least once to Wolf Jaw Base. But we'd heard nothing. No confirmation. No rescue on the way. Just the endless, patient waiting as our air and power slowly dwindled.

In those quiet hours, with Sofia's breathing the only sound beyond the soft hum of the ship's systems, my mind wandered to unexpected places. I found myself pondering the meaning of birth and death, the cosmic joke of consciousness in an indifferent universe.

I'd never been religious—agnostic at best, skeptic at worst. If there was a god out there somewhere, watching over all this, they'd done a remarkable job of hiding their tracks. And if they did exist, I wasn't sure I wanted to meet them—we'd have some pointed questions to discuss about their design choices. Why seizures? Why sickness at all? Why make a universe so vast if we were meant to care about each individual life?

Death itself didn't frighten me. It struck me as merely a transition to another state of being, just as birth was. The universe recycled everything eventually—stars, planets, people. The atoms that made up Sofia and me had once been part of ancient stars. We were cosmic hand-me-downs, wearing particles that had seen billions of years of history.

I traced a finger gently along Sofia's arm, following the blue lines of veins under her skin. What a miracle that these particular atoms had assembled themselves into her—pragmatic, brave, beautiful her. What terrible cosmic wastage it would be to lose her now.

It occurred to me that immortality, which so many humans seemed to crave, was fundamentally selfish. If nobody died, where would the space come for new life? The universe was vast, but not infinite in its resources. Striving to live forever seemed like hogging the buffet table at a party where new guests were constantly arriving.

Yet despite this philosophical acceptance of mortality, I found myself longing for more time. Not endless time—just enough. Enough to see what came next. Enough to maybe have children someday.

The thought surprised me, bubbling up from some previously unexplored part of my psyche. Children. A family. With Sofia.

I'd never seriously considered it before, had always been too focused on my life, on survival, on the next mission. But lying there in the dim light of our quarters, Sofia's hand in mine, I could suddenly see it so clearly—a little girl with Sofia's blonde hair and serious blue eyes, a boy with her steady hands and my inability to sit still.

Sofia would make an excellent mother. She had that perfect combination of protective instinct and unwavering patience. Like a mother bear—dangerous to anyone threatening her cubs, but gentle beyond measure with those she loved. The image made me smile despite our circumstances.

It was the first time I'd considered developing our relationship into something deeper—a true partnership in parenthood. How would I even bring up such a subject with her? "Hey, Sof, once we're not dying slowly in an asteroid, want to make some babies?"

Perhaps it would have to wait until she was better. And only if she was equally enthusiastic, of course. I wouldn't pressure her. Maybe she'd never wanted children. We'd never really discussed it, always too busy with immediate concerns, like not getting shot at or blown up.

And would we marry? Did it matter? The ceremony itself seemed less important than the commitment behind it. I imagined exchanging vows without all the pomp and circumstance—just promises of monogamy for as long as we chose to be together. No "till death do us part" when death felt so uncomfortably close these days.

Sofia stirred in her sleep, murmuring something unintelligible. I pressed a kiss to her forehead, feeling the slight fever burning beneath her skin. "Hang in there," I whispered. "We've got plans to make."

The next day brought the first noticeable decrease in air quality. The atmosphere aboard *Luminara* had grown noticeably stale, carrying a hint of recycled breath and machinery that hadn't been there before. My lungs felt like they were working harder for less reward, like running uphill when you're already tired.

I found Captain Borlo and Queen Zeta on the bridge, engaged in what appeared to be a serious discussion. They paused when I entered.

"Something wrong?" I asked, though the question felt redundant. Everything was wrong.

"Borlo regrets to inform Commander Drake that our oxygen reserves have fallen below acceptable parameters," the captain said, his cube pulsing dimly. "We can no longer afford to vent the ship's atmosphere."

"Meaning what, exactly?"

"Meaning we must conserve what oxygen remains," Zeta replied, her plasma form swirling more rapidly within her octahedral capsule. "The carbon dioxide scrubbers are functioning at reduced efficiency due to a shortage of Xenon-129 and our power constraints prevent use of the nanoforge."

I ran a hand through my hair, which was getting greasy from too many days without a proper shower. "So we're officially suffocating, just very slowly."

"The Queen does not appreciate Commander Drake's flippancy in this matter."

"Sorry, Zeta. It's just my way of processing bad news." I moved to the navigation console, pulling up a map of our location. "What if we relocate to Luna? We could attempt to mine oxygen there."

Zeta's capsule drifted closer. "Zeta wonders why Kory suggests Luna when HideyRock itself is rich in iron oxides. We could mine oxygen here."

"Do we have the equipment for that?"

"Borlo confirms that *Luminara* carries basic extraction tools," the captain interjected. "However, the power requirements would be substantial."

"Which we don't have," I finished for him. "So we're stuck."

"Zeta prefers to think of it as being committed to our strategy," Zeta said. "We decided to wait at HideyRock for a reason. *Thunder* may yet appear."

She was right, of course. We couldn't afford to leave HideyRock behind, not when it was our rendezvous point with *Thunder*—if *Thunder* was even out there looking for us. For all we knew, they may not have received our message. Or even worse, the ship could have been destroyed or captured since the last time I exchanged messages with Destiny.

"The drone should have reached Earth by now," I said, more to myself than to them.

"Zeta has faith in your drone's mission," Zeta said, her tone softening slightly. "We must be patient."

I nodded, though patience had never been my strong suit. Especially not when Sofia was getting worse by the hour and our air was slowly poisoning us.

"Patient," I echoed. "Right. We'll just sit here and breathe shallowly while we wait to be rescued."

Borlo's cube rotated in what I took to be disapproval. "Borlo suggests Commander Drake might wish to check on Warrant Officer Kohl. Medical telemetry reports she is awake."

I was already moving toward the door before he finished speaking. "Let me know if anything changes," I called over my shoulder. "Or if you suddenly remember we have a magical oxygen generator hidden somewhere on this ship."

As I made my way back to Sofia, I tried to focus on the future I'd imagined the night before—children, a home, a life beyond this crisis. It helped, a little. But with each labored breath of the increasingly stale air, that future felt more like a dream than a plan.

Still, a dream was better than nothing. And nothing was exactly what we'd have if someone didn't find us soon.

9

I jammed the long-handled brush deeper into the filter housing, my face twisted in disgust behind my protective mask as a clump of matted kavreni fur broke free and splashed into the collection bucket. The stench somehow found its way through my filtration system—a sour, ammonia-tinged odor that made my eyes water. A year of commanding *Thunder* hadn't prepared me for the glamor of cleaning waste filters on a royal yacht. But idle hands make for a restless Kory Drake, and Captain Borlo had been "generous" enough to find me this particular task.

"You're welcome," I muttered to myself, scraping at another stubborn mass of hair. Kavreni shed like it was their sacred duty, their fine fur working its way into every conceivable nook and cranny of *Luminara*'s systems. Without regular cleaning, the entire ship would probably grind to a halt under the weight of alien dander.

The protective gloves—three layers thick and still somehow not quite enough—squished unpleasantly as I worked. I'd been at it for nearly two hours, moving methodically from one filter to the next, a strange sort of meditation in maintenance. Not exactly how I'd pictured myself spending time on a royal igna vessel, but beggars couldn't be choosers, and I was definitely begging for something—anything—to do.

Thunder was my ship. My crew. My purpose. Without them, I was just a tall guy with surprisingly adept plumbing skills and increasingly pruned fingers.

I'd spent most of my time hovering around Sofia, watching, hoping she was recovering from the head injury. Her normally sharp blue eyes had been foggy, unfocused. Her precise, accented speech slurred. Sofia assured me she was improving, but the worry gnawed at me like acid on metal. Even after three days, she still had moments when she seemed lost, forgotten in the middle of a sentence.

And so I'd asked Borlo for a job—any job—to keep me from pacing a groove into the floor of our cabin. I'd expected something that used my skills as a starship captain. Maybe tactical analysis. Strategic planning. Hell, I'd have taken navigation calculations.

Instead, I got fur-clogged waste filters.

"Truly, you've outdone yourself, Captain Drake," I said to my reflection in a particularly shiny bit of drain pipe. "The UHC Armada would be so proud."

The light above the bathroom door flashed red, and the ship's PA system crackled to life.

"Commander Drake to the bridge," Borlo's voice announced. "Commander Drake will report to the bridge immediately."

I dropped the brush, my heart rate kicking up several notches. No one had called me to the bridge since we'd tucked ourselves into this asteroid's canyon. Something had changed.

I tugged off the gloves with a wet sucking sound and pulled the mask from my face, allowing myself one deep breath of relatively cleaner air. The janitorial cart would have to wait—I wouldn't be so cruel as to leave this mess for someone else to clean up. I stowed the supplies against the wall where they wouldn't be in the way and hurried toward the bridge.

The corridors of *Luminara* were narrow compared to *Thunder,* designed with thin kavreni bodies and igna capsules in mind. I had to duck through several hatchways, the top of my head brushing against the frame despite my careful movements. The ship hummed with the quiet efficiency of emergency power conservation—half the lights dimmed, environmental systems running at minimum capacity.

The bridge door slid open at my approach, revealing a scene of controlled tension. Captain Borlo's white cube capsule hovered at the central command station, the plasma within shifting in patterns I couldn't begin to interpret. The kavreni crew worked silently at their stations, their enormous ears twitching occasionally as they monitored systems.

"Commander Drake has arrived," Borlo announced, his capsule rotating slightly to face me.

"I came as quickly as I could," I said, wiping my still-damp hands on my pants. "What's happening?"

"*Luminara* has received a message," Borlo said. "A radio transmission over low-rate spread spectrum tight beam. The sender claims to be *Thunder.*"

My pulse jumped. "*Thunder*? Are you sure?"

"Borlo cannot authenticate. The message was received in packet form, likely to avoid Kergan detection."

"Let me talk to them," I said, stepping toward the

communications station. "I can verify if it's really *Thunder*."

"That is not possible," Borlo said. "As Borlo explained, it was a one-way transmission—a data packet. No real-time communication was established."

I tried to mask my disappointment. "What did the message say?"

Borlo gestured with a corner of his capsule, and a nearby kavreni handed me a tablet. I scanned the brief text displayed:

"*Thunder* acknowledges message from *Luminara*, in transit to your location, ETA 28 hours."

That was it. No authentication codes, no personal message from my crew. Just bare-bones information that could have come from anyone who knew we were here. But who else would know? Who else would be looking?

"Thank you," I said, handing the tablet back. "If it is *Thunder*, is 28 hours quick enough for our situation?"

"It is not," Borlo stated flatly. "At current consumption rates, Luminara has life support for approximately 12 hours. The oxygen recyclers were damaged during our escape. The carbon dioxide scrubbers are functioning at 18% efficiency."

I let that sink in. Sixteen hours short. Not a small gap to bridge.

A shimmer of golden light drew my attention to the far side of the bridge where Zeta's capsule hovered, her plasma form glowing with royal radiance. Unlike Borlo's cubic container, Zeta's octahedral housing was ornate, with subtle patterns etched into the transparent material that contained her stellar form.

"The queen suggests putting most of the kavreni crew into torpor," she said, her formal third-person speech even more pronounced than Borlo's. "This will reduce oxygen requirements significantly."

"Borlo has already ordered this measure," the captain replied. "Even with 80% of kavreni crew in torpor state, *Luminara* will exhaust breathable atmosphere before *Thunder*'s arrival."

"What options do we have?" I asked. "Can we further reduce power consumption? Shut down more systems?"

"All non-essential systems are already inactive," Borlo said. "*Luminara* operates at minimum viable functionality."

"The queen will power the nanoforge," Zeta announced abruptly.

The bridge fell silent. Even the minimal background noise of tapping and clicking from the kavreni crew ceased.

"The queen cannot—" Borlo began.

"The queen can and will," Zeta interrupted, her plasma form flickering with intensity. "The nanoforge can extract oxygen from HideyRock's iron oxides. The queen's body contains sufficient energy to power this process."

I glanced between the two igna, sensing the tension in their exchange despite the alien nature of their communication.

"Such a task is beneath the queen," Borlo argued. "There must be alternative solutions."

"The queen asks Captain Borlo to suggest these alternatives," Zeta replied coolly.

Borlo's plasma swirled in agitation. "Borlo cannot power the forge because Borlo must command the ship. But the queen will be vulnerable during the process. The queen will be unresponsive to external stimuli. If there is danger —"

"The queen notes that danger already exists," Zeta said. "The queen will not allow her subjects to perish from lack of oxygen when she possesses the means to prevent it."

"Borlo objects to this course of action," he insisted.

"The queen appreciates Captain Borlo's concern," Zeta said, her plasma form settling into calmer patterns. "However, the queen is making this an order, not a suggestion. Zeta will power the nanoforge. Commander Drake will accompany the queen. Preparations will begin immediately."

Borlo's capsule dipped slightly. "Borlo obeys," he said, his tone conveying resigned acceptance.

I looked at Zeta's capsule, trying to read anything from the swirling patterns of plasma inside. I couldn't help but admire her willingness to put herself at risk.

"Lead the way, Zeta," I said with a slight nod.

I followed Zeta's floating octahedral capsule through *Luminara*'s narrow corridors, our odd procession illuminated by the golden glow of her plasma body. The ship hummed with the depleted energy of a vessel on its last legs. We were headed to the nanoforge compartment—a room I'd passed a dozen times without giving it much thought. Funny how a place could suddenly become the difference between life and death. Then again, that seemed to be the recurring theme of my life since becoming *Thunder*'s captain.

The nanoforge compartment was adjacent to the chromatic battery banks—logical, considering the massive energy requirements of atomic-level fabrication. As the door slid open, I was struck by how modest the setup looked for something so technologically advanced. The nanoforge itself resembled an industrial washing machine crossed with a medical scanner—all gleaming surfaces and inscrutable displays that blinked with multicolored status indicators.

"I've never seen this nanoforge in action," I admitted, running my hand along its smooth exterior. "Much less powered by royalty."

"The queen rarely serves as a power source," Zeta replied, her capsule rotating slightly toward me. "But these are unusual circumstances."

"How exactly can you power it?" I asked. "I mean, I know igna are basically walking stars, but there must be limits."

Zeta's plasma form shifted inside her capsule, golden waves rippling in what I recognized as contemplation.

"The queen's body exists in entanglement with the quantum foam that underlies reality," she explained. "In theory, igna have access to unlimited energy—we feed on the constant creation and annihilation of virtual particles in the vacuum of space."

"In theory?" I raised an eyebrow.

"In practice, there are biological limits," Zeta conceded. "Drawing too much power too quickly is... painful. The queen's neural patterns become disrupted. Imagine your nervous system being used as electrical conduits."

I winced. "Sounds unpleasant."

"The queen is willing to endure discomfort if it means saving her subjects," Zeta said, and I couldn't help but admire her resolve. In my experience, rulers who put themselves at risk for their people were rare indeed.

"What do you need from me?" I asked.

"The queen requires only a kavreni technician to operate the nanoforge," she replied. "Once connected, the queen will be unconscious—unable to control the fabrication process."

A kavreni engineer entered the compartment, ducking his head as he passed through the doorway. His enormous ears twitched nervously, and his tail swished behind him as he bowed deeply to Zeta.

"Do you really want to do this?" I asked her quietly while the engineer prepared the console. "There's no other way?"

"The queen does not want to do this," Zeta admitted, her plasma form flickering briefly. "But the queen sees no alternative that ensures the survival of all aboard *Luminara*."

I nodded, understanding all too well the weight of command decisions. Sometimes the only options were bad and worse.

The kavreni engineer gestured to a metallic frame standing next to the nanoforge—an igna walker. Unlike the floating capsules that igna typically used to navigate terrestrial environments, the walker was humanoid in shape, with articulated limbs designed for manual manipulation.

Zeta's capsule floated toward the walker, settling into a harness at its center. With surprising grace, the mechanical arms of the walker reached up and positioned cables against Zeta's octahedral housing. I watched, fascinated, as the cables seemed to meld with the transparent material—no visible ports, yet they connected as naturally as if they'd been designed for this very purpose.

"The queen is initiating power transfer," Zeta announced, her voice already sounding distant. "The queen entrusts her safety to Captain Drake and Engineer Tikrit."

The kavreni—Tikrit—took his seat at the control console, his long fingers dancing across the interface. The nanoforge began to vibrate, a low hum that quickly rose in pitch and intensity. The surrounding air shifted, growing warmer as the massive machine drew power from Zeta's stellar body.

I caught a whiff of ozone, sharp and electric, followed by a rush of hot air that tousled my hair. The lights in the compartment flickered momentarily, then stabilized at a brighter intensity than before—as if the excess energy from

Zeta was bleeding into Luminara's systems.

"Zeta?" I asked, but received no response. Zeta's plasma had condensed into a tight, brilliant core within her capsule—no longer swirling in the complex patterns. She was already unconscious.

"System initiated," Engineer Tikrit announced, his voice high-pitched and clipped. "Nanobot swarm activation complete. Energy flow stable."

I leaned against the wall, crossing my arms as I settled in for what was clearly going to be a waiting game. "How do you feel about this?" I asked the engineer. "Your queen powering a machine like a battery?"

Tikrit's ears flattened against his head briefly—embarrassment or discomfort, I couldn't tell which.

"The greatest ruler is not the one who sits highest on the throne," he replied, eyes still fixed on his console, "but the one who bends lowest to lift others." His long tail flicked thoughtfully. "Our queens have always taught that to rule is to serve. Today, Her Majesty demonstrates this truth most literally."

I hadn't expected such philosophical depth from a ship's engineer. Then again, I'd learned long ago not to underestimate any sentient being based on their job title.

"Nanobot survey underway," Tikrit reported. "Mapping external composition of HideyRock in immediate vicinity of *Luminara*."

Minutes stretched into a quarter hour with little visible change. The nanoforge continued its gentle hum, occasionally punctuated by mechanical adjustments and the soft beeping of Tikrit's console.

"Oxide ores located," he announced finally. "Starting extraction sequence."

The display screen above the console flickered to life,

showing microscopic views of what appeared to be dust particles. As I watched, they transformed into swarming dots that arranged themselves in complex patterns—nanobots harvesting oxygen atoms from the rocky material outside our hull.

"How long before we see results?" I asked.

"Oxygen partial pressure should begin to increase within the hour," Tikrit replied. "I have also programmed the nanoforge to split carbon dioxide molecules. We will reclaim oxygen while reducing harmful CO2 levels."

I nodded, impressed. "Smart thinking."

"The queen selected this engineer personally," Tikrit said, his chest puffing slightly with pride. "This engineer trained at the Vireliean Academy of Atomic Manufacturing."

Another hour passed, and true to Tikrit's prediction, the ship's atmospheric displays showed a gradual increase in oxygen levels and a decrease in CO_2 levels. The emergency warnings that had been flashing on his console dimmed to cautionary status.

I must have dozed in my chair. I opened my eyes and found a very different scene. Engineer Tikrit was frantically tapping commands into his console, his ears flattened against his skull in distress. The nanoforge was emitting a high-pitched whine that set my teeth on edge, and the air had grown uncomfortably hot.

"What's wrong?" I demanded, rushing to his side.

"Overheating in primary conversion chamber," Tikrit replied, his words tumbling out in a panicked rush. "I have reduced conversion rate by sixty percent, but thermal regulation is still failing."

"Did something break?"

"Damage to cooling subsystem," he confirmed, tail lashing anxiously. "Possibly sustained during our escape from Arctis's forces. I did not detect it during diagnostics."

"Is there going to be enough air?" I asked, eyeing the atmospheric readouts on his screen.

"I... believe so," Tikrit said, though his hesitation was far from reassuring. "But cannot guarantee optimal levels."

"What about Zeta? Is she in danger?"

Tikrit's enormous eyes blinked rapidly. "The queen is stable. Her vital patterns show stress but remain within acceptable parameters."

Before I could ask another question, *Luminara* lurched violently beneath our feet. I staggered, grabbing the edge of the console to keep from falling. A tremendous bang reverberated through the hull, followed by a series of smaller impacts that reminded me of hail on a tin roof—if the hail were the size of bowling balls.

"What the hell was that?" I shouted, struggling to regain my balance as the deck continued to shift beneath us.

Tikrit's ears swiveled toward the ceiling, his sensitive hearing picking up details my human ears couldn't detect.

"Impact on exterior hull," he reported, voice tight with fear. "Multiple impacts. Something has struck *Luminara*."

10

I raced through *Luminara*'s corridors, my heart hammering against my ribs with each new rumble and groan from the ship's hull. The sounds of shifting rock and metal under stress chased me like hungry predators. Sofia's face filled my thoughts—her pale complexion, the lingering confusion in her eyes. If a rock slide had damaged the ship's life support systems, her already fragile condition would... No. I wouldn't let my mind go there. First, find Sofia. Then, solve the latest disaster in what was becoming an increasingly ridiculous series of unfortunate events in the life of Captain Kory Drake.

The mess hall was empty, the chairs still askew from where she had been sitting earlier. I pivoted and sprinted toward our cabin, ducking through hatches and narrowly avoiding a collision with a maintenance drone.

More kavreni crew members rushed past me, their enormous eyes wide with alarm, their normally precise movements frantic. I called out to one, asking what had happened, but he charged past without acknowledging me, his attention fixed on some urgent task ahead.

Outside our cabin door, I paused to catch my breath, forcing myself to appear calmer than I felt. The last thing Sofia needed was to see me panicking. I straightened my shoulders, arranged my face into what I hoped was a reassuring expression, and pressed the entry panel.

The door slid open to reveal Sofia propped up in bed, a tablet in her hands. Her blonde hair was pulled back in a loose ponytail, revealing the fading bruise at her temple. She looked up, her blue eyes sharpening with concern as she took in my disheveled appearance.

"What's happening?" she asked, setting aside the tablet.

I moved to her side, quickly checking her over for any signs of distress. "Just some asteroid turbulence. Are you okay?"

"I'm fine," she said, her German accent clipping the words. "The ship moved suddenly. I heard impacts."

"I'm heading to the bridge to find out exactly what's going on," I told her, squeezing her hand. "Stay here, alright? Rest."

Sofia's eyes narrowed. "You're going to do something stupid, aren't you?"

I pressed my hand to my chest in mock offense. "Me? Never. Well, rarely. Okay, occasionally, but only when absolutely necessary." I managed a crooked smile. "I'll be back as soon as I can."

Her fingers tightened around mine. "Be careful, Kory," she said, her voice softening. "I'm still not in shape to save you if you get into trouble."

I kissed her forehead. "Noted. No trouble requiring rescue."

Back in the corridor, I broke into a run again, heading for the bridge. The ship continued to groan around me, the metal frame settling under new pressures. More kavreni rushed past, their long limbs carrying them with a strange, stilted grace despite their obvious haste.

The bridge door slid open, revealing a scene of controlled chaos. Captain Borlo hovered near the main display, his cubic capsule rotating rapidly—the igna equivalent of pacing. The few kavreni crew members still awake worked feverishly at their stations, their enormous ears twitching with stress.

"What's going on?" I demanded, striding to Borlo's side.

"Tidal forces from Earth have affected HideyRock's structural integrity," Borlo replied, his plasma body swirling agitatedly inside his cube. "The canyon walls surrounding Luminara have shifted. A partial collapse has occurred."

"Show me," I said.

Borlo gestured toward the main display. The screen cycled through external camera views, but each showed the same thing—darkness, occasionally interrupted by static as the cameras attempted to recalibrate.

"I can't see anything," I said.

"Because there is nothing to see," Borlo replied. "Debris blocked the cameras. The canyon wall has collapsed onto Luminara."

My stomach dropped. "Are we being crushed?"

"No," Borlo assured me. "HideyRock's gravitational force is insufficient to compress *Luminara*'s hull. The danger is not from pressure but from entombment."

"So we're buried alive," I summarized grimly.

"Affirmative. And the debris is likely covering *Luminara*'s sensor arrays and communication antennas."

The implications hit me like a fist to the gut. "We have no way to contact *Thunder*."

"Correct," Borlo confirmed, his plasma form dimming slightly. "If *Thunder* cannot locate *Luminara,* rescue becomes exponentially more difficult."

I ran a hand through my hair, thinking fast. "We need to dig ourselves out before *Thunder* arrives."

"Borlo concurs with this assessment."

"I'll handle it," I said, already turning toward the door.

"Commander Drake," Borlo called after me. "Borlo advises caution. The debris field is unstable. Further collapses are possible."

I nodded. "Understood. I'll be careful."

I made my way quickly to *Luminara*'s main airlock, my mind racing through possibilities. The ship's storage lockers contained several suits of protomatter armor—multi-purpose protective gear that would shield me from the vacuum of space and provide enhanced strength and endurance. Not as robust as military-grade combat suits, but more than adequate for my current needs.

The closest locker yielded what I was looking for—a formless blob of matte black nanobots that seemed to pulse with potential energy. I stripped out of my coveralls, stepped forward, and pressed my palm against the mass, feeling a slight tingle as the protomatter recognized my biometric signature.

Without hesitation, I stepped into the seemingly amorphous blob. The nanobots responded instantly, flowing up my legs like water in reverse gravity. They spread across my skin, conforming perfectly to every contour of my body. The sensation was oddly intimate—cool at first, then warm as the protomatter established connectivity with my nervous system.

The black substance flowed up my torso and along my arms, encasing me in a flexible second skin that was only a centimeter thick but would protect me from vacuum, radiation, and physical impact. When the nanobots reached my head, they formed a rigid helmet with a transparent diamond faceplate that offered an unobstructed view of my surroundings.

Information scrolled across my field of vision as the suit's systems came online. Oxygen levels, power reserves, structural integrity—all optimal. I flexed my fingers, feeling the subtle amplification of my movements as the suit's muscle enhancement calibrated itself to my body.

"Bridge, this is Drake," I said, testing the suit's communication system. "I'm suited up and ready."

"Borlo acknowledges," came the captain's response. "*Luminara* will deactivate artificial gravity in affected sections. This will minimize the risk of debris falling into the ship when you open the airlock."

"Copy that," I replied. "Cutting gravity in three, two, one..."

The familiar sensation of weightlessness took hold, my body drifting slightly off the deck. I'd spent enough time in zero-g during my years commanding *Thunder* that it felt almost natural. I secured my footing using the suit's magnetic boots, then approached the airlock control panel.

"Opening inner door," I announced, tapping the sequence.

The airlock door slid open with a soft hiss. I stepped inside, sealed the inner door behind me, and prepared to face whatever lay beyond the outer hatch.

After pumping air out of the chamber, I said, "Opening outer door," more for my own benefit than for Borlo's.

The outer door slid sideways into its recess in the hull—and I found myself staring at a wall of dark gray gravel and dust. Small particles immediately began drifting into the airlock, dancing in the beam of my helmet lights like demented fireflies.

It occurred to me how much danger I was in. If debris fell into the chamber, I wouldn't be able to close the outer hatch. And if I couldn't close the outer hatch, I couldn't repressurize the chamber and open the inner hatch. I would be trapped here until my air ran out and I died.

I stood motionless, carefully assessing the situation. The debris looked like a solid mass, but in HideyRock's minimal gravity, it was more like a cloud of particles held together by the barest whisper of attraction. The problem wasn't that it was heavy—it wasn't. The problem was that there was so much of it.

How thick was the layer? Centimeters? Meters? Dozens of meters? I had no way to know for certain, but based on the canyon's dimensions that I'd observed during our arrival, I guessed we were dealing with a debris field at least ten to twenty meters thick.

We didn't have time to dig out the entire ship—that would take days we didn't have. What we needed was a tunnel—a passage to the surface where we could establish communications with *Thunder* and create an evacuation route if necessary.

"Bridge, I'm looking at a wall of gravel blocking the airlock," I reported. "I need to create a tunnel to the surface. I'm going to start moving debris into the cargo hold."

"Borlo understands," came the reply. "Cargo hold has been prepared. Be advised that two kavreni crew members are en route to assist. Borlo has awakened them from torpor."

"Copy that. I'm starting now."

I reached out and scooped a handful of gravel, the material behaving like thick liquid in the minimal gravity.

The problem became immediately apparent—there was nowhere to put it. I couldn't just shove it aside; the particles would drift back into place. I needed to physically relocate every bit of debris I moved.

Turning back toward the inner airlock door, I sealed the outer hatch temporarily and cycled through, carrying my handful of asteroid material. Once inside, I made my way to the cargo hold—a relatively small space on a yacht like *Luminara*, but it would have to do.

I deposited the gravel in a corner of the hold, where Borlo had erected a containment field to keep the debris from floating freely around the ship. One handful down, about a million to go.

By my third trip, the two kavreni crew members had arrived. They wore smaller versions of protomatter armor adapted to their unique physiology, their enormous eyes visible behind their faceplates.

"Commander Drake," the first one greeted me, his voice tinny through the comm system. "I am Engineer Sorril. This is Technician Visk. We are here to assist."

"Glad to have you," I said sincerely. "I was just realizing what a monumental task this is going to be."

"We have brought capture nets," Sorril said, holding up what looked like a mesh bag attached to a collapsible frame. "They will help transport larger quantities of debris."

"Perfect," I nodded. "Let's get to work."

We established a system—I would excavate the debris, filling the capture nets that Sorril and Visk would then transport to the cargo hold. Working together, we made better progress, but the task remained daunting. For every cubic meter we cleared, there seemed to be ten more waiting.

After two hours of backbreaking labor, we had

managed to tunnel perhaps five meters into the debris field. My suit's power reserves had dropped to 68%, and my muscles ached despite the armor's enhancement. Sweat trickled down my face inside the helmet, impossible to wipe away.

"There has to be a better way," I muttered, watching as Visk disappeared down our makeshift tunnel with another load of gravel.

Sorril tilted his head, his enormous ears twitching inside his helmet. "Commander Drake, this technician has an observation. The debris behaves like a fluid in microgravity. Perhaps we should use fluid dynamics principles."

"What do you mean?"

"Instead of removing all debris, we could create a moving bubble," he suggested. "Push the material outward and upward, allowing it to close behind us as we ascend."

I considered this. "Like swimming through it, letting it flow around us?"

"Precisely," Sorril confirmed. "It would require less total work and achieve our objective more quickly."

It was a brilliant idea. Instead of fighting the properties of the debris field, we'd use them to our advantage.

"Let's try it," I decided. "When Visk returns, we'll explain the new plan."

With our revised approach, we made faster progress. I took the lead position, using wide sweeping motions to push the gravel outward and upward. Sorril and Visk followed, reinforcing the bubble of space I created. As we moved forward, the debris flowed around and behind us, filling in the space we'd vacated.

The work was still exhausting, but we were moving more efficiently now. My mind wandered as my body settled into the repetitive motion of clearing a path. I thought of Sofia lying in our cabin, still recovering from her injury. I thought of *Thunder*, racing toward us, unaware that we were now buried under tons of asteroid material. I thought of Zeta, her consciousness submerged as her body powered the nanoforge that was keeping us all alive.

So many lives depending on my ability to dig a hole. It wasn't exactly the heroic scenario I'd imagined when I first took command of *Thunder*.

"Commander Drake, are you well?" Sorril's voice broke into my thoughts. "Your movements have slowed."

I realized I'd been pushing debris with decreasing efficiency as my mind wandered. "I'm fine," I said, shaking myself back to full alertness. "Just pacing myself."

"This technician estimates we have penetrated approximately twelve meters," Visk reported from behind me. "Based on sensor readings prior to the collapse, we may be halfway to the surface."

Halfway. Only halfway after nearly three hours of work. My shoulders burned with fatigue, and my lungs labored despite the suit's oxygen supply. The protomatter armor was excellent, but it couldn't eliminate the physical toll of sustained exertion.

Just as I was preparing to push forward again, the debris ahead of me shifted suddenly. A cascade of gravel rushed toward us, filling our carefully maintained bubble and forcing me backward into Sorril.

"Stability breach!" Visk called out unnecessarily.

I braced myself against the sudden pressure, the suit amplifying my strength as I fought to hold my position. "Everyone okay?" I asked, once the flow had stabilized.

"Affirmative," Sorril replied. "But we have lost approximately three meters of progress."

Three meters. Almost an hour of work, gone in seconds. Frustration boiled up inside me, but I pushed it down. Anger wouldn't get us to the surface any faster.

"Let's keep going," I said. "We'll recover the lost ground."

We resumed our methodical progress, but I could feel fatigue settling deeper into my bones. My suit's power levels had dropped below 50%, and my concentration was beginning to slip. I thought of Sofia again, wondering if she was still reading in our cabin or if she'd fallen asleep. I imagined her face when I told her about this adventure—her eyes rolling at yet another Kory Drake special situation.

Another small collapse set us back, but we pushed through it with grim determination. The debris seemed to be changing texture—becoming finer, more dust-like. Could that mean we were nearing the surface?

"Commander Drake," Visk called from behind me. "This technician's sensors are detecting a change in pressure gradient. The surface may be near."

Hope surged through me, giving fresh energy to my tired muscles. I increased the pace of my digging, pushing the debris upward with renewed vigor.

"I think I see something," I said, as my helmet lights reflected differently off the material ahead. "The consistency is changing."

I pushed forward with one final, powerful thrust—and my hands broke through into empty space. Dust and small pebbles drifted out into the star-filled void beyond HideyRock. I had reached the surface.

"We're through!" I announced, relief flooding through me. "I can see stars!"

I enlarged the opening, pushing aside more material until it was wide enough for my helmet to fit through. As I emerged onto the surface of HideyRock, the silent majesty of space—endless darkness punctuated by distant stars and the looming blue-white curve of Earth on the horizon—greeted me.

"Bridge, this is Drake," I transmitted, hoping *Luminara*'s internal communications could relay my message. "We've reached the surface. I'm going to remain here to await *Thunder*'s arrival."

The canyon that had hidden us was now a jumbled mess of asteroid material, with no visible sign of the ship buried beneath. But we had our tunnel now—our lifeline to the surface.

I extracted a small device from my suit's utility compartment—an anchor. As I activated it, root-like extensions shot out and penetrated deep into the loose gravel.

I floated on the irregular surface of HideyRock, surrounded by the quiet emptiness of space, and allowed myself a moment of satisfaction. We weren't safe yet—not by a long shot. We still had to evacuate everyone through this narrow tunnel, and Sofia's condition remained a concern. But we had a fighting chance now.

"Commander Drake to bridge," I said, my voice steady despite my exhaustion. "Mission accomplished. Now let's get ready to welcome *Thunder*."

11

The regolith crunched under my boots as I nudged the last chunk of rock out of the tunnel. It tumbled soundlessly into the void, glinting once in Earth's reflected light before vanishing among the stars. Two days marooned on this glorified pebble, and finally—maybe—our ticket home was approaching. If it was *Thunder.* If they'd received our message. If they weren't Kergan. That was a lot of ifs between me and a hot shower.

"Clear passage confirmed, Commander Drake," chirped one of the kavreni engineers through my comms. Her stilt-like limbs carried her effortlessly in the microgravity as she tapped at a handheld scanner. "Tunnel integrity at ninety-seven percent."

I nodded inside my helmet, more for my own benefit than hers. "Good work. Let's get that epoxy applied before the next micro-quake decides to redecorate."

The two kavreni engineers scuttled around me with the careful precision of creatures who'd evolved to hang from cave ceilings. Their long, thin arms manipulated canisters of vacuum-drying epoxy, spraying it along the rough-hewn walls of our escape route. The substance emerged as a clear mist that immediately began to harden, transforming into a glossy shell that reinforced the tunnel's integrity.

"Fascinating material," I remarked, watching the molecules lock into place. "Works in total vacuum?"

"Yes, Captain," the second engineer replied, his oversized ears twitching beneath his helmet. "Quantum bonding occurs more efficiently without atmospheric interference. The valence properties allow—"

"Save the chemistry lesson," I interrupted, not unkindly. "Just make sure it holds until everyone's out."

We worked methodically for another hour, clearing the rest of the spoil and reinforcing the walls. Each scoop of debris we ejected into space represented another step toward freedom from this cosmic prison. HideyRock—a name I'd coined in a moment of either brilliance or oxygen deprivation—was barely 300 meters across, a tumbling potato satellite with just enough mass to provide a hint of gravity. Perfect for hiding *Luminara* after our hasty retreat from *Inferis*, terrible for long-term habitation.

When the tunnel was finally secure, I floated back to the airlock where our makeshift sanctuary waited beneath tons of collapsed rock. Once inside *Luminara*, I cycled through decontamination and peeled off my protomatter suit with a sigh of relief. The yacht's systems, though damaged, still maintained basic life support in the intact sections.

I made my way to the galley, nodding to the passing kavreni crew. They gave me a wide berth—part respect for my rank, part because humans apparently smell awful to their ultra-sensitive noses. Fair enough. After a full day sealed in a suit, I wasn't exactly a bouquet of roses.

The synthesizer hummed to life and dispensed

something optimistically labeled "meat soup." It tasted like salty plastic laced with existential dread, but it was hot and packed with calories—basically a gourmet feast under current conditions. I downed it, followed by two nutrient bars and a full liter of water. Spacewalks had a way of torching energy reserves like dry kindling.

Afterward, I checked on Sofia in our quarters. She was unconscious and covered in vomit—another seizure, likely while I was in the tunnel. Panic flared in my chest, but I forced it down. Right now, the only thing I could do for her was get her to *Thunder* and make sure we reached someone who could help.

I cleaned her up with a damp rag and carefully strapped her into the bed to prevent injury if another seizure struck. I stood over her for a moment, feeling utterly helpless. Then I swallowed my fear, turned away, and started prepping my suit for another trip to the surface.

Twenty minutes later, freshly suited and fully topped off on oxygen and power, I climbed back through the tunnel. It now looked almost professionally built—a quiet testament to kavreni engineering. I stepped out onto HideyRock's bleak, cratered surface and clipped myself to the anchor point near the tunnel entrance: a simple metal spike hammered deep into the regolith, with a tether that kept me from drifting off into the void.

And then, I waited.

Earth hung in the void before me, a blue-white disc about twice the size of my thumb at arm's length. Four hundred thousand kilometers away—tantalizingly close in cosmic terms, impossibly distant without a functioning ship. The homeworld I'd rarely seen from space before Zeta recruited me into this interstellar mess. The planet I'd spent my childhood roaming, first in orphanages, then on the streets.

I thought about my parents—or rather, the absence of them. The memories Ban'ach had stolen from me. Not that I'd had many to begin with; I'd been just three when they died in the car crash. Most of what I "remembered" were actually stories Destiny had told me since my memories were lost. How my mother had sung me to sleep every night. How my father had carried me on his shoulders through a park I couldn't name. Whether these memories were real or Destiny's kind fabrications to give an orphaned kid some sense of having been loved, I couldn't say anymore. Ban'ach had made sure of that when she'd rifled through my mind and stolen the real ones. All I had now were memories of Destiny's memories of what I had told her in years past.

My throat tightened with a familiar ache that had nothing to do with the recycled air I was breathing. I'd survived so much—street life, space battles, alien conspiracies—but sometimes the simple absence of memories hurt worse than any wound.

A flash of movement jerked me from my reverie.

Something had moved against the star field—a dark shape momentarily occluding the distant pinpricks of light. I held my breath, scanning the blackness, my suit's enhanced optics struggling to make sense of the visual data.

There—a ship, running completely dark. No navigation lights, no thermal signature. Running silent. Just a black silhouette slightly darker than the surrounding void.

Thunder? Or Kergan?

In vacuum, distance was difficult to estimate. The object could have been a kilometer-long dreadnought fifty kilometers away, or a basketball-sized probe barely a hundred meters from me. I squinted, trying to gauge its motion relative to the fixed stars behind it.

Based on parallax and my rough estimate of its velocity, I calculated it was approximately a kilometer away, making the ship about two hundred meters long. That seemed too big for *Thunder,* significantly larger than when I'd last seen her. Had Destiny mentioned upgrades in one of our spotty communications? I couldn't remember—our messages had become increasingly intermittent over the months since I was assigned to *Inferis*.

Doubt crept in, cold and unsettling. What if it wasn't *Thunder*? What if the Kergans had intercepted our transmission and arrived instead? My hand drifted to the small sidearm magnetically attached to my suit—a pathetic defense against a warship, but it was all I had.

The black ship appeared to stop its relative motion, hanging motionless against the stars. No, not stopped—its apparent size was gradually increasing. It was approaching, directly toward HideyRock, directly toward me.

I had to decide. The timing aligned with our planned rendezvous with *Thunder.* The dimensions, though large, seemed plausible. And if it was Kergan... well, I was already trapped on a rock with no escape.

Taking a deep breath, I set my tactical radio to low power—no sense broadcasting our position to the entire system—and transmitted, "Calling *UHSS Thunder,* this is *Luminara*, do you read me, over."

The silence that followed seemed to stretch for an eternity. I counted five heartbeats before trying again.

"*Thunder,* this is *Luminara*. Commander Kory Drake transmitting. Do you copy?"

Nothing. The dark shape continued its approach, growing perceptibly larger against the star field. I transmitted again, and again, repeating my message a dozen times over the next five minutes while the ship drew ever closer.

Just as I was about to give up, a burst of static crackled in my headset, followed by a voice that made my heart stutter.

"*Luminara,* this is *Thunder,* we read you. Request immediate SITREP and location."

The voice wasn't Destiny's—probably their comms officer—but it was unquestionably human, unquestionably using UHC protocol. I couldn't stop the grin that spread across my face, so wide it hurt my cheeks.

One of the kavreni engineers was nearby, securing equipment. I switched to local comms. "Engineer, I have contact with *Thunder.* Inform Captain Borlo immediately." I didn't have direct radio contact with the igna captain through all that rock, but the message would reach him.

Switching back to the tactical frequency, I composed myself and transmitted our status: "*Thunder,* this is Commander Kory Drake, transmitting. Current position: surface of HideyRock. Tidal forces have triggered a canyon wall collapse on *Luminara*—vessel is buried. Tunnel is prepped for ship evacuation. On board: twenty-seven personnel (two humans, two igna, twenty-three kavreni). One human requires immediate MEDEVAC. Request your vectors on my beacon, over."

I enabled my suit's tactical transponder, trusting *Thunder*'s navigation suite to lock onto my signal. The sleek black shape had resolved into a recognizable silhouette now—definitely a warship, definitely not Kergan design.

Another burst of static, and then: "*Luminara, Thunder,* acknowledge twenty-seven souls with one human requiring medical evac. Homing on your beacon now."

There was a brief pause, and then a fresh voice. "Good to

hear your voice again, Kory!"

My chest tightened at the unmistakable sound of Destiny's voice—professional yet edged with a warmth that cut through the vacuum between us. My hands were trembling inside my gloves, but I felt a heat in my chest, a rush of relief that left me momentarily speechless.

"Likewise, *Thunder,*" I finally managed, my voice steadier than I felt. "Been one hell of a year."

"Save the reunion for when you're aboard," she replied, but I could hear the smile in her voice. "Stand by for approach and extraction. *Thunder,* out."

As the transmission ended, I took another look at Earth hanging in the distance, then back to the approaching warship. Soon I'd be leaving this rock behind. Soon I'd see familiar faces again. Soon I'd get Sofia the medical help she desperately needed.

I just had to hope "soon" would be soon enough.

I watched *Thunder*'s approach with a sense of disbelief that grew with every passing minute. This was not the modest corvette I'd left behind. The warship that loomed overhead was at least twice that size—an elongated ellipsoid bristling with weapons blisters and sensor arrays that reminded me of a porcupine having a really bad hair day. Her hull was matte black, absorbing starlight rather than reflecting it, with running lights extinguished for stealth. She was beautiful in the way apex predators are beautiful—sleek, lethal, and perfectly evolved for her purpose.

Over the next ten minutes, I tracked *Thunder*'s cautious approach. Her maneuvering tractor pods fired in controlled bursts, sensed only as slight vibrations coupling into HideyRocks regolith as she aligned herself precisely with my position. The ship's hull eclipsed the stars above me, casting me in its shadow. At this range, I could make out dozens of weapons emplacements—railgun turrets recessed into the hull, missile tubes sealed behind armored doors, and laser point defense blisters that dotted her surface like watchful eyes.

Thunder came to an abrupt stop directly above the tunnel mouth, hovering with impossible precision. An airlock on her underside dilated open, spilling light onto HideyRock's dark surface. A figure appeared in the opening, their armored silhouette stark against the bright interior. A powerful beam of light swept across the surface, found me, and held steady.

I waved both arms over my head, feeling suddenly like a castaway on a cosmic desert island.

The figure didn't hesitate. They pushed off from the airlock with practiced confidence, traversing the twenty meters of empty space between us in a graceful arc. The figure's descent was controlled by subtle bursts from suit thrusters, bringing them to a perfect landing beside me.

Up close, I could see the suit was far more advanced than the protomatter model I wore—a proper combat hardsuit with integrated weapons systems and reinforced plating. The faceplate was mirrored, showing me my own distorted reflection, but somehow I knew exactly who was inside.

Without warning, the figure grabbed me in a bear hug that would have crushed my ribs if not for our respective suits. I felt the solid thump as they pressed their helmet against mine, creating a temporary contact that allowed sound vibrations to pass between us without radio.

"Hey, Captain, it's Busto!" The familiar, gruff voice reverberated through my helmet.

I let out a whoop of joy that no one but me could hear in

the vacuum and returned the embrace with equal enthusiasm. When we separated, I noticed a cluster of mission patches slapped onto his chest plate—some official, some clearly improvised.

"Trying to start a fashion trend, or did a supply crate explode on you?" I asked, the vibrations carrying through our still-touching helmets.

"Just about everything between here and Mars," Busto replied, and though I couldn't see his face, I heard the grin in his voice. He stepped back, all business now. "We need to get you aboard ASAP. Captain Austin is about to wear a hole in the deck, pacing."

"Can't do that yet," I responded, gesturing toward the tunnel. "I've got twenty-six others down there, including one critical medical case."

Busto nodded. "Roger that. We'll extract them all, but right now, Destiny needs to talk with you." His use of her first name rather than her rank told me this wasn't just ship's business. "I'll take over here. Lieutenant Rowbottom's squad is already suiting up to assist with evacuation."

I hesitated, torn between my responsibilities to *Luminara*'s crew and my desire to reunite with my own people.

"Go," Busto insisted, giving me a gentle push toward *Thunder*. "I've got this. That's an order, sir." The irony of him ordering his superior officer wasn't lost on either of us.

With a final nod, I leaped across the gap between HideyRock and *Thunder*, using my suit tractors to guide my trajectory. I sailed through the open airlock and landed inside with a magnetic clunk as my boots engaged with the deck.

The outer door sealed behind me, and atmosphere hissed into the chamber. Status lights shifted from red to amber to green, and the inner door slid open to reveal a welcoming committee.

I was immediately engulfed in a wave of bodies as the crew members waiting there surged forward. Hands clapped my back, voices called my name, and I laughed in surprised delight at the enthusiastic reception. As I retracted my helmet, the familiar recycled ship's air—with its unique blend of ozone, metal, and the indefinable scent of too many humans in too small a space—filled my lungs.

"Make room, you animals, that's an order!" A commanding voice cut through the hubbub, and the crowd parted to reveal Destiny Austin, her familiar figure instantly recognizable despite the commander's uniform she now wore. Her curly black hair was cropped shorter than I remembered, and a recent scar traced a thin line along her jawline, but her dark eyes sparkled with the same intelligence and humor.

"Well, well, look what the cosmic cat dragged in," she said, arms crossed, mouth twitching with suppressed emotion.

"Destiny," I managed, suddenly choked up at seeing my oldest friend after so long apart.

She closed the distance between us in two quick strides and wrapped me in a fierce hug that spoke volumes. "Lordy, Kory," she whispered against my shoulder, "I was worried I'd never see you again."

"Takes more than a buried spaceship and a year on an alien planet to get rid of me," I quipped, returning her embrace.

When we separated, I noticed Phoebe Brooks hovering just behind Destiny. She looked mostly the same—her brown hair pulled back in a practical ponytail, her slim figure now dressed in a lieutenant's uniform with engineering insignia.

"Phoebe," I said, opening my arms.

She stepped forward with a warm smile, hugged me tightly, and then surprised me with a quick kiss on the cheek. As she pulled back, her nose wrinkled. "Yuck, you stink, Captain."

"What's new?" Destiny added with a grin.

I laughed, suddenly self-conscious about my less-than-fresh condition after a long day in the same suit. "First order of business when everyone's safe will be the longest shower in human history."

A stocky woman with close-cropped blonde hair and the no-nonsense demeanor of someone who's seen everything twice pushed forward. "Good to have you back, Captain," she said, offering a crisp handshake instead of a hug. "Medical bay's prepped and ready."

"Doc Montana," I greeted her warmly. "Thanks. We've got one critical coming up who'll need your expertise."

The reunions continued for another minute before I raised my hands. "I want to catch up with everyone, I really do, but we've got *Luminara*'s crew to evacuate, and someone who needs urgent medical attention."

Destiny's expression shifted immediately to professional concern. "Who's injured?"

"The other human aboard—a woman I met in Astrithon. She's been with me the past year." I tried to keep my tone neutral, but something in my voice must have given me away.

Destiny's eyebrow arched knowingly. "Sounds like there's a story there you haven't shared in your transmissions."

"Her name is Chief Warrant Officer Sofia Kohl," I replied, feeling a flush creep up my neck. "Former German military police, brilliant officer. She has a head injury from the battle at Virelia. She's having seizures, complaining of headaches."

"We'll take care of her," Doc Montana assured me. "I'll examine her as soon as she's transferred to medical."

"Thanks, Doc." I turned back to Destiny. "How many crew do you have now? We've got twenty-seven to evacuate."

"Twenty-four total," she replied. "Nearly triple what we had when you left. *Thunder*'s been upgraded to a frigate class. We've got a proper FTL drive now, artificial gravity—the works. Can cross the entire system in days instead of weeks."

"And you've got nine Marines," added a deep voice from behind Destiny.

"Ensign Rowbottom!" I said, recognizing the former Army Scout who had joined Busto's MARDET.

"It's Lieutenant Junior Grade now, sir," he replied with a grin.

I smiled and shook his hand.

"My squad is prepping for extraction duty now," Rowbottom said.

I nodded my thanks to the Marine.

As the evacuation preparations continued around us, Destiny guided me toward a striking figure standing slightly apart from the others. A dodecahedral capsule of crimson metal hovered at waist height, clearly containing an igna.

"This is Nicobe," Destiny explained. "She's a Heliacal Templar of the Collective Dominion. My... consort, I guess you'd say. Assigned to me after you and Zeta left."

The crimson dodecahedron bobbed slightly in what I took to be a greeting. "Nicobe is pleased to meet the famous Captain Drake," came a melodious voice from a speaker on the capsule's surface. "Destiny speaks highly of you, when she is not cursing your name for leaving her with all the paperwork."

I laughed, immediately liking the igna's direct humor. "The paperwork was my most diabolical revenge plan."

"Nicobe serves as Thunder's chief engineer as well," Destiny added, a note of pride in her voice. "She's the reason we've got half these upgrades working."

Before I could respond, a hush fell over the crowded corridor. The crew members straightened imperceptibly, and even Destiny's posture shifted to something more formal. I turned to see what had caused the change.

An elegant octahedral capsule of pure white metal floated through the inner airlock door. Unlike Nicobe's relatively simple design, this capsule was etched with intricate glyphs that pulsed with a subtle blue-white light. I recognized it immediately.

"Queen Zeta," I said, inclining my head in respect.

"Commander Drake," the familiar formal voice replied from the capsule. "Zeta is pleased to see you have survived another adventure. Your resilience continues to impress."

I felt Destiny stiffen beside me, her expression carefully neutral as she performed a correct but minimalist bow. "Your Majesty."

There was a subtle tension in the air that hadn't been there moments before. I knew its source—Zeta's involvement in having me charged with sydereal assault had driven a wedge between her and Destiny. Though Zeta had formally pardoned me when the full circumstances came to light, Destiny was not one to quickly forgive anyone who threatened her friends.

Nicobe, however, immediately rotated her capsule in a complex pattern. "Your Majesty, Nicobe is honored by your presence. Nicobe hopes her service has been worthy of the Collective Dominion."

"Zeta has heard excellent reports of your service, Templar Nicobe," Zeta replied, her capsule performing a corresponding pattern. "Zeta congratulates you on *Thunder*'s many successes. The rightful Dominion remembers its faithful servants."

I watched the exchange with interest, noting how the human crew members reacted to Zeta's presence. There was respect, certainly, even awe—Zeta was, after all, the legitimate queen of the most powerful stellar empire in known space. But there was something else, too. Hope, perhaps. Determination. These people had aligned themselves with an exiled monarch against overwhelming odds.

Destiny must have read my thoughts. "A lot's changed since you've been gone," she said quietly. "The Collective Dominion civil war has spread. Arctis's forces have taken three more systems. The Kergan Empire has forced Earth to declare official neutrality, but..." She gestured around at the diverse crew. "Some of us have chosen sides."

Before I could process this new information, my comms unit beeped. "Captain Drake," came Busto's voice, "we've got your people moving through the tunnel now. First evacuees will reach *Thunder* in approximately five minutes."

"Copy that," I replied, then said to Destiny. "Alright, I'm getting back to work. I've got people to save."

As the group dispersed to their stations, I couldn't help but feel a surge of pride. This was still my crew, still my ship—changed, upgraded, expanded, but fundamentally the same in all the ways that mattered. We'd been through hell together before, and it seemed the universe wasn't done testing us yet.

With one last look at Zeta's glowing capsule, I turned to descend back down the tunnel to find Sofia and get her out of *Luminara*.

12

The route back to *Luminara* felt longer than it had just hours before, each step weighted with a new urgency. I'd left Sofia stable but unconscious in our shared quarters after her most recent seizure, tucked into a makeshift harness on our bed fashioned from blankets and spare clothing. Her most recent seizure had left her lips blue and her breathing shallow. I pushed those images away as I descended through the tunnel, focusing instead on the fact that help was finally here, that Doc Montana was waiting with medical equipment and human medical expertise. All I had to do was get Sofia safely to *Thunder*.

The tunnel's epoxy-reinforced walls glistened under my helmet light, the surface oddly organic despite its artificial nature. I passed several kavreni heading toward *Thunder*, each carrying personal effects or essential equipment. They acknowledged me with respectful nods, but didn't slow their pace. Everyone understood the stakes—get out before the next structural shift buried us all permanently.

Luminara's remaining functional airlock cycled me

through with a wheeze of protesting hydraulics. Inside, the damaged yacht was a shadow of its former elegance. Emergency lighting cast everything in a sickly amber glow, and the air tasted stale and metallic. Power was being rationed to essential systems only, and even those were failing incrementally as the ship's systems degraded.

I made my way through tilted corridors where the artificial gravity fought with HideyRock's minimal natural pull, creating a disorienting sensation of constantly walking slightly uphill. Debris had been cleared from the main pathways, but dark smears on the walls and floors told their own story of the chaos when the canyon wall had collapsed onto *Luminara*.

Our quarters were in one of the less damaged sections, tucked away from the worst structural failures. I palmed open the door, my heart jumping into my throat when I found Sofia exactly as I'd left her—unmoving, pale, her honey-blonde hair spread across the improvised pillow like a halo.

"Sofia," I called softly, kneeling beside her. I gently stroked her cheek, noting the clammy coolness of her skin. "Sofia, help is here. We're going to get you proper medical attention."

Her eyelids fluttered but didn't open. A small crease appeared between her brows, as if she were trying to process my words through layers of pain and confusion.

"I need to move you now," I explained, though I wasn't sure how much she comprehended. "We have to get to *Thunder*. Doc Montana is waiting."

No response. I swallowed hard against the knot in my throat and began the careful process of preparing her for transport. First, I gathered her limp form into my arms, cradling her against my chest as I'd done so many times before—though never in these circumstances, never with this terrible weight of fear pressing down on me.

Sofia's protomatter suit lay ready beside the bed, its advanced fabric capable of conforming to any body shape and providing life support in hostile environments. I'd already programmed it for minimum pressure and maximum stability—essential for someone in her condition.

"This is going to feel strange," I murmured to her, knowing from experience how disorienting it could be to have protomatter flow across your skin. "Just breathe normally. The suit will do all the work."

First, I stripped her naked. Then, with practiced movements, I activated the suit and guided the responsive material over her body. The protomatter rippled like liquid mercury, flowing up her legs, around her torso, and finally encasing her head in a transparent bubble that would maintain pressure and oxygen levels. The suit's medical subsystems immediately activated, small lights blinking as they monitored her vital signs.

Once she was fully enclosed, I lifted her again. She felt lighter now, the suit tractors compensating for gravity and providing structural support to her limbs. Her head lolled against my shoulder, but the helmet kept it stable, preventing any dangerous movement.

"Let's get you home," I whispered, though the words caught in my throat. Home. What did that even mean anymore? For the past year, home had been wherever Sofia and I had found ourselves together—a luxury that had seemed absurd when set against the backdrop of interstellar war, but which had kept me sane through the darkest times.

The journey back through *Luminara*'s tilted corridors was slow and careful. I avoided jostling Sofia as much as possible, each step measured and deliberate. Several kavreni crew members offered to help, but I declined with terse thanks. This was my responsibility. My fault, in ways I couldn't fully articulate even to myself.

The tunnel seemed narrower with Sofia in my arms, the low ceiling forcing me to hunch uncomfortably. The epoxy coating glistened wetly in my helmet light, occasionally bulging in places where it hadn't fully cured. Above us, HideyRock's minimal gravity tugged erratically as we passed through density variations in the asteroid.

When we finally emerged onto the surface, I saw that *Thunder* had extended a proper docking tube to the tunnel entrance, creating a secure pathway between the ships. Two Marines in combat hardsuits stood guard at the entrance, their weapons at ready position.

"Commander Drake," one acknowledged, stepping aside. "Medical team is standing by."

I nodded my thanks and entered the tube, feeling the artificial gravity take hold as we crossed the threshold into *Thunder*. The weightless sensation of the asteroid surface gave way to a solid one-g pull, and I adjusted my stance to compensate for Sofia's weight.

Inside *Thunder*, the corridors were brightly lit and humming with activity as crew members assisted with the evacuation. They parted before us, conversations falling silent as they noted my burden and the grim determination on my face. A few offered encouraging nods or murmured support, but no one delayed us.

Thunder's medical bay occupied a significant section of Deck 3, much larger than I remembered. The doors slid open automatically as we approached, revealing a space that resembled a small hospital more than the modest sickbay I'd left behind. Multiple treatment areas lined the walls, each equipped with advanced diagnostic equipment and surrounded by privacy screens.

Doc Montana was waiting, her boyish face set in

professional lines as she gestured to an examination table. "Put her here, Captain."

I laid Sofia down with infinite care, my hands lingering on her shoulders, before reluctantly stepping back. Montana immediately moved in, her fingers dancing over the protomatter suit's control interface.

"Let's get this off her for proper assessment," she said, entering a command that caused the suit to recede, flowing away from Sofia's body like water down a drain until she lay bare and vulnerable on the examination table.

I heard a soft intake of breath behind me and turned to find Destiny standing in the doorway, her eyes fixed on Sofia's unconscious form as Montana covered her with a blanket. A complex emotion passed across Destiny's face—surprise, perhaps, mixed with something harder to define.

"She sure is a pretty woman," Montana remarked as she gently cupped Sofia's cheek, turning her head slightly to examine the fading bruise at her temple.

"What's wrong with her?" I asked, unable to keep the edge of desperation from my voice.

Montana's blue eyes flicked up to meet mine. "Let's start with what happened. Tell me her symptoms and when they began."

I drew a deep breath, organizing my thoughts. "We were on *Inferis* when the spectrals ambushed us. Our flagship took torpedo hits, and part of the ceiling collapsed during the bombardment. Sofia was hit—broken leg and a nasty bump on the head." I gestured to the faint discoloration at her temple. "The leg healed fine, but her head's been getting worse. Seizures started about three days ago, getting more frequent and severe. Headaches. Sometimes her speech slurs. Her personality changes—she gets confused, irritable."

"Any scans or treatment so far?" Montana asked, already reaching for a handheld medical scanner.

"We did what we could on *Luminara*. The ship's physician identified increased fluid around her brain, but he didn't have expertise in human physiology." I swallowed hard. "The kavreni aren't usually trained for humans."

"And you two are..." Destiny let the question hang in the air, her tone carefully neutral.

I met her gaze directly. "Together. Since Astrithon. She helped to protect me on Virelia."

Destiny nodded slowly. "I see." A beat passed between us, loaded with unasked questions, before she added, "I'll leave you to it. Find me when you're ready to talk."

As she turned to leave, Montana called after her, "Captain Austin, I may need authorization for emergency procedures, depending on what I find."

"You have it," Destiny replied without hesitation. "Do whatever's necessary." She cast one last unreadable look at Sofia before the doors closed behind her.

Montana turned her full attention to Sofia, running the scanner methodically over her body, starting at her head and working downward. The device emitted a soft hum, occasionally beeping as it registered something of note. Montana's expression gave nothing away as she worked, her movements efficient and practiced.

"How long have the seizures been lasting?" she asked without looking up.

"Thirty seconds to as much as five minutes. The most recent one was nearly five minutes. She was having trouble breathing and her face turned blue."

Montana nodded grimly. "And recovery time between episodes?"

"Getting longer. At first, she'd be back to normal in an

hour or so. The last few, it's been closer to half a day before she's fully lucid."

The examination continued in silence for several long minutes. I stood at the foot of the bed, hands clenched behind my back to keep from fidgeting, watching every flicker of expression on Montana's face for clues. The medic occasionally muttered to herself, too low for me to catch the words, as she directed the scanner to take more detailed readings of Sofia's brain.

Finally, Montana straightened and moved to a nearby console. She transferred the scanner data to the larger system and began manipulating a three-dimensional holographic image of Sofia's brain that appeared above the workstation.

"This is a real-time neural tomography," she explained, gesturing me closer. "See this dark area here, between the brain and the skull?"

I nodded, noticing a crescent-shaped shadow on one side of the image.

"That's blood. She has what we call a subdural hematoma—bleeding directly under the skull that's creating a pool of blood that's pressing on her brain." Montana rotated the image, highlighting different sections. "The initial trauma caused blood vessels to tear, and they've been slowly leaking. The pressure is causing her symptoms, and it's gradually getting worse."

My mouth went dry. "Can you fix it?"

Montana's expression turned apologetic. "I can administer medications to reduce inflammation and prevent further seizures, but..." she hesitated. "I'm not qualified to perform the necessary surgical intervention. She needs a craniotomy to evacuate the hematoma."

"In English, Doc," I said, my voice tight.

"She needs brain surgery to drain the blood and repair the torn vessels." Montana held up her hands in a gesture of helplessness. "I'm a combat medic with expanded qualifications, not a neurosurgeon."

"But it's treatable?" I pressed, grasping at the implied hope.

"Completely treatable," Montana confirmed. "With proper surgical intervention, patients typically make a full recovery." She hesitated again. "Once we get back to Wolf Jaw Base, the nurse practitioner there might have additional options. Alternatively, we could attempt to reach a major medical center in one of the cities."

I nodded slowly, relief and anxiety warring in my chest. "So you're saying she'll be okay, but we need to find her a brain surgeon?"

"Essentially, yes. In the meantime, I can make her comfortable and manage her symptoms." Montana moved to a supply cabinet and began gathering materials. "I'll start her on medications to reduce brain swelling. We'll insert an IV for fluids and monitoring."

Together, we transferred Sofia to a proper patient bed in one of the private treatment areas. Montana worked with quiet efficiency, inserting the IV line and connecting monitors that immediately began displaying Sofia's vital signs. She administered several medications through the IV port, explaining each one as she went.

"This will help reduce the inflammation," she said, injecting a clear solution. Another syringe, another medication. "We'll keep her sedated for now—it's safer given her condition."

When everything was set up, Montana stepped back with a sigh. "That's all I can do for the moment, Captain. She's stable, and the medications should help, but..."

"But she needs surgery," I finished.

"Yes. That's my opinion."

I gazed down at Sofia's pale face, her expression peaceful now that the pain medications had taken effect. Her hair spilled across the white pillow, and I gently brushed a strand away from her forehead. Our fingers had brushed countless times over the past year—in tenderness, in passion, in simple companionship—and each time I'd felt that spark between us. Now her hand lay limp in mine, and I felt only the coolness of her skin.

"Thank you, Doc," I said finally, not taking my eyes from Sofia. "For being honest, and for doing what you can."

Montana squeezed my shoulder briefly. "I'll continue monitoring her. We'll get her the help she needs, Captain. *Thunder*'s faster now—we'll be back to Wolf Jaw Base before you know it."

I nodded, knowing she was right, knowing that Sofia at least had a fighting chance now. But as I sat beside her bed, holding her unresponsive hand, I couldn't shake the fear that had taken root in my chest. We'd survived so much together—political intrigue on Astrithon, the fall of *Inferis*—only to face this invisible enemy that I couldn't fight on her behalf.

"Hold on," I whispered, pressing my lips to her knuckles. "Just hold on a little longer."

13

My fingers tapped a nervous rhythm against my thigh as I sat bolt upright in the jump seat, eyes fixed on Destiny's profile. She stood at the helm of *Thunder* with the casual confidence of someone who'd been born to command warships, not someone who'd spent her formative years picking pockets beside me in San Jose's undercity. The bridge hummed with the quiet efficiency of a vessel that knew its business, even if its business now included hauling twice as many people as it was designed for. I shifted uncomfortably. If this seat got any more cramped, they'd have to pry me out with a crowbar and a stick of butter.

"Status report," Destiny said, her voice carrying that edge of authority that still caught me off guard sometimes. Hard to believe this was the same girl who once helped me steal a crate of protein bars from a military supply depot. Now she was Lieutenant Commander Austin, and the transformation never ceased to amaze me.

The tactical officer—a wiry woman whose name I couldn't remember—responded without looking up from her console. "Approach vector steady. Stealth systems nominal. Earth perimeter defenses haven't spotted us yet."

I glanced around *Thunder*'s bridge, taking in the tightly packed array of stations, each occupied by a focused crew member. Even with the expanded bridge of this Collective Dominion vessel, the space felt claustrophobic with the addition of our twenty-seven refugees from *Luminara*. Earlier that day, I'd spotted a group of kavreni crew members being redirected to the cargo hold—their long, thin limbs and bat-like heads bobbing as they chattered in their clicking language. The poor things looked like walking stilts with furry torsos balanced on top, their reversed knees giving them that distinctive gait that always reminded me of marionettes. They hadn't complained, but their oversized eyes had held a resigned acceptance that made my stomach knot.

The tension between *Thunder*'s original crew and us *Luminara* refugees simmered just below the surface. This morning, I'd overheard a grizzled mechanic with oil-stained knuckles recounting how he'd almost come to blows with one of *Thunder*'s engineers over the use of an access bay as a temporary sleeping berth.

"So I tells him, 'Look, buddy, I didn't ask to be rescued only to sleep on the hard floor of your fancy ship,'" the mechanic had said, gesturing with hands that trembled slightly from fatigue or anger, I couldn't tell which.

Small misunderstandings, magnified by stress and close quarters. I understood too well how quickly those could escalate.

My thoughts drifted to Sofia, lying unconscious in the infirmary. Doc Montana had induced a coma to protect her from the head injury. I kept picturing her face—that heart-shaped face with blue eyes that could see right through my bullshit—now slack and unresponsive. The doctor had assured me it was temporary, but each hour that passed felt like a small eternity.

"You're going to wear a hole in that armrest," Destiny remarked without turning around.

I realized I'd been digging my fingernails into the padding. "Sorry," I muttered. "Just thinking."

"About Sofia?"

"Among other things." I gestured vaguely at the forward viewport where Earth hung like a blue-green jewel. "Like how we're supposed to sneak twenty-seven extra people onto a planet under Kergan occupation."

The weight of our mission pressed down on my chest. We weren't just running home with our tails between our legs—we were carrying the queen of the Collective Dominion. And Sofia, damn her noble heart, had nearly died.

Destiny opened her mouth to respond, but was cut off by a shrill alarm that shot through the bridge like an electric current.

"Heatsink overloaded!" Nicobe's voice rang out from the engineering station. The crimson dodecahedron that housed her igna form pulsed with urgency. "The stealth systems are compromised!"

I'd never fully understood how an intelligent ball of plasma could operate computer controls, but Nicobe managed it somehow through her mechanical capsule. The igna was Destiny's consort—a military assignment that had evolved into something more complex.

"How bad?" Destiny spun toward Nicobe, all trace of casual posture vanishing.

"Nicobe regrets to inform the captain that the primary heatsink has exceeded thermal capacity by thirty-seven percent," the igna responded with that formal third-person speech that somehow managed to convey dry humor, even in a crisis. "Stealth field integrity has dropped to forty-three percent."

Destiny's fingers flew over her command console. "Can we dump the sink and switch to secondary?"

"Not without leaving a thermal signature visible to any watching eyes," Nicobe replied. "Nicobe suggests recalibration of the absorption matrix while maintaining minimal output."

I watched the exchange of technical jargon with growing unease. I wasn't an engineer, but I'd spent enough time on ships to know that compromised stealth systems while approaching a hostile-controlled planet was about as bad as it got without actually being shot at.

The sensor officer's voice crackled over the comm. "Commander, we're being scanned by an acquisition radar. Pattern suggests Kergan military."

My heart rate doubled in an instant. Acquisition radar was the first step before weapons lock.

"Source?" Destiny demanded.

"Patrol vessel, corvette class, bearing two-seven-delta-four."

The communications officer—a young man with a perpetual crease between his eyebrows—turned in his chair. "Commander, we're being hailed by the Kergan patrol."

Destiny's jaw tightened. "No response. Maintain comm silence."

"They'll know we've received it," the officer warned.

"I'm aware," Destiny replied, her tone leaving no room for debate. She turned to address the bridge crew. "I'm sorry, folks, but our stealthy approach is completely botched. We need to run."

I gripped my harness as Destiny gave the order to accelerate. *Thunder* responded immediately, her drives lighting up with a vengeance that pressed me deep into my acceleration couch. Eight gees of acceleration hit like a linebacker, and I felt the inertial dampeners struggle to compensate. The pressure on my chest made breathing an exercise in determination.

"Kergan corvette has altered course," the sensor officer reported, her words slightly strained under the g-forces. "They're in pursuit, but we're pulling ahead."

"They will not catch us," Destiny said with grim confidence. "Not in that bucket."

I remembered from briefings that Kergan corvettes were sturdy but slow—unlike *Thunder,* which had been designed by the Collective Dominion with an emphasis on speed and maneuverability. But then:

"Commander, I've got eight Kergan fighters lifting off from a base south of Denver," the sensor officer called out. "They're on an intercept course."

"Shit," Destiny muttered, then louder: "Tactical display."

The main viewscreen switched to show our position relative to Earth and the approaching fighters. Even I could tell they would reach us long before we could break orbit.

"We can't outrun these," Destiny admitted. She turned to the tactical officer. "Weapons free. Deploy intercept missiles."

"Engaging," the tactical officer confirmed, fingers dancing across her console.

Destiny turned to Nicobe. "Energize the bolsters and enable LPD turrets."

"Activating defensive systems," Nicobe confirmed. Bolsters were a quantum field that strengthened the chemical bonds of ship armor, greatly enhancing its stopping power. The LPDs—laser point defense turrets—were more straightforward: high-powered lasers designed to pick off incoming missiles.

"*Thunder* no longer needs to maintain the pretense of being an unarmed cargo vessel?" Nicobe asked, a hint of amusement in her synthesized voice.

"Cat's out of the bag now," Destiny replied. "Let's show them some teeth."

I felt a subtle vibration through the deck as *Thunder*'s weapons systems came online. On the tactical display, I watched our intercept missiles tear through space toward the incoming fighters. Two bright flashes indicated hits, and the number of hostile targets dropped from eight to six.

"Two fighters down," the tactical officer reported. "Remaining six have launched antiship missiles. Twelve incoming."

"Intercept pattern alpha," Destiny ordered. "LPDs to support."

Thunder's defensive systems roared to life. More missiles streaked away from our ship, while the LPD turrets created a series of popping noises that vibrated through the bridge as they fired. Lasers, of course, were silent in space, but the power draw and heat dissipation systems made their presence known through the ship's structure.

Destiny hit the ship-wide comm. "All hands, prepare for evasive maneuvers! Everyone, restrain yourselves and brace for acceleration!"

I barely had time to tighten my harness before *Thunder* lurched violently to port. The g-forces jerked me sideways, then pressed me back into my seat as Destiny executed a complex series of maneuvers that no human pilot should have been able to pull off. Each change in direction sent fresh waves of pressure through my body.

On the tactical display, Kergan missiles exploded in succession, some hit by our interceptors, others vaporized by the laser defense grid. Thunder fired another salvo, taking down a third fighter and forcing another to retreat with damage. But that still left four on our tail, and our missile reserves weren't infinite.

"Commander," the sensor officer called, her voice tight. "Six additional Kergan fighters lifting off from Texas. ETA four minutes."

"We can't fight this many," Destiny said, her fingers never pausing on the controls.

I scanned the tactical display, desperate for options, when my eyes caught the navigation screen. A massive storm system was approaching Denver, towering thunderheads reaching thousands of meters into the atmosphere.

"The storm!" I shouted, pointing. "Can we use it for cover?"

Destiny glanced at the navigation display, then back at me. A slow smile spread across her face. "That sounds like a good idea."

She adjusted our course, plunging *Thunder* deep into the atmosphere. Warning prompts flared across the status display as the bolsters strained to reinforce the hull from the crushing pressure and searing heat of entry at orbital velocity. The screens dimmed automatically, filtering out the brutal UV light radiating from gas superheated to ten thousand degrees as the hull rammed into the air, instantly ionizing nitrogen and oxygen molecules.

But *Thunder* held steady—unshaken, unbothered—and dove straight toward the churning storm below. Through the external cameras, we saw a towering wall of cloud lit from within by wild forks of lightning, dancing and snapping with savage grace.

"Brace for turbulence," Destiny warned as we dove into the storm.

The external displays went dark almost immediately, filled with swirling clouds and sheets of rain. *Thunder* shuddered as powerful winds buffeted her hull. I felt each gust as a physical push, despite the ship's mass and stabilization systems. Destiny guided us lower, closer to the ground.

"Find us someplace to hide on the ground, now!" she ordered the navigation officer.

Minutes stretched like hours as we rode the storm downward, the ship bucking and rolling in the turbulence. Lightning flashed so close that the electromagnetic interference caused momentary glitches in the bridge displays.

"There!" The navigation officer's voice was taut with relief. "Gorge, ten klicks northeast. Marking on tactical."

The Kergan fighters had vanished from our sensors, either unable to track us through the storm or unwilling to follow us into it. Smart move on their part—*Thunder* was designed to handle atmospheric conditions that would tear apart small fighters.

"Nicobe, dump the overloaded heatsink and begin transferring to the new unit," Destiny ordered as she guided us through the last layer of storm clouds.

"Transferring thermal load now," Nicobe confirmed. "Stealth systems reengaging."

I exhaled a shaky breath I hadn't realized I was holding. Below us, a deep river gorge came into view, its steep walls providing natural cover from above. Destiny brought *Thunder* down with impressive precision, settling us on a sandy bar with the aft section partially submerged in the rushing river.

"Activating surface camouflage," Nicobe announced. "*Thunder* is entering sleep mode to minimize signature."

The lights on the bridge dimmed to emergency levels as non-essential systems powered down. In the new quiet, I could hear the creaks and groans of *Thunder*'s hull as it cooled and settled. Outside, rain pattered against the viewport, the storm's remnants providing additional cover.

We sat in tense silence as passive sensors continued to scan. My nerves felt frayed, heart still pounding from the constant near-miss of enemy detection. On the tactical display, Kergan fighters and warships appeared again—but they were hundreds of kilometers away, obviously searching in the wrong place.

"They've lost us," the sensor officer whispered, as if afraid to jinx our luck.

Destiny leaned back in her command chair for the first time in what felt like hours. "For now," she said. "We'll wait until nightfall, then attempt to reach Wolf Jaw Base."

I stared at the tactical display, watching the red dots of Kergan ships move in futile search patterns far from our position. A strange mix of relief and disbelief washed over me. We had made it. Or at least, we had survived round one.

"Nice call on the storm," Destiny said, glancing back at me with a tired smile.

I shrugged, trying to ignore the tremor in my hands. "I've always had a talent for finding shelter in a shitstorm. Literal or figurative."

A few exhausted chuckles rippled across the bridge. The tension didn't disappear, but it eased enough for us all to breathe again. I looked out at the rushing river beside us, Earth's water flowing past a ship built by aliens, carrying humans and kavreni and ignas.

Sofia would appreciate the irony when she woke up. When, not if. I had to believe that.

For now, we were hidden, we were alive, and we had made it to Earth. Step one complete. I just hoped the next steps wouldn't involve quite so many missiles.

14

The steady beep of Sofia's vitals monitor was the only sound in the infirmary, a metronome counting down hours I couldn't afford to lose. I slouched in my chair, uniform wrinkled from eight hours of continuous vigil, my eyes scratchy from lack of sleep. The overhead lights cast Sofia's face in a bluish glow that made her look more corpse than coma patient. I'd faced down Kergan warships with less fear than what churned in my gut now, watching the woman I loved drift in unconsciousness, her brain swelling inside her skull like a time bomb.

Eight hours since we'd slipped between Kergan patrols like a ghost through walls, finding refuge in this narrow Colorado gorge. Eight hours of relative safety, with *Thunder* nestled against rock walls that scrambled enemy sensors. Eight hours that should have brought relief, but only deepened my anxiety.

I reached out and brushed a strand of blonde hair from Sofia's forehead. Her skin felt cool and dry beneath my fingertips. Too still. Sofia Kohl was never still—always alert, always scanning, always processing. The former German military police officer had taught me more about tactical awareness in our months together than all my time under Clemen Busto's tutelage. Now she lay before me, her brilliant mind locked away behind swollen neural tissue and scalp lacerations.

"Come back to me," I whispered, knowing she couldn't hear me but needing to say it, anyway.

Somewhere above us, Destiny was running my ship. Well, her ship now. *Thunder* had changed hands while I was away on Virelia, training and fighting legal battles. The thought of Destiny Austin in command brought a flicker of pride through my exhaustion. From street rats to starship captains - neither of us had seen that coming when we'd huddled together for warmth in San Jose alleyways.

I knew she wanted to talk, to properly reunite after our year apart. I wanted that too. Destiny wasn't just my oldest friend; she was the sister I'd never had by blood but found in the trenches of survival. But every time I considered leaving Sofia's side to seek out Destiny, the monitor would beep, or Sofia's eyelids would flutter without opening, and I'd be anchored again by guilt and fear.

My head dipped forward as exhaustion won a brief battle. Dreams and reality blurred: Sofia smiling at me across a Virelian cafe table; Sofia firing a flechette rifle down *Inferis*'s damaged corridor during a Kergan boarding action; Sofia's stern face as she taught me a better way to disarm an assailant.

I jerked awake with a stiff neck and the taste of copper in my mouth from where I'd bitten my cheek.

Nothing had changed. Sofia's face remained slack, expressionless in her coma. The seizures that had racked her body aboard *Luminara* had at least stopped. Doc Montana had said that was a good sign, but her guarded expression told me more than her words.

I stretched, feeling vertebrae pop, and looked at Sofia's still form. Humans are social creatures, I thought. Impossible to understand in isolation. A person isn't just a collection of traits and experiences, but a node in a web of relationships. I'd built one web on Virelia during my time at Officer Training School—instructors, fellow candidates, people like Sofia. Another web existed here on Earth—Destiny, Lieutenant Busto and his Marines, the engineering team, the base personnel.

And Sofia—Sofia existed at the intersection. She'd been part of my Virelian life, saving me from traffic and thugs alike. Now she was here, about to meet the most important person from my Earth life, when she woke up. When, not if. I clung to that distinction like a lifeline.

Would they get along, Sofia and Destiny? Both were skilled, both fierce in their loyalties. Both had seen me at my worst. The thought of my two worlds connecting brought an unexpected comfort. Despite *Thunder*'s unfamiliar upgrades, despite the crew changes, despite the looming Kergan threat, I felt a sense of rightness being back among humans. Among my people.

The thought had barely formed when Sofia's body suddenly went rigid.

"No," I breathed, lunging forward as her back arched unnaturally. Her limbs stiffened, then began to tremble with increasing violence. "Doc!" I shouted, my voice cracking. "Doc Montana!"

I reached for Sofia's shoulders, trying to stabilize her as her head began to thrash against the pillow. The beeping of the monitor accelerated to a frantic pace, matching my own pulse.

"She's seizing again!" I shouted toward the infirmary

door. "Doc!"

Footsteps pounded against the metal deck plates, and Cindy Montana burst through the doorway, her close-cropped blonde hair still damp from a shower. She took in the situation with one professional glance and moved with practiced efficiency.

"Hold her head—gently," Montana ordered, her voice cutting through my panic. "Don't restrain her limbs completely, just keep her from striking anything."

I cradled Sofia's head between my palms, trying to provide cushioning without restriction. Her body bucked against the bed, muscles contracting with a strength that seemed impossible from someone who'd been unconscious for hours. Her face, previously pale, flushed a dangerous crimson. Veins stood out against her temples, and a thin line of spittle escaped from between her clenched teeth.

"She can't breathe," I said, horror climbing up my throat. "Doc, she can't—"

"I see it." Montana was already reaching for a transparent mask connected to an oxygen tank. "Her breathing's strained from the muscle contractions. Keep her head steady."

Sofia's eyes had rolled back, showing only white beneath partially open lids. I'd faced combat, I'd stared into the void of space, I'd confronted alien species bent on my destruction, but nothing had prepared me for the helplessness of watching someone I loved suffer while I could do nothing but hold on.

Montana fitted the mask over Sofia's nose and mouth, then cranked a dial on the tank. The hiss of oxygen joined the cacophony of medical alerts. "Talk to her," Montana said, adjusting a setting on one of the monitors. "Familiar voices can sometimes help, even in a seizure."

"Sofia," I said, my voice steadier than I felt. "It's Kory. You're on *Thunder*. You're safe. We're going to get through this." I kept talking, repeating reassurances, not knowing if they helped her, but knowing they helped me maintain some semblance of control.

Two minutes stretched like an eternity before Sofia's trembling began to subside. Her breathing, harsh and irregular through the seizure, gradually eased into a more natural rhythm. The rigid tension in her limbs melted away, leaving her once again limp against the sweat-soaked bedding.

The sudden stillness felt almost as alarming as the violent motion had been.

"I thought she was getting better," I exclaimed, not caring that my voice cracked. "The seizures had stopped. You said that was a good sign."

Montana's hand landed on my shoulder, squeezing gently. Her face, normally professional to the point of stoicism, softened with compassion. "Brain injuries don't work in neat, predictable patterns, Commander. Progress isn't linear."

I realized I was crying only when a tear splashed onto Sofia's arm. I wiped at my face roughly, embarrassed and not entirely sure why. "Will she—" I couldn't finish the question.

"I won't lie to you," Montana said, checking Sofia's pupils with a penlight. "The repeated seizures are concerning. But she's young, she's healthy, and she's fighting." She adjusted the oxygen flow and added, "The fact that the seizures are spaced farther apart is still a positive indicator, even with this setback."

I nodded, not trusting my voice.

"Commander," Montana said, and something in her tone

made me look up. "You need rest."

"I'm fine."

"With all due respect, sir, you're not." She nodded toward my trembling hands. "I understand why you're upset. Anyone would be. But there's nothing you can do here that I can't, and wearing yourself to collapse won't help Chief Kohl."

I opened my mouth to argue, but Montana raised her eyebrows in that way medical professionals have perfected over centuries—the look that says they know better and they know you know it too.

"I'll call you immediately if there's any change," she promised. "But you need to eat something that isn't from the replicator, shower, and at least try to sleep for a few hours."

"I don't think I can sleep," I admitted.

"Then at least shower and change out of that uniform. You've been wearing it since the evacuation." Montana turned away to check Sofia's readings, our conversation clearly over in her mind.

I stood reluctantly, legs stiff from hours in the chair. My hand lingered on Sofia's, feeling the warmth that reassured me she was still alive, still fighting. Then I forced myself to turn and walk out of the infirmary.

The corridor outside felt too bright, too normal. Crew members moved with purpose, nodding respectfully as I passed. I should have acknowledged them properly—I was a commanding officer, after all, even if currently without a ship—but I couldn't muster the energy. My thoughts remained in the sterile room behind me, with the woman whose life hung in precarious balance.

I wouldn't sleep. Couldn't. But I could find Destiny. After a year apart, after everything that had happened, I needed my oldest friend. It was time to find her.

The bridge of *Thunder* was a hive of focused activity when I arrived. Faces I recognized mixed with new crew members I'd yet to properly meet. I scanned for Destiny, but didn't see her among the officers' monitoring stations. Instead, I spotted Lieutenant Busto conferring with a communications tech, his perpetual scowl firmly in place.

"Commander Drake," Busto said with a curt nod when he spotted me. "Captain Austin's in her ready room." He gestured toward the door off to the side of the bridge, then added in a quieter tone, "Good to have you back, sir."

I was still getting used to the shift in tone. Before Astrithon, Busto had just called me by name. Now it was all "Commander" this and "Captain" that—from him and everyone else. I figured with a bigger crew and more complex missions, Destiny and Busto had tightened up the discipline, reinforcing the chain of command. It made sense. It was smart. Still, I missed the early days—just the four of us: Destiny, Busto, Zeta, and me, crammed into our little Raider-class strike fighter, picking fights with the Kergan Empire.

I nodded my thanks and walked to the ready room. I paused before knocking, suddenly struck by the fact that this used to be my space—my refuge. Now it belonged to Destiny. I raised my hand and knocked gently on the metal door.

"Enter," Destiny's voice called from within.

She sat behind the desk, surrounded by holographic displays showing damage reports, navigational charts, and communication logs. Her curly black hair was pulled back in a tight bun, regulation-perfect except for a few rebellious strands that escaped around her temples. The captain's insignia gleamed on her collar, and for a moment, I saw her as her crew must—commanding, competent, authoritative.

Then she looked up, saw me, and instantly transformed

back into the Destiny I knew. Her sharp face broke into a wide grin, and she waved me in with characteristic impatience.

"Shut the door, you idiot," she said, already rising from her seat.

I did, and the moment the door closed behind me, Destiny crossed the room in three quick strides and threw her arms around me. She was small—five-foot-four to my six-foot-four—but her embrace felt like the most solid thing in the universe. I hugged her back, tight enough that she grunted in protest, and we stood there, clinging to each other like the lost kids we'd once been.

"I thought you were dead," she murmured against my chest. "When the *Inferis* was destroyed, and we heard about the coup... God, Kory."

"I'm hard to kill," I said, aiming for lightness but landing somewhere near choked emotion.

Destiny pulled back and punched my arm hard enough to sting. "Don't you ever disappear on me like that again. You hear me? A year, Kory. A goddamn year with barely any communication."

"Interstellar bureaucracy," I said with a weak smile. "You know how it is."

She snorted and returned to her desk, gesturing for me to take the seat opposite. "How's your girlfriend?"

"Stable. Mostly." I sank into the chair, suddenly aware of how exhausted I truly was. "She had another seizure just now."

Destiny's face softened with genuine concern. "Montana's the best. If anyone can pull her through, it's Doc."

"I know." I rubbed my face, feeling the stubble that had accumulated over the last day. "It's just... hard to watch."

"Tell me about her," Destiny said, leaning back in her chair. "How did Lieutenant Commander Kory Drake, former street rat, manage to snag a German military police officer?"

Despite everything, I found myself smiling. "She saved my life, actually. My first day on Virelia, I almost got flattened by a transport truck. Sofia pulled me out of the way."

"Sounds romantic," Destiny deadpanned.

"It got better. Some local thugs tried to mug me a few days later. Sofia intervened, kicked their asses, then nursed me through a concussion." I shook my head, remembering. "She was assigned to my case as an undercover close protection specialist. Spent months keeping me safe, then followed me to *Inferis* when I was assigned there."

I told Destiny about Sofia's quiet competence, her dry humor, how she'd volunteered to join the *Inferis* to follow me despite having the option of a comfortable posting on Virelia. How she'd saved my life again during the battle, how she'd been injured during enemy action.

"I think I love her, Des," I admitted finally.

Destiny smiled and shook her head. "I never thought I'd see the day. The great Kory Drake, brought low by a woman."

"What's that supposed to mean?"

"Nothing bad," she said with a laugh. "Just that I wasn't even sure you liked girls. You never showed interest in anyone back in the day."

"We were trying not to starve to death back in the day," I pointed out.

"True enough." Her expression sobered. "She'll pull through, Kory. And when she does, I'll make sure she knows exactly what she's getting into with you."

"Should I be worried about that conversation?"

"Terrified," Destiny confirmed with a wicked grin. Then, more seriously: "It could be worse, you know."

"How's that?"

Destiny's eyes darkened, and for a moment, she looked away. "Sofia could be a captive of the Kergans."

The simple statement landed like a physical blow. "Des..."

"They caught me about six months ago," she said, her voice deliberately casual. "A raid on a supply dump went sideways. Bad intel, worse luck." She picked up a stylus from her desk and twirled it between her fingers. "Had me for three days before Busto and his marines pulled off a rescue."

I stared at her, processing this new information. "What did they—" I couldn't finish the question.

Destiny didn't answer immediately. The stylus danced between her fingers, faster and faster. "The weird thing is, I don't remember much of it," she finally said. "Doc says it's probably emotional trauma, my brain protecting itself." She shrugged. "Honestly, I don't want to remember."

The stylus stilled, and Destiny met my eyes again. "So yeah, Sofia could have it worse. She's injured, but she's with people who care about her. Who'll protect her."

I nodded, understanding the message beneath her words. Destiny had endured something she couldn't even bring herself to remember, yet here she was, commanding a starship, fighting on. If she could do that, Sofia could recover from a head injury.

A knock interrupted us before I could respond. Destiny called out permission to enter, and the door swung open to reveal a slim woman with long brown hair.

Phoebe Brooks stepped into the ready room, her eyes lighting up when she saw me. "Commander Drake! It's so good to see you back." Her smile was warm, perhaps a touch too warm, before she turned professional again. "Captain, I wanted to report that repairs on the starboard quarter bolster are complete. *Thunder* is ready to depart whenever you give the order."

"Thank you, Lieutenant," Destiny said, standing. "Tell engineering to prepare for lift-off in thirty minutes."

Brooks nodded and left, but not before giving me another smile. I remembered, distantly, that Destiny had once mentioned Phoebe had a crush on me. The thought felt irrelevant now, with Sofia lying unconscious in the infirmary.

Destiny stretched, then adjusted her uniform collar. "Time to get this bucket of bolts moving," she announced. "Wolf Jaw Base is expecting us, and I don't want to keep Commander Brooks waiting. Lynda's been kind enough to tolerate our presence; the least we can do is show up without her having to send out a search party."

She started toward the door, then paused and looked back at me. "It's damn good to have you back, Kory. Even under these circumstances."

"It's good to be back," I said, and despite everything—Sofia's condition, the looming Kergan threat, the uncertainties ahead—I meant it. I was home.

15

The massive bulk of *Thunder* sliced through the sky above the Sierra Nevada, her engines a steady purr beneath my feet. After months of exile, training, and fighting for my life, the sight of actual Earth terrain—jagged mountains, feathery pine forests, and the glinting mirror of Huntington Lake—hit me with a nostalgia I hadn't expected. My hands gripped the command rail, knuckles white, as if I might float away without an anchor. Funny how "home" could be a place I'd only spent a few months at before everything went sideways.

"Coming up on Wolf Jaw Base, Captain." The helmsman's voice cut through my thoughts.

I nodded, eyes fixed on the main display.

Destiny said, "Take us in nice and slow. No need to announce our return with a sonic boom."

The journey across multiple states had been mercifully uneventful—a rarity in my life lately. We'd maintained low altitude and subsonic speeds, keeping *Thunder*'s advanced stealth systems engaged. The Kergans still held most of

Earth, and while they hadn't yet discovered our new base location, flaunting our presence would be idiotic.

"Captain, receiving landing protocols from Wolf Jaw Control," the comms officer announced.

"Acknowledge and proceed," Destiny said.

Most of the crew I'd known had apparently rotated out during my year-long absence. Just one more reminder of how much had changed.

Below us, Huntington Lake's surface glimmered like polished metal under the light of a half-moon. As we banked toward the western shore, a section of the mountainside suddenly split open, revealing the gaping maw of the underground hangar. I'd been briefed that after the Kergans discovered and raided our original Wolf Jaw Base north of town, they'd relocated everything to this more defensible position.

"That's... significantly larger than I remember," I muttered, watching the hangar doors yawn wide.

Destiny, who'd been silently piloting from the command chair—her command chair—flicked me a sardonic smile. "What, did you think we'd just sit around moping while you were off playing criminal on Virelia?"

"Lieutenant Commander Austin," I corrected with mock formality, "I assumed you'd be far too busy keeping *Thunder* in one piece to undertake massive construction projects."

"Multitasking is a specialty of mine." Her eyes sparkled with the same mischief that had kept us both alive on the streets of San Jose all those years ago. "Just wait till you see what else we've been up to."

Thunder glided into the cavernous space, her hull clearing the opening with room to spare. Overhead lighting blinked on sequentially, illuminating a space easily three times larger than our original base hangar. The landing cradles extended to receive us with mechanical precision. With a barely perceptible bump and the hiss of settling struts, we touched down. Above us, the massive hangar doors began their slow closure, sealing us away from prying eyes with a reverberating thump I felt in my chest.

Home. Sort of.

My thoughts immediately turned to Sofia. She'd been unconscious since our narrow escape from the HideyRock. Doc Montana had kept her stable, but we needed the more advanced medical facilities here at the base.

"Lieutenant Commander Drake." Montana's voice crackled over my comm unit. "If you're finished admiring the view, I could use a hand transferring our patient to the infirmary."

"On my way," I replied, already moving toward the lift.

The ship's corridors felt narrower than I remembered, or maybe I'd just gotten used to the sweeping halls of the Space Warfare School. I made it to the infirmary in record time, finding Montana and an orderly preparing Sofia for transport. Her hair spilled over the edge of the gurney, her face peaceful despite the neural monitors attached to her temples.

"She's stable," Montana said without preamble, her eyes clinically assessing my reaction. "But I want her in a proper medical bay with actual equipment, not this glorified first-aid kit."

I nodded, swallowing the lump in my throat. "What can I do?"

"Help us navigate this oversized torpedo tube you call a ship," she said, handing me a portable med monitor. "And try not to look so much like a lost puppy. She's tough."

"Never suggested otherwise." I positioned myself at the head of the gurney, trying not to focus on Sofia's still form.

Her hand had fallen slightly off the edge, and I gently tucked it back beside her. My fingers lingered on hers for just a moment—cool but not cold. "Ready when you are."

Maneuvering through *Thunder*'s tight passageways was a delicate operation. The orderly—a stocky man with arms like tree trunks—proved surprisingly graceful as he guided the front of the gurney while I handled the rear. Montana walked alongside, monitoring Sofia's vitals with the intensity of a hawk tracking its prey.

We reached the main airlock and waited as the ramp extended to the hangar floor. The vast space outside buzzed with activity—ground crew swarming around *Thunder*'s hull, maintenance techs already setting up diagnostic equipment, security personnel establishing a perimeter. Dozens of unfamiliar faces, all moving with the choreographed efficiency of a well-trained military unit.

"Quite the welcome committee," I muttered.

Montana snorted. "They've been preparing for days. Word got out that the prodigal son was returning."

"Terrific." I felt a flush creep up my neck. "Nothing like a little pressure."

We descended the ramp to a small reception party waiting at the bottom. I recognized Baxter Brooks—husband of Lynda Brooks and father of Phoebe—who gave me a quick, professional nod before turning his attention to *Thunder*'s exterior. The rest were strangers, though they all wore UHC insignia with the distinctive Wolf Jaw Base patch—a stylized wolf's head superimposed over a hydroelectric dam.

"Lieutenant Commander Drake," one of them began, stepping forward with a clipboard.

Montana cut him off with a glare that could have melted steel. "Medical emergency. Paperwork later."

The welcoming committee scattered like leaves in a windstorm, clearing a path to a set of double doors across the hangar. The orderly picked up the pace, and I matched him stride for stride.

The base itself was both familiar and alien—same utilitarian design principles as the original, but with subtle differences in layout and scale. The corridors were wider, the ceilings higher, everything built with the confidence of people who believed they'd be staying for the long haul. We passed several junction points where base personnel stopped to stare at our little procession. I kept my eyes forward, focused on the task at hand.

We reached a freight elevator with doors wide enough to accommodate the gurney without difficulty. Inside, Montana punched the button for level B2.

"Medical's down one floor now," she explained, noticing my confusion. "More space, better radiation shielding."

"Smart," I agreed, watching the numbers blink downward. "How many levels does this place have?"

"None above ground, five below. Plus, some specialized areas I don't have clearance to know about." She shrugged. "Above my pay grade."

The elevator doors opened onto a corridor with soft amber lighting recessed into the ceiling—easy on the eyes and distinctly different from the harsh white illumination of the upper levels. We followed signs for the infirmary, passing several labs and what looked like physical therapy rooms before arriving at a set of double doors marked with the universal medical symbol.

The infirmary itself was impressive—a hospital in miniature, with a central nursing station surrounded by examination areas, private rooms, and medical equipment. Clean, efficient, and far more comprehensive than anything we'd had at the old base.

A stern-faced woman with steel-gray hair cut in a severe bob intercepted us just inside the entrance. Her uniform marked her as medical staff, though her bearing suggested someone accustomed to command.

"Exam Room 2," she directed, pointing to our right. "Already prepped and waiting." Her gaze swept over Sofia's still form, assessing and cataloging with professional detachment. "I'm Nurse Practitioner Kovac. I run this facility."

Montana stepped forward, transferring the medical datapad to Kovac. "Patient is Chief Warrant Officer Sofia Kohl, twenty-six, suffering from a head wound following the battle of Virelia. She's been stable but unresponsive for approximately forty-eight hours."

Kovac nodded, scanning the information. "I've received her complete file. We'll take good care of her." She glanced at me, eyes narrowing slightly. "And you are?"

"Lieutenant Commander Kory Drake," I said, straightening instinctively under her scrutiny. "I'm—"

"He's the patient's partner," Montana interrupted, giving me a look that clearly said, “shut up and let me handle this.”

Kovac's expression softened fractionally. "I see. Well, Commander Drake, we need to get Chief Kohl settled and begin our assessments. Perhaps you could return in, say, three hours?"

I opened my mouth to protest, but Montana's hand on my arm stopped me. "You'll just be in the way," she said quietly. "Let Kovac do her job."

The rational part of my brain knew they were right. The rest of me wanted to plant my feet and refuse to leave Sofia's side. But I'd spent enough time in military hospitals to know that hovering relatives—even ones with rank—were at best a distraction and at worst an active hindrance.

"Three hours," I agreed reluctantly. "But I want updates if anything changes."

Kovac nodded. "Of course, Commander. Now, if you'll excuse us..."

I watched them wheel Sofia away, the doors to Exam Room 2 swinging shut behind them with a soft pneumatic hiss. My chest tightened with an uncomfortable heat that I recognized as helplessness—a feeling I'd become all too familiar with during my time on Virelia.

"She's in expert hands," Montana assured me. "Kovac's reputation precedes her. Twenty years Navy Medical Corps before joining the UHC. Served on three different aircraft carriers."

"Thanks, Doc," I said, managing a weak smile. "I'll try not to pace a groove in the floor while I wait."

"Do that." She clapped me on the shoulder. "I need to get back to *Thunder*. Post-landing checks won't run themselves."

Left alone in the infirmary's waiting area, I suddenly realized I did not know where to go or what to do with myself. The base was largely unfamiliar, and my few possessions were still aboard *Thunder*. I decided to head back upstairs and see if I could find someone to give me a proper briefing on the base layout.

The elevator deposited me back on the main level, and I picked a direction at random, figuring I'd eventually find something useful. The corridors were busier now, with personnel moving purposefully between sections. No one stopped me or questioned my presence, though I caught a few curious glances. Apparently, my reputation—or at least my face—had preceded me.

After about ten minutes of aimless wandering, I caught

the distinctive murmur of multiple voices engaged in serious discussion. I followed the sound down a side passage and through an open doorway into what was clearly the base's command center.

The room was spacious, dominated by a large holographic display table in the center showing a detailed 3D rendering of the base and surrounding terrain. Workstations lined the walls, each monitoring different aspects of base operations. And gathered around the main display were four familiar figures, deep in conversation.

Destiny Austin stood with her arms crossed, her sharp chin jutting forward in the way it always did when she was about to win an argument. Beside her floated the crimson dodecahedron that housed Nicobe, the Heliacal Templar's containment field, humming softly. Across from them, Queen Zeta's octahedral vessel glowed with internal plasma light, casting warm patterns across the tactical display. And completing the group was a woman I recognized immediately despite the additional lines at the corners of her eyes—Lynda Brooks, who had commanded the original Wolf Jaw Base before their hasty relocation.

They all looked up as I entered, conversation halting mid-sentence.

"Well, look what the cat dragged in," Lynda said, a smile spreading across her face. She stepped forward, extending her hand. "Welcome back from exile, Kory. You're looking surprisingly well-fed for someone who's been held captive on an alien planet."

I shook her hand, returning the smile. "They fed me well on Virelia. Military doctrine holds that hungry students make poor strategists. How have you been, Commander Brooks?"

"It's been... eventful," she replied, her expression turning wry. "But we persevere. Baxter sends his regards. He's running a security drill on the perimeter and should be back shortly."

"And Ricki?" I asked, remembering her son—a gangly teenager with a knack for mechanical systems.

Her face softened with maternal pride. "Working in the power plant as an apprentice engineer. He's got quite the gift for plasma systems." She laughed lightly. "Gets that from his father, not me."

"I'm glad they're both well." I glanced around at the others. "I don't mean to interrupt. Sounds like you were in the middle of something important."

"Merely discussing the allocation of resources," Zeta intoned. "The Queen is pleased to see her former companion returned safely to Earth's embrace."

"What Her Majesty means," Destiny translated with an eye roll, "is that we're trying to figure out where to put all the kavreni refugees we picked up from *Luminara*. The base isn't exactly designed for non-human habitation."

"A temporary inconvenience," Zeta declared. "As the rightful sovereign of the Collective Dominion, the Queen hereby grants permission to expand this facility to accommodate our allies." Her octahedron rotated slightly, focusing one of its faces toward Nicobe. "Furthermore, we authorize Nicobe, as Heliacal Templar and consort to Commander Austin, to oversee the construction."

Nicobe's dodecahedron pulsed with acknowledgment. "Nicobe is honored by Her Majesty's trust. The expansion will proceed according to UHC protocols while incorporating Dominion efficiency standards."

"And where exactly are we getting the resources for this expansion?" I asked, stepping further into the room to examine the base schematic.

Ignoring my question, Zeta continued. "The Queen has

also granted access to the Marauder class of Dominion warships," she said, her tone suggesting this was a tremendous boon—which, knowing the Dominion's protective attitude toward their military technology, it absolutely was. "*Thunder* shall be upgraded accordingly."

I blinked in surprise. "The Marauder class? That's... significant."

"Light cruiser equivalent," Destiny explained, unable to hide her excitement. "Improved armor, enhanced weapons systems, and a fusion reactor for extended range." Her eyes gleamed. "She'll be faster, deadlier, and able to operate independently for months if necessary."

"Nicobe has already begun preliminary assessments," the Templar added. "The work will require *Thunder* to be docked for approximately two weeks. The assault shuttles will be deployed to the hangar to allow complete access to the hull integration points."

Lynda pointed to several areas on the holographic display. "We're planning to add additional habitation pods here and here, expand the primary hangar, and construct a secondary hangar for escort vessels." She glanced at me. "Assuming Dominion intelligence is correct about the Kergan patrol patterns, we should be able to complete the work without detection."

"The Queen's intelligence is beyond question," Zeta stated, managing to sound affronted despite her plasma form having no actual facial expressions.

"Of course, Your Majesty," Lynda replied smoothly. She'd clearly prepared to navigate Zeta's royal sensitivities.

I nodded along, absorbing the plans while still wrapping my head around the fact that *Thunder*—my ship, though technically not anymore—was about to get a serious upgrade. She was about to become something far more formidable. The strategic implications alone...

Still, one issue nagged at me. "Do we even have enough tribute points for that?" I asked.

Every head turned to Zeta. The queen inclined her capsule slightly.

"Commander Drake, the situation is unprecedented," she said. "You are no longer merely insurgents fighting for the liberty of your people. You now carry the weight and authority of the Collective Dominion. Zeta is dissolving the system of tribute points and instead granting you full access to the finest technology my people possess—limited only by what your crew can operate."

Destiny exhaled. "Yeah, well, people are the problem. We're recruiting like mad, but we're not exactly staffed to run a battleship."

"Or a fleet," I added. "But we can hope for that one day." I turned to Zeta. "Thank you, Zeta. We accept your offer."

"There's one more thing we need to discuss," Destiny said suddenly, interrupting my train of thought. She straightened, her expression shifting from casual to formal in an instant. "Now that Kory's back, I'm relinquishing command of *Thunder* to him."

The statement hit me like a physical blow. "What?"

"You heard me," she said, holding my gaze. "I'm giving you back your ship."

"That's—no," I stammered, genuinely stunned. "Destiny, you're *Thunder*'s commanding officer. I'm not going to waltz back in and take that from you after everything you've done."

"You're not taking anything," she countered. "I'm giving it back. It was always meant to be temporary."

"But—"

"But nothing," she cut me off. "You've spent the last year

training with the best tacticians and strategists in the Dominion. You've served under Celestarch Kaelith himself. Meanwhile, I've been running guerrilla operations with what we had available." She shook her head. "I'm good, Kory. You know I am. But you've got the formal education now to back up your natural instincts."

"Destiny is correct," Zeta interjected. "The UHC selected you specifically for command training because they recognized your potential. It would be wasteful not to use that investment."

I looked between them, searching for signs of reluctance or resentment, finding none. "What about UHC High Command? Don't they have something to say about this?"

Destiny shook her head. "We've been out of contact with High Command since the fall of Virelia to Arctis's forces. I think we're on our own now."

Zeta's octahedron pulsed dismissively. "Zeta is taking command of your forces until communication is reestablished with your commanders. Even when that happens, they are unlikely to contradict both the Queen's recommendation and Commander Austin's own request."

"It's what I want," Destiny said firmly. "I'll stay on as your XO, of course. Someone has to keep you from doing anything monumentally stupid."

A laugh escaped me despite my confusion. "Well, when you put it that way..."

"Then it's settled," she declared, satisfaction clear in her voice.

I turned to Zeta, another question forming. "Will you be resuming your position as my Heliacal consort?"

"The Queen regrets that her duties prevent such an arrangement at this time," Zeta replied. "The civil war requires her direct attention. However, Nicobe will continue to serve as Destiny's consort and provide technical support to *Thunder*."

"Nicobe is pleased to maintain this service," the Templar confirmed.

I stood there, looking at each of them in turn—Destiny with her confident smirk, Zeta with her regal bearing, Nicobe's subtly pulsing containment field, and Lynda's approving smile. My people. Despite a year's absence, despite everything that had changed, they still considered me one of their own. They still wanted me to lead.

The realization settled in my chest, a warmth that chased away the lingering chill of uncertainty. I was home, not just to a base or a planet, but to a purpose and a crew that believed in me.

"Alright," I said finally, standing a little straighter. "I accept. But I expect full briefings on everything I've missed, and I mean everything."

"Wouldn't have it any other way, *Captain*," Destiny replied, emphasizing the title with a hint of her street-kid drawl.

Captain. Again. The word echoed in my mind, both familiar and strange, like returning to a childhood home to find the furniture rearranged but the foundations unchanged. *Thunder* was mine once more. Despite everything—the exile, the trials, the battles—I'd come full circle.

And this time, I was ready.

16

I gripped the edge of the medical console until my knuckles matched the sterile white of the examination room. Sofia lay on the scanning bed, her hair stark against the dark cushion, her usually alert blue eyes glazed with pain. Doc Kovac moved with the efficiency of someone who'd seen too much trauma to be rattled by one more emergency, but I caught the slight furrow in her brow as she studied the initial readings. My stomach twisted into a knot that would've made a boy scout cry and possibly voided a warranty.

"Lieutenant Commander Drake, I need you to step back," Kovac said, her steel-colored bob not moving an inch as she turned to face me. "You're hovering."

I backed away, hands raised in surrender. "Sorry, Doc. Just worried."

"We all are," she replied, softening slightly. "But I need space to work."

Wolf Jaw Base's medical bay was several cuts above *Thunder*'s cramped sickbay. Real hospital beds lined one wall, while advanced diagnostic machines hummed with purpose rather than complaint. The room smelled of antiseptic and that peculiar scent that all medical facilities share—fear mixed with hope.

Sofia winced as Kovac checked her pupillary response with a penlight. "Is the light causing pain?" Kovac asked.

Kovac had brought Sofia out of her induced coma in order to better evaluate her condition.

"Yes," Sofia said, her German accent thickened by discomfort. "Like knives behind my eyes."

I crossed my arms to keep from reaching for her. "Her speech has been—"

"Slurred," Sofia finished for me, the word itself slightly blurred at the edges. "I can speak for myself, Kory."

"Sorry," I muttered, feeling useless. Being a starship commander didn't count for much in a medical bay. Here, I was just the worried boyfriend, relegated to the sidelines while professionals did the real work.

Kovac nodded, making notes on her tablet. "What other symptoms have you experienced, Chief Kohl?"

Sofia took a deep breath, clearly collecting her thoughts. "Headaches. Severe ones. Nausea. Sometimes I cannot... find the right words." She paused, frustration flashing across her face. "And I am angry all the time. For no reason."

"Personality changes are consistent with your injury," Kovac said, her tone matter-of-fact but not unkind. "Let's get you into the scanner so we can see what's happening inside that head of yours."

The scanner was a sleek white arch, nothing like the clunky medical equipment I'd seen during my brief, unpleasant encounters with Earth's healthcare system before the invasion. This was Collective Dominion tech specifically modified for scanning humans.

"Please remain completely still," Kovac instructed as

Sofia slid into the machine. "This won't hurt, but any movement will blur the images."

I watched Sofia's face disappear into the scanner and felt a pang of helplessness sharper than any physical pain. The woman I loved was suffering, and all my supposed power as a UHC officer meant nothing. I couldn't fight this enemy with railguns or tactical maneuvers.

"How long has she been experiencing these symptoms?" Kovac asked me quietly as the scanner hummed.

"The headaches started right after we escaped from *Inferis,*" I said. "When the ship was hit, she took a blow to the head. But everything else—the seizures, the mood changes—that's been escalating for the past week."

Kovac's lips thinned. "And you waited until now to seek proper medical attention?"

I felt heat rise in my face. "We've been running for our lives, Doc. Sofia saw Cindy on *Thunder,* but we didn't have access to this kind of equipment until now. Or human medical specialists."

"Lieutenant Montana is a good field medic, but she's not a neurologist," Kovac replied, her eyes on the screen where ghostly images of Sofia's brain were beginning to appear. "And this..." she pointed at a crescent-shaped shadow on the display, "is why you need specialists."

The scanner completed its work with a soft chime, and Sofia was slowly slid out. Her face was pale, a thin sheen of sweat on her forehead despite the cool air in the medical bay.

"Can I sit up now?" she asked.

"Slowly," Kovac instructed, helping her to a seated position. "Commander Drake, please assist Chief Kohl to the consultation area. I need to review these scans in detail."

I helped Sofia to a small alcove with comfortable chairs

and a desk. She leaned heavily against me, her usually sturdy frame seeming fragile under my hands. I could feel tremors running through her muscles.

"I'm fine," she insisted, though the slight slur in her words betrayed her.

"Sure you are," I agreed, because sometimes the kindest thing is to let someone keep their pride. "Just humor me by sitting down before you fall down."

We waited in silence, Sofia's hand gripped tightly in mine. Her fingers were icy, and I rubbed them gently, trying to warm them with friction. Outside the window, I could see the underground hangar of Wolf Jaw Base, where *Thunder* rested in her berth like a predator taking a brief nap before the next hunt.

Kovac returned with a tablet and a grim expression that made my heart rate spike. She pulled up a chair across from us and tapped the screen, projecting a three-dimensional image of Sofia's brain in the air between us.

"Chief Kohl," she began formally, "I'm seeing a chronic subdural hematoma here." She pointed to the crescent-shaped dark area. "This is fluid—most likely blood—trapped between your brain and your skull. It's putting pressure on your brain tissue, which explains all of your symptoms."

Sofia's grip on my hand tightened painfully. "How serious is this?" she asked, her voice steady despite the fear I could feel radiating from her.

"Very," Kovac said bluntly. "The initial injury likely caused a small bleed that has continued or recurred over time. The pressure has been building gradually, which is why your symptoms have been escalating."

I forced my voice to work past the tightness in my throat. "Can you fix it?"

Kovac's face hardened, and I knew the answer before she spoke. "No. This requires neurosurgical intervention—a procedure to drain the fluid and repair the damaged blood vessels. I'm not qualified to perform brain surgery, Lieutenant Commander Drake. This base isn't equipped for it."

"But—" I started.

"I can manage the symptoms," she continued. "Diuretics to reduce the fluid buildup, corticosteroids to decrease inflammation, anti-seizure medications to control the seizures. But these are stopgap measures, not a cure."

Sofia's face was expressionless. "How long do I have?" she asked, the question clinical, as if she were discussing someone else's prognosis.

Kovac hesitated, and in that pause, I heard the answer I didn't want to hear.

"With medication, I estimate two to three weeks before you begin to suffer permanent neurological damage," she finally said. "The pressure will continue to increase. Eventually, it will affect critical brain functions. Memory. Motor control. Respiratory regulation."

My vision tunneled briefly, the edges going dark as the implications hit me. Sofia could die. Sofia could die within weeks. The thought was incomprehensible, like trying to imagine *Thunder* navigating without stars.

"There must be someone," I said, my voice sounding distant even to my own ears. "A surgeon. Someone who can help. In Wolf Jaw, maybe?"

"Before the invasion, certainly," Kovac acknowledged. "But now..." She shook her head. "The UHC has few medical specialists. Most were trapped on Earth during the Kergan takeover."

Sofia straightened in her chair, military discipline

asserting itself. "What medication do I need to start immediately?"

I admired her calm even as I wanted to scream at the unfairness of it all. We'd survived battles, a coup, the destruction of a starship, and now this—an invisible enemy we couldn't fight with all our technology and weapons.

Kovac tapped on her tablet. "I'm prescribing dexamethasone for the swelling, furosemide as a diuretic, and levetiracetam for the seizures. You'll need to monitor for side effects—increased thirst, frequent urination, dizziness when standing. The anti-seizure medication may cause fatigue."

"Will I be combat effective?" Sofia asked, and I nearly laughed at the absurdity of the question. Leave it to Sofia to worry about her duty when her life was in danger.

"No," Kovac said firmly. "You are not cleared for duty, Chief. These medications will help, but you're at high risk for sudden severe symptoms—including loss of consciousness or prolonged seizures that could be life-threatening."

Sofia's jaw tightened, but she nodded once, accepting the verdict.

"I'll have these medications ready within the hour," Kovac continued. "In the meantime, I want you to rest. No physical exertion, no stress if possible." She glanced at me with a look that clearly communicated how unlikely she found that last instruction. "And Commander Drake, I want to speak with you privately."

Sofia gave my hand one final squeeze before releasing it. "Go. I will wait here."

I followed Kovac to the far side of the medical bay, dread pooling in my stomach.

"You need to find her a neurosurgeon," Kovac said

without preamble. "This isn't optional, Commander. The medications will buy time, but not much."

"I understand," I said, my mind already racing through possibilities. "Is there anyone in the UHC forces? Anyone who escaped Earth with medical training?"

"I've already checked our personnel databases," she replied. "We have three doctors with neurological training, but none with the surgical expertise required for this procedure. This isn't like patching up a bullet wound. Brain surgery requires years of specialized training and experience."

I ran a hand through my hair, frustration making my movements jerky. "So what you're saying is that we need to find a surgeon on Earth. Under Kergan occupation."

"Yes." Her eyes held mine steadily. "And you need to find one quickly."

I glanced back at Sofia, who sat perfectly upright in the chair, her face composed despite everything. Her discipline only made me love her more, which made the thought of losing her unbearable.

"Two to three weeks," I repeated. "You're sure?"

"That's an optimistic estimate," Kovac said. "It could be less time. The brain is unpredictable. One severe seizure could cause a catastrophic increase in pressure."

My hands were numb, but I felt a heat in my chest, an uncomfortable burning that I recognized as fear mixed with determination. I'd faced impossible odds before. I'd fought Soul Ravagers and survived the destruction of a starship. I'd be damned if I'd lose Sofia to something as mundane as a medical condition.

"I understand," I said again, with more conviction this time. "Thank you, Doc."

"Don't thank me," she replied, turning away. "Just find

her a surgeon. I'll do what I can here, but..." she let the sentence hang unfinished, the implication clear.

I returned to Sofia's side, schooling my features into something resembling confidence. I wouldn't add to her burden by showing my fear.

"We need to call a meeting," I told her. "Destiny, Zeta, Busto—we need a plan."

"To find a neurosurgeon," Sofia said. It wasn't a question.

"Yes."

"I'm sorry to be such a burden," she said. "What must your friends think of me?"

I gently nudged her. "It'll be fine. Don't worry about it."

Her blue eyes met mine, clear and determined despite the pain I knew lurked behind them. "Okay. But don't forget that I'm just one person."

Nurse Kovac had some paperwork to complete and medications to issue before Sofia could be released, so I left them and walked out of the base infirmary. As I moved through the corridor alone, the weight of Kovac's prognosis hung over me like a shadow. Two weeks to find a specialized surgeon on an occupied planet, extract them from Kergan control, and perform a delicate brain surgery.

Just another impossible mission for the crew of *Thunder.* I almost smiled at the thought, because sometimes gallows humor is all you have left.

17

The command center of Wolf Jaw Base hummed with quiet efficiency, screens casting blue-white reflections across faces that had seen too much war to show outright concern. I stood at the head of the holotable, my reflection fractured across its dark surface like the pieces of the plan I was desperately trying to assemble in my head. The meeting had been hastily arranged, the chairs around the table filled with the only people in the galaxy I trusted with Sofia's life —and the impossible task of saving it.

Destiny sat to my right, her dark curls framing a face set in the particular expression she reserved for when things were truly dire—a studied nonchalance that didn't reach her eyes. Beside her, Nicobe's crimson dodecahedron hovered silently, occasional flickers of light within suggesting the igna's attentiveness. Lieutenant Commander Brooks occupied the seat opposite me, her thin frame rigid with military bearing, brown-gray hair pulled back so severely it seemed to be doing double duty as a facelift.

Zeta's octahedral vessel floated at the far end of the

table, its crystalline surfaces reflecting fragments of light that danced across the ceiling. In the Collective Dominion, her presence would have commanded immediate deference. Here, she was—well, still royalty, but royalty in exile, which meant she actually had to listen to the rest of us occasionally.

Busto was the last to arrive, striding in with his characteristic military precision, uniform pressed to within an inch of its life.

"Lieutenant," I acknowledged as he took his seat.

"Sorry for the delay, sir," he said, though his expression suggested it was our fault for starting early rather than his for being late. "I was checking our security perimeter. Old habits."

"Appreciated, Lieutenant," Brooks said. "This base has been secure for three months, but vigilance never hurts."

I cleared my throat, drawing their attention. "I've called this meeting because we have a situation." My voice sounded steadier than I felt, a small victory. "Sofia's... Chief Kohl's condition has been diagnosed. It's serious."

The room quieted, the background hum of equipment suddenly more noticeable.

"How serious?" Destiny asked, her carefully constructed facade slipping for a moment.

"Life-threatening," I replied, forcing myself to maintain eye contact. "She has a chronic subdural hematoma—blood trapped between her brain and skull. It's causing seizures, personality changes, cognitive issues. According to Nurse Kovac, without surgical intervention, she has two weeks before she starts suffering permanent brain damage."

Destiny swore softly, an inventive combination of English and street slang I hadn't heard before.

"Can the base medical staff perform this surgery?"

Brooks asked, practical as always.

I shook my head. "Kovac was clear—this requires a neurosurgeon with specialized training. She can manage the symptoms temporarily with medication, but Sofia needs surgery."

"The Collective Dominion has exceptional medical facilities," Zeta's voice emanated from her vessel, formal and measured. "However, reaching them would require a journey of considerable distance through space now patrolled by forces loyal to the usurper Arctis."

"Not to mention the time it would take," I added. "Kovac was emphatic about the timeline. We don't have weeks to spare for interstellar travel, even if we could safely reach Dominion space."

Busto leaned forward, elbows on the table. "So we need a neurosurgeon, and we need one fast. What are our options within UHC resources?"

Brooks tapped her tablet, bringing up a personnel directory on the central holodisplay. "I've already consulted our databases. We have three personnel with neurological training in the entire UHC Armada. One is specialized in neurochemistry, not surgery. Another is a neurologist with no surgical experience. The third has performed basic neurosurgical procedures but lacks the expertise for this specific operation and his last known location is Virelia."

"Nicobe believes there is another option worth considering." The igna's voice was surprisingly soft, coming from the crimson dodecahedron. "Earth."

A weighted silence fell over the room. Earth—our homeworld, under Kergan occupation. The place we'd all fought to protect. The place now crawling with marac soldiers and mindjacked humans and human collaborators.

"Earth must have thousands of neurosurgeons," Destiny

said, voicing what we were all thinking. "Or at least it did before the invasion."

"If they haven't all been killed or taken off-world," Busto countered grimly.

"Actually," Brooks said, tapping her tablet again, "we have intelligence suggesting something interesting about medical personnel on Earth." The holodisplay shifted to show a series of reports, witness testimonies, and fragmented data streams. "Over the past six months, our intelligence network has noted a pattern. The Kergans have been systematically rounding up medical specialists—particularly surgeons, and more specifically, neurosurgeons and neurologists."

I frowned, scanning the reports. "Rounding them up for what?"

"That remains unclear," Brooks admitted. "Possibly for treating high-value Kergan personnel, possibly for research purposes. Some reports suggest they're being forced to work on mindjacking technology improvements."

"Makes sense," Busto said. "Neurologists would understand brain structure better than anyone. If the Kergans want to refine their mindjacking tech, that's who they'd want."

I felt a chill at the thought. Mindjacking—the Kergan technology that turned humans into compliant slaves—was horrific enough in its current form. The idea of them improving it with the forced help of human doctors was nauseating.

"So the Kergans are collecting brain doctors," Destiny summarized, her fingers drumming a restless pattern on the table. "That actually works in our favor, doesn't it? Instead of having to track down individual surgeons who might be dead or hidden, we know the Kergans are keeping them somewhere."

"Not just somewhere," Brooks said, zooming in on one report. "We have confirmed locations for several medical detention centers. They're keeping specialists in regional hospitals, under guard but generally in good condition. They need their skills intact."

Hope flickered in my chest for the first time since Kovac's diagnosis. "Do we have names? Specific surgeons we could target?"

Brooks nodded, bringing up a personnel file that expanded in the air above us. The image showed a woman in her fifties, Asian features, with steel-rimmed glasses and a no-nonsense expression that reminded me, oddly, of Sofia herself.

"Dr. Eleanor Chen," Brooks said. "Before the invasion, she was one of the most respected neurosurgeons on the west coast, specializing in traumatic brain injuries. She was the department head at UC Davis Medical Center in Sacramento. Our latest intelligence confirms she's being held at the Sacramento VA Medical Center, now under Kergan control."

"Sacramento," I murmured, mentally calculating. "That's what, 200 kilometers from here?"

"233 kilometers by the most direct route," Busto corrected. "But that direct route passes through multiple Kergan controlled airspaces and a heavy patrol zone around the city perimeter."

Destiny leaned back in her chair, eyes narrowed in thought. "So we need to break into a Kergan-controlled hospital in the middle of an occupied city, extract a high-value specialist without getting killed or captured, and get her back here to perform brain surgery on Sofia."

"That summarizes the situation accurately," Zeta

confirmed, apparently missing Destiny's sarcasm.

"Piece of cake," Destiny said, rolling her eyes. "We've done harder things before breakfast."

"Actually, we have," I pointed out. "The mission to Lindblad Crater was objectively more difficult."

"Lindblad Crater didn't have marac patrols on every street corner," Busto countered. "And we had a much larger force. Four corvettes worth of crew. Don't forget that for the moment, *Thunder* is unavailable while it's being rebuilt."

"Zeta wonders if a direct assault is the wisest approach," the queen said, floating her vessel slightly closer to the table. "Perhaps subterfuge would serve better than force in this instance."

I nodded, grateful for her input. "Agreed. We need more information before we can plan an extraction. We need to know the hospital's security protocols, patrol schedules, how Dr. Chen is monitored, and whether she'd be willing to come with us."

"She might not have a choice," Destiny pointed out. "If it's between helping us or staying as a Kergan prisoner..."

"We cannot assume," Nicobe interjected. "Some cooperate with occupiers to protect others. Some resist in ways we cannot see. Nicobe suggests learning Dr. Chen's disposition before assuming her compliance."

Busto nodded approvingly. "Good point. We need human intelligence—someone inside that hospital or with access to it."

"The resistance networks in Sacramento have been particularly active," Brooks offered. "We've maintained limited contact through dead drops and encrypted communications. They might be able to get someone inside, or may already have people working there."

I felt the beginnings of a plan taking shape. "So we reach

out to the Sacramento resistance, gather intelligence on the hospital and Dr. Chen specifically, then formulate an extraction plan based on what we learn."

"While simultaneously preparing our assault shuttles for a potential rapid deployment," Busto added. "If things go sideways, we might need air support or a quick extraction."

"And we'll need to prepare the medical bay here for the surgery," I continued. "Kovac will know what equipment is required."

"Zeta will provide any necessary medical technology from the Collective Dominion's resources," the queen offered. "The nanoforge can fabricate advanced medical equipment that may supplement what is available here."

I looked around the table, noting the determined expressions on each face—even Zeta's capsule seemed to pulse with purpose. "Then we're agreed. Our mission is to extract Dr. Eleanor Chen from Sacramento and bring her here to perform surgery on Sofia."

"On a compressed timeline," Destiny reminded us. "Two weeks isn't much margin for error."

"Which is why we start immediately," I said firmly. "Commander Brooks, please establish contact with the Sacramento resistance network. We need eyes inside that hospital within 48 hours."

"I'll send a courier today," she confirmed.

"Lieutenant Busto, I want a security assessment of Sacramento—patrol patterns, checkpoints, response times, everything we can gather from our intelligence sources."

He nodded. "I'll coordinate with our recon teams, sir."

"Destiny, you and Nicobe work with Kovac to prepare a list of equipment and supplies needed for the surgery. If we're going to extract a surgeon, we need to make sure she has everything required once she's here."

"On it," Destiny said, while Nicobe's vessel bobbed in agreement.

"Zeta will consult her knowledge of neural medicine," the queen said. "The Collective Dominion has advanced understanding of brain traumas that may be relevant."

"Thank you, Your Majesty," I said, genuinely grateful. "I'll coordinate the overall operation and keep Sofia informed. She deserves to know what we're planning, and she may have insights that could help us."

"And one of our own," Destiny added softly.

I glanced at her, feeling a surge of gratitude for the reminder. "Yes. One of our own. Which means we do whatever it takes to save her."

The meeting broke up with a purposeful energy, each person moving off to tackle their assigned tasks. I remained at the holotable, studying the image of Dr. Eleanor Chen still rotating slowly above it. Her serious expression revealed nothing about whether she'd be an ally or an obstacle in our plan. Would she help willingly, or would we need to coerce her? The thought made me uncomfortable, but for Sofia, I realized I'd cross lines I'd previously considered inviolable.

"You're worried," Destiny said, having lingered behind as the others left.

I didn't bother denying it. "Of course I am. Sofia's dying, and our solution is to kidnap a doctor from a Kergan-controlled hospital."

"When you put it that way, it sounds insane," she agreed, coming to stand beside me. "But we've pulled off crazier stunts."

"Have we?" I asked, genuinely curious.

She pretended to consider. "Well, there was that time we stole a freighter from the Kergan Empire."

"We failed the first time. It took two attempts," I

corrected.

"And the time we bombed that airbase in Montana."

"We nearly died."

"And the time we walked away from a crash in Arizona."

"Again, nearly died. In fact, Zeta *did* die."

Destiny rolled her eyes. "Temporarily." She punched my arm lightly. "See? Compared to all that, this is just a minor illegal extraction from hostile territory. Practically a milk run."

Despite everything, I felt a smile tug at my lips. "Your definition of a 'milk run' needs serious recalibration."

"Probably," she conceded, then pointed a finger at me. "But here's the thing, Kory. I bet you'd do the same for any of us without blinking. Hell, if one of us needed that surgeon, I'd expect you to already be halfway to Sacramento—with a fake ID, a stolen uniform, and some completely unconvincing alias like 'Doctor Not Suspicious.'"

She was right, and we both knew it. This wasn't just about Sofia. My loyalty to my people was absolute. And if our positions were reversed, my people wouldn't waste time worrying about their motivations—they'd act.

"I know," I mumbled. "That's why we can't fail."

"We won't," Destiny said with a confidence I envied. She squeezed my shoulder once before heading for the door. "Go check on her. We've got this part covered."

Left alone in the command center, I took one last look at Chen's image before shutting down the holodisplay. The doctor's stern face vanished, leaving only my own reflection in the dark surface—tired eyes, worry lines I hadn't noticed before, the weight of command settling heavier than usual on my shoulders.

Two weeks to find a surgeon, extract her from enemy

territory, and save Sofia's life. All while avoiding Kergan patrols, maintaining our secrecy, and not starting an incident that could compromise Wolf Jaw Base and the fragile human resistance movement on Earth.

Just another impossible mission. But as I headed back to the infirmary to find Sofia and tell her about our plan, I realized something that almost made me smile: impossible missions were becoming something of a specialty for the crew of *Thunder*. And we had yet to fail when one of our own was on the line.

18

The antiseptic smell of the infirmary clung to my nostrils as I watched Sofia sign her release forms, her hand trembling just enough for me to notice but steady enough to maintain her dignity. A day without a seizure—a record since the injury—and the cloud of confusion that had fogged her eyes since waking from the coma had lifted like morning mist. It was almost enough to make me believe in miracles, except for Nurse Kovac's stern expression as she handed over the medication bottle.

"Three times daily, without fail," Kovac instructed, her steel-gray bob swinging as she nodded for emphasis. "One missed dose and we could be back to square one."

Sofia accepted the bottle with military precision, tucking it into the pocket of the fresh fatigues someone had scrounged up for her. "Understood."

"Commander Drake," Kovac turned to me, her eyes hardening like cooling metal. "I need you to understand something. The medication is treating symptoms, not the cause. That subdural hematoma is still there, pressing on her brain, and it's a ticking time bomb."

I nodded, the weight of responsibility settling across my shoulders like a tactical vest. "I understand."

"No strenuous activity," Kovac continued, her gaze now pinning Sofia. "Rest. Take it easy. Your brain needs time to heal, but what it really needs is surgery."

Sofia sat straighter on the edge of the examination table. "I am feeling much better, Nurse Kovac. The headaches are manageable, and my thoughts are... clearer." Her German accent curled around the words, stronger than usual when she was tired.

"That's the medication talking, Chief Kohl," Kovac replied, unmoved. "Don't mistake symptom management for recovery."

I stepped forward, eager to extract Sofia before Kovac could paint an even bleaker picture. "We'll follow your instructions to the letter. And we're working on securing that surgical support."

Kovac's expression softened fractionally. "See that you do. You're released, Chief. Don't make me see you in here again until that surgery."

Sofia slid off the table with deliberate care. I hovered nearby, resisting the urge to steady her with a hand at her elbow. She'd hate that—the implication she couldn't manage on her own. But when she swayed slightly, my hand shot out of its own accord.

"I've got you," I murmured.

Her blue eyes flashed with momentary irritation before softening. "Thank you, Kory."

We left the infirmary, emerging into the utilitarian corridor of Wolf Jaw Base. The quartz walls felt close and confining, though they were more expansive than the alien corridors of *Luminara*. Sofia walked slowly but steadily beside me, her tall frame just a few inches shorter than mine.

"Where are my quarters going to be?" she asked suddenly, breaking the comfortable silence between us.

The question caught me off guard. I'd assumed—well, I hadn't really thought it through. On *Luminara,* we'd shared quarters out of necessity and convenience. It was the first time we'd ever shared a room, and it was because we had no other choice, not because we'd intended it that way. But here...

"Uh, well," I began, eloquent as ever. "The thing is, quarters are pretty limited right now. We've got a lot of the kavreni still sleeping on *Thunder,* and..."

I trailed off, suddenly aware of how intensely she was watching me fumble through this explanation. My face felt warm.

"There aren't any private quarters available for you," I finally managed. "But if you don't mind, you could stay in mine. I can sleep on the floor, or—"

Sofia's laugh cut me off, a warm sound that made my stomach flip. "Are you always this awkward about sleeping arrangements, Commander?"

"Only with you," I admitted.

"You snore less than most of my former roommates," she said with a smirk. "And you don't steal the covers... much."

I felt my face flush deeper, suddenly aware that while we were undoubtedly in a romantic relationship—the kisses we'd shared on *Luminara* had confirmed that much—we hadn't exactly been sleeping together, despite sharing quarters. If you know what I mean. She was injured. The distinction felt important somehow, a line we'd crossed only twice on Virelia. I didn't want to just assume anything about the status of our relationship.

"Is that a yes?" I asked.

"It's not a no," she replied, her blue eyes twinkling with mischief.

We continued walking, taking it slow for Sofia's sake. The base was a maze of quartz-lined tunnels and chambers, and my assigned habitation pod was tucked away in a quieter section—a small mercy given Sofia's condition.

When we reached my quarters, I keyed the entry pad and ushered her inside. The space was spartan: a narrow bed against one wall, a small desk with a chair, a compact dresser, and a tiny attached bathroom. What it lacked in luxury, it made up for in privacy—a rare commodity in the base granted me because I was *Thunder*'s commanding officer.

"Home sweet home," I said, suddenly self-conscious about the rumpled sheets and the uniform jacket draped over the chair.

Sofia stood in the center of the room, swaying slightly. Before she could protest, I gently guided her to the bed and helped her lie down, pulling the covers up over her.

"Doctor's orders," I reminded her when she frowned. "Rest, remember?"

"I've been lying in a bed for days," she grumbled, but settled back against the pillow.

I grabbed the chair from the desk and positioned it beside the bed, sitting down and leaning forward with my elbows on my knees. Sofia studied me with a bemused expression.

"Are you really going to sleep in that chair?" she asked, eyebrow quirked.

"I want you to be comfortable," I replied, the chair already digging into my back in a way that promised a night of misery.

She patted the space beside her. "The bed is a little small, but there's room for you if you want it." Her lips curled into a smile. "Besides, if I have another seizure, you can catch me before I fall off."

The joke landed like a punch to the gut, a stark reminder of what we were facing. I tried to smile, but the expression felt brittle on my face.

"Hey," she said softly, reaching out to touch my cheek. "That was a poor joke. I'm sorry."

I caught her hand and held it, marveling at the warmth of her skin against mine. My throat felt tight, words backing up behind a sudden swell of emotion. This woman—this strong, brave, brilliant woman—had wormed her way into my heart so completely that the thought of losing her made my chest ache.

"Sofia, I—" I started, then stumbled. My tongue felt three sizes too large, clumsy and uncooperative. "I need to tell you something."

She watched me expectantly, her expression open and patient despite the shadow of pain that never quite left her eyes these days.

"I have feelings for you," I finally managed, the words tumbling out in a rush. "Strong feelings. And I know the timing is terrible, with everything that's happening, but I—I couldn't bear it if something happened and I never told you."

Sofia looked away, her cheeks flushing pink. Her hands twisted together in her lap until her knuckles turned white. For a moment, I was sure I'd made a terrible mistake, pushed too far, too fast.

Then she turned back to me, her gaze so intense it nearly pinned me to the chair. "Kory Drake," she said, her voice low and serious, "shut up."

Before I could respond, she leaned forward, grabbed the front of my uniform, and pulled me into a kiss that sent electricity coursing through my veins. Her lips were soft but insistent against mine, her hands sliding up to tangle in my hair. I found myself responding with equal fervor, my arms wrapping around her, drawing her closer.

Time suspended as we melted into each other. The feel of her body under my hands, the subtle floral scent of her hair, the little sound she made when I deepened the kiss—these details consumed me, driving all other thoughts from my mind.

When we finally pulled apart, both breathless, she kept her hands on my shoulders, her blue eyes searching mine.

"I am very fond of you, Kory," she breathed. "I trust you. You are loyal and strong, and you want to do good in this broken world." Her thumb traced my jawline. "I feel safe with you. I enjoy spending time with you."

The words were simple, straightforward—so typically Sofia—but they hit me with the force of a fusion drive igniting. I covered her hand with mine, turning to press a kiss to her palm.

"I love you," I said, the words emerging with surprising ease now that the dam had broken. "And I don't want to lose you."

The silence that followed stretched between us, taut with unspoken emotion. Sofia stared at me, her expression unreadable. Then, to my horror, tears welled in her eyes and spilled down her cheeks in glistening trails.

"Sofia, I'm sorry," I said hastily, fumbling for the tissue box on the nightstand. "I didn't mean to upset you."

She took the offered tissue and wiped at her eyes, a sound escaping her that was half-laugh, half-sob. "I'm not crying because I'm sad, you idiot."

"Oh," I said, eloquent as ever.

She looked up at me, her eyes shining. "Those are the most beautiful words anyone has ever said to me."

I blinked, surprised. "You mean nobody's ever said they love you?"

She chuckled, sniffling slightly. "Sure, other people have said it. But none of them were you." Her voice softened. "It's you saying it that makes it special."

Something inside me expanded, a balloon of warmth and light filling my chest until I thought I might float away. I reached for her hands, holding them gently in mine.

"I love you too, Kory," she said, her gaze steady on mine. "I want to be a part of your life. I hope..." Her voice caught. "I hope we won't soon be separated."

The unspoken reality of her condition hung between us —the ticking time bomb Kovac had mentioned. But in that moment, I refused to let fear rule us.

"Let's make a promise to each other," I said, squeezing her hands. "That we'll be there to love and support each other, and be faithful to one another, no matter what comes."

She nodded, a new tear tracking down her cheek.

"I promise to do these things," I continued, my voice growing stronger with each word. "To love you as my partner, and only you, if you'll have me."

"I promise the same," she whispered, and the simple words carried the weight of a formal vow.

I leaned forward to kiss her again, tenderly at first, then with growing passion as she wound her arms around my neck and drew me down onto the bed with her. I found myself lying atop her, careful to support my weight on my elbows, our bodies fitting together as if designed for this purpose.

As we lost ourselves in each other, one thought crystallized in my mind with perfect clarity: I had never loved another person this much before. The happiness that flooded through me was so intense it was almost painful—a sharp-edged joy that cut through the darkness of our uncertain future like a beacon, guiding us home.

19

I slipped out of bed as silently as possible, watching Sofia's chest rise and fall in the steady rhythm of deep sleep. The dim red night lighting of my quarters cast blood-tinged shadows across her face, softening the worry lines that had become a permanent fixture since her injury. For a few seconds, I let myself simply watch her—this miracle of a woman who had somehow decided I was worth loving—before pulling on a fresh utility uniform and heading out to face whatever fresh disasters the morning had brought.

The corridors of Wolf Jaw Base were quiet in the early hours, with only the occasional off-duty personnel nodding respectfully as I passed. I made my way to the mess hall, guided by the promising aroma of actual coffee—a luxury I hadn't expected to find. The dining facility was nearly empty, with just a handful of bleary-eyed resistance fighters nursing cups of caffeine at scattered tables.

Lynda Brooks sat alone at a corner table, her thin frame hunched over a data pad as she methodically worked through a plate of scrambled eggs. I grabbed a tray and helped myself to a surprisingly generous breakfast—real eggs, bacon that was actually from a pig, and pancakes that hadn't come from a synthesizer. Minor victories.

"Mind if I join you?" I asked, approaching Brooks' table.

She looked up, tucking a strand of graying brown hair behind her ear. "Commander. Please." She gestured to the empty chair across from her.

I sat down and dug into my breakfast with an enthusiasm that bordered on indecent. After months of Collective Dominion food—perfectly nutritious but designed for beings who considered taste an unnecessary evolutionary quirk—this was heaven.

Brooks watched me with amusement. "Enjoying the local cuisine, sir?"

"Remind me to thank whoever's running your kitchen," I said around a mouthful of pancake.

"That would be Sergeant Menendez. Former chef at some fancy restaurant in San Francisco before the invasion." Brooks sipped her coffee. "How's Chief Kohl this morning?"

I swallowed before answering. "Better. The medication seems to be helping." I didn't elaborate on the more personal developments of the previous night.

Brooks nodded, then glanced back at her data pad. "We need to talk about personnel, Commander. I've been running the numbers."

"Hit me," I said, spearing a piece of bacon.

"We're severely understaffed for an operation of this size," she said, sliding the pad toward me. "Between expanded base operations, *Thunder*'s new crew requirements, and the security contingent, we need at least another 120 trained personnel."

I studied the figures, mentally calculating the logistical challenges. "And we need them yesterday."

"Preferably." She tapped the screen. "I've started preliminary screening of the Wolf Jaw civilians and surrounding refugee communities, but training will take time we may not have."

I pushed my empty plate aside and leaned forward. "I'm putting you in charge of recruitment and training, Lynda. Full authority to establish whatever protocols you deem necessary."

She straightened, her blue eyes sharp. "Yes, sir. I'll start interviews today."

"What about the base expansion?" I asked. "Last I heard, we were still operating at about sixty percent capacity."

Brooks' expression lightened. "Your igna friends have been busy. Nicobe and Queen Zeta haven't stopped working since they arrived." She shook her head in amazement. "They excavated a new tunnel system just last night—took them hours, not days. And they're expanding the main hangar to accommodate *Thunder*'s rebuild into a Marauder-class vessel."

I whistled low. "Sometimes I forget what they're capable of."

"Wish I had half their energy," Brooks said.

I drained my coffee cup. "All of us humans wish that."

After finishing breakfast and reviewing a few more operational details with Brooks, I decided to inspect the construction progress firsthand. I made my way through the base, nodding to personnel who snapped to attention as I passed. It still felt strange, being the one in command, having people look to me for guidance. Sometimes I wondered if they could sense the impostor lurking beneath my confident exterior.

The new tunnel system branched off from the main corridor, its walls smoother than the older sections—a testament to the precision of Collective Dominion technology. The air smelled of wet earth and hot stone, with an underlying metallic tang that tickled the back of my throat. Long, slimy tendrils of nanobots streamed along the floor and walls, carrying raw materials from the base's nanoforges to where they were needed. They moved like living things, pulsing and undulating with purpose, leaving behind faint, iridescent trails that gradually faded.

I followed the main flow of nanobots toward the hangar, occasionally stepping aside as human and kavreni workers hurried past with equipment and supplies. The closer I got to the hangar, the louder the ambient noise became—the steady hum of power tools, the rhythmic clanking of mechanical systems, and the high-pitched whine of nanoforges reshaping matter.

The hangar doors were wide open, and I paused at the threshold to take in the organized chaos within. The cavernous space had nearly doubled in size since my last visit, with new support beams arching overhead and work platforms extending along the far wall. In the center of it all stood *Thunder*, my ship—our ship—her sleek ellipsoid hull bearing the scars of our recent adventures.

I walked the perimeter of the hangar, making my way toward *Thunder*. Engineers and technicians swarmed around her like bees tending to their queen, removing excess equipment and personal belongings to prepare for the ship's rebuild. I trailed my fingers along her outer hull as I circled her, feeling the scratches and dings left by micrometeorites and battle damage. Each mark told a story, a testimony to her resilience.

"We've been through a lot together, haven't we, old girl?" I murmured, patting her hull affectionately.

Thunder couldn't answer, of course, but sometimes I swore she had a personality—stubborn and loyal, like the best of her crew. Pride swelled in my chest as I considered what we'd accomplished with this remarkable vessel. She wasn't just a ship; she was home, sanctuary, and weapon all wrapped into one elegant package.

Off to the side of the hangar, partially concealed by stacks of supply crates, rested *Thunder*'s two assault shuttles. The Albatross-class vessels weren't much to look at—squat, utilitarian craft designed for function over form—but they were crucial to our operations. Each could transport a full squad of armed personnel to and from orbit, or anywhere on the planet, with enough firepower to make any Kergan patrol think twice about interference.

I made a mental note to have Phoebe run a full system check on both shuttles. If we needed to evacuate in a hurry, those birds would be our lifeline.

With a last glance at *Thunder*, I left the hangar and made my way toward the command center, snagging a fresh cup of coffee from a makeshift break station along the way. The bitter liquid scalded my tongue, but the jolt of caffeine was worth the momentary discomfort.

The command center occupied the heart of the base, its walls lined with a hodgepodge of Earth and Collective Dominion technology. Busto and Destiny stood hunched over the central holographic display, engaged in what appeared to be a heated discussion. Neither noticed my entrance until I cleared my throat.

"Well, look who finally broke free from the love nest," Destiny said, her dark eyes sparkling with mischief. "We were beginning to think you'd forgotten about us common folk."

I ignored the jab, focusing instead on the tactical display they'd been studying. "What's the situation?"

Busto straightened, his perpetual scowl deepening.

"Reconnaissance team reported in an hour ago, sir. They've identified what appears to be a Kergan listening post on a peak approximately twelve kilometers northeast of our position."

"Show me," I said, stepping closer to the display.

Busto tapped a series of commands, and the hologram zoomed in on a topographical rendering of the surrounding mountains. A red marker pulsed on one of the higher peaks.

"The post is perfectly positioned to observe operations around Wolf Jaw," Busto continued, his voice clipped and professional. "They've got line of sight to our main access points and enough signal-processing equipment to potentially detect and intercept our wireless communications in the area."

I studied the display, mentally calculating firing solutions. "Why don't we just eliminate it? One missile strike and problem solved."

"That's what I said," Busto muttered.

Destiny shook her head, her curly black hair bouncing with the movement. "Bad idea. All that would do is confirm to the Kergans that there's something worth investigating in this area. They'd send in a full battalion to secure the region and sweep every cave and crevice until they found us."

"Has this been an issue before?" I asked, glancing between them.

"Increasingly," Busto replied grimly. "The Kergans have been expanding their surveillance network across North America for months. The listening posts start, then come the drones, then the patrols."

Destiny crossed her arms. "I think it's time we seriously consider moving our operations off-planet, Kory. The insurgency lost two entire bases to Kergan anti-insurgency operations last month alone." She gestured to the display. "It's only a matter of time before they find us again, and I don't fancy another last-minute evacuation with Kergans breathing down our necks."

I sipped my coffee, considering our options. An off-world base had its advantages—harder for the Kergans to locate, easier to defend with our space-based assets. But it also meant abandoning Earth, at least partially, and that didn't sit right with me.

"Maybe an asteroid would work," I mused aloud. "Plenty of raw materials, natural radiation shielding..."

"Like the Belters," Destiny said, grinning. "You know, from The Expanse?"

Busto stared at her blankly.

"The TV show?" Destiny prompted. When Busto's expression remained unchanged, she groaned. "Lordy, you are so out of touch with reality."

I couldn't help but laugh at Busto's bewildered expression. "I wouldn't mind being a Belter if that's what it takes to secure our position and give the Kergans hell," I said. "But right now, our priority is rescuing that neurosurgeon and getting them back to base."

Destiny's expression softened. "How is Sofia this morning?"

"Stable," I replied, grateful for her concern. "The medication is helping, but she still needs that surgery."

Busto nodded. "We'll have the extraction team prepped and ready as soon as possible. Weather forecast for the target area is favorable for the near future, and our intelligence suggests minimal Kergan presence at the hospital complex. It's controlled by the HCD."

"HCD?" I asked.

"Oh, that's right," Busto said. "You weren't here when

that all happened. HCD. Human Compliance Directorate. The HCD are the Kergans' secret police. It's staffed with human collaborators tasked with internal security of the Kergan Military Authority here on Earth. The Kergans have suddenly taken a more hands-off approach to dealing with human affairs and turned that job over to the HCD."

"They sound friendly."

Destiny huffed. "If you think the Gestapo were friendly, then you're not too far off the mark."

"Okay," I said. "No Kergans to worry about, but we have HCD forces in the area. Keep me updated on any changes to the plan. And maintain surveillance on that listening post—I want to know the second their activity patterns change."

They acknowledged their orders, and I left them to work out the operational details. As I headed back toward my quarters to check on Sofia, I couldn't help reflecting on my priorities. I should probably feel guilty about devoting so many resources to helping my partner—my partner. I still couldn't believe I had one—but that's just the way things were going to be.

It was my fault for falling in love with that woman, but I didn't regret it for one second. We all needed something worth fighting for. I hadn't felt this happy, this purposeful, since before I lost the memories of my parents.

The war against the Kergans would continue. The resistance would fight on. But for now, Sofia was my mission, and I would move heaven and earth—or even relocate to an asteroid belt—to save her.

20

I drummed my fingers on the edge of the console, watching the screens flicker with incoming data like digital confetti at the world's most depressing party. The command center of Wolf Jaw Base hummed with the quiet intensity of people trying not to look nervous, but I could feel the tension crackling between us like static electricity. This intel drop wasn't just another mission parameter—it was our first solid lead on Dr. Eleanor Chen, the neurosurgeon whose skills might be the only thing that could save Sofia's life. And mine, by extension, because a world without Sofia wasn't one I was prepared to navigate.

"Sir, transmission coming through now," announced a technician, her face bathed in the blue glow of her monitor. "Decryption protocols engaged."

"About damn time," I muttered, straightening up. My back cracked in three places, a reminder that I'd been hunched over these displays for the better part of six hours.

Destiny appeared at my elbow, a cup of something that pretended to be coffee in her hand. "You look like hell warmed over, Kory."

"Thanks. I was going for 'hell frozen over,' but I'll take what I can get." I accepted the cup and took a swig, immediately regretting it. "Blazes, Des, did you make this or did you wring it out of an old boot?"

Her lips quirked up at one corner. "Military-grade caffeine. It's not supposed to taste good; it's supposed to keep you vertical."

"Mission accomplished," I replied, taking another sip despite my better judgment.

Around us, the intelligence team leaned forward in their chairs, eyes fixed on their screens as the encrypted transmission continued to filter through our systems. The Sacramento recon team had been silent for three days—a necessary precaution while they established surveillance on the VA Medical Center. Now, finally, they were sending what they'd found.

The air in the room felt charged as the first images began populating the main display—high-resolution scans of the medical center, personnel schedules, security rotations. The data scrolled past faster than I could process, but our analysts were already on it, fingers flying over keyboards, cross-referencing and compiling.

"Got her," announced a young woman with hair pinned up in a severe bun. She tapped her screen, and the main display shifted to show a grainy image. "Facial recognition confirms 94% match to Dr. Eleanor Chen. Image captured yesterday at 1547 hours."

I stepped closer, squinting at the image. It showed a middle-aged Asian woman in a white lab coat, escorted by two guards in the distinctive gray and blue uniforms of the Human Compliance Directorate. Her face was composed, professional, but there was something in her eyes—a hardness, a calculation—that told me Dr. Chen wasn't a willing participant in whatever the HCD had her doing.

"Location?" I asked, my voice sharper than I intended.

"Sacramento VA Medical Center, third floor, east wing," replied the analyst. "According to our source, that entire section has been converted into a research facility."

Busto, who'd been leaning against the wall with his arms crossed, pushed off and approached the display. "What's security look like?"

Another analyst, a former NSA employee we'd rescued from a labor camp outside Fresno, pulled up a schematic. "Two checkpoints to reach the third floor. Key card access, retinal scanners at research wing entrance. HCD personnel stationed at all access points, with roving patrols on a fifteen-minute rotation."

"Tight, but not impenetrable," Busto commented, his expression giving away nothing.

I stared at the image of Dr. Chen, trying to reconcile this composed professional with the near-mythical figure Nurse Kovac had described—the neurosurgeon whose pioneering work on neural interfaces had made her a prime target when the Kergans invaded.

"So the HCD's star brain tinkerer is being kept in a VA hospital," I said, unable to keep the edge of bitterness from my voice. "There's a special kind of irony in using a veterans' hospital for alien tech research."

"They're not just holding her there," said another analyst, pulling up a new file. "She's working for them. Our source says she's heading up a research project on neural implant technology."

The room went quiet. We all knew what that meant. The Kergans' mindjacking technology—the implants that turned humans into remote-controlled puppets—was devastating but still limited in scope and reliability. If they had someone of Chen's caliber working to refine it...

"Is she a collaborator?" Destiny asked the question no one wanted to voice.

The analyst shook his head. "According to our source, they're holding her family as leverage. Husband and two teenage children, kept in a separate facility. She cooperates, they live."

My hands clenched at my sides.

"Classic HCD playbook," Destiny said. "Find the pressure point and push until it breaks. We've seen it too many times. Do we know where her family is being kept?"

"No, ma'am," the analyst replied.

"Then find out," I said. "The only way to ensure Chen's cooperation is if she knows her family is safe from HCD retaliation."

"Yes, sir. Uh... one more thing: The source believes Dr. Chen is subtly sabotaging her own research," the analyst continued. "Progress reports show delays, equipment failures, unexpected complications in test subjects. Nothing obvious enough to trigger suspicion, but enough to slow things down."

"Smart woman," Busto muttered.

A tall, rangy technician raised his hand. "Sir, I've got the full hospital layout now. Transferring to the main display."

The screen shifted to show a detailed 3D rendering of the medical center, with highlighted areas indicating security checkpoints, patrol routes, and—most importantly—Dr. Chen's lab and living quarters.

"Our source says she's never allowed to leave the facility," the technician explained. "She works sixteen-hour days and sleeps in a converted patient room adjacent to the lab."

"Keeping their prize researcher on a short leash," I said, unable to suppress a grimace. "Any chance we can get to her there?"

"Negative," Busto replied immediately. "Too well guarded, too many variables."

The official announcement came from the head analyst, a former FBI data specialist with prematurely gray hair: "Dr. Eleanor Chen confirmed at Sacramento VA Medical Center, third floor research wing, under HCD supervision."

A murmur ran through the room—a mixture of relief at finally locating our target and apprehension about what came next.

Destiny stepped forward, pulling up a new file on the display. "Our hospital source has provided an infiltration option," she said, her voice taking on the crisp efficiency she used when presenting mission parameters. "They're suggesting we use ambulances—specifically, three ambulances with patients requiring emergency care."

"We're going to fake emergencies?" I asked, raising an eyebrow.

"Yes, fake," Destiny replied, her expression light. "Get your makeup ready. The ER staff includes several resistance sympathizers who've agreed to help us get inside. They'll recognize specific trauma profiles and direct those patients to appropriate areas, creating distraction and cover."

Busto nodded slowly. "EMTs coming and going wouldn't draw attention. It's a hospital, after all."

"Exactly," Destiny said. "Our hospital source has secured access to three ambulances. Once we're in, the ER team will help guide us through the service corridors to the third floor."

"What about getting Chen out?" I asked.

"Same way we came in," Destiny replied. "Our source

says there's a service elevator that leads directly from the third floor to the ambulance bay. Not commonly used, minimal security coverage."

I studied the schematic, tracing the proposed route with my eyes. It could work, but there were a lot of moving parts, a lot of places where things could go sideways.

"How reliable is this source?" I demanded. "If they're feeding us bad intel—"

"They've been vetted," Destiny cut in. "Their information has been solid for months. They've helped move half a dozen high-value targets through Sacramento without incident."

"But never from inside an HCD-controlled facility," Busto pointed out.

Destiny conceded the point with a slight nod. "True, but they've provided accurate details on security protocols, patrol patterns, everything we've been able to verify."

I paced a tight circle, my mind working through scenarios. We needed Chen—not just for Sofia, but also for the intelligence she could provide on Kergan neural tech. My partner's condition was deteriorating, and Chen was possibly the only neurosurgeon left in the area with the skills needed to help her.

But rushing in half-cocked was how people got killed. How missions failed.

"When can we move?" I asked.

Busto cleared his throat. "With respect, sir, I'd like at least six days for additional recon. We need to verify patrol patterns, identify potential alternate routes, establish communication protocols with the hospital source."

Six days. That would put us close to the two-week window Kovac had given us. I didn't like pushing the schedule so far out. Kovac had said her estimate was probably optimistic and that Sofia could take a turn for the worse at any moment. The knot in my stomach tightened.

"Six days is pushing it, Busto," I said, not bothering to hide my concern. "Sofia's condition—"

"I understand, sir," he interrupted, his normally stern face softening just a fraction. "But a rushed extraction could leave us with nothing. If we get caught, if Dr. Chen is killed or moved to another facility..."

He didn't need to finish the thought. We'd have lost our only chance to help Sofia, and potentially handed the HCD a major intelligence coup about our operations.

The weight of command settled heavy on my shoulders. This was the part nobody tells you about being in charge—sometimes there are no good choices, just a selection of bad ones with varying degrees of terrible consequences.

"One more thing," Busto said.

"Go ahead," I replied.

"We need to recover Dr. Chen's family before we go in there for her, but not so soon that it tips the HCD off and they increase security around Chen. We're talking about two extraction operations now, sir, that must happen nearly simultaneously. That's why I need those six days."

I looked around the room at the grim faces of my team. They were all thinking the same thing: this was a high-risk operation, and it was all being done for one person, Sofia. If things went bad and my people got killed, their blood would be on my hands.

My hands were cold, but there was a heat in my chest—a burning sensation that felt uncomfortably like guilt tangled with fear. I knew what Sofia would say if she were here. She'd tell me to do it right, to protect the mission and the team first. To be the commander, not the desperate partner.

"Six days," I agreed finally, forcing a tight smile that felt like it might crack my face. "But not a minute more. We move next Tuesday in the morning."

Busto nodded, satisfaction and relief briefly flashing across his features before his professional mask slipped back into place. "Yes, sir. My teams will be ready."

As the command center erupted into activity—analysts pulling data, tactical teams beginning their planning—I stepped back, suddenly needing space. The coffee in my cup had gone cold, much like the feeling spreading through my chest.

Six days was simultaneously too long and not nearly enough time. For Sofia's sake, I hoped we weren't making a mistake. For all our sakes, I hoped Dr. Chen was worth the risk.

21

The infirmary lights were too bright—the kind of sterile fluorescence that made everyone look halfway to the grave. Sofia squinted against them as I helped her sit up on the exam table, her honey-blonde hair falling across her face. It might've been endearing in any other context, but here, with the shadows under her eyes and the faint tremor in her hands, it just made my stomach twist.

She'd claimed to feel better that morning—a lie I pretended to believe. Arguing with Sofia was like trying to persuade a mountain to scoot a few feet to the left: technically possible with enough explosives, but rarely worth the fallout. Still, I'd managed to nudge her into seeing Nurse Kovac after it became clear the meds weren't cutting it. No new seizures, thankfully, but the other symptoms were stacking up: irritability, dizziness, slurred speech, memory lapses. None of it good.

"The doctor will be here in a minute," I said, trying to keep my voice light. "You know how it is—always running late. Probably dealing with someone who thinks a paper cut requires emergency surgery."

Sofia didn't laugh. She just nodded, wincing slightly as the movement sent a wave of pain through her head. I could see it in the tightening around her eyes, the subtle clench of her jaw. The subdural hematoma was getting worse, not better, despite what the med staff kept telling me about "plateauing symptoms" and "expected fluctuations."

"We found Dr. Chen," I said, partly to distract her, partly because I needed her to know we were making progress. "She's in Sacramento. We're planning the extraction now."

Sofia's eyes brightened momentarily. "That's good," she said, her German accent more pronounced than usual—a telltale sign of her fatigue. "When will you—"

She stopped mid-sentence, her body suddenly going rigid. Her eyes widened, vacant and unseeing, and then rolled back in her head.

"Sofia?" My voice sounded strange in my ears, distant.

The seizure hit her like a lightning strike. One moment she was sitting there, the next her body was convulsing violently, limbs rigid and jerking with a strength that seemed impossible from her slender frame. She pitched sideways off the examination table before I could catch her, her skull making a sickening crack against the metal cart beside the bed.

Blood—bright arterial red—immediately began pooling beneath her head.

"I need help in here!" I shouted, dropping to my knees beside her. "Medical emergency!"

The infirmary erupted into motion. Two nurses and a medic burst through the door, pushing me aside with practiced efficiency. I stumbled back, watching in horror as Sofia's body continued to convulse, her limbs beating a terrible rhythm against the linoleum floor. Blood and sweat mingled beneath her, creating pink-tinged smears as the medical team tried to stabilize her.

"Grand mal seizure," snapped one of the nurses, a stocky woman with forearms like a weightlifter. "Get me five milligrams of lorazepam, now!"

"She's got a laceration on the temporal region," reported the medic, his hands already pressing gauze against the side of Sofia's head. "Bleeding heavily."

I stood frozen, useless, as the medical team worked. They rolled Sofia onto her side, injected medication, called out vital signs in a clinical shorthand that my brain couldn't process. All I could see was Sofia's face—contorted, unrecognizable, a grotesque mask that bore no resemblance to the woman I loved.

The seizure seemed to last forever, though the rational part of my brain knew it was probably less than two minutes. When it finally subsided, Sofia went limp, unconscious, but still breathing in shallow, irregular gasps.

"Let's get her on the table," ordered the stocky nurse. "Careful with her head."

They lifted Sofia's limp form back onto the examination table, now reclined flat. Blood had soaked through the gauze pressed to her temple, and more streaked her face like war paint. The front of her coveralls was damp with sweat, and something else—I realized with a sick jolt that she'd lost control of her bladder during the seizure.

"What happened?" I managed, my voice a rasp.

The medic glanced up at me, his face professionally blank. "Seizure. Worse than her previous ones."

"I can see that," I snapped, immediately regretting it. "Sorry. I mean, what caused it? Is she going to be okay?"

Nurse Kovac rushed in. Her face was grim as she checked Sofia's pupils, pulse, and the wound on her head.

"The increased intracranial pressure from the hematoma likely triggered the seizure," she explained, not looking up from her examination. "The impact with the cart caused a scalp laceration, but I'm more concerned about potential additional trauma to the brain."

She straightened up and issued rapid-fire orders for an immediate CT scan, additional medication, and continuous monitoring. Then, finally, she looked at me.

"Commander Drake, I need to be direct with you," she said, her voice quieter now. "Chief Kohl's condition is deteriorating more rapidly than we anticipated. This seizure was significantly more severe than her previous episodes."

My throat felt like I'd swallowed glass. "What are you saying?"

"I'm saying that we need to put her in a medically induced coma again to reduce brain activity and hopefully slow the progression of her symptoms," she replied. "And I'm saying that without proper neurosurgical intervention soon, the prognosis is not good."

I nodded mechanically, feeling like I was suddenly operating my body from a great distance. "Do what you need to do."

Nurse Kovac's expression softened slightly. "We'll take good care of her, Commander. But I want to be clear—she needs more than we can provide here. She needs a specialist."

"I know," I said. "We're working on it."

She nodded and turned back to her patient, issuing more orders as nurses prepared medication and monitoring equipment. I was ushered out of the room, left standing in the hallway like a piece of obsolete machinery—present but without purpose.

I don't remember walking to my quarters or staring at the wall for what must have been an hour. The next clear memory I have is of returning to the infirmary, where Sofia lay unnaturally still under a web of monitoring wires and IV lines. They'd shaved a small patch of her head to stitch the laceration, the stark white of the bandage contrasting sharply with her honey-blonde hair. Her face was slack, peaceful in a way that wasn't reassuring at all.

I sat beside her bed, taking her hand in mine. It was warm but unresponsive—the strong, capable hands that had killed and healed with equal precision now limp in my grasp.

"I'm going to fix this," I told her, knowing she couldn't hear me but needing to say it anyway. "I'm going to get Dr. Chen and bring her back here, and she's going to fix whatever's broken inside your head."

My voice cracked on the last word. The truth was, I'd never felt more helpless in my life—not during the Kergan invasion, not while captaining *Thunder* through impossible battles, not when facing down Ban'ach in the Syderealium, and not even when I was stuck in the Dominion legal system as a charged criminal. Those were situations I could fight my way through. This was something else entirely—an enemy I couldn't see or touch or outsmart.

I pressed Sofia's hand to my forehead, closing my eyes. "Don't you dare leave me," I whispered. "That's an order, Chief."

The monitors beeped steadily in response, the rhythm of machines keeping her stable while her brain rested. Nurse Kovac had explained that the induced coma would prevent further seizures and reduce the metabolic demands on her brain, potentially buying us time. But how much time, she couldn't say.

The helplessness curdled inside me, transforming into

something harder, more focused. Anger. Determination. Purpose.

I gently placed Sofia's hand back on the bed and stood up. "I'll be back soon," I promised, then turned and walked out of the infirmary with a clear destination in mind.

"I need the command staff in the conference room immediately," I told the first officer I encountered in the hallway.

Twenty minutes later, I stood at the head of our small conference table, looking at the grim faces of my senior staff. Destiny sat to my right, her usual sarcastic demeanor subdued. Busto was to my left, his expression professionally neutral, but his eyes watchful. The rest of the chairs were filled with others.

"Sofia's condition has deteriorated," I said, skipping any warm-up. "Nurse Kovac's put her in a medically induced coma to stop the brain damage from getting worse. But it's just buying us time—nothing more."

I paused, letting the weight of it settle over the room. I knew I was asking more than was fair. Most of them barely knew Sofia—she'd barely stepped off the ship before being confined to bed. No shared stories, no camaraderie, just a name and a medical chart. Any willingness to help now wasn't about her. It was about me.

And that gnawed at me.

Because the deeper fear, the one I hadn't said out loud, was that this whole mission to save Dr. Chen wasn't just about Sofia. It was about me needing to do something, needing to feel like I hadn't already failed. And maybe, just maybe, I was dragging everyone along on a rescue built more on guilt than hope.

"We've located Dr. Eleanor Chen at the Sacramento VA Medical Center," I continued. "She's the neurosurgeon we need—not just for Sofia, but for our understanding of the Kergan neural implant technology. As of now, I'm accelerating our timeline. We're launching the extraction mission immediately."

The declaration hung in the air like a grenade with the pin pulled. No one spoke for a long moment, the only sound the rattle of a loose air vent somewhere above us.

Busto cleared his throat. "With respect, sir, immediate deployment would be a mistake."

I turned to him, my jaw tight. "Explain."

"Look, I asked for six days. I know things happen, and sometimes timelines have to be sped up, but my recon team needs at least another 48 hours to confirm the intel we've received," he said, his voice firm but not confrontational. "We need to verify patrol patterns, establish secure communication with our source inside the hospital, run a thorough background check on the ER staff who supposedly will help us, and most important of all, allow time for our assets to get in place. Remember, we've got two parallel rescue ops planned for: One to rescue Dr. Chen, and the other to rescue her family."

"We don't have 48 hours," I countered, pacing away from the table and then back again, unable to keep still. "Every hour we delay puts Sofia at greater risk."

"And rushing in blindly puts the entire mission at risk," Busto replied. "If we fail, if we lose Dr. Chen, if we expose our hospital source—"

"I know the risks," I snapped, more harshly than I intended.

Destiny leaned forward. "Kory, we all understand what's at stake here. But Busto's right. The HCD isn't something we can just bulldoze through. They're methodical, paranoid, and they've got Kergan tech backing them up."

The rational part of my brain knew they were right. The part of me that had just watched Sofia convulse on the infirmary floor wanted to grab a rifle and head to Sacramento right now.

"Two days won't significantly change Sofia's prognosis," added Nurse Kovac, who had just joined us for the meeting. "The coma is keeping her stable. What will change her prognosis is a failed rescue attempt that leaves us with no neurosurgeon at all."

I paced the length of the conference room, my imagination running wild with images of Sofia's condition worsening beyond repair while we sat here debating logistics. Every fiber of my being screamed for immediate action, but the commander in me—the part that had gotten us through impossible situations before—knew better.

"Forty-eight hours," I finally said, the words feeling like rocks in my mouth. "Not a minute more. I want round-the-clock surveillance, multiple ingress and egress plans, and full profiles on every HCD officer in that facility."

Busto nodded, relief briefly showing on his normally impassive face. "Yes, sir. We'll be ready."

"Destiny, coordinate with the medical team on patient transportation requirements," I continued. "I want every detail of this operation locked down by this time tomorrow."

"On it," she replied.

I looked around the table, making eye contact with each of my officers. "Make no mistake—this mission is not optional, and failure is not acceptable. In 48 hours, we're getting Dr. Chen out of that hospital, no matter what stands in our way."

The meeting broke up, my staff filing out with

determined expressions. I remained at the head of the table, staring at the map of Sacramento that had been projected on the wall throughout our discussion.

Destiny lingered behind, approaching me once the others had gone. "You made the right call," she said quietly. "I know it doesn't feel like it, but you did."

I managed a tight, grim smile that felt more like a grimace. "Let's hope so. Because if we're wrong, and Sofia—" I couldn't finish the sentence.

Destiny squeezed my shoulder. "Sofia looks like a tough person. She'll hold on."

I nodded, not trusting myself to speak. The prospect of 48 more hours of waiting felt simultaneously necessary and unbearable. But I'd made my decision as a commander, setting aside my personal feelings for the good of the mission. It was what Sofia would have expected of me.

But after that, nothing in this world or any other would stop me from bringing Dr. Chen back to save Sofia—even if I had to tear the entire Human Compliance Directorate apart with my bare hands to do it.

22

I watched the nanobots work, thick ropes of them slithering across the cave floor like mechanical pythons with a serious work ethic. Each one was wider than my thigh and made a soft, rhythmic, chugging sound as they transported materials to the expanding walls of our makeshift hangar. The air reeked of wet earth and hot stone, like some primordial soup getting ready to birth a military base. Queen Zeta floated nearby in her octahedral capsule, a living star contained in geometric precision, directing the expansion with the casual ease of someone who could have been building secret bases for centuries.

The nanobots deposited excess material on the surface, gradually coating the new walls with a crystalline layer of quartz that caught what little light we had and amplified it. It was beautiful, in a military-industrial-meets-alien-technology kind of way. The reflected light cast rippling patterns across Zeta's containment vessel, making her plasma form shimmer even more brilliantly than usual.

I approached her, careful to step over a particularly

enthusiastic strand of nanobots that seemed determined to trip me. "Zeta, the work is coming along impressively fast."

"Good day to you, Kory," Zeta replied, her plasma form pulsing with what I recognized as pleasure. "Zeta is taking a moment to recalibrate the construction parameters. The nanobots require occasional supervision to prevent architectural... enthusiasms."

I chuckled, watching as one nanobot tendril appeared to be attempting to create something that looked suspiciously like a decorative arch. "I see what you mean. Destiny has an aunt who can't help adding doilies to everything. Looks like your nanobots have similar design aspirations."

"Indeed. Zeta finds that all creations eventually develop personalities of their own." Zeta's capsule rotated slightly, adjusting her view of the construction. "How fares Sofia Kohl this day?"

My smile faltered. "The same. The doctors have her in an induced coma. The hematoma is getting worse. She's..." I searched for the right words.

"The queen understands the burden of watching those we care for suffer." Zeta's plasma form darkened momentarily, a gesture I associated with sympathy or sadness. "Whatever happens, time will heal your own pains."

I nodded, grateful for her understanding but eager to change the subject. "Speaking of time, I've been meaning to ask—what's next for you, Zeta? Once we're more established here, I mean."

The plasma within Zeta's containment field swirled more intensely, like a star going through a minor eruption. "The queen has duties that extend beyond Earth's boundaries. As queen-in-exile of the Collective Dominion, Zeta must unite her people against the usurper Arctis and restore the legitimate government to power."

Her voice remained formal, but I detected an undercurrent of raw emotion—something rare for Zeta.

"The murder of the queen's mother at Arctis's command must be answered. Justice must be served not only upon Arctis himself but upon all who collaborate with his illegitimate regime." The plasma in her container glowed white-hot for a moment before settling back to its usual golden hue. "This is the burden of the crown, even a crown in exile."

I nodded, trying to imagine the weight of an entire interstellar civilization on my shoulders. My problems with *Thunder* seemed trivial by comparison. "I understand. Is there anything I can do to help? Anything we can do?"

"You and your people have your own sacred duties," Zeta said, her voice softening. "To Earth and its inhabitants. Zeta would not presume to divert resources from humanity's fight for liberation."

She paused, and her containment vessel drifted slightly closer to me.

"However, the queen would make a request of Kory Drake. Zeta must return to Dominion space to gather her allies and rally the royalist faction. For this, the queen requires *Luminara*."

"Your yacht?" I asked, remembering the elegant vessel that had saved Sofia and me after the destruction of *Inferis*.

"Indeed. The queen wishes to recover *Luminara*, complete necessary repairs, and depart for Dominion space." Her plasma form pulsated in what I recognized as hesitation. "The queen seeks your blessing for this endeavor."

I blinked in surprise. "Zeta, you're a queen. You don't need my permission to take your own ship and go where you need to go."

"This is true," Zeta acknowledged, a ripple of amusement passing through her plasma form. "The queen requires no permission. And yet, Zeta would value your blessing, nonetheless. Our paths have become intertwined by fate and shared purpose. Zeta would not sever this connection lightly."

I felt a strange warmth in my chest—not guilt this time, but something like pride mixed with humility. Here was a being who could live for centuries, who governed worlds, and she was asking for my blessing as though my opinion mattered.

"You have my blessing, Your Majesty," I said, meeting the bright center of her plasma form where I imagined her eyes would be if she had them. "But if you could wait until *Thunder*'s rebuild is complete and when we're sure Sofia is safe, I'd be grateful. We need your expertise, and frankly, your presence is a morale booster for the crew."

"Of course," Zeta's plasma form brightened. "The queen would not abandon allies in their time of need. Zeta will remain until *Thunder* flies again and Sofia Kohl's recovery is assured."

I nodded, surprised at the relief I felt. "Thank you. I wish we could go with you when the time comes. Help you fight Arctis and put you back on your throne."

"In time, this may come to pass," Zeta said, her voice taking on a prophetic quality. "The stars have brought our peoples together for a purpose. The queen believes this purpose extends beyond Earth's liberation."

Before I could respond, the base's PA system crackled to life with a sound like someone dragging sandpaper across a microphone.

"Commander Drake to the base command center. Commander Drake to command, priority one."

I winced at the volume. "Duty calls, Your Majesty. We'll talk more later."

"The queen will continue her work here," Zeta replied, already turning her attention back to the nanobots, which had started to form what looked suspiciously like a decorative cornice along one wall.

I made my way through the expanding hangar, dodging work crews and equipment being shuttled from one end to the other. Our base was growing by the hour, transforming from an insurgent outpost into something resembling an actual military installation. The smell of wet earth gave way to the antiseptic tang of filtered air as I entered the more established sections.

I picked up my pace to a fast walk, not quite running, but making it clear I wasn't taking the scenic route. Officers and enlisted personnel alike flattened themselves against the walls as I passed. Whether out of respect or self-preservation, I couldn't tell. When you're six-four and built like someone who takes anger management advice from brick walls, people tend to give you space.

The command center was a hive of activity when I arrived. Destiny stood at the central table, her curly black hair pulled back into a tight bun that meant serious business. Lieutenant Busto was beside her, his perpetual scowl etched a little deeper than usual. Around them clustered a group of intelligence specialists, all hunched over datapads and holographic displays like fortune tellers trying to divine the winning lottery numbers.

"What's the situation?" I asked, sliding into place beside Destiny.

She looked up, her dark eyes sharp with concentration. "We just received an intelligence update from our people in Sacramento. Doctor Chen is scheduled to be moved tomorrow to an unknown location in Maryland."

"You're sure?" I asked.

"Yes," Destiny confirmed. "Our people inside the Sacramento VA Medical Center say they're prepping for transfer. They're keeping it pretty quiet, but it's definitely happening tomorrow."

"Do we know when, exactly?" I asked, scanning the intelligence reports scrolling across the nearest display.

Destiny shook her head, frustration evident in the tight set of her jaw. "That's the problem. We don't have a specific time, just 'sometime tomorrow.' Could be dawn, could be midnight."

I ran a hand through my hair, weighing our options. It felt like there weren't any.

"We need to move now," I decided. "I'm sorry for the rush, but we can't risk losing her. The rescue operation launches immediately."

Busto let out a groan that sounded like it had started somewhere around his boots. "Commander, with respect, we need at least three hours to get everything in position. We still have to position the ambulances we're using and coordinate with the hospital staff who are helping us. And the team extracting Chen's family needs time to get to the house where they're being held."

I looked at him, taking in the lines of exhaustion around his eyes. Busto had been working non-stop, planning this operation down to the smallest detail. The man was thorough to a fault.

"You've got three hours," I conceded. "Get your tactical team together. I'm coming with you."

Busto's eyebrows shot up. "Sir, is that wise? With all due respect—"

"It wasn't a suggestion, Lieutenant," I cut him off. "We'll travel by Albatross shuttle to the outskirts of Sacramento, just south of the airfield near the Medical Center. From there, we'll rendezvous with the ambulances."

I turned to Phoebe Brooks. "I want both Albatross shuttles prepped and ready. They'll stand by to provide emergency air cover and extraction if needed."

Phoebe nodded, already tapping commands into her tablet.

"That's the rough plan," I said, looking each person in the eye. "Any questions?"

Destiny raised an eyebrow. "Just one. Does Sofia know you're going?"

I felt my expression freeze. "Of course not. She's in a coma."

She muttered something I couldn't hear.

I ignored her and addressed the room. "We're on the clock, people. Execute the plan. Busto, I want your team and equipment ready in three hours. Destiny, you're with me for the final briefing in two. Let's move."

The command center erupted into controlled chaos as everyone moved to their assigned tasks. I caught Busto muttering something that sounded suspiciously like a prayer in Spanish as he hurried out.

Destiny lingered by my side as the room cleared. "You sure about this, Kory? You're not exactly inconspicuous. The HCD probably has your face plastered on every wall from here to the East Coast."

I gave her a lopsided grin. "That's why I'll be wearing a helmet. Besides, someone needs to make sure you all don't have too much fun without me."

She rolled her eyes but couldn't quite suppress a smile. "Right. Because breaking into an HCD-controlled medical facility is my definition of a good time."

"Three hours," I reminded her, already turning toward

the door. "And Destiny? Make sure the medical bay is prepped for Dr. Chen. No telling what condition she'll be in when we get her out."

"Already on it," she assured me, and I knew she was. Destiny was always three steps ahead, which was why she made a great XO.

As I headed out to prepare for the mission, I tried not to think about the risks we were incurring by moving the clock up so drastically. But we didn't have a choice. Dr. Chen was running out of time, and so was Sofia. We might not get another chance. Sometimes being in command meant making the hard calls and living with the consequences.

And I'd gotten pretty good at living with consequences.

23

My palms weren't sweating. At least, that's what I kept telling myself as we closed in on the Sacramento VA Medical Center—three ambulances in formation, lights off, gliding through the dark like sharks on silent approach. The insertion had gone smoothly so far. Our contacts in the local resistance had the ambulances ready, right place, right time. It should've been reassuring.

It wasn't.

I knew how ops like this went. When everything started off too clean, it just meant the chaos was waiting for a better entrance.

The weight of the protomatter armor pressed against my chest beneath the baggy orderly uniform—a constant, quiet reminder of what this really was. Not a rescue. Not exactly. It was a heist, and the prize was a person.

Dr. Eleanor Chen: gifted neurosurgeon, reluctant HCD collaborator, and possibly the only one who could save Sofia's life.

"Two minutes to checkpoint," the driver of our

ambulance muttered, his eyes fixed on the road ahead.

I nodded, checking the safety on my concealed laser pistol one last time before tucking it back under the uniform. Busto sat across from me, his face a mask of professional indifference. Only the tight set of his jaw betrayed any tension.

"Remember," I said, keeping my voice low, "we're transferring critical patients from County General. Emergency neurological cases. We have all the paperwork."

"Copy that, Commander," Busto replied, not looking up as he adjusted his orderly's cap. "My boys are ready."

My boys. Eight Marines and myself split between three ambulances, all of them wearing protomatter combat armor beneath hospital scrubs or orderly uniforms. The armor could stop most conventional weapons and even some energy weapons, but it wouldn't do us any good if we got caught at the gate.

Busto tapped the side of his helmet as the radio crackled in our ears. He turned slightly away from us, one hand cupping the receiver.

“Whiskey Team, this is Zulu Team, in position,” came the hushed voice. “Initiating extraction on target’s family now.”

“Copy that,” Busto replied. “Keep it quiet. We need a final confirmation once you’ve got them.”

The channel went silent.

He turned back to us with a curt nod. “They’re moving.”

A tight breath escaped my chest before I even realized I’d been holding it. “Good,” I said. “At least something’s going according to plan.” We needed Chen’s family safe and under our control to ensure Chen’s cooperation.

The ambulance slowed as we approached the outer perimeter checkpoint. Through the windshield, I could make out the illuminated gatehouse, two guards visible inside, their HCD armbands glowing faintly blue in the darkness.

"Game faces, everyone," I murmured.

The driver rolled down his window as a guard approached, flashlight in hand. My heart rate kicked up a notch, but I forced my breathing to remain steady. The guard's face appeared in the window, bored and tired. Good.

"Patient transfer from County General," our driver said, handing over a clipboard with the forged paperwork. "Three critical cases for Dr. Chen's team."

The guard scanned the paperwork, flipping through pages with practiced indifference. The seconds stretched like hours.

"Neurological cases, huh?" he said, shining his light briefly into the back of the ambulance where I sat beside what appeared to be a patient on a gurney—actually a Marine named Rodriguez wrapped in blankets with an IV drip of saline for show.

"Yes, sir," I said, adopting the deferential tone of a medical technician. "Implant rejections. Dr. Chen requested immediate transfer."

The guard nodded, seemingly satisfied. "The other two ambulances with you?"

"Yes, sir. Same situation. We've got six total transfers tonight."

He handed back the clipboard and waved us through. "Building C, emergency entrance. They're probably expecting you."

My shoulders relaxed slightly as the gate lifted and we pulled through. The other two ambulances followed close behind. Phase one complete. Now came the tricky part.

"That was almost too easy," Busto muttered as we

circled toward Building C.

"Don't jinx it," I replied, checking my watch. "Our contact should be waiting at the side entrance. Two minutes, tops."

The ambulances pulled up to the designated entrance, a nondescript door marked "Emergency Staff Only." I counted to thirty in my head, then nodded to Busto. We moved quickly, unloading the "patients" and medical supply boxes containing our real equipment.

Right on cue, the door opened. A woman in scrubs stood there, her eyes darting nervously.

"You're Drake?" she whispered.

I nodded. "Are we clear?"

"For now. Night security does rounds every twenty minutes. You've got about twelve until they come back through this section." She held the door wider. "Hurry. Dr. Chen is finishing an operation on the fourth floor."

We moved with practiced efficiency, wheeling our "patients" through the door while three members of the Sacramento resistance stayed behind with the ambulances. Inside, the sterile hospital corridor smelled of antiseptic and fear. Our contact led us to a service elevator, swiping her badge to grant us access.

"The surgical suite is restricted," she said as we crowded into the elevator. "I can get you to the fourth floor, but you'll need these to get through the final checkpoint." She handed me three ID badges. "They're temporary passes for visiting specialists. They'll work on the scanner, but won't stand up to close inspection."

I took the badges, handing one to Busto and keeping one for myself. "What about cameras?"

"We've looped the feeds in the main corridors, but the surgical floor has independent systems. You'll be visible once you're up there."

The elevator doors opened, revealing another white corridor, this one busier, with night staff moving between stations. Our contact stepped out first, gesturing for us to follow with our "patients."

"Act like you belong," I whispered to the team. "Eyes forward, move with purpose."

We split into our pre-arranged groups, three "patients" with medical handlers, moving down different corridors to avoid looking like a convoy. Busto took two Marines and headed left toward what we'd identified as a secondary access point to the surgical floor. I took my group straight ahead, toward the main checkpoint.

The night nurse at the station barely looked up as we approached, too busy with paperwork to pay much attention to yet another patient transfer. I swiped the temporary badge, holding my breath until the light turned green. The doors unlocked with a soft click.

"We need to get these patients prepped for Dr. Chen's team," I said, infusing my voice with medical urgency.

The nurse nodded absently. "Room 4, they're finishing up with the previous case. Should be ready in twenty."

I pushed through the doors, the Marines following with our "patient" and equipment. Once we were through and around the corner, I allowed myself a small smile.

"So far, so good," I muttered.

"Commander," one of the Marines whispered, "we've got movement ahead."

I peered around the corner to see two HCD officers standing outside what appeared to be a break room, coffee cups in hand. They weren't looking our way, but we'd have to pass them to reach the surgical suite.

"Change of plan," I whispered. "We continue the patient

act until we reach the surgical floor. Martinez, you're still our patient. Jenkins, help me get these supplies unpacked once we're in position."

We rolled forward, passing the HCD officers with professional nods. My fingers itched to reach for the weapon hidden in the supply box, but discipline kept them steady on the gurney handle. We turned another corner and found ourselves in a small prep area outside several operating rooms.

A doctor emerged from one of the rooms, a surgical mask hanging loose around his neck. He looked at us with mild surprise.

"Another transfer? I didn't think we had any more scheduled tonight."

I felt a flicker of panic before smoothly replying, "Emergency cases from County. Dr. Chen requested immediate transfer for her research program."

The doctor frowned. "She's in OR-3 right now with an HCD official. Won't be finished for at least an hour."

My mind raced. This wasn't part of the plan. We needed Chen now, not in an hour when security would definitely have noticed something amiss.

"We were told to prep the patients and wait," I said, improvising. "Is there a recovery room we can use?"

He pointed to a door across the hall. "Use Recovery 2. It's empty tonight." With that, he turned and walked away, apparently too tired to question us further.

Once inside Recovery 2, I pulled out my secure communicator. "Busto, we've got a situation. Target is in surgery with an HCD official. We may need to adjust the timetable. Have you heard anything from Zulu Team?"

His voice came back, tense but controlled. "Copy that. No, no word yet from Zulu Team. We're in position on the west corridor. How long do you need?"

"Doctor says an hour, but we can't wait that long. We need to get eyes on her, assess the situation."

"Should we move to the extraction point and reschedule?"

I considered it for a moment. Abort now, return another day? The risk seemed tempting, but we had limited intelligence on Dr. Chen's schedule, and this might be our only chance. Plus, we could have control of Chen's family at any moment, and once that happened, it could trigger the HCD into upping the security around Chen.

"Negative. We proceed as planned, but carefully. Get your team to Recovery 2. We'll regroup and approach the surgical suite together."

Just then, my radio crackled, and I heard a call. "Whiskey Team, this is Zulu Team. Amber Latch! I say again, Amber Latch!"

"Amber Latch" was our prearranged codeword meaning Chen's family had been secured and safely extracted. Delighted, I called Busto. "Did you hear that, Whiskey-One?"

"Got it, Whiskey-Nine. The op is a go. Moving now."

I turned to the Marines with me, who were already unpacking our real equipment from the medical boxes. Protomatter armor configurations were being adjusted beneath clothing, weapons checked and safeties confirmed.

"This just got more complicated," I said, unable to keep a hint of grim humor from my voice. "Either we've stumbled into the worst timing possible, or the best possible intelligence coup."

One of the Marines raised an eyebrow.

"Think about it," I continued, checking the charge on my own weapon. "Dr. Chen operating on an HCD official?

Whatever she's doing in there could yield some incredible intelligence."

Five minutes later, Busto arrived with his team. We gathered around a small table where I'd sketched a rough layout of the surgical floor.

"Our intel suggests OR-3 is here," I said, pointing. "Two entrances—main doors and a scrub room access. We'll split into two teams. I'll take the scrub room approach with two Marines. Busto, you take the rest and cover the main entrance. We observe first—no engagement unless absolutely necessary."

Busto nodded, his expression grim. "And if Chen is unwilling?"

I met his gaze steadily. "She no longer has a choice. We have her family in custody, though she doesn't know that yet. We extract her, willing or not."

"Copy that, Commander."

As we prepared to move out, I felt that familiar mixture of anticipation and dread settle in my stomach, the same feeling I'd had before every combat drop since joining the resistance. The cold certainty that things were about to go sideways, coupled with the determination to complete the mission anyway.

"This is either the best ambulance ride ever," I said, checking my weapon one last time, "or a one-way ticket to a mess. Let's find out which."

With that, we moved into position, ready to extract the doctor who would save Sofia's life. One way or another, Dr. Eleanor Chen was leaving with us tonight.

24

We never made it to the surgical suite. As we rounded the corner from Recovery 2, the unmistakable sound of boots—too many boots—echoed down the corridor ahead. I raised my fist, the universal signal for "freeze," and my team went statue-still behind me. The footfalls grew louder, accompanied by the crackle of comms and the distinctive clinking of HCD tactical gear. I pressed myself against the wall, mind racing through options that were evaporating by the second. This wasn't a routine patrol—this was a full security detachment, and they were headed straight for us.

"Back," I whispered, motioning toward an alcove housing a cleaning cart. "Now."

We retreated silently, sliding into the shadows as flashlight beams swept around the corner we'd just abandoned. Through the narrow gap between wall and cart, I counted six—no, eight—HCD officers moving in formation. Their black uniforms seemed to absorb what little light existed in the corridor, making them appear like moving holes in reality. Each carried a Kergan-issue flechette rifle, the kind that could turn protomatter armor into smoking slag with a well-placed burst.

One of them spoke into his comm unit, his voice carrying clearly in the silent hallway. "Level four sweep commencing. Teams Alpha and Bravo converging on surgical wing per Controller's orders."

My blood went cold. This wasn't a coincidence. Either something had tipped them off, or our intel on tonight's security layout had been dead wrong from the start. Then it hit me—Chen's family. Maybe that was the trigger. If the HCD had caught wind of the extraction, the whole hierarchy in Sacramento was probably scrambling by now.

Busto appeared at my shoulder, his breath a controlled whisper against my ear. "Trap?"

I shook my head slightly. "Unknown. But we can't stay here, and we can't abort." I studied the HCD formation as they moved past our position. They were thorough, checking each room, but moving with purpose toward the surgical wing. "We need to split up."

Busto's jaw tightened, but he nodded. In our line of work, splitting up often meant some people didn't come back together.

I sketched a quick diagram on my palm with my finger, indicating positions. "Take Martinez, Jenkins, Rodriguez and Patel. Head back to the service corridor, create a diversion at the far end—something noisy, but controllable. Draw as many of them away from the surgical suite as possible. Then circle back through the east stairwell."

"And you?"

"I'll take Alvarez and the Diaz twins. We'll push forward once your diversion pulls their attention. We rendezvous at point Charlie, if separated."

Busto checked his weapon, a compact flechette gun

hidden under a baggy smock. "Timeline?"

"Ten minutes for the diversion. After that, we extract the doctor regardless of the situation. The ambulances won't wait forever."

With a sharp nod, Busto gathered his designated team members with a series of hand signals. They began to move back down the corridor we'd come from, each step measured, each movement precise. Marines might not be known for subtlety in conventional warfare, but these were members of *Thunder*'s MARDET, trained for exactly this kind of infiltration. They disappeared around the corner like ghosts.

I turned to my remaining team. "Alvarez, take point. Diaz One and Two, cover our six. We shadow the HCD patrol, stay just out of sight, and move when they move to mask our sounds."

Alvarez, a wiry woman whose previous life as a gymnast made her uniquely suited for close-quarters stealth work, nodded and shifted to the front of our formation. The Diaz twins—a brother and sister—took up the rearguard positions.

We moved like this for what felt like hours but was probably only minutes, a careful dance of advance and hold, always staying just behind the HCD patrol. They were moving systematically through the fourth floor, room by room, but their primary focus seemed to be ahead, not behind.

"They're looking for something specific," I whispered to Alvarez during one hold period. "Or someone."

She nodded. "Not us, though. They'd have locked down the floor if they knew we were here."

A thought struck me. "The doctor. Something's happening with Chen."

Before I could develop this theory further, my comm unit vibrated twice against my wrist. Busto's signal that they were in position. I checked my watch—seven minutes since we'd split up. He was moving faster than expected, which either meant things were going well or very badly.

I sent back a single vibration. Acknowledged.

We waited, pressed against the wall of a darkened patient room. The HCD patrol had paused at a junction ahead, their leader conferring with someone over their comm system. I could make out terse phrases—"negative contact" and "expand the search perimeter"—but not enough to understand what exactly they were looking for.

Then chaos erupted from the far end of the floor.

An alarm blared, followed by the sound of breaking glass and shouting. Emergency lights began to pulse, bathing the corridor in alternating darkness and bloody red illumination. The HCD patrol reacted instantly, their leader barking orders.

"Teams Alpha and Gamma, converge on the disturbance! Bravo team, maintain position at the surgical suite!"

They split, six officers racing toward the commotion while two remained behind, taking up defensive positions at the junction. It was better than I'd hoped—Busto had drawn off three-quarters of the immediate threat.

"Move up," I ordered, and we slipped forward, using the pulsing emergency lights to time our advancement. Three seconds of darkness, two seconds of red light. Move in the dark, freeze in the red.

We reached the junction where the two remaining HCD officers stood guard. They were facing away from us, attention focused on the corridor where their comrades had disappeared. The surgical suite lay just beyond them, its double doors visible at the end of the passageway.

I indicated our weapons, then the guards. My team understood immediately. We couldn't risk gunfire—the sound would bring the entire HCD contingent down on us—but we couldn't leave the guards conscious, either.

Alvarez moved first, a shadow among shadows. She closed the distance to the first guard during a darkness pulse, then struck as the red light flooded back. Her arm wrapped around his throat in a practiced choke hold, cutting off both air and blood flow. Then her other arm punched a knife up under his ribs and directly into his heart, killing him instantly.

The second guard turned at the sound of scuffling, but the Diaz twins were already on him. Maria seized his rifle arm, yanking it downward as Carlos stepped in, driving a sharp, practiced blow to his throat. The guard staggered back, choking and clutching at his crushed larynx, his breath reduced to a rasping wheeze. Carlos slipped behind him, locking in a choke hold with ruthless efficiency. Within seconds, the guard went limp. He wouldn't be getting back up.

"Drag their bodies into that supply closet," I ordered, pointing to a door beside us. "We've got maybe two minutes before someone notices they're not responding to comms."

While my team handled the guards, I scanned our surroundings. The surgical wing was eerily quiet, despite the alarm still blaring in the distance. Either the staff had evacuated, or they were hunkered down inside the operating rooms.

"Clear," Alvarez reported as they finished securing the guards.

"Good. Now we—"

My comm unit vibrated three times in rapid succession.

Busto's emergency signal. Something had gone wrong.

I cursed under my breath. "Change of plans. We need to move faster. Alvarez, get to that surgical suite and confirm if Chen is inside. Diazs, cover the junction in case any HCD circle back this way."

They moved to their assignments while I tried to raise Busto on the comm.

"Whiskey-Nine to Whiskey-One, status report," I whispered, using our mission call signs.

Static, then Busto's voice, tight with tension: "Whiskey-One to Whiskey-Nine. Diversion successful but we've been spotted. Four HCD in pursuit. Cannot reach rendezvous point Charlie. Proceeding to alternate extraction."

My mind raced through the implications. Busto's team would head for the emergency stairwell at the far end of the building, then try to reach the ambulances directly. They might make it, they might not. Either way, my team was now on its own for the primary objective.

"Copy that, Whiskey-One. Proceed to extraction. We'll secure the package and follow."

"Roger that. Good hunting, Commander."

The comm went silent. I hurried to where Alvarez was peering through the small window in the surgical suite doors.

"She's there," Alvarez confirmed. "Operating on someone. Two nurses, one anesthesiologist, and what looks like an HCD observer in the corner."

I looked for myself. The operating room was brightly lit, a stark contrast to the dim corridor. Dr. Eleanor Chen stood over a surgical table, her hands steady as she manipulated some kind of delicate instrument near the patient's open skull. Her face was largely hidden behind a surgical mask, but her eyes were intense with concentration. The HCD observer stood against the wall, arms crossed, watching every move.

"We need to wait until she's finished," I decided. "We can't risk interrupting brain surgery, even for extraction."

"Commander," one of the Diaz twins called softly from the junction. "Movement from the east corridor. More HCD incoming."

I swore under my breath. "How many?"

"At least four, maybe more."

Our options were evaporating by the second. We couldn't fight our way past that many HCD without risking Chen and alerting the entire facility. We couldn't retreat without abandoning the mission. And we couldn't stay where we were without being discovered.

Then I noticed the scrubs hanging on a hook near the supply closet.

"New plan," I said. "We're going to hide in plain sight."

Working quickly, we donned the medical scrubs over our tactical gear. The protomatter armor was thin enough to be concealed, but our weapons were another matter. We distributed them among our medical supply boxes, each disguised as equipment.

"Alvarez, you're a nurse now. Diaz One, you're a technician. Diaz Two, orderly. I'll be Dr. Brown, neurological consultant." I grabbed a clipboard from the nurse's station and scribbled meaningless notes on it. "Remember, look busy, look tired, and for god's sake, look like you belong here."

We had barely settled into our roles when four HCD officers rounded the corner, weapons at the ready. I stepped forward, clipboard in hand, channeling every arrogant doctor I'd ever met.

"Can I help you, gentlemen?" I asked, infusing my voice

with professional irritation, though I hadn't a clue about what an actual doctor would say. "We're preparing for a secondary procedure here."

The lead officer regarded me suspiciously. "We're conducting a security sweep. There's been an incident on this floor."

I sighed dramatically. "Yes, we heard the alarms. Very disruptive to our work. I assume you need to check the surgical suite?"

He nodded.

"Fine, but I must insist you maintain sterile protocols. Dr. Chen is performing delicate neural integration work for your superiors, and I won't have it compromised by security concerns, however valid they might be." I gestured to Alvarez. "Nurse, please provide these officers with appropriate coverings if they intend to enter the surgical area."

Alvarez, bless her adaptive thinking, immediately moved to a cabinet and retrieved surgical masks and covers, handing them out with practiced efficiency. The HCD officers looked uncertain, caught between their security protocols and the apparent medical necessity.

"Who exactly are you?" the lead officer demanded.

My mind scrambled to remember the name printed on my fake ID. "Dr. Hugo Brown, neurological specialist. I've been brought in to consult on this particular case." I tapped my forged ID badge. "You can verify with Director Mercer if you wish, though I imagine he's occupied with whatever security situation you're addressing."

I held my breath as the officer scrutinized my badge. Our forgeries were good, but they wouldn't withstand serious investigation. After what seemed like an eternity, he handed it back.

"We'll need to check the adjacent rooms," he said, seemingly satisfied with my credentials.

"Of course. My staff will assist you. We have nothing to hide here, Officer. Just important work to complete."

The HCD team moved past us, checking the nearby rooms while scrupulously avoiding disrupting what they believed to be legitimate medical procedures. I caught Alvarez's eye and gave a small nod. We'd bought ourselves some time, but not much.

As the HCD officers disappeared down the hallway, I let out a breath I hadn't realized I was holding. "That was too close."

"Commander," Carlos Diaz said quietly from beside me, "I think we have another problem."

25

I pressed my face close to the reinforced window, taking in the scene with a growing sense of dread. This wasn't just any operation—the patient on the table wore the distinctive collar insignia of an HCD Deputy Commander. We weren't just interrupting brain surgery; we were interrupting brain surgery on one of the enemy's highest-ranking officers.

"Holy shit," Alvarez whispered beside me, her eyes wide as she took in the scene. "That's Deputy Commander Voss. He's in charge of the entire Northern California HCD division."

The Diaz twins exchanged glances laden with meaning. We all understood the implications instantly. This wasn't just a complication—it was potentially an intelligence gold mine. Whatever Chen was doing to Voss's brain could be crucial information for the resistance.

"Options," I said quietly, stepping back from the window. "Go in now and extract Chen, risk the patient dying and bringing the entire HCD down on us. Or wait until the surgery concludes and risk missing our extraction window."

Alvarez checked her watch. "Busto's team is probably at the rendezvous point by now. Ambulances were instructed to wait fifteen minutes past the extraction time, which gives us... seven minutes."

"Not enough time for brain surgery to wrap up," I muttered.

I returned to the window, studying the scene more carefully. Dr. Chen was working with incredible focus, her hands moving with the precision of someone who had performed this procedure many times before. She was manipulating something near the frontal lobe—a small device that caught the surgical lights and reflected them in metallic glints. An implant of some kind.

The HCD observer stood with rigid posture, occasionally consulting a tablet in his hands. Two nurses assisted Chen, handing instruments and monitoring equipment, while an anesthesiologist monitored vital signs at the head of the table. The room was filled with the quiet beeping of medical equipment and the metallic sounds of surgical tools.

"I think she's almost done," I said after watching for another minute. "She's closing up whatever access point she created."

"Commander," one of the Diaz twins whispered urgently. "More movement in the east corridor."

I cursed under my breath. We were running out of time and options. "How many this time?"

"Can't tell. But it sounds like a lot."

I made a rapid calculation. If we waited for Chen to finish, we'd likely be discovered by whatever HCD reinforcements were heading our way. If we burst in now, we risked killing a high-ranking HCD official on an operating table—which would result in a manhunt that might make our escape impossible.

"We need a third option," I murmured, more to myself than my team.

As if in answer, Dr. Chen suddenly looked up from her work, her eyes finding the window where we stood. Her gaze locked with mine for the briefest moment, and I saw something flash across her face—recognition? Fear? Calculation? She looked away just as quickly, returning to her work without missing a beat, but I knew she had seen us.

"She made us," Alvarez whispered.

"Maybe," I replied, my mind racing. "Or maybe she was expecting someone like us."

A new thought struck me. Chen was being forced to work for the HCD—our intelligence suggested her family was being held as leverage. What if she'd found a way to send a message to the resistance? What if this operation wasn't what it appeared to be?

I studied her movements more carefully. Her hands were steady, her actions precise, but there was something deliberate in the way she positioned herself, always keeping the observer from having a clear view of exactly what she was doing with the implant.

"I think she's sabotaging it," I blurted. "The implant. She's doing something the observer can't see."

Alvarez looked skeptical. "That's a hell of a gamble, Commander."

"So is bursting into an operating room with guns drawn," I countered. "We need to wait just a little longer."

The sound of approaching footsteps grew louder. The Diaz twins took up defensive positions at each end of the corridor, their hands hovering near their concealed weapons.

Inside the operating room, Dr. Chen was finishing her work, closing the surgical site with practiced efficiency. She applied some kind of sealant—not sutures, I noted—and stepped back, removing her gloves.

"Patient is stable," I could hear her say faintly through the door. "The integration is complete."

The observer stepped forward, examining the tablet in his hands. "Neural links are registering. Baseline functions appear normal." He looked up at Chen. "Activation timeline?"

"Twenty-four hours minimum," she replied, her voice clinical and detached. "The neural pathways need time to accept the interface. Attempting activation sooner could cause synaptic cascade failure."

The observer seemed displeased, but nodded. "Very well. Prepare him for recovery and generate your usual reports. Director Mercer will want to review the procedure details personally."

Chen nodded, then turned to the medical team. "Prepare for transport to recovery. Standard post-neural protocols."

This was our moment. As the medical team began disconnecting monitoring equipment and preparing the patient for transfer, Chen would be the least occupied and the room at its most chaotic.

"New plan," I whispered to my team. "When they move the patient, we go in as medical transport. Alvarez, you and I will approach Chen directly. Diazs, secure the observer—non-lethal takedown only. We extract Chen, leave everyone else."

We waited in tense silence for what felt like hours, but was probably only fifteen minutes. Fortunately, the sound of boots we'd heard earlier had faded, the HCD patrol somehow missing us. Finally, Chen stepped back from the table, stripping off her bloody gloves and surgical gown. She spoke briefly to another surgeon, who nodded and continued the closing procedure.

After washing her hands, Chen pushed through the door into the hallway. She startled slightly at the sight of us but quickly composed herself. The woman had a professional poker face that would put career gamblers to shame. And she was coming to us without Voss. That required yet another change of our plan.

I improvised on the spot, stepping forward. "Dr. Chen, you're coming with us."

Her eyebrows lifted a fraction of an inch—the medical professional's equivalent of gasping in shock. "I most certainly am not. I have another procedure scheduled in an hour."

"That's been canceled. I'm with the resistance." I kept my voice low, conscious of potential ears everywhere. "We're here to extract you."

"The resistance," she repeated flatly, as if I'd told her I was the tooth fairy. Her eyes darted toward the nearest security camera, then back to me. "How thoughtful. However, I must decline your invitation."

"It's not an invitation."

"You don't understand," she said, her voice dropping to barely a whisper. "My family. My husband and daughters. They're hostages. If I don't comply—"

"They were hostages," I corrected her. "As of 30 minutes ago, they're in resistance custody. Safe."

The mask of professional detachment cracked, just slightly. Hope and disbelief warred in her eyes. "You're lying."

I pulled out the tactical radio I'd kept hidden in my

stolen lab coat. "Dogbone-One, this is Whiskey-Nine, you copy?"

The radio crackled with Phoebe's voice, who was piloting Zulu Team's assault shuttle. "Reading you five by five, Whiskey-Nine."

"Put Mr. Chen on the line."

A brief pause, then a man's voice came through, tense with emotion. "Hello? Eleanor?"

Chen's composure crumbled. She snatched the radio from my hand with surprising strength. "David? David, is that really you?"

"Eleanor! Oh my God, Eleanor, it's really me. The girls are here too. We're safe. These people, they came in the night —"

I gently reclaimed the radio. "Sorry to cut the reunion short, but we're on a clock here."

Tears glistened in Chen's eyes, but she nodded, squaring her shoulders. "I understand."

"Dogbone-One, we're moving to extraction point. Make sure our ride is hot."

"Already on it, Whiskey-Nine. Mother says to hurry. The diversion teams can't hold much longer."

I pocketed the radio and gestured toward the emergency stairwell. "This way, Doctor."

We started moving, the Diaz twins taking point while Alvarez guarded our rear. Chen kept pace beside me, her face now set with determination.

"Wait," she said suddenly as we approached the stairwell. "I need to make a stop."

I didn't even try to hide my exasperation. "We don't have time for detours."

"If you want my full cooperation, you'll make time." Her voice was steel. "There's something I need to retrieve—

something you'll want."

"What could possibly be worth—"

"Technology. Research. The reason they took my family hostage in the first place." Her eyes met mine, unflinching. "Trust me, Commander. This is worth the risk."

I considered for exactly three seconds, weighing the increasing sounds of chaos from other parts of the hospital against the determined set of Chen's jaw.

"You've got two minutes," I conceded. "Diaz, Diaz—cover position. Alvarez, with us."

Chen led us down an adjacent corridor to a heavy steel door with multiple security warnings plastered across it. A keypad and retinal scanner guarded the entrance.

"Let me guess," I said. "You don't have access."

"No," Chen replied, "only the Chief of Surgery does."

"So we need another way in."

I pulled a small breaching charge from my hidden equipment pouch. Modern problems, ancient solutions. I placed it carefully around the locking mechanism.

"Stand back," I warned, guiding Chen behind the cover of a nearby supply cabinet. "This will be loud."

The charge detonated with a sharp crack, filling the hallway with acrid smoke. My ears rang as the door swung open on damaged hinges. Chen darted past me into what appeared to be a large storage room lined with shelves of small plastic containers, each meticulously labeled.

"What is all this?" I asked, following her inside while keeping watch on the door.

Chen grabbed a plastic sack hanging by the entrance and began stuffing containers into it with frantic efficiency. "Neural implant prototypes. The Kergans have been forcing me to develop them—brain-machine interfaces for controlling human subjects."

The implications sent a chill down my spine. "Mind control?"

"Essentially, yes." She moved methodically along the shelves, selecting specific containers. "Though I've been sabotaging the research where I could. The ones I'm taking are the functional prototypes—the ones that work as they're supposed to, not as I've told the Kergans they work."

The bag bulged with her selections. In the distance, I heard boots pounding on tile. Our distraction was wearing thin.

"Time's up, Doctor," I urged.

"Hold on!" She frantically scanned the back shelves. "Where is it? Where—ah!" She lunged for a container partially hidden behind others. "Here it is!"

"What's so special about that one?"

She stuffed it into her already overflowing bag. "I'll tell you later."

I nodded toward the door. "Let's move."

"Wait," Chen said, surveying the room. "Can we destroy this place? If the HCD recovers this research..."

I glanced at Alvarez, who was already two steps ahead, pulling thermite grenades from her pack.

"Plant them deep," I ordered. "We want nothing salvageable."

Alvarez nodded grimly, moving to strategic points in the storage room as Chen and I backed out.

From down the hallway came the sound of weapons being readied. The Diaz twins opened fire without hesitation, their flechette rifles coughing out lethal swarms of metal shards. An HCD security team dropped before they could even raise their weapons.

"Alvarez, move it!" I shouted.

She sprinted from the storage room, slamming the

damaged door. "Ten seconds!" she warned.

We ran for the stairwell as white-hot light began to seep through the cracks around the storage room door. Behind us, the thermite ignited with a distinctive whoosh, heating rapidly to temperatures that would reduce everything inside to unrecognizable slag.

We'd barely made it twenty yards when four more HCD security personnel rounded the corner ahead, weapons raised. One spotted Chen and his eyes widened in recognition.

"Halt! Hands up!" he barked. "Dr. Chen, step away from those people immediately!"

Chen froze beside me, genuine fear flashing across her face. Our cover was thoroughly blown.

"Weapons free!" I shouted, drawing my sidearm. "Move!"

As the corridor erupted in gunfire, Chen screamed, genuine horror in her voice. "There are patients and medical staff on this floor!"

I grabbed her arm, pulling her behind a medical cart for cover as my team returned fire. "We must deal with these monsters, Doctor, or we're all dead. I'm sorry, but we're doing our best to minimize collateral damage."

She didn't answer, but when I tugged her toward the stairwell, she followed without resistance, clutching her precious bag of technology.

"Western loading dock," I ordered as we pounded down the stairs. "Commander Austin has our extraction there."

26

We hustled Dr. Chen down the stairwell. The thunder of boots echoing up from below told me our problems were about to get a whole lot more immediate. We'd hit the second-floor landing when the first HCD helmet appeared below us, and just like that, our escape route vanished in a heartbeat.

"Contact front!" I hissed, shoving Dr. Chen behind me against the wall. "Hostiles coming up!"

The HCD squad—six of them in matte black armor with those ridiculous blue armbands—spotted us the same moment we spotted them. What followed was that microsecond of mutual surprise where everyone's brain catches up with their eyes. Unfortunately, their brains were quicker.

The lead HCD trooper snapped his weapon up and fired first, the harsh crack of his flechette rifle bouncing off concrete walls. I felt the air stir as tiny metal darts zipped past my head.

"Diaz, suppressing fire! Alvarez, get the doctor back!" I

yelled, raising my own rifle and squeezing off three rapid bursts.

The twins moved in perfect sync—probably some weird sibling thing—laying down a wall of flechettes that forced the HCD troops to duck behind the railing. Alvarez, bless her jumpy nerves, had already grabbed Chen and was pulling her toward the landing door.

More flechettes pinged against the walls around us. The Diaz twins alternated fire, never leaving an opening. Classic leapfrog suppression, just like we'd drilled a hundred times. At least someone was paying attention during Busto's boring-as-hell tactical sessions.

I backed up, keeping my body between Chen and the incoming fire. "Move, move, move!" I shouted, feeling the doctor's hesitation behind me.

Then the HCD squad tossed something small and cylindrical up the stairwell.

"Grenade!"

I didn't think—just reacted. I spun and lunged at Chen, wrapping my arms around her and using my body as a shield. The concussive blast hit a moment later, throwing us both forward onto the landing. The ringing in my ears almost drowned out the sudden burst of gunfire.

Pain exploded across my left side, sharp and electric. Something punched through my protomatter armor—which was supposed to be goddamn flechette-resistant—and buried itself deep in my torso. The impact knocked the wind out of me, and for a disorienting second, my vision sparkled with dancing black dots.

"Commander's hit!" someone shouted—probably Alvarez, though it was hard to tell through the ringing.

I tried to push myself up, but my left arm collapsed under me. A cool female voice spoke in my helmet:

"WARNING: ARMOR BREACH DETECTED. BIOLOGICAL PENETRATION CONFIRMED. ADMINISTERING EMERGENCY PROTOCOLS."

My suit went to work immediately, the sensation of microscopic needles deploying into my flesh, barely registering against the white-hot agony in my side. A cool rush spread through my veins—anticoagulants to prevent bleeding out, painkillers to keep me functional, and stimulants to counteract shock.

Hands grabbed me roughly under my armpits, and I was suddenly being dragged backward through the door to the second floor. Alvarez, grunting with effort, pulled me into the corridor as the Diaz twins provided covering fire. Through the narrowing gap of the closing door, I saw them toss what looked like plasma grenades down the stairwell. The blue-white flash was followed by screams.

"They got the commander," Alvarez said, her voice tight with panic. "He's bleeding."

"I'm fine," I grunted, the drugs already kicking in and dulling the edge of the pain. I tasted copper in my mouth but forced myself to my feet, swaying slightly. "Just a scratch."

Dr. Chen's face appeared in front of mine, her eyes wide behind those wire-rimmed glasses. "You're wounded! There's blood leaking through your armor!"

I glanced down. A dark stain was indeed spreading across my left side where the shrapnel had punched through. Not good, but not immediately fatal either. My suit was already compensating, hardening around the wound to create a pressure seal.

"No time to play doctor," I said, forcing a grin despite the pain. "We need to move. Now."

The twins burst through the door behind us, breathing hard. "Bought us maybe two minutes," one of them said—

Maria.

I keyed my radio. "This is Whiskey-Nine. Primary exfil compromised. Moving to evac route Bravo. Over."

Static crackled for a second before Destiny's voice came through, tense but controlled: "Copy that, Dodger-One Actual. Be advised, we're facing heavy air defense. ETA uncertain."

Perfect. Just perfect.

"Alvarez, take point. Get us to the alternate evac." I straightened, ignoring the warning flashes in my HUD showing my dropping blood pressure. "Let's move, people!"

We set off at a run down the wide, sterile hallway of the hospital's second floor. My side screamed with each step, but the cocktail of drugs pumping through my system kept me upright and moving. The protomatter armor was doing its job, stiffening around the wound and maintaining pressure, but I could feel something hard and jagged shifting inside me with every movement. The shrapnel was still in there—not ideal, but extraction would have to wait.

Alvarez led us around a corner into a narrow service corridor—the kind of hallway hospitals use to stash laundry carts and awkward conversations. The flickering fluorescent lights overhead did their best impression of a haunted house, casting twitchy shadows across the industrial tile floor. Our boots echoed like we were marching through a tin can.

"How're you doing, Commander?" Maria Diaz asked, eyeing the blood soaking my side.

"Never better," I lied. "Might take up ballroom dancing after this. Something low-impact."

She snorted, but didn't slow down. We pushed through a set of double doors and barreled into what had clearly become a makeshift shelter. The space had cafeteria bones—

folding tables pushed aside, cots and blankets strewn across the floor, and that faint institutional smell of despair and old coffee. Dozens of civilians and medical staff turned to gape as we stumbled in, covered in blood and bristling with weapons like action figures someone had chewed on.

A woman in scrubs screamed. A man lunged for the wall phone like it was a game show buzzer.

"Don't mind us!" I called out, waving one bloodied hand. "Just your friendly neighborhood assault team—door-to-door service with a smile!"

People dove for cover. Some screamed, some froze, and one guy just sort of slowly slid under a table like his soul had given up.

An unarmed security guard took one heroic step forward—then wisely reconsidered when the Diaz twins leveled their weapons at him in eerie sync.

"Apologies for the mess!" I added over my shoulder, already halfway to the next set of doors. "Send the cleaning bill to the Human Compliance Directorate—tell 'em *Thunder* says hi!"

We burst through the far doors and into another empty corridor, leaving behind chaos, confusion, and probably a few therapy bills. My breath came in ragged gasps, but I wasn't about to slow down. Not yet.

"Secondary stairwell should be just ahead," Alvarez called back, checking the schematic on her wrist display.

We reached the stairwell and descended quickly, the sound of our footsteps echoing in the concrete chamber. No sign of pursuit yet, but that wouldn't last. I checked the wound as we moved—the bleeding had slowed, but my suit indicators were flashing amber warnings about internal trauma. Not good.

We exited onto the ground floor into an empty lobby on

the south side of the building. Through the glass doors, I could see a four-story parking garage across an open lot. Our destination. The alternate exfil point.

"There it is," I said, pointing. "That's our ticket out of here. Alvarez, take the doctor. Diaz twins, covering fire if needed. Ready? Go!"

We burst through the doors and sprinted across the pavement. My side felt like it was on fire with each pounding step, but I kept my weapon up and scanned for threats. We'd made it halfway across when a side door of the hospital slammed open and a squad of HCD security forces stumbled out, looking disoriented but very much armed.

"Contact right!" I shouted, grabbing Chen by the collar of her lab coat and practically throwing her behind a line of parked cars. "Get down!"

The air filled with the sharp crack of flechette rifles as both sides opened fire simultaneously. I pressed myself against the hood of a dented Toyota, checking that Chen was safely huddled behind the engine block.

"Stay low," I told her, then keyed my radio. "Whiskey-Nine to Dodger-One. We're pinned down outside the secondary exit. Moving to LZ Bravo now. Will be on the roof momentarily."

"Copy that," Destiny's voice came back, strained over the sound of what might have been anti-aircraft fire. "We're ten clicks out and catching hell from Kergan air defense. Working on it."

"Work faster!" I snapped, then immediately regretted it. Destiny was doing her best. "Sorry. Just... hurry if you can."

"Always do, boss," she replied, and I could hear the eye-roll in her voice.

I signaled to Alvarez and the twins, pointing toward the

garage. "We move car to car, leapfrog. Maria, you first!"

Maria Diaz darted forward, making it to the next row of vehicles before dropping into a crouch. Her brother laid down covering fire, his weapon spitting deadly metal shards toward the HCD forces.

"Go, go, go!"

We worked our way across the parking lot in a deadly dance, each of us covering the others as we advanced. Chen kept up surprisingly well for a civilian, following my directions without question. The woman had guts—I had to give her that. Pretty much any other civilian in these circumstances would be catatonic with fear.

We reached the base of the parking garage, ducking into the relative safety of the concrete structure. The gunfire behind us intensified as more HCD forces joined the fight.

"Stairs!" I pointed to the emergency stairwell. "All the way to the roof!"

We began climbing, the enclosed space amplifying our labored breathing. I was feeling light-headed, the stimulants in my system fighting a losing battle against blood loss. Each landing we passed felt higher than the last.

We'd just rounded the third-floor landing when a burst of flechettes tore through the air from below. Carlos Diaz—Maria's brother—cried out as several hit him on the back of his legs, sending him sprawling onto the stairs.

"Carlos!" Maria screamed, turning back.

I grabbed her arm. "Keep moving! Alvarez, get the doctor to the roof!"

Alvarez hesitated for only a second before nodding and pushing Chen ahead of him up the stairs. Maria tore free from my grip and dropped to her brother's side. Blood pooled beneath him, spreading across the concrete steps.

"Go," Carlos gasped, his face contorted in pain as he

fumbled for a grenade on his belt. "I'll hold them."

"No!" Maria gripped his tactical vest. "I'm not leaving you!"

The sound of boots on stairs grew louder below us. We had seconds, maybe less.

"We can't carry him," I said, the words tasting bitter. "Maria, we have to move."

She looked up at me, her eyes fierce and wet. "Then I'm staying too."

Carlos shook his head violently. "No, sis. You get out. Complete the mission." He pressed something into her hand. "For Mom."

Maria's face crumpled, but she shoved whatever he'd given her into her pocket, leaned forward and kissed Carlos on his helmet faceplate, then grabbed her rifle. "Let's go," she said to me, her voice hoarse.

We continued up the stairs, leaving Carlos behind. We'd barely made it to the next landing when the distinctive crack of his rifle echoed up the stairwell, followed by shouts and screams.

I keyed my radio as we climbed. "Whiskey-Nine to Dodger-One. Be advised, we've lost Whiskey-Seven."

"Which one?" Destiny's voice came back immediately.

"Carlos," I replied, glancing at Maria's rigid back as she climbed ahead of me. "His sister's still with us."

We reached the door to the roof just as a deafening explosion shook the stairwell. Maria paused, her hand on the door handle, her face turned toward the sound below.

"For Earth," she whispered.

I put my hand on her shoulder. "For Earth."

She nodded once, then pushed through the door onto the roof.

The open air hit us like a wall after the enclosed

stairwell. The garage roof was mostly empty—a few abandoned cars scattered across the concrete expanse. Alvarez had positioned herself and Chen behind a huge Ford pickup near the center, her rifle trained on the stairwell door.

"Spread out," I ordered, moving toward them while scanning the sky for any sign of our extraction. "Maria, watch our six."

I dropped behind the truck next to Chen, my legs finally giving out as the adrenaline ebbed. The pain in my side had transformed into a dull throb that worsened whenever I moved. I pressed my hand against the wound and felt only an entry hole—no exit wound. The shrapnel was still inside me, probably tearing things up with every movement.

"Let me look at that," Chen said, reaching for the breach in my armor.

"Later," I grunted, keying my radio again. "Whiskey-Nine to Dodger-One. We are at LZ Bravo awaiting retrieval. LZ is hot with multiple armed hostiles in pursuit. Where's our ride?"

Destiny's voice came back, clearer now: "We've been delayed, but help is on the way."

I frowned. "What do you mean, 'help'? I thought you were our one and only taxi service?"

"No time to explain. Just be ready."

Great. Cryptic responses were always so reassuring.

"Any word from Whiskey-One?" I asked, suddenly remembering the other half of our team.

"Nothing since they reported reaching the primary extraction point," Destiny replied. "Comms have been spotty with all the Kergan jamming."

I cursed under my breath. Busto had four good Marines with him. I couldn't afford to lose them too.

The door to the stairwell burst open, and an HCD soldier charged through, weapon raised. I squeezed off a burst of flechettes before he could fire, watching as the tiny metal darts tore through his body armor and sent him crumpling to the ground.

"Move!" I shouted to Chen, pulling her behind the bed of the pickup as more HCD troops flooded onto the roof.

Alvarez had taken position behind a nearby Honda Accord, her rifle barking in controlled bursts. Maria was somewhere to our left, her fire joining hers. The HCD forces spread out, using cars and concrete barriers for cover as they advanced.

I popped up to fire, then ducked back down as return fire pinged against the truck's body. My vision swam, the edges darkening. I pressed my hand to my side again and found it slick with fresh blood. The wound had reopened with the exertion.

My stomach cramped suddenly, a wave of nausea washing over me. Not good. Internal bleeding, most likely. My suit's medical systems were fighting a losing battle.

"Commander!" Alvarez called out. "I'm on my last mag!"

I checked my own ammunition—less than half a magazine left. Maria couldn't be doing much better. The gunfire was getting closer, HCD troops advancing under covering fire from their comrades.

Sixty seconds. Maybe less. That's all we had.

I looked at Dr. Chen, her face pale but composed. She'd known the risks when she agreed to come with us. Hell, she probably knew better than any of us what the HCD did to those who betrayed them.

"Doctor, I—" I began, intending to apologize for getting her into this mess, for failing to get her out.

The surrounding air suddenly throbbed, a deep

vibration that I felt in my chest more than heard. A blinding flash lit up the daylight, followed immediately by the deafening crack of railgun slugs hitting concrete. The entire rooftop shook as explosions blossomed where the HCD forces had been advancing moments before.

"What the hell?" I gasped, peering over the truck bed through clouds of concrete dust and smoke.

Alvarez was on her feet, cheering wildly. "Take that, *caras de culo*!"

I looked up and felt my jaw drop. A frigate-sized warship of Dominion design hovered overhead, its weapon systems fully engaged. The sleek vessel's point-defense lasers flashed repeatedly, picking off HCD soldiers with surgical precision while its main railguns demolished their cover. A second identical warship orbited further away, launching a brace of intercept missiles that streaked off toward some unseen target.

The first frigate descended toward our position, its ventral airlock opening as a boarding ramp extended to touch down on the garage roof. An igna in an armored walker marched down the ramp, the mechanical limbs moving with startling grace as it trained a heavy flechette rifle on the remaining HCD forces.

"Get your team inside!" the igna shouted, its voice amplified through external speakers.

I staggered to my feet, supporting myself against the truck. "Who the hell are you?"

The igna's capsule pulsed with blue-white energy as it replied: "Dominion Royal Guard, under direct orders from Queen Zeta. Now move!"

I signaled to Alvarez and Maria, who helped Dr. Chen up the ramp. I followed, stumbling slightly as my legs threatened to give out. The igna in the walker provided covering fire, the heavy flechette rifle cracking in sustained bursts that kept the regrouping HCD forces pinned down.

Once we were inside, the igna backed up the ramp, still firing. The airlock cycled shut behind us, and I felt the subtle shift in gravity as the frigate began to move.

We stood in a pristine, gleaming corridor that screamed "Dominion military" with its efficient design and subtle blue lighting. An igna officer—her capsule housed in a tetrahedral configuration that marked her as female—floated toward us.

"Lieutenant Loroso of the Dominion Royal Guard," she introduced herself, her plasma body pulsing with each word. "Welcome aboard the Royal Guard frigate *Dedicated.*"

I opened my mouth to respond, but the words wouldn't come. The adrenaline that had kept me going finally ebbed away, and darkness crept in from the edges of my vision. The last thing I saw before collapsing was Dr. Chen's concerned face leaning over me, her lips moving in words I couldn't hear.

27

I came to with the familiar antiseptic smell of an infirmary burning my nostrils and the distant drone of medical equipment humming in my ears. My side felt like someone had tried to carve a turkey with me as the main course. Before I could even pry my eyes open, I was already forming words, my throat sandpaper-dry but urgent. "My team. What happened to my team?" Typical Drake behavior—worried about everyone else while potentially bleeding out. Some leadership habits die hard.

"Commander Drake, welcome back to the land of the living." Nurse Kovac's no-nonsense voice cut through the fog in my head. She appeared at my bedside, her steel-gray bob framing a face that had perfected the art of professional compassion.

I tried to sit up, but a bolt of pain convinced me that was a terrible idea. "Busto? His squad? The extraction?" I croaked, my memories of the mission fragmented but alarming.

"Lieutenant Busto and his team were successfully

exfiltrated aboard one of the Royal Guard frigates," Kovac said, checking something on my monitor with practiced efficiency. "All personnel are accounted for and stable, excluding Specialist Diaz."

My stomach dropped. "Carlos?"

Kovac's expression softened almost imperceptibly. "Didn't make it. Took hostile fire covering the exfil. Two others wounded, including yourself. Everyone else is safe."

Carlos. Dammit. I closed my eyes for a moment, remembering the sacrifice the Marine made to save my team. Another name to carve into my mental wall of the fallen. We'd have to do a proper memorial when things settled down.

"And Sofia?" I asked, opening my eyes again. "Chief Kohl—how is she?"

"Still unconscious but stable," Kovac replied, her professional demeanor firmly back in place. "Dr. Chen is monitoring her condition."

Only then, with everyone else accounted for, did I finally think to ask, "What about me? How bad is it?"

Nurse Kovac almost smiled—almost. "Deep slicing wound to your left flank. Significant blood loss, but no vital organs compromised. We've closed and healed the lacerations using Dominion nanites and topped off your blood supply with donations from the base personnel. You're technically ready for duty, though I'd advise taking it easy for the next twelve hours. Your muscles are probably tender."

She could say that again. I nodded, making a mental note to find out who had donated blood. That was a debt I'd need to repay. "Thank you for your service, Nurse Kovac."

She gave a clipped nod and moved on to her next patient, efficient as always.

After convincing Kovac I was steady enough to move around—which involved a series of humiliating tests to prove I wasn't going to face-plant the moment I stood up—I made my way to the base's main office. My side ached with each step, the nanite healing leaving me whole but sensitive, like a fresh bruise stretched across my ribs.

I wished healing Sofia would be as easy as pumping her full of Dominion nanites. But apparently the human brain was too complex for existing nanites to operate on.

I found Destiny hunched over a tactical display, her curly black hair pulled back in a no-nonsense bun. When she looked up, her expression shifted from concentration to relief to irritation in the span of a second.

"Look who decided to rejoin the living," she said, straightening up. "How's that hole in your side? Got enough room to store snacks in there now?"

"Good to see you too, XO," I replied, easing myself into a chair across from her. "What's the sitrep on the Albatross shuttles?"

Her face darkened. "We encountered unexpected resistance from Kergan air defense units. Had to withdraw before we could reach the extraction point."

"So, who the hell pulled our asses out of the fire?" I asked, wincing as I shifted in my seat.

Destiny's lips quirked into a half-smile. "That would be our royal friend's entourage. Apparently, units of the Dominion Royal Guard followed Zeta all the way from the Ignisara System. They appeared at Wolf Jaw a few hours after your rescue mission kicked off."

I blinked. "Zeta ordered the Royal Guard here?"

"She commanded them to provide air cover for your rescue mission," Destiny confirmed. "Two frigates of the Royal Guard appeared just in time to extract you and

Busto's teams. Talk about dramatic timing."

I let out a low whistle. "Remind me to send Her Majesty a fruit basket or whatever the igna equivalent is. Maybe a small star?"

"The appropriate gift is probably your continued survival, which was very much in question," Destiny said, her tone sharpening. "I warned you we were rushing that mission, Kory. If the Royal Guard hadn't shown up when they did..."

Her words trailed off, but they didn't need to be finished. I knew exactly what would have happened. We'd all be dead or captured, with Dr. Chen back in Kergan hands and no hope for Sofia.

"You were right," I admitted, the words tasting like ashes in my mouth. "I pushed too hard, too fast. We got lucky."

Destiny looked genuinely surprised by my admission. "Did that head wound affect your brain? You never admit I'm right."

"Don't get used to it," I muttered, but the humor felt hollow. The reality of how close I'd come to getting over a dozen people killed—including myself—was settling in my gut like a lead weight. Some hotshot commander I was, nearly destroying the very team I was responsible for.

Destiny must have read something in my expression because her tone softened. "Hey, we got the doctor out. That's what matters."

"Speaking of which," I said, grateful for the change of subject, "where is Dr. Chen now?"

"In the library. She's turned it into her personal research lab," Destiny said with a roll of her eyes. "Books on one side, mysterious brain implants on the other. Very cozy."

I pushed myself to my feet, ignoring the protest from my

side. "I should go see what progress she's made with Sofia."

"Try not to bleed on any important documents," Destiny called after me as I headed for the door.

The library was a room intended for research and included both shelves of books and computer workstations. When I arrived, Dr. Eleanor Chen was bent over a table strewn with what looked like silver mechanical spiders and various medical displays showing technical data I couldn't begin to comprehend.

"Dr. Chen," I said by way of greeting.

She looked up, her sharp eyes assessing me through wire-rimmed glasses. "Commander Drake. I see your medical staff is quite competent. I'm glad you're up and about."

"How is your family settling in?" I asked, moving closer to examine the devices scattered across the table. Each one looked like a nightmarish cross between an insect and a circuit board.

She gave a dry laugh. "My husband's pretending he's not terrified. The girls are trying to make friends with every alien they see, and I'm just hoping none of them bring one home like a stray dog."

"What exactly are you doing here?" I asked, gesturing to the technological menagerie.

"Taking inventory," she replied simply, picking up one of the smaller devices and examining it under a magnifying glass. "Each implant has specific functions and compatibility parameters."

"Do you know the main reason I authorized that mission to rescue you?" I asked, cutting to the chase.

Chen set down the device carefully. "Yes, I do. Lieutenant Commander Austin briefed me on Chief Kohl's condition. The chronic subdural hematoma is causing her seizures, slurred speech, personality changes, and severe headaches."

"And can you help her?" I pressed.

"I am qualified to perform the necessary surgery," Chen confirmed. "However, I lack the proper surgical equipment. I've sent word to Wolf Jaw to see if they can scrounge up what I need."

"Which is?"

"At a minimum: a neurosurgical drill, cranial fixation plates, and a bipolar cautery," she listed off.

I gave her a blank look. "I have no idea what any of those are."

"Without those tools, operating on Chief Kohl's subdural hematoma would be reckless," Chen explained, turning back to her work. "I'm waiting for word from the town."

I felt a surge of frustration watching her calmly tinker with her devices while Sofia lay unconscious in the infirmary. "So you're just going to sit in here playing with your implants while Sofia is dying down the hall?"

Chen's eyes snapped up to mine, sharp and unflinching. "No, Commander. I am not 'playing.' I am monitoring Chief Kohl closely and have already altered her care regimen. Nurse Kovac is implementing my instructions precisely."

My temper flared. "My team risked their lives to get you out of that facility. Carlos Diaz gave his life for you. And now you're in here, comfortable and taking your sweet time while—"

"These," Chen interrupted, pointing at the devices before us, "may be necessary for saving Chief Kohl's life. That is why I am studying them."

That caught me off guard. "What do you mean?"

Chen picked up one of the implants—a silver-plated

spider-like thing safely contained in a protective plastic bag. "I made unauthorized modifications to many of these implants to make them compatible with human brains and to provide certain physiological benefits."

She held the bagged implant up to the light. "This particular model could help Chief Kohl's brain heal and might be necessary for the surgery."

I took an instinctive step back. "You want to put a machine in Sofia's brain? One based on Kergan tech that was originally designed for mindjacking?" My voice rose with each question. "Are you planning to mindjack her?"

Chen's expression hardened. "You're oversimplifying a complex topic, Commander. Yes, these implants can be used to enslave a human, but the same technology can also be used for a human's benefit. That's what I've been secretly doing at the Sacramento VA Medical Center for the last eighteen months."

She set the bagged implant down carefully. "I've been figuring out how to modify human mindjack implants to give them a backdoor that allows the host human to benefit instead of being enslaved. With the proper signals, a human with one of my backdoor-equipped implants can be easily freed and given extensive augmentations."

I felt myself calming down as I listened to her lecture, my initial anger giving way to a wary curiosity. Still, I moved closer, using my height to loom over her slightly. "I'm trusting Sofia's life to your hands, Doctor. And I have no way to confirm any of the claims you're making."

Chen looked up at me, unintimidated. "I would never lie about one of my patients, Commander Drake."

Then she did something unexpected. She rested her hands on my shoulders and spoke in a gentler tone. "I understand your concern. Chief Kohl means a great deal to you, and you've already been through so much. But I promise you, I am doing everything in my power to save her life."

Something about her words, the simple humanity in them after months of military jargon and crisis management, pierced straight through my defenses. I felt a sudden burning in my eyes and a tightness in my throat that I couldn't swallow away.

To my horror, I felt hot tears spill down my cheeks. I turned away quickly, embarrassed beyond words. A commanding officer crying in front of a civilian? Might as well hand in my rank insignia now.

"I'll let you proceed as planned," I said, my voice rough. "For now."

I left the library quickly, wiping my sleeve across my face, hating the weakness, but knowing it came from a place I couldn't—and maybe shouldn't—control. Sofia was everything to me, and the thought of losing her was the one thing that could crack my carefully maintained facade.

As I walked back toward the infirmary, I steeled myself. Sofia needed me to be strong, not falling apart. I would be there for her, whatever came next.

28

I sat in the hard plastic chair beside Sofia's bed, watching the gentle rise and fall of her chest. Her face pale but peaceful. The steady beep of the heart monitor had become the soundtrack to my vigil, a mechanical lullaby promising that she was still with me. I reached for her hand—it felt cool and lifeless in mine, so unlike the warm, firm grip I was used to. The distance between us felt vast, measured not in inches but in consciousness. I was right here next to her, and yet she was worlds away.

"Come on, Chief. The paperwork's piling up without you."

The monitor continued its rhythmic beeping, unimpressed by my attempt at humor. I rubbed my thumb across her knuckles, remembering how those same hands had once dispatched three Kergan Imperial Marines in under thirty seconds. Sofia Kohl was a force of nature when healthy—precise, efficient, unstoppable. Seeing her like this felt fundamentally wrong, like watching a lion caged and sedated.

I was about to reach for the water cup on her bedside table when I noticed her fingers twitch. At first, I thought it was my imagination—or maybe just my own pulse making her hand move. Then her eyelids fluttered.

"Sofia?" I leaned forward, hope surging through me.

The flutter became a tremor, spreading from her eyelids to her face, her neck, her shoulders. The heart monitor's beeping sped up, its steady rhythm deteriorating into a frantic, irregular staccato.

"Nurse Kovac!" I shouted, standing so quickly my chair crashed to the floor behind me. "Something's happening!"

Sofia's body went rigid, then convulsed violently. Foam appeared at the corners of her mouth, her eyes rolling back to show only white. The seizure was nothing like the previous ones—this was a full-system rebellion, her body at war with itself.

Nurse Kovac burst through the door with two medical techs in tow. "Move aside, Commander!" She shoved me roughly away from the bed as the team swarmed around Sofia.

"Tonic-clonic seizure," Kovac barked. "Duration?"

"Twenty seconds since I noticed," I responded automatically, military training kicking in despite my panic.

"Get me five of lorazepam," Kovac ordered one of the techs. "And padding for the rails."

I stood frozen, watching as they worked to protect Sofia from hurting herself, inserting a foam block between her teeth to prevent her from biting her tongue. The seizure continued, her body bucking against the restraints they hastily applied.

Then the heart monitor flatlined, its shrill, continuous tone cutting through the room like a knife.

"She's coding!" Kovac shouted. "Code Blue! Get the crash cart in here now!"

My blood turned to ice as the words registered. Code Blue. Cardiac arrest. Sofia's heart had stopped beating.

A team of four more medical personnel rushed in, pushing a cart loaded with emergency equipment. I was forced back against the wall, becoming part of the room's architecture as they fought for Sofia's life.

"Starting compressions," a male tech announced, positioning himself over Sofia's chest and beginning CPR. His movements were precise and mechanical, pressing down with enough force that I could hear the crack of her ribs. A necessary brutality.

"Push one of epi," Kovac ordered, her voice calm but urgent.

"Epi in," a female tech confirmed, injecting something into the IV line.

"Charge to 200," Kovac said, taking the defibrillator paddles from another tech.

"Charged to 200."

"Clear!"

Everyone stepped back from the bed as Kovac pressed the paddles to Sofia's chest. Sofia's body jerked upward with the shock, then fell back limp.

"Still asystole," someone reported, looking at the monitor.

"Continue compressions. Another round of epi, and charge to 300," Kovac directed.

The male tech resumed compressions, counting under his breath. I watched, paralyzed, as a human metronome tried to force life back into the woman I loved. My throat closed up, my vision narrowing to just Sofia's face, still and waxen under the harsh infirmary lights.

"Epi in."

"Charged to 300."

"Clear!"

Another shock. Another violent rise and fall of Sofia's body. The monitor remained stubbornly flat.

"Come on, Sofia," I whispered, my voice barely audible over the controlled chaos. "Fight."

"No response. Continue compressions. Let's intubate," Kovac decided.

A tech positioned herself at Sofia's head with a laryngoscope and endotracheal tube, working quickly to establish an airway. "Tube is in, confirming placement."

"Amiodarone 300 mg IV push," Kovac ordered. "And charge to 360."

I'd fought gangbangers in the street with nothing but a knife. I'd been in firefights, space battles, and hand-to-tentacle combat with marac marines. I'd faced death more times than I could count. But nothing had ever made me feel as helpless as this moment—watching Sofia die while a team of professionals used every trick in their arsenal to drag her back from the brink.

"Charged to 360."

"Clear!"

Another shock. The longest second of my life. Then—

Beep. Beep. Beep.

"We have sinus rhythm," someone announced, relief clear in their voice.

"BP coming up, 90 over 60," another reported.

"Pupils equal and reactive," the tech at Sofia's head added.

The room collectively exhaled. I realized I'd been holding my breath so long my lungs burned.

"She's back," Kovac confirmed, her professional

demeanor cracking just enough to reveal the human beneath. "For now."

Dr. Chen strode into the room then, her wire-rimmed glasses reflecting the overhead lights. She moved directly to Sofia's side, checking the monitors and examining her pupils herself.

"What happened?" she asked Kovac.

"Tonic-clonic seizure progressing to cardiac arrest," Kovac reported crisply. "Down for three minutes, forty seconds. Required three rounds of epi and three shocks at escalating voltage."

Chen's expression remained neutral, but I saw her fingers tighten on her tablet. "We can't afford another seizure like that."

"Agreed," Kovac said, looking pointedly at Sofia's vitals. "But we have no word on when the surgical equipment you requested will be found. And there's no other hospital we can move to—not with the Kergan patrols increasing since the rescue mission."

"I thought Zeta or Nicobe were going to fabricate the necessary instruments using the nanoforge," I said.

"There hasn't been time to get them the mechanical and electrical specifications," Kovac replied. "Just because we can name the device doesn't mean it shows up magically in their nanoforge database. They have to be told how to fabricate each instrument so the nanoforge can be programmed. I'm sorry."

I pushed away from the wall, finding my voice at last. "We need to do something," I said, my tone edged with desperation. "We're going to lose her."

Chen looked at me, then at Kovac, and finally back to Sofia. Her expression was contemplative, her mind clearly working through variables and probabilities. After what felt like an eternity, she nodded once, decisively.

"I'll work with what we have here," she said. "It's not ideal. Normally I'd have specialized drills and neuro-grade hemostatics, but..." she trailed off, studying Sofia's monitors. "If we don't act now, we risk permanent brain damage or death."

Chen turned to me, her gaze sharp and direct. "Do you understand how big of a risk we're taking with your partner's life?"

"I do," I replied without hesitation. "But it would be even riskier to do nothing."

Chen nodded, seeming satisfied with my answer. "You're right."

Kovac stepped forward. "What do you need, Doctor?"

Chen tapped her fingers on the nearby table, the staccato rhythm betraying her tension despite her calm demeanor. "An orthopedic drill, thoroughly sterilized. The smallest scalpels and forceps you have—they'll be crude compared to neurosurgical tools, but they'll have to do."

She continued listing items, each one painting a clearer picture of the improvised surgery they were about to attempt. "We don't have bipolar cautery, so we'll use monopolar on the lowest setting possible. Infection risk is high, so everything must be sterile. Triple-check each instrument."

Kovac was taking mental notes, her expression growing grimmer by the second.

"We lack an ICP monitor," Chen added, "so we'll have to use clinical signs, such as pupil response, to monitor intracranial pressure. It's primitive, but we'll manage."

The medical team dispersed to gather supplies, leaving me alone with Chen and Sofia for a moment.

"Will it work?" I asked quietly.

Chen didn't sugar-coat her response. "I don't know. But I've performed this procedure hundreds of times in optimal conditions. The principles remain the same, even if the tools are... suboptimal."

I nodded, appreciating her honesty. "Thank you for trying."

"Don't thank me yet," she replied, already focusing on the tablet in her hands. "If you want to be present for the surgery, you'll need to be dressed in sterile garments and stay completely out of the way. Can you do that?"

"Yes." I'd stand on my head in the corner if that's what it took to be there for Sofia.

The next hour was a blur of activity. Sofia was carefully transferred to the makeshift surgical theater—really just a repurposed exam room with better lighting. The small space was transformed with sterile drapes and makeshift equipment stands. I was ushered into a corner after being draped in a sterile gown, mask, and cap that made me look like a misplaced blue ghost.

Chen ordered another CT scan to pinpoint the exact location of the hematoma. The portable scanner hummed and clicked as it mapped the inside of Sofia's skull, revealing the dark pool of blood pressing against her brain.

Once the scan was complete, Nurse Kovac approached Sofia with a set of electric clippers. My heart clenched as she began shaving away Sofia's beautiful honey-blonde hair on one side, revealing a pale patch of scalp over the right side of her head.

"Standard craniotomy approach," Chen murmured, more to herself than anyone else. "Minimal disruption to surrounding tissue."

Kovac coated the exposed scalp with Betadine, the orange-brown liquid making Sofia look like some kind of tribal warrior with partial war paint. The smell of antiseptic grew stronger, mingling with the metallic scent of the surgical tools and the underlying hint of fear-sweat from everyone in the room.

Then Chen picked up a scalpel, and I had to force myself not to look away.

"Making initial incision," she announced, her hand steady as the blade bit into Sofia's skin.

A thin line of red appeared, tracing the path of the scalpel. Chen worked methodically, peeling back layers of skin and connective tissue to expose the skull beneath. Each layer was clamped back with small metal clips that reminded me absurdly of the binder clips Sofia used to organize our mission reports.

The orthopedic drill whined to life, its high-pitched scream making my teeth ache. Chen positioned it carefully against Sofia's exposed skull.

"Beginning burr hole," she said.

The drill bit ground against bone, producing a sound and smell I knew would haunt my nightmares—a combination of burning dust and something primal that triggered every evolutionary instinct to run. Fine white powder mixed with blood created a pinkish paste that Kovac continuously suctioned away.

Chen worked slowly, creating several small holes in Sofia's skull before using a different tool to connect them, essentially cutting a window into her head. The removed bone section was carefully placed in a sterile solution.

And then I could see it—Sofia's brain, pulsing gently beneath a thin, bulging membrane, the surface crisscrossed with blood vessels. Something about the sight was both mundane and miraculous. That wrinkled mass of tissue held everything that made Sofia who she was—her memories, her skills, her love for me.

"Dura looks intact," Chen observed, using a tiny instrument to delicately open the membrane covering the brain. "There's the hematoma."

I could see it too—a dark, swollen area beneath the surface, like an underwater shadow. Chen worked with impossible precision, using instruments that seemed comically large for such delicate work, yet somehow managing to navigate the microscopic landscape of Sofia's brain.

The smell in the room had changed—copper and salt from the blood, a faint electrical scent that might have been my imagination, and the continued sharp bite of antiseptic. The only sounds were the soft beep of monitors, the occasional metallic clink of instruments, and the whispered exchanges between Chen and her makeshift surgical team.

I stood perfectly still, barely breathing, as if any movement from me might disrupt the delicate procedure. My legs had gone numb hours ago, but I wouldn't have moved for anything.

Suddenly, Chen cursed—the first unprofessional thing I'd heard from her. "There's bridging vein damage extending further than the scan showed. The bleeding won't stop with conventional techniques."

She looked up at Kovac. "Get me the implant. The modified A7-series."

Kovac hesitated for only a fraction of a second before retrieving the spider-like device from a sterile container. Chen took it carefully, examining it under the surgical light.

"This is not how I planned to use this," she muttered, "but it's our best option for stopping the bleeding and preventing further damage."

I watched, my heart in my throat, as Chen positioned

the implant against Sofia's exposed brain. The metallic spider gleamed under the harsh lights, its legs seeming to flex of their own accord.

"Releasing adhesion protocol," Chen said, pressing something on the implant's center.

The thing came alive, its leg-like tendrils stretching and burrowing beneath the surface of Sofia's brain, seeking anchor points under her skull. It moved with disturbing organic fluidity for something mechanical, settling into place until it sat flush against her brain tissue, nearly invisible except for a small silver disc at its center.

"Implant is self-embedding," Chen reported. "Get me another CT to confirm placement."

The portable scanner was repositioned, and we all held our breath as it completed another scan. Chen studied the results on her tablet, her expression unreadable.

"Placement is optimal," she finally said. "The implant is already forming connections with the damaged vessels. Bleeding is slowing."

Over the next hour, Chen meticulously closed the various layers of Sofia's head—replacing the skull section, suturing the dura and other membranes, closing the scalp with neat stitches that would leave only a thin scar hidden by her hair when it grew back.

By the time the final bandage was placed, the tension in the room had shifted from desperate to cautiously hopeful. Sofia's vitals remained stable throughout the procedure, and there were no further seizures.

"Administer 2 grams of ceftriaxone IV," Chen instructed Kovac as Sofia was transferred back to the recovery area. "And continue the anti-seizure medication at current dosage. She'll need to remain in the medically induced coma until we're sure the bleeding has completely stopped and the swelling has subsided."

I followed them back to Sofia's room, my legs wobbly after standing for so many hours. Sofia looked somehow smaller with her partially shaved head and the white bandage wrapped around it, but her color was better, and the monitors showed steady, strong readings.

"How long until she wakes up?" I asked Chen, my voice rough from disuse.

"At least 48 hours," she replied, checking Sofia's pupils one last time. "Maybe longer. We need to give her brain time to heal."

I nodded, sinking into the chair beside Sofia's bed. The adrenaline was wearing off, leaving me hollow and exhausted.

Chen rested a hand briefly on my shoulder. "Get some rest, Commander. There's nothing more you can do for her right now."

"I'm fine," I lied automatically.

Chen's expression told me she wasn't buying it. "You've been through a traumatic experience and you're still recovering from your own injuries. Your body needs sleep to heal, just like hers does."

I wanted to argue, but my eyelids felt like they had weights attached to them. "Just for a few hours," I conceded. "And someone comes to get me if anything changes."

"Of course," Chen agreed. "Now go."

I stood reluctantly, leaning down to press a gentle kiss to Sofia's forehead, careful to avoid the bandages. "See you soon, Chief," I whispered.

As I walked back to my quarters, I tried not to think about the metallic spider now living inside Sofia's head, or what it might mean for her when she woke up. For now, it was enough that she would wake up at all. The rest we could figure out together.

29

I counted Sofia's breaths like they were my own lifeline. Two days had passed since Dr. Chen had drilled into her skull and installed that Kergan implant, and still Sofia floated in some twilight world between consciousness and whatever dark corner comas occupy. My fingers had gone numb from holding her hand, but I felt a persistent ache in my chest—not guilt exactly, but something adjacent to it, as if I'd somehow failed to protect her from this moment.

The medical bay in Wolf Jaw Base wasn't exactly state-of-the-art, but it was clean and functional, with just enough equipment to serve as an adequate field hospital. The walls were the generic white that was supposed to make everything appear clean and pure. The soft beeping of the monitors provided a rhythm that was both comforting and maddening.

"Her vitals are stabilizing nicely," Dr. Chen said on her third visit that morning, checking the monitors with practiced efficiency. "The implant is integrating with her neural pathways as expected."

"But will she wake up?" I asked for what must have been the hundredth time.

Dr. Chen gave me the same measured look she'd been giving me since the surgery. "Commander, the brain is complex. We won't know the extent of any damage until she regains consciousness."

I nodded, because what else could I do? There were military operations I could plan, the rebuild of *Thunder* I could supervise, but this—waiting, hoping—was beyond my control. And I hated it.

"You should go back to work," Dr. Chen suggested, not unkindly. "You have other people who depend on you."

"It's fine," I lied.

Her expression told me she didn't believe me, but she didn't push. After adjusting Sofia's IV, she left me alone with the beeping monitors and my thoughts.

When the pressure of the waiting room became too much, I'd occasionally step out to check on *Thunder*'s progress. It gave me something to focus on besides the endless tick of the clock and Sofia's unchanging face.

Zeta and Nicobe had transformed the underground hangar into something between a shipyard and a science experiment. They had stripped *Thunder*'s familiar hull completely away, the exposed inner structure now encased in an undulating mass of nanobots that resembled nothing so much as a ship-shaped blob of silver jelly. The sight was both fascinating and unsettling.

"Zeta is pleased by the progress of the vessel," the igna queen announced as I approached. She hovered in her octahedral containment unit, the plasma of her form shifting in patterns of satisfaction.

"It's... bigger," I observed, noting how the ship's frame was being extended at both ends.

"The vessel requires additional capacity for integrating advanced propulsion and defense systems," she explained. "Zeta has determined that the increased size is optimal for the missions that await."

I tried to care about propulsion systems and mission capabilities, but my mind kept drifting back to the medical bay. "How much longer until she's flight-ready?"

"Approximately ten Earth days," Zeta replied. "Perhaps less if resources are prioritized effectively."

I nodded absently, already turning back toward the corridor that led to the medical bay. "Keep me updated."

"Zeta wishes to express her concern for Sofia Kohl," she called after me, her formal tone softening slightly. "The human's recovery is important to the mission and to you."

"Thank you," I managed, surprised by the gesture. Sometimes I forgot that beneath all that plasma and formality, Zeta had something approximating a heart.

Back in the medical bay, I resumed my post by Sofia's bed, continuing my vigil. I must have dozed off at some point because a small sound jerked me awake—a sigh, different from the steady breathing I'd been listening to for days.

Sofia's eyelids fluttered.

I leaned forward, my own breath caught in my throat. "Sofia?"

Her eyes opened slowly, unfocused at first, then gradually finding my face. There was confusion there, but recognition too.

"Kory?" Her voice was a cracked whisper.

I hit the call button for Dr. Chen so hard I nearly broke it, then took Sofia's hand in mine. "I'm here. You're in Wolf Jaw Base. You had surgery."

She blinked several times, processing. "My head hurts."

I laughed, a sound that was half relief and half something close to hysteria. "Yeah, that happens when someone drills into your skull."

Dr. Chen arrived at a run, pushing me aside to examine Sofia, checking her pupils with a penlight and running through a series of quick neurological tests.

"Can you tell me your name?" she asked.

"Sofia Kohl," came the reply, stronger now.

"Do you know where you are?"

"Wolf Jaw Base. Kory just told me." A hint of Sofia's usual precision was there, which made my heart leap.

"Do you know what year it is?"

Sofia answered correctly, then followed Dr. Chen's finger with her eyes, squeezed hands, and answered several more questions about her background and recent events.

"Remarkably well," Dr. Chen concluded, allowing herself a small smile. "The surgery appears to have been successful, and your initial neurological responses are excellent. You'll need to remain under observation, but I'm cautiously optimistic."

Sofia nodded slightly, then winced at the movement. "What about the seizures?"

"The implant should prevent them by regulating the pressure and neural activity. We'll monitor you closely, but I believe the worst is behind you."

I could have kissed Dr. Chen at that moment. Instead, I squeezed Sofia's hand and felt her squeeze back, weaker than normal but definitely there.

The next few days passed in a blur of improvement. Sofia recovered with the same focused determination she approached everything in life. By the third day, she was sitting up and having full conversations. By the fifth, she was insisting on walking short distances around the medical bay, with me hovering anxiously at her side.

But along with the recovery came something unexpected—the flashbacks.

The first episode happened during lunch on the fourth day. We were in her room in the infirmary talking about *Thunder*'s redesign when Sofia suddenly went rigid, her eyes unfocused.

"There's a room," she whispered. "Gray walls. A Kergan officer—I don't know his rank—talking to humans in strange uniforms. They're looking at maps of something underground."

"Describe the uniforms the humans are wearing," I said.

"Black military uniforms with blue armbands."

"HCD," I said. Sofia had likely never seen a member of the HCD before. How was she seeing one now?

Then, as quickly as it came, the vision passed, and she blinked at me in confusion.

"Sofia?" I prompted.

"I've never seen that place," she said, her voice shaking slightly. "I've never seen those people. But it felt like... like a memory."

I reported it to Dr. Chen, who examined Sofia again but found nothing physically concerning. "It could be a side effect of the trauma or the medication," she suggested, but I caught a flicker of something—worry, guilt?—in her eyes.

The visions and flashbacks continued and intensified. Sometimes they were brief flashes—a Kergan data terminal, an unfamiliar face, a snippet of conversation in a language Sofia didn't speak but somehow understood. Other times they were longer, more coherent—a secret meeting in what looked like a repurposed human office building, HCD officers discussing deployment patterns, a Kergan scientist explaining something about human neural compatibility.

After a particularly intense episode that left Sofia shaking and disoriented, I cornered Dr. Chen in the small office that Lynda Brooks had found for her.

"What the hell is happening to her?" I demanded, closing the door behind me with more force than necessary.

Dr. Chen's calm medical demeanor slipped for a moment. She looked tired, the weight of her captivity and forced work with the HCD showing in the lines around her eyes.

"It's the implant," she admitted after a long pause.

"I figured that much out myself. What I want to know is why, and whether it's going to get worse."

She sighed and gestured for me to sit. I remained standing.

"The implant I gave Sofia isn't just a standard neural regulator," she explained, her voice low. "It's a modified version of one that the HCD was developing for their highest-level human collaborators—a way to access and store sensitive information directly in the brain."

My blood ran cold. "You put HCD tech in Sofia's head? Without telling us?"

"I had limited options," Dr. Chen countered. "The standard implants wouldn't have been powerful enough to manage her condition. This one was the most advanced neural interface I had access to. It was capable of far more precise regulation than anything else available."

"So you decided to experiment on her."

"I decided to save her life," Dr. Chen shot back, a rare flash of emotion breaking through her professional facade. "The implant I chose was the one with the highest chance of success."

I leaned across her desk. "And you didn't think to mention that it might come with a side of Kergan brainwashing?"

"It's not brainwashing," she said firmly. "The implant contains a secure HCD database—I knew that—but it was supposed to be dormant. The data was encrypted and isolated from the therapeutic functions."

"Well, it's clearly not dormant now," I growled.

Dr. Chen nodded. "The encryption appears to be breaking down as the implant integrates with her neural pathways. The database is slowly decrypting and... interacting with her consciousness."

"Blazes." I ran a hand through my hair. "So you recklessly dumped this—this thing—into my partner's brain, and now she's having visions of HCD secret meetings? What happens when the encryption fails completely? Will she become some kind of HCD sleeper agent?"

"No," Dr. Chen said quickly. "That's not how it works. The implant can't override her consciousness or free will. It's just... sharing information."

"Information that could be dangerous for her to have. Information that could put a target on her back if the HCD ever finds out."

"I made a choice in an emergency situation," Dr. Chen said, her voice tight. "Sofia was dying. The seizures were increasing in frequency and severity. I used the most capable tool I had available. Would you rather I had let her die instead?"

That stopped me short. The anger was still there, but beneath it was the undeniable truth that Sofia was alive because of Dr. Chen's decision.

"What are the consequences going to be?" I asked, my voice lower now. "Long-term. What does this mean for her?"

"I don't know," Dr. Chen admitted. "This is unprecedented. The implant was never meant to be used this way. We'll have to wait and see what information emerges and how her brain processes it."

"Can it be removed?"

"Technically, yes. Practically..." She shook her head. "The implant has already integrated with her neural tissue. Removing it now would likely cause significant damage—possibly worse than what we were treating in the first place."

I closed my eyes, trying to process everything. "So we're stuck with it."

"For now, yes. But Sofia is strong, and her mind is resilient. She's young and healthy. She's already adapting to the flashbacks. And there may be unexpected benefits—the database could contain valuable intelligence about Kergan and HCD operations."

"She's not a damn intelligence asset," I snapped. "She's a person who deserved to know what was being put in her head."

Dr. Chen held my gaze. "In an ideal world, yes. But we're at war, Commander. Sometimes the choice isn't between right and wrong—it's between risky and certain death."

I wanted to argue further, to rage against the impossible situation, but what would be the point? The implant was there, integrated into Sofia's brain, decrypting its secrets bit by bit. The only path now was forward.

"If anything changes—anything at all—you tell me immediately," I said. "And you explain everything to Sofia. She deserves to know."

Dr. Chen nodded. "Of course."

I left her office feeling like I'd lost a battle I didn't even know I was fighting. Sofia was alive and recovering, but at what cost? Only time would tell, and waiting had never been my strong suit.

30

Sofia ran her palm over her freshly shaved scalp, fingertips lingering on the raised line of the surgical scar. A week had passed since she'd woken up, and the physical recovery had been remarkable—Dr. Chen's implant had done its job, at least where the seizures were concerned. The mental side effects were another matter entirely. "Think I should grow it back or keep it like this?" she asked, turning to catch my reflection in the small bathroom mirror. Our eyes met, and despite everything—the base, the war, the alien tech in her head—I felt that familiar pull between us, like gravity but far less predictable.

"I loved your hair," I admitted, coming up behind her and placing my hands gently on her shoulders. "But this has a certain... intensity to it."

She snorted. "That's diplomatic. I look like a recruit on day one of bootcamp."

The truth was, without her long blonde hair framing her face, Sofia looked different—younger somehow, more vulnerable. The sharp angles of her cheekbones stood out prominently, and her blue eyes seemed larger, more luminous. The scar itself was thin but angry red, curving from just above her ear to disappear into her hairline—or where her hairline would have been.

"You look like you could kick my ass," I said, and she rewarded me with a small smile.

"I always could kick your ass, Kory. The hair was just a distraction." She turned away from the mirror with a sigh. "It's going to take years to grow back."

"We've got time," I said, though in truth, time felt like the one commodity we couldn't count on anymore. Not with the Kergans occupying Earth, not with Sofia experiencing increasingly vivid flashbacks from the HCD database in her head, not with the constant pressure of knowing we were some of the few forces actively fighting back.

She must have read something in my expression because she reached up and squeezed my hand where it rested on her shoulder. "I had another one this morning," she said quietly.

"A flashback?"

She nodded. "I saw a facility—somewhere in what used to be eastern Europe, I think. They were testing something on human subjects. Something about neural compatibility with Kergan tech." She shuddered. "It was clearer than before. I could read documents, understand conversations."

I tried not to show my concern. "Did you tell Dr. Chen?"

"Yes. She took more scans. Says the integration is progressing faster than she expected." Sofia turned to face me, her expression determined. "But I'm fine, Kory. These are just... recordings. They can't hurt me."

I wasn't so sure about that, but I nodded anyway. "Movie night still on?"

Her smile returned, small but genuine. "Wouldn't miss

it. Busto threatened to make us watch a documentary on ancient Roman battle tactics if we're late."

"Well, we can't have that," I said, matching her lighter tone. Some semblance of normalcy, even if just for an evening, seemed suddenly precious.

As we descended to the lower levels of the base, we passed dozens of unfamiliar faces. Commander Brooks and her team had brought in a wave of new recruits over the past week, gearing up to crew the rebuilt *Thunder*. They were raw, barely trained—but they were our future. It was good to see them and I stopped to shake hands with a few and ask about them.

The recreation room was the closest thing Wolf Jaw Base had to a living room, and someone—probably Phoebe, who could make a bunker feel like a bed-and-breakfast—had worked her magic. She'd scattered mismatched cushions across the benches, draped a couple of throw blankets with heroic optimism, and somehow coaxed a handful of scrappy plants to thrive under the sterile glare of artificial lighting. The centerpiece was a battered but beloved large screen, acquired in a trade with a local civilian who'd driven a hard bargain—apparently, antibiotics had more street value than entertainment.

Destiny was already sprawled across one end of the sectional like she owned it, her legs somehow managing to occupy three times the space her body logically allowed. The initial meeting between her and Sofia after Sofia's recovery had gone surprisingly well—suspiciously well, in fact. The two of them had slipped into easy conversation within minutes, like long-lost co-conspirators finally reunited.

I knew I was doomed the moment I heard them laughing and trading stories about my allegedly "quirky" habits—like how I organize ration packs by color, or that time I tried to fix a power relay with chewing gum and optimism.

Destiny tossed a kernel of popcorn into her mouth when she saw us. "Well, if it isn't my favorite invalid and her nursemaid."

"Careful," Sofia warned, lowering herself onto the middle of the sofa with only a slight wince. "This invalid might still kick your ass."

"Not in movie night jurisdiction," Destiny countered, shifting her legs just enough to make room. "In here, I'm the admiral of entertainment."

"God help us all," I muttered, dropping down next to Sofia and letting my arm rest casually behind her.

Phoebe arrived next, carrying what looked like homemade cookies on a tray. "Special occasion," she explained when she saw my raised eyebrows. "Our Sofia with her fancy new haircut deserves proper refreshments."

"It's not a haircut, it's a scalping," Sofia corrected, but she reached for a cookie with genuine appreciation.

Busto was the last to arrive, punctual to the second, as always. He wore the standard military-issue off-duty clothes, but somehow still managed to look like he was in uniform. "Kory," he nodded to me, then to my partner. For once, he dropped the formalities. Tonight, instead of UHC officers, we were simply a group of friends. "Sofia. Good to see you vertical."

"Good to be vertical, Clemen," Sofia replied. Busto had tried—so far unsuccessfully—to get Sofia to call him Busto. He complained that only his mother called him "Clemen."

With everyone assembled, Destiny hit play, and the familiar opening of *The Incredibles*—a movie we'd watched enough times that it had become a group ritual rather than entertainment—filled the screen.

"'I never look back, darling,'" Destiny and Phoebe quoted

in unison with Edna Mode, "'it distracts from the now.'"

Even Busto, who pretended to be above such things, murmured, "No capes," at the appropriate moment, earning a delighted cackle from Destiny.

As the movie progressed, I watched my crew—my friends—more than the screen. Destiny with her razor-sharp wit and infectious laugh. Phoebe, who noticed everything and found joy in the smallest details. Busto, whose stern exterior hid a deep loyalty to all of us. And Sofia beside me, alive, healing, her shoulder pressed against mine.

A year ago, I had been in Astrithon, a human thrust into the complex politics of the Collective Dominion. I'd been alone, separated from everything familiar, fighting battles I barely understood. Now, sitting here with these people who had become my family, I felt a contentment that seemed almost dangerous in its completeness.

Sofia's hand found mine in the dim light, our fingers intertwining. It was a small gesture, but it grounded me—reminded me of what we were fighting for. Not just survival, but moments like this. The right to sit in a room with people you love and laugh at a movie you've seen a dozen times before.

The explosion ripped through that moment like tissue paper.

The floor beneath us vibrated violently, and a dull boom echoed through the base. We all froze, the movie continuing its cheerful soundtrack in surreal contrast to our sudden tension.

Then the base alarm blared—three short bursts followed by one long, the signal for an internal security breach.

"What the—" Destiny was already on her feet.

"Security stations," I ordered, military training kicking in instantly. "Now!"

We scattered. Sofia moved to follow me, but I caught her arm. "Medical bay," I said firmly. "You're still recovering."

Her eyes flashed with that stubborn determination I knew so well. "I'm fine, Kory."

"That's an order, Chief," I said, hating myself for pulling rank but unwilling to risk her safety.

Something that might have been hurt crossed her face, but she nodded curtly. "Aye, sir."

There was no time to smooth it over. I was running for the control room, the sound of distant gunfire spurring me faster. The corridors of Wolf Jaw Base, usually so orderly, were now filled with personnel moving purposefully to battle stations, their faces tight with the controlled focus of trained military.

The control room door slid open at my approach. Inside, Lieutenant Commander Lynda Brooks stood at the central console, her thin frame radiating tension as she directed the base's response. Technicians worked frantically at monitoring stations, their faces illuminated by the blue glow of screens.

"Report," I demanded, moving to stand beside her.

Lynda's eyes were fixed on the main tactical display. "Security breach, D-sector. Marine detachment responding." Her voice was clipped, professional, but I could hear the strain underneath.

Another burst of gunfire, closer this time, made several technicians flinch.

"Hostiles?"

"Unknown number. We lost visual in that sector when the first explosion hit." She tapped a command, bringing up a different view. "Possible sabotage of internal systems as well. We're getting anomalous readings from the hangar."

"The hangar?" My thoughts immediately went to *Thunder*, still under renovation. "What kind of readings?"

Before she could answer, the gunfire outside the control room intensified, then abruptly ceased. The sudden silence was almost more unnerving than the shooting had been.

The door slid open again, and Busto strode in, transformed from the off-duty officer of minutes ago. He was encased in protomatter armor, the matte black fabric clinging to his muscular frame like a second skin. The helmet was retracted, showing his grim face, but the diamond visor was visible as a thin ring around his neck, ready to deploy in microseconds. The flechette rifle in his hands looked oversized, but he carried it with the easy familiarity of an extension of his body.

"Lieutenant," I acknowledged, relieved to see him. "Status?"

"Hostiles neutralized," he reported, his voice carrying that particular calm that only came from years of combat experience. "One enemy KIA, two of ours wounded, stable."

"Enemy?" Lynda pressed.

Busto's expression hardened. "Private Blazek. Security team B."

The news hit like a physical blow. "One of ours?"

"Not anymore," Busto said grimly. "Placed an explosive device on the hangar hatch mechanism. Wounded Specialist Han and Private Tobin before we took him down."

Lynda's face went pale. "Sabotage."

"We've been compromised," Busto confirmed.

"But why the hangar specifically?" I asked, though I was beginning to form a sickening theory.

Lynda turned back to the tactical display, her fingers flying over the controls. The screen shifted to an external view, showing the terrain surrounding Wolf Jaw Base. What I saw made my blood run cold.

Dozens of heat signatures were moving toward the base from multiple directions. The movement patterns were too coordinated, too purposeful to be anything but a military operation.

"That's why," Lynda said softly. "We've been betrayed."

"HCD?" I asked, though I already knew the answer.

"And Kergan support units," she confirmed, highlighting several larger signatures moving more slowly behind the human forces. "Blazek must have been their inside man. The hangar hatch is jammed shut—we can't launch shuttles or deploy *Thunder*."

The realization hit me like a physical blow. They knew about *Thunder*. They knew where we were. And they had just sealed our most powerful asset underground like a cork in a bottle. Not that *Thunder* could fly yet, but we couldn't launch our shuttles to provide air cover.

"Commander Brooks," I said, falling back on formal address to mask my racing thoughts, "initiate base defense protocols and try to get that hangar hatch unjammed. I need to speak with Zeta."

"Yes, sir," she responded, already turning to relay orders.

I sprinted for the hangar, pushing past personnel rushing to defensive positions. The corridors seemed endless, my mind calculating options and finding too few that ended with all of us surviving.

The hangar was a hive of activity when I arrived. The explosion had left the massive hatch door visibly damaged, its hydraulic systems sparking and spitting fluid. A thin smoke hung in the air. Engineers were already swarming over the hatch, but one look told me it wouldn't be opening anytime soon.

Thunder dominated the center of the space, dramatically changed from the ship I'd once commanded. Her sleek form had nearly doubled in length, the outer hull restored but now stretched to accommodate new systems. The surface gleamed with the distinctive sheen of recently formed armor plates, sections still showing the swirling patterns of nanobots completing final adjustments.

Zeta's octahedral containment unit hovered near what would be the bridge, directing the final phases of reconstruction.

"Zeta!" I called, jogging toward her. "We need *Thunder* flying. Now."

The plasma within her container shifted in a pattern of concern. "Commander Drake, Queen Zeta regrets to inform you that *Thunder* is not yet prepared for flight operations. The power distribution systems remain incomplete, and critical propulsion elements are still being integrated."

"We don't have time for incomplete," I said urgently. "The base is under attack. HCD and Kergan forces are inbound, and they've trapped us down here. We need options."

Zeta's form pulsed thoughtfully. "The vessel's structural integrity is sound, and the navigational systems are operational. Primary weapons are at approximately sixty percent capacity." She paused, calculations almost visible in the shifting patterns of her plasma. "A partial launch may be possible, though with significant risk."

"Define 'significant,'" I pressed.

"Power fluctuations could result in system failures during flight. Weapons targeting may be unreliable. And without full propulsion capability, maneuverability will be severely compromised."

Not great odds, but better than being sitting ducks. "Make it happen. We need *Thunder* ready to fly the moment that hatch opens—if it opens."

"Zeta will prioritize essential systems," she agreed, already directing nearby technicians with precise instructions.

I hurried back to the control room, where the tactical situation had deteriorated further. The enemy forces were now visible on multiple surveillance feeds, HCD troops in their distinctive black armor moving in practiced formations, backed by the hulking forms of Kergan armored units.

"They're jamming our communications," Lynda reported as I entered. "We can't get a signal out to warn other resistance forces."

"Status on the hangar hatch?"

"Engineering says the explosion severed the main hydraulic lines and fused the emergency release mechanisms. They're working on it, but..." She didn't need to finish the sentence. We both knew what "working on it" meant when facing an imminent assault.

"Defensive positions?"

"All personnel deployed. External turrets are online and engaging distant targets." As if to emphasize her point, the base shuddered slightly as the automated defense systems opened fire.

I moved to the tactical display, studying the enemy approach. The pattern was clear now—this wasn't just an attack; it was an encirclement operation. They weren't trying to destroy the base; they wanted to capture it. Capture us.

"They know about *Thunder*," I hissed. "The sabotage, the jamming of the hangar—this entire operation is designed to trap *Thunder* underground and intact."

Lynda's eyes widened with understanding. "The technological advantage..."

"Would be devastating if they captured her," I finished. "Especially with Zeta's rebuild."

The base shuddered again as the turrets fired another salvo. On the screens, I could see the first wave of HCD troops taking cover, but more were moving up behind them. They had numbers and time on their side.

"We need to hold them off until we can get that hatch open," I said, already formulating a plan. "And if we can't open it..."

"Sir?" Lynda prompted.

I met her gaze steadily. "Then we need to make sure *Thunder* never falls into enemy hands."

The implication hung in the air between us—a last resort that neither of us wanted to contemplate. But before the moment could stretch further, the tactical display flashed with new warnings as the enemy launched their first coordinated assault on our outer defenses.

The battle for Wolf Jaw Base had begun, and with it, a desperate race against time.

31

The tactical screen showed a sea of red dots swarming toward our position like digital ants to a picnic. Wolf Jaw Base had been compromised three different ways before breakfast, and now we were looking at enough Kergan firepower to turn our little mountain hideout into a smoking crater. I drummed my fingers on the edge of the console, my mind racing through a catalog of terrible options.

"Commander Brooks," I said, forcing my voice into something resembling calm authority, "what happened to the Royal Guard frigates that followed Queen Zeta to Earth? The ones that helped us rescue Dr. Chen?"

Lynda Brooks straightened slightly. The fine lines around her eyes deepened as she answered.

"The frigates were scouting for a location to construct a Dominion base somewhere in the Sol system, sir. Last communication indicated they were evaluating certain near-Earth asteroids, but that was days ago." She hesitated. "I don't have their current coordinates."

I nodded, trying not to let disappointment show. Those

warships had firepower that could even the odds against what was bearing down on us. "Issue a distress call over the syderealdyne transceiver. Request immediate assistance and transmit our tactical situation."

"Yes, sir." Brooks' fingers flew over her console, the blue light illuminating her aging face. Her brown hair—more steel than brown these days—was pulled back in a regulation bun that hadn't moved a millimeter despite the base's state of alert.

I reached for the intercom controls. "Queen Zeta, this is Commander Drake. What's the status of *Thunder*?"

There was a pause before Zeta's distinct, formal voice resonated through the speakers. "The Queen and Nicobe have identified a method to restore *Thunder* to flight capability. However, it will require the Queen and Nicobe to interface directly with the vessel's power systems to energize critical components that remain incomplete."

I leaned closer to the speaker. "And the risks?"

"The procedure would temporarily immobilize both the Queen and Nicobe. Should *Thunder* sustain damage during this period, we would be unable to disengage without significant harm to our plasma forms."

Great. Just great. I suppressed a sigh. "Do what you need to do, Your Majesty. We're running out of options here."

"The Queen understands. We shall begin immediately."

The intercom clicked off as I returned my attention to the tactical display. The red mass had grown, spreading out to encircle our position. HCD infantry supported by Kergan armored walkers—a full-scale assault force with enough firepower to punch through our mountain bunker in hours, not days.

The command room door hissed open, and Destiny Austin strode in like she owned the place. Her curly black hair was pulled back from her face, and her dark eyes quickly assessed the tactical display before landing on me.

"Well, we're royally screwed," she announced without preamble, leaning against the console next to Brooks. Despite her small stature, Destiny always managed to fill a room with her presence.

"Thanks for the tactical assessment, XO," I replied dryly. "Any constructive suggestions?"

Destiny's expression turned serious. "The base is completely compromised, Kory. Even if we somehow beat back this attack, which—" she gestured toward the screen, "—seems highly unlikely, they'll just come back with more. Probably within days."

"So, what do you suggest?"

"We evacuate. Now." Her voice was firm, her eyes unwavering.

I spread my hands. "And go where, exactly? In case you hadn't noticed, we're a little short on friendly territory these days."

"I don't know," she admitted. "But not here. Here is definitely about to become a smoking hole in the ground."

Before I could respond, an alarm blared from the tactical system. Brooks' fingers raced across her console.

"New contact!" she called out. "Coming in fast from high orbit!"

My stomach clenched. Another enemy force? But then Brooks' face transformed, the grim line of her mouth shifting into disbelief.

"It's... it's one of the Royal Guard frigates, sir!"

The overhead screen shifted to show a real-time feed from our remaining external cameras. The sleek, elliptical shape of a Dominion warship streaked through the sky, its gleaming hull catching the morning sunlight. Before I could even process its arrival, lances of brilliant energy erupted from its weapons ports.

The effect on the approaching enemy was immediate and devastating. A Kergan armored walker took a direct hit through its cylindrical torso, the impact sending a white-hot flash across the screen. The walker exploded in a shower of burning debris, raining down on the HCD infantry formations below. Hypervelocity railgun slugs slammed into the terrain with mathematical precision, each impact vaporizing rock and flesh alike, leaving behind craters large enough to swallow a semi-truck.

The command room erupted in cheers as the display showed enemy formations breaking apart, their neat tactical formations dissolving into chaos. The Royal Guard frigate moved with an elegant brutality, systematically targeting the largest concentrations of enemies.

"Second contact!" Brooks called out, her voice rising with excitement. "The other Royal Guard frigate just dropped out of high atmosphere!"

The second warship appeared on our displays, taking up a patrol pattern overhead, its weapons systems tracking any movement below. Between the two of them, they'd established complete air superiority over the battlefield.

I slapped my palm against the console, allowing myself a moment of pure relief. "They've bought us time. If we can get the hangar hatch operational, we can fly *Thunder* out of here." I turned to Brooks. "What's the status on that hatch?"

Brooks pressed her comm unit to her ear. "Engineering reports they should have it operational within fifteen minutes, sir."

"Good. Start loading base personnel onto *Thunder*." I turned to Destiny. "I need you to get to *Thunder* and prep it for flight. I'll meet you there after I get to medical."

Destiny nodded sharply. "On it."

"Commander Brooks," I continued, "coordinate the evacuation and keep me updated on the enemy situation. Those frigates won't be able to hold them off forever."

"Yes, sir." Brooks was already on the comm, her voice steady as she began issuing orders.

I sprinted from the control room, my boots echoing down the corridor as the base PA system crackled to life behind me: "Attention all personnel, this is a mandatory evacuation order. Proceed immediately to the hangar bay for transport. This is not a drill. Repeat, proceed immediately to the hangar bay for transport."

As I ran, my mind raced. *Thunder* wasn't completed yet —we'd only managed to restore about sixty percent of her systems before the Kergans found us. With all the base personnel, she'd be packed to capacity and beyond. I just hoped her newly expanded hull configuration could handle the load. The reconstruction had doubled her internal space, but many internal systems were still exposed, waiting for components we hadn't yet had time to install.

I rounded the corner into medical, nearly colliding with Nurse Kovac, who stood like a sentinel outside the infirmary waiting room.

"Commander," she acknowledged with professional crispness.

"We're evacuating," I said between breaths. "Get your patients and staff to the hangar immediately. Priority on Dr. Chen—the Kergans want her back in the worst way. Don't forget her family."

Kovac nodded, her steel-gray bob swinging with the motion. "We've already begun preparations. Dr. Chen is gathering her research materials and has her husband and daughters with her."

I moved past her into the waiting room where Sofia sat.

"Time to go, dear," I called to her.

She looked up, her blue eyes finding mine.

"I heard the announcement." She rose and placed her hand on my shoulder, her touch steadying both of us. "I'm ready."

We joined the flow of medical personnel making their way toward the hangar. Dr. Chen walked ahead of us, her family in tow, each carrying a slim case or other article.

"We need to get to the armory first," I told Sofia, guiding her down a side corridor. I didn't want to go into battle unprepared.

The armory was deserted, the weapons racks already picked clean by the base security teams. I punched my code into the protomatter storage locker, and the door slid open to reveal the black, fluid-looking suits inside.

We stripped efficiently, the cold air raising goosebumps on my skin as I pulled off my uniform. The protomatter armor felt alive as I stepped into it, the nanobots adjusting to my body contours, sealing seams and hardening in strategic locations while remaining flexible at the joints. Sofia struggled briefly with her suit, and I moved to help her, holding her steady as the black carbon nanobots flowed up her body.

The diamond helmet formed around my head, the heads-up display blinking to life with system diagnostics. We looked at each other through our faceplates, two black-clad figures ready for battle.

"Let's move," I said, my voice slightly distorted through the helmet's comm system.

We made our way to the hangar, passing groups of personnel hurrying in the same direction. The massive space was organized chaos, with base staff being directed by *Thunder*'s crew into assigned sections. The ship itself dominated the center of the hangar, its elliptical hull gleaming under the harsh lights.

Thunder had once been sleek and compact, but the reconstruction had expanded her profile. New hull plates covered sections that hadn't existed before, and even from the outside, the hasty nature of her rebuild was evident in the mismatched plating and exposed access points.

We boarded through the main airlock, making our way through corridors crowded with evacuees. *Thunder*'s internal spaces were in even worse shape than her exterior—exposed conduits hung from ceilings, and in some sections, wall panels hadn't yet been installed, revealing the complex network of systems that made up a starship's guts. We passed one corridor where a gaping hole exposed an entire section of power conduits, still waiting for their protective shielding.

The command deck was alive with activity when we arrived. Destiny stood at the tactical station, firing off orders to the crew members who scrambled to bring systems online. She looked up as we entered.

"Cutting it close," she said. "Nicobe and Zeta are both tied into *Thunder*'s power systems. They're currently unresponsive—fully engaged in getting the critical systems powered up."

I nodded, moving to the command chair. "Status?"

"Engineering reports all essential systems are green, but that's about all we've got," Destiny reported. "Life support, propulsion, minimal bolsters. Weapons are offline, and most of our sensors are still non-functional."

The navigation officer—a young lieutenant whose name temporarily escaped me—looked up from her station. "Sir, where are we headed once we clear the hangar?"

I gripped the arms of the command chair. "Right now, our priority is getting safely away from the base."

Destiny frowned. "Without most of our sensors, how are we supposed to know where to go? We'll be flying blind."

Before I could answer, Sofia stiffened beside me, her hand shooting out to grip my shoulder. Her eyes had gone distant, staring at nothing, her body rigid. My heart skipped a beat, thinking it was a seizure. At the worst possible time! But then I recognized the signs of another flashback. The Kergan neural implant Chen had placed in her brain was active again, and there was nothing I could do but wait for it to pass.

32

For a moment that stretched like taffy, Sofia remained frozen, her eyes fixed on something none of us could see. The command deck fell silent as everyone pretended not to notice. I held my breath, feeling the familiar helplessness that came whenever the implant took hold of her. Then she blinked, life flowing back into her face like color returning to a photograph, and her grip on my shoulder tightened with sudden purpose.

"I know where we need to go," she said, her voice suddenly clear and focused, the slight slurring that had plagued her since her injury completely absent.

I turned to face her fully. "Where?"

"There are gaps in the Kergan air defenses near Tijuana." Her eyes were bright with certainty, her hands moving as if tracing invisible maps. "If we fly *Thunder* on a route over the mountains, then from there west to Tijuana, I can guide us through. I can see the safe corridor."

The command deck remained eerily quiet. Sofia continued, her words coming in a rush, as if afraid the knowledge might slip away. "Their surveillance network has blind spots—created by terrain features and atmospheric conditions the Kergans haven't fully accounted for. If we follow the right path, we can slip through undetected."

Destiny stepped forward, her expression a mixture of suspicion and concern. "How the hell do you know all this?" She looked from Sofia to me. "Kory, what's going on?"

I met Destiny's gaze and saw the worry tucked behind her sharp question. We'd known each other long enough that I could read her like a book—this wasn't hostility toward Sofia, it was concern, plain and simple. That's when it hit me: I hadn't told my sister about the strange visions and flashbacks Sofia had been getting from the implant. A glaring oversight—and one I was definitely going to get chewed out for the moment she cornered me in private.

"It's a long story," I said, aware of the eyes of the entire command crew on us. "But right now, we need to trust Sofia."

"Trust her?" Destiny's voice dropped to a fierce whisper. "She's talking about Kergan defense systems that even our intelligence officers don't have mapped."

Sofia stood straighter, her chin lifting slightly. "I know it sounds impossible, but I can see it. Like a tactical overlay in my mind."

I placed my hand over Sofia's where it still rested on my shoulder. The cool material of our protomatter suits prevented actual contact, but the gesture connected us nonetheless. At that moment, I made my decision.

If I followed Sofia's suggestion, I was putting *Thunder* and everyone aboard—my crew, the base personnel, Zeta, Nicobe, Dr. Chen—into the hands of her neural implant. The same implant fabricated by the HCD from Kergan technology. The same implant that triggered flashbacks and visions that left her staring into space. The same implant that could, for all I knew, be feeding information directly back to the enemy.

But what choice did we have? Stay and die? Try to outrun the Kergan fleet on our own? I'd spent days being afraid of what that implant might mean, what it might do to Sofia. Maybe it was time to stop being afraid and start using the one advantage it gave us.

"We're going with Sofia's plan," I announced, loud enough for everyone to hear. I returned to the command chair and activated the ship-wide comm. "All hands, prepare for immediate departure. Secure all stations and passengers."

I looked toward the helm. "Lieutenant Howard, transfer flight control to the command chair. I'm taking us out personally."

"Aye, sir," Howard responded, her fingers dancing across her console.

Destiny moved closer, her voice low. "I hope you know what you're doing."

I gave her a tight smile. "When have I ever?"

That earned me a reluctant grin before she turned to her own console. "All crew report to stations. Base personnel, secure yourselves in designated areas. Prepare for possible combat maneuvers."

The minutes ticked by with agonizing slowness. Finally, Destiny turned to me. "All crew at stations. Base personnel loaded and secured. Engineering reports the hangar hatch is ready to open."

I nodded. "Open the hatch."

The massive doors above us groaned as they slid apart, revealing a slice of blue sky. Sunlight streamed into the hangar, catching dust motes in golden beams.

I settled into the command chair, feeling the familiar flight controls under my hands. *Thunder* hummed beneath me, her systems responding to my commands with a willingness that belied her incomplete state.

"Powering main pods to twenty percent," I announced. "Lifting off."

Thunder rose from the hangar floor with surprising grace. The ship's expanded mass meant she responded more sluggishly than I remembered, but she was still responsive enough for what we needed. I guided her upward through the opening, the hull clearing the edges with mere meters to spare.

As we emerged into daylight, the tactical display showed our two Royal Guard escorts hovering nearby, their weapons still tracking targets below. I opened a channel to them.

"Royal Guard vessels, this is Commander Drake on *Thunder*. We have Queen Zeta on board and secured. Request you follow and provide escort. We're evacuating all personnel from Wolf Jaw Base."

A crisp, formal voice responded immediately. "*Thunder,* this is Royal Guard frigate *Dedicated*. We acknowledge your request and will provide escort. Be advised, enemy reinforcements are inbound from the north."

"Understood, *Dedicated*. We're proceeding southeast along the mountain range. Please cover our retreat."

I turned to Sofia, who now stood at the auxiliary navigation console. "Guide us."

She nodded, her eyes calm and focused. "Set course one-six-five, following the Sierra Nevada ridgeline. Maximum altitude three thousand meters to use the terrain as cover."

I input the course, feeling *Thunder*'s engines surge as we

accelerated southward. Behind us, the Royal Guard frigates fell into formation, their sleek hulls gleaming in the morning sun.

We hadn't made it five kilometers before the first warning came.

"Enemy fighters approaching from north-northeast," reported *Dedicated.* "We will intercept."

Through *Thunder*'s exterior view screens, I watched as one of our escorts broke formation, climbing sharply. Seconds later, the sky lit up with the bright flashes of interceptor missiles streaking toward unseen targets. The Royal Guard frigate's point defense lasers created a web of deadly light, cutting down approaching Kergan missiles before they could reach us.

I kept *Thunder* low, hugging the contours of the mountain peaks, our speed deliberately subsonic to minimize our heat signature. The ship shuddered occasionally as we hit turbulence from the rough terrain below, but held together despite her incomplete state.

Without most of our sensors operational, I felt half-blind, relying on visual observation and the tactical data relayed from our escorts. It was like trying to drive through fog with only occasional glimpses of the road ahead. Every instinct screamed at me to climb higher, to gain room to maneuver, but Sofia's directions kept us low and hidden.

"Turn to heading one-four-zero," Sofia instructed. "Maintain current altitude. There's a Kergan sensor station ahead we need to avoid."

I adjusted our course, guiding *Thunder* through a narrow mountain pass that scraped uncomfortably close to our expanded hull. The ship groaned in protest, but the structural integrity held.

For nearly an hour, we continued this nerve-wracking

flight, Sofia calling out course corrections, our Royal Guard escorts engaging the occasional pursuing fighters that managed to track us. We emerged from the Sierra Nevada range and continued southeast over the Mojave Desert, the harsh landscape blurring beneath us.

"Turn to heading two-seven-zero," Sofia said when we reached a point east of Yuma. "We're approaching the Mexican border. Once we cross, adjust altitude to one hundred meters above ground level."

I glanced at her. "That's cutting it close."

She nodded, her expression unchanged. "The Kergan ground radar has a blind spot there. They expect threats from above, not something skimming the surface."

Trusting her—trusting the implant—I took *Thunder* into a banking turn that pointed us west, then dropped our altitude until we were practically scraping the desert floor. We crossed the Mexican coast south of Tijuana, the sprawling city visible in the distance to our north.

The Pacific Ocean appeared ahead, the blue expanse promising open space after the claustrophobic terrain-hugging flight. We'd seen no pursuit for the last forty-five minutes, and it had been even longer since our escorts had fired a shot in our defense.

"We're clear of the immediate threat zone," Sofia announced. "Once we're over the Pacific, set course west-southwest and increase speed to four thousand kilometers per hour."

Destiny raised an eyebrow. "You want us to go supersonic over open water? We'll light up every Kergan sensor in the hemisphere."

Sofia shook her head. "There's a gap in their ocean surveillance network. If we stay below five hundred meters altitude, their tracking algorithms will classify us as anomalous weather patterns, not a ship."

I looked between them, then made my decision. "Taking us up to four thousand kph."

Thunder's tractor pods roared as I pushed them harder, the ship accelerating smoothly despite her patchwork construction. The ocean blurred beneath us, our altitude so low that I could see the white caps of waves as we streaked past them. The hull vibrated with the strain, but held together.

For two hours, we flew west-southwest, following Sofia's precise directions. Occasionally, she would call for minor course adjustments, her voice never wavering. Finally, she pointed to a speck on the horizon.

"There. Isla Perdana."

As we approached, the island revealed itself—a crescent-shaped volcanic formation rising dramatically from the ocean. Steep basalt cliffs surrounded most of its perimeter, with a single southern cove featuring a white-sand beach. A dormant volcanic peak dominated the center, surrounded by dense tropical vegetation.

"This is our destination?" I asked.

Sofia nodded. "The island's natural magnetic properties interfere with Kergan scanning technology. The volcanic rock contains minerals that absorb and scatter their sensor sweeps. The dense fog banks that regularly form here provide natural visual concealment. It's... perfect."

I guided *Thunder* into a gentle descent, aiming for the open beach area. Our Royal Guard escorts took up positions overhead, standing watch as we settled onto the sand with a soft bump. Through the view displays, I could see waves lapping at the shore just meters from our landing struts.

"Power down non-essential systems," I ordered as the pods spun down. "Minimum power to life support and security only."

The command crew moved with practiced efficiency, shutting down systems in sequence. As the background hum of *Thunder*'s systems faded to a whisper, a palpable sense of relief spread through the command deck. We'd made it. For now, at least, we were safe.

That relief was short-lived.

Destiny turned from her console, her eyes fixed on Sofia with an intensity that could have melted steel. "Alright, now that we're not about to die, would somebody please explain what the hell just happened?" She moved closer to Sofia. "How did you know about Kergan defense systems, sensor gaps, and this convenient little island hideaway? Because last I checked, you were a German military police officer, not a tactical analyst with access to classified enemy intelligence."

Sofia met her gaze steadily, but said nothing.

I stepped between them, holding up my hands. "This isn't a conversation we should have on the command deck." I glanced meaningfully at the curious eyes of the crew watching us. "Let's take this to my ready room."

Without waiting for agreement, I headed for the small office adjacent to the command deck. Sofia followed immediately, her steps steady but slow. After a moment's hesitation, Destiny joined us, her lips pressed into a thin line of frustration.

As the ready room door slid shut behind us, I prepared myself for what promised to be an extremely difficult conversation about trust, secrets, and the enemy technology embedded in my partner's brain.

33

I drummed my fingers on the ready room table, my eyes darting between Sofia's composed face and Destiny as she sauntered in, her curly black hair bouncing as she dropped into a chair. At nineteen, my executive officer and oldest friend looked tired but alert, her dark eyes immediately picking up on the tension between Sofia and me.

"So," she said, crossing her arms like a judgmental cactus, "talk to me before I assume the worst and make it worse."

I almost laughed. "Des. It's—"

"It's about my head." Sofia cut in, her voice clinical and detached, as if she were discussing someone else's medical condition. "The Kergan implant Dr. Chen installed to save my life after my head injury."

Destiny's eyebrows shot up. "Wait, what? I knew about the implant, but... Kergan?"

I nodded grimly. "Dr. Chen didn't exactly advertise its origin. She was—is—a neurosurgeon the Kergans, and the HCD forced to work on neural integration technology."

Sofia tapped her temple with one finger. "The implant is not just healing my brain injury. It's accessing an encrypted HCD database."

"You're telling me," Destiny said slowly, leaning forward, "that you've got hostile alien tech wired into your brain? Tech from the guys who conquered our planet and are currently hunting us down?" Her eyes widened. "That's just... great. Perfect. Should we be concerned about, I don't know, mind control? Tracking? Spontaneous head explosions?"

Despite the gravity of the situation, I felt my lips twitch. This was classic Destiny—confront the apocalypse with sarcasm.

"Dr. Chen believes the implant is standalone," Sofia said. "It cannot communicate externally. It was designed for HCD leaders who, for security reasons, couldn't be connected to a network because of the sensitivity of the information stored in the implant."

"Well, that's comforting," Destiny muttered. "So you just have enemy property in your brain, accessing what—enemy secrets?"

I nodded. "Human Compliance Directorate data. Names, locations, operations."

Destiny let out a low whistle. "So Sofia's basically a walking, talking intel drop." She looked at my partner with newfound concern. "How does it feel? Can you control it?"

Sofia's blue eyes met Destiny's. "Sometimes I access it. Sometimes it... accesses me." Her hands, usually so steady, trembled slightly. "I have flashbacks. Information downloads without warning."

"That doesn't sound safe," Destiny said, her sarcasm giving way to genuine concern.

"It isn't," I acknowledged. "But Dr. Chen says removing

it now could kill her."

Destiny rubbed her face with both hands like she was trying to erase her own expression. "Okay. So we've got a ticking information bomb. Awesome. Maybe later we can adopt a live grenade and name it Sparky."

"The intel could be invaluable," Sofia said. "Locations of HCD facilities, command protocols, access codes."

"Assuming we can trust it," Destiny countered. "Hell, assuming we can trust your brain while it's under the influence."

Sofia's jaw tightened. I knew that look—her pride was wounded, but she was too professional to show it. I intervened before the situation could escalate.

"We're telling you because you need to know," I said. "As my XO and as our friend. If Sofia starts behaving strangely or reciting information, you need to recognize what's happening."

Destiny considered this, then nodded. Her expression softened as she looked at Sofia. "Does it hurt?"

Sofia's clinical façade cracked slightly. "Sometimes. Not physically. But... it's disorienting to suddenly have memories that aren't mine."

"Well," Destiny said with a sigh, "I suppose if we're going to have alien tech in our midst, better in Sofia's organized brain than mine. I'd probably end up with the coordinates to the nearest alien fast-food joint rather than anything useful."

I snorted despite myself. Even Sofia's lips curved upward.

"Thank you," Sofia said quietly.

Destiny shrugged. "For what? Making inappropriate jokes about your life-threatening condition?"

"For understanding," I answered for Sofia. "And for

trusting us."

"Yeah, well." Destiny stood up. "That's what we do, right? Trust each other with the weird stuff. Been that way since we were eating discarded tacos behind that restaurant in San Jose." She snapped her fingers. "What was it called again?"

"Taco Nova," I said, without missing a beat. I had fond memories of that taco stand.

Destiny smiled and slapped her thigh. "Yeah, that's it."

After Destiny left, Sofia and I exchanged a long look. "That went better than expected," I said.

"She's afraid," Sofia replied. "But she's practical. Like me."

I reached for her hand. "Like us all."

The irony of this meeting was that not long after, we would find out that Destiny had her *own* troubling secrets, ones that she wasn't even aware of, but would soon threaten everything.

The next few days blurred together in a haze of activity. Our impromptu base on the uninhabited island—little more than a rocky outcrop in the Pacific—buzzed with purpose as Zeta and Nicobe resumed their work on *Thunder*.

Zeta's octahedral capsule hovered near *Thunder*'s hull, brilliant light emanating from her plasma form as she supervised the installation of the last weapons systems. "The Queen is pleased with the progress," she announced, her speech carrying across the makeshift landing pad where we'd set down.

Beside her, Nicobe's crimson dodecahedron bobbed in what I recognized as excitement. "Nicobe believes the propulsion system will exceed expectations," she said, her dry humor evident as she added, "Assuming the humans do not meddle with her perfect calculations."

I watched them work, marveling at the ignas' ability to manipulate matter and energy. *Thunder* was already a formidable ship when we'd arrived on Earth, but with the ignas making modifications, she was becoming something else entirely—a representation of the pinnacle of Dominion warship technology.

The two Royal Guard frigates that had accompanied Zeta's yacht now maintained a perimeter around our island, their sleek forms barely visible through advanced cloaking technology. Occasionally, their patrol patterns would shift, and I'd catch a glimpse of their formidable weaponry—a reminder that we weren't just hiding; we were preparing.

Our crew and the base personnel kept busy. Some assisted with *Thunder*'s reconstruction, while others constructed temporary shelters or cataloged our supplies. Sofia spent most of her time with Dr. Chen, monitoring the implant's integration and documenting the information it revealed.

I found Lynda Brooks standing on a rocky outcrop, gazing out at the endless blue of the Pacific. The base commander's brown hair, now streaked with more gray than when I'd first met her, whipped around her face in the sea breeze.

"Beautiful spot," she said as I approached. "Defensible, isolated. It would make an excellent location for a permanent base."

I surveyed the island—barely three square miles of volcanic rock and sparse vegetation. "It's too small," I replied. "And nowhere on Earth is truly safe now. The Kergans have a planetary detection grid. It's just a matter of time before they find this place."

Lynda turned to face me, her expression thoughtful. "You're probably right. But we need somewhere to regroup, to plan our next move."

"Our next move." I repeated the words, tasting their weight. "That's what I've been thinking about."

"And?" Lynda prompted.

I hesitated, then decided that if I couldn't trust her, there was no one I could trust. "We need to take our operation off-world."

Lynda's eyebrows rose, but she didn't dismiss the idea outright. "Bold thinking, Kory. Very bold."

"Bold is all we've got left," I said, watching a flock of seabirds wheel overhead. They were free to come and go as they pleased—a luxury we no longer had on our own planet.

That night, alone in my quarters, I pored over star charts and the limited intelligence we'd gathered on Kergan patrol patterns. The idea that had formed in my mind during the conversation with Lynda seemed simultaneously absurd and inevitable. Earth was compromised, but space was vast. With *Thunder*'s capabilities and Zeta's resources, we could establish a base somewhere the Kergans wouldn't look—or couldn't reach.

The question wasn't whether we should leave Earth. The question was where we could go, and whether humanity's best hope for resistance lay among the stars we'd barely begun to explore. As I studied the charts, one thought kept circling: home wasn't a place anymore; it was the people I was determined to protect—Sofia, Destiny, and everyone who'd placed their trust in me.

We needed a sanctuary. And if it didn't exist, we'd have to create one.

34

The command tent flapped gently in the Pacific breeze, the canvas walls filtering the morning sun into a diffuse glow that made everyone look slightly jaundiced. I leaned against the makeshift table—a sheet of *Thunder*'s hull plating balanced on supply crates—and watched my senior officers file in. Five days on this uninhabited rock, and we'd already established a pecking order for the coffee rations. Destiny clutched her mug like it contained liquid salvation, while Busto, ever the Marine, stood at parade rest with his own cup positioned at a precise forty-five-degree angle from his chest. We were stranded, rebuilding, and somehow maintaining military protocol—humans are strange animals.

"Good morning, exiles," I said once everyone had settled. "Welcome to day five of our unplanned vacation on Isla Perdana."

Sofia snorted from her position near the tent flap. Her clothing was wrinkled and a sheen of sweat shined on her forehead. Even disheveled, she maintained that air of

German efficiency that had first caught my attention.

"Some vacation," she said. "I've got sand in places I didn't know I had places."

"Queen Zeta finds the locale quite pleasing," said the white octahedral capsule, floating serenely at the far end of our table. Inside, the plasma form of our royal ally pulsed slightly, as if agreeing with her own statement. "The solar radiation is most invigorating."

"Easy for you to say," Destiny muttered into her coffee. "You don't have to sleep on the ground."

I cleared my throat. "As much as I'd love to continue comparing notes on our accommodations, we have more pressing matters. Specifically, where do we go from here?"

Through the open tent flap, I could see *Thunder* resting on the beach like a beached metallic whale. The ellipsoid cruiser was impressive even in its current state, with scaffolding surrounding sections of the hull where final rebuild work continued. The 300-meter warship dominated the white sand beach, its normally sleek profile broken by the occasional worker crawling across its surface like a tick on a dog.

"There's been talk about setting up on an asteroid," I continued, pulling my attention back to the task at hand. "But before we make any decisions, I want to hear what each of you thinks. We're in this together, and I need your input."

Lieutenant Commander Lynda Brooks, now lacking a base to command, raised her hand like we were in a classroom. "Permission to speak candidly, sir?"

"We're sitting on supply crates in a tent, Lynda. I think we can dispense with some of the formalities."

She nodded, the lines around her eyes crinkling slightly. "An asteroid is a deathtrap waiting to happen. If something goes wrong—and something always goes wrong—we're stuck in the cold vacuum with nowhere to go."

"Precisely why it's perfect," Destiny countered, setting her coffee down with enough force to splash a few drops onto the table. "The Kergans are looking for us. They have thermal imaging, atmospheric sensors—planets are big bullseyes. An asteroid gives us cover."

Busto, who had remained in his parade rest stance despite my attempt to lighten the mood, finally shifted his weight and crossed his arms. "With respect, Commander Austin, asteroids have minimal resources. No atmosphere, limited water if any, completely dependent on supply lines that could be cut at any moment."

I watched the debate unfold, feeling like a tennis referee at a particularly aggressive match. My XO and security chief stared at each other across the table, both convinced of their position.

"We've got fabricators," Destiny said, leaning forward. The curls of her black hair bounced with the movement, contrasting sharply with the intensity in her dark eyes. "We can recycle virtually everything. Water included."

"Until something breaks," Busto countered, his muscular frame tensing as if preparing for physical rather than verbal combat. "Then we're breathing vacuum and drinking our own processed urine until it runs out."

Sofia tapped her finger on the table rhythmically, a habit she'd developed since receiving the Kergan brain implant. Sometimes I wondered if it was morse code, her subconscious trying to communicate something from the alien data swirling in her head.

"Asteroid's defensible," she said finally. "Limited approach vectors. Easy to monitor. Tactically sound."

"Thank you, Chief Kohl," I said, nodding to my partner.

Her tactical assessment wasn't surprising, but I noticed she hadn't firmly come down on either side.

Nicobe's crimson dodecahedron capsule shifted slightly, rotating to face the group. "Nicobe believes the asteroid proposition contains merits, but also significant limitations. The chief concern would be concealment versus sustainability."

"Exactly," Lynda interjected. "And let's not forget recruitment. At Wolf Jaw, we had a community to draw from. We need people—engineers, marines, pilots—and those don't grow on asteroids."

I rapped my knuckles on the table to regain control of the conversation, which was threatening to devolve into multiple arguments. "One at a time. Destiny, you were saying about concealment?"

My XO and oldest friend straightened, shifting into her professional mode despite the casual setting. "The Kergans have Earth locked down tight, but their resources aren't unlimited. The asteroid belt gives us thousands of potential hideouts, all within striking distance when we need to hit back."

"And we will hit back," Busto added, his voice low and determined. The former Marine Raider had a personal stake in this fight, having watched the Kergan invasion from the sidelines while waiting for a call to arms that never came.

"Queen Zeta must consider the political implications as well," our royal ally spoke, her capsule drifting slightly closer to the center of our gathering. "The Collective Dominion's resources are stretched thin in our own conflict with Arctis. While we support Earth's resistance, we cannot provide unlimited resources to an isolated asteroid base."

I felt the weight of command pressing down on my shoulders. Five days ago, we'd barely escaped Wolf Jaw with *Thunder* only partially rebuilt. This hidden island had been a stroke of luck—isolated enough to avoid immediate detection, yet close enough for the incomplete starship to limp here. But we couldn't stay. It was only a matter of time before Kergan patrols expanded their search perimeter.

"What about a compromise?" I suggested, running a hand through my shaggy brown hair. "What if we don't choose between an asteroid or a planetary base, but find something in between?"

Six pairs of eyes focused on me with varying degrees of curiosity and skepticism.

"Mars," I said simply. "Or rather, one of its moons."

The tent fell silent as my officers considered this option. I could practically hear the gears turning in their heads.

"Nicobe, what do you think?" I asked, turning to our Heliacal Templar engineer.

The crimson capsule pulsed briefly before responding. "Nicobe finds merit in this solution. Deimos is the smaller of Mars' moons, yet large enough to establish meaningful infrastructure. Its irregular shape and composition would make it difficult for Kergan sensors to distinguish from other natural celestial bodies in the area."

"And it's still close enough to Earth for our purposes," Destiny added, warming to the idea. "We could reach it in what, a week with *Thunder* at full capacity?"

"Two days, fourteen hours at standard cruise given Earth's and Mars's current orbital positions," Nicobe corrected.

Busto remained skeptical. "Resources are still an issue."

"Less so than an asteroid," I countered. "We have an entire planet nearby."

Lynda's thin frame shifted as she leaned forward. "It's still isolated, though. Recruitment will be a challenge."

"True," I acknowledged, "but we're not in a position to be picky. We need somewhere safe to regroup and plan our next moves."

The tent fell silent again as everyone considered the proposal. Outside, the sound of plasma cutters and metallic hammering provided a constant reminder of our ticking clock. Every hour spent on this island increased our risk of discovery.

Queen Zeta's capsule brightened slightly, drawing our attention. "The Queen believes Commander Drake's suggestion has merit. A Martian moon offers an acceptable balance of security and sustainability. Furthermore, Mars itself could provide additional resources if needed."

I looked around the table, gauging reactions. Destiny was nodding, already on board. Sofia seemed convinced, possibly influenced by whatever information the implant had provided. Busto and Lynda remained reserved, but not openly opposed. Nicobe's capsule pulsed in what I recognized as approval.

"Deimos it is, then," I declared, feeling a small weight lift from my chest. At least we had a destination now. "Destiny, I want you to work with the navigation officer to plot our course and identify the best landing site based on whatever information you both have. Nicobe, please help them."

"Nicobe shall comply with enthusiasm," the Heliacal Templar responded, her capsule bobbing slightly in acknowledgment.

"Lynda," I continued, "inventory our supplies and prepare a list of what we'll need to establish a base on Deimos. Assume minimal existing infrastructure. I also need you to work with Destiny on personnel. Once we're on Deimos, we'll need to establish watchbills, assign quarters, the works."

"We can handle that," Destiny said, speaking for both of them. Lynda's tight smile suggested she wasn't entirely pleased with the pairing, but she didn't object.

"Queen Zeta," I said, turning to our royal ally, "if there's anything the Collective Dominion can provide to help establish our base, now would be the time to mention it."

The igna's plasma form swirled thoughtfully within her capsule. "Zeta and Nicobe will employ nanoforges to construct the base from Deimos's own material, as we have done previously."

"Thank you, Zeta," I said, inclining my head slightly in respect. "Your help is appreciated."

I took a deep breath and looked around at my team—an eclectic mix of humans and aliens united by a common cause. Five days ago, we'd been fleeing for our lives. Now we were planning a resistance base.

"Our priority is getting *Thunder* space-worthy," I said, my tone hardening with urgency. "We need to be off this island as soon as possible. The longer we stay, the more likely the Kergans are to find us."

I glanced through the tent flap at the cruiser on the beach. Despite its incomplete status, *Thunder* was still one of the most formidable vessels in Earth's vicinity—a Marauder-class cruiser built by the Collective Dominion and handed over to the human insurgency.

"Commander Austin, Chief Kohl, with me," I said, standing up straight. "Let's check on *Thunder*'s progress. The rest of you, dismissed to your tasks."

As the group dispersed, I caught Sofia's eye and gave her a small smile. The strain of command was always there, pressing down on my shoulders, but having her at my side made it bearable.

"So," Destiny said as we exited the tent, squinting

against the bright Pacific sun, "we're really going to live on a moon named after the god of terror and dread? That doesn't strike you as a bad omen?"

I laughed despite myself. "Would you prefer Phobos? The god of panic and fear?"

"Fair point," she conceded, her lips quirking up at one corner.

As we walked toward *Thunder*, I felt a strange mixture of dread and hope churning in my gut. We had a plan now—tenuous as it might be—and a crew crazy enough to follow me into the void. Whether Deimos would be our salvation or our tomb remained to be seen, but at least we were moving forward.

And in war, standing still is just another way to die.

That night, in the small tent we shared on the beach, Sofia sat cross-legged on her cot, her fuzz of cropped blonde hair begging to be rubbed. It made her look both younger and more vulnerable than the military police officer who faced down an alien implant in her brain without flinching.

I handed her a mug of something that claimed to be tea. "How are you? Really?"

She accepted the mug, cradling it between her palms. "Functional."

I raised an eyebrow. "That's not what I asked."

A small smile flickered across her face. "It's strange to have memories that aren't mine. To know things I shouldn't know." She took a sip of the tea. "Like looking through someone else's eyes at scenes I never witnessed."

I sat beside her, careful not to jostle the tea. "Is it getting worse?"

"More frequent," she corrected. "Not necessarily worse. Dr. Chen believes the neural pathways are stabilizing, which is why I'm experiencing more conscious access to the database."

I wanted to ask if she was scared, but I already knew the answer. Sofia wasn't fearless—she was simply disciplined enough to function despite fear. It was one of the many things I admired about her.

"I had another flashback," she blurted. "While you were meeting with Lynda about supply coordination."

My heart skipped. "Why didn't you say something earlier?"

"Because it was... personal. Not tactical." She set the mug down on our small side table with careful precision. "I saw Destiny."

Something cold settled in my stomach. "Destiny?"

Sofia nodded, her eyes distant as she accessed the memory. "In an HCD detention facility. Being interrogated."

"We knew she'd been captured before," I intoned. "While you and I were in Astrithon. She doesn't talk about it much."

"There's a reason for that." Sofia's voice dropped lower. "She doesn't remember it. Not all of it. The interrogator was Ban'ach."

The name sent a chill down my spine. Ban'ach—the female marac Soul Ravager I'd wounded in combat in the Syderealium. The reason I'd been charged with sydereal assault in the first place. The person who stole my memories of my parents.

"Are you sure?" I asked, though I didn't doubt her. Sofia didn't make claims without certainty.

She nodded. "The memory was from an observation room. HCD scientists watching the interrogation through one-way glass. They were documenting Ban'ach's methods."

My hands clenched involuntarily. "What did she do to Destiny?"

"Sydereal manipulation," Sofia said. "The memory didn't show the entire process, but the scientists were noting that Ban'ach was selectively erasing and altering memories."

"Shit." The word felt inadequate, but it was all I could manage. My mind raced through implications, each worse than the last. "Why? What was she after?"

Sofia met my eyes directly. "Information about you. Your background, your abilities, your weaknesses. The memory showed Destiny resisting, but..."

"But even Destiny has limits," I finished for her. The icy feeling in my stomach had spread throughout my body. I felt numb, but there was a heat in my chest—an uncomfortable weight that I recognized as guilt. If Ban'ach had targeted Destiny, it was because of her connection to me.

"There's more," Sofia said quietly. "The scientists were discussing something called 'deep-pattern conditioning.' They seemed pleased with Ban'ach's progress."

The implications hit me like a physical blow. "You think Ban'ach programmed her? Conditioned her to... what? Spy on us? Betray us at some critical moment?"

Sofia's face remained carefully neutral, but I could see the concern in her eyes. "It's a possibility we need to consider. Destiny escaped HCD custody under circumstances that, in retrospect, seem convenient."

I stood up abruptly, unable to sit still with this knowledge churning inside me. "Destiny is the most loyal person I know. We grew up together on the streets. She saved my life more times than I can count."

"I'm not questioning her loyalty," Sofia said gently. "I'm concerned that her loyalty might have been weaponized against her will."

I paced the small confines of our tent, three steps one

way, three steps back. "If you're right, what do we do? How do we even begin to untangle something like that?"

"Dr. Chen might have insights," Sofia suggested. "She was forced to work on neural manipulation for the Kergans. She might recognize signs, know countermeasures."

I stopped pacing. I talked to myself out loud. "Does Destiny show any symptoms? Any behavioral changes I've noticed?"

Sofia considered this. "If Ban'ach was as skilled as the HCD scientists believed, the conditioning would be designed to remain dormant until triggered."

"A sleeper agent," I muttered. "And she wouldn't even know it."

"It might not be that dramatic," Sofia cautioned. "It could be as simple as an implanted suggestion to overlook certain information, or to make specific decisions under specific circumstances."

That was almost worse. The idea that Destiny's choices might not be fully her own, that her mind had been subtly nudged in directions serving our enemies—it violated something fundamental.

"We need to tell her," I said finally.

Sofia raised an eyebrow. "Are you sure? If there is conditioning, confronting her with it might trigger unpredictable responses."

"She deserves to know," I insisted. "She deserves the chance to fight it, just like you're fighting the implant's influence."

Sofia was quiet for a long moment, then nodded. "You're right. But we should approach it carefully."

I sat back down beside her, suddenly exhausted. "Tomorrow," I decided. "We'll talk to Chen first, then Destiny. Together."

Sofia leaned against me slightly, her warmth a contrast to the cold dread that had settled in my chest. "Together," she agreed.

I wrapped an arm around her shoulders, drawing strength from her presence even as my mind raced with new threats and complications. Ban'ach had gotten to Destiny once. I wouldn't let the Soul Ravager's influence hurt my oldest friend again—even if that influence now lived inside Destiny's own mind.

We had faced impossible odds before. We would face them again. But this time, the enemy wasn't just out there in the vastness of space or hiding in Kergan strongholds on Earth. This time, the enemy might have hidden themselves inside one of our own.

35

The door hissed shut behind Sofia, leaving Destiny and me alone in my ready room. The three of us had just finished telling Destiny about what Sofia learned about Destiny's interrogation. Destiny had immediately asked to speak with me in private.

The ambient hum of *Thunder*'s systems filled the silence between us, a mechanical heartbeat that usually comforted me but now only emphasized the heavy quiet. The ship wasn't quite complete, but the ready room was available and I didn't want to have a sensitive conversation like this in a tent. Destiny sat rigid in her chair, her fingers drumming an anxious rhythm against her thigh—a habit she'd had since we were kids on the streets of San Jose, one that only emerged when something really got under her skin.

"You're doing the thing," I said, nodding toward her hand.

She stopped immediately, clenching her fist instead. "What thing?"

"The drumming. The one that tells me you're about to either punch someone or steal their wallet." I tried for lightness, but it fell flat against the tension in the room.

Destiny's dark eyes flickered up to meet mine, then darted away. She shifted in her seat, her shoulders hunched forward as if bracing against an invisible wind. The executive officer's insignia on her collar caught the light—a reminder of how far we'd both come from scavenging dumpsters behind restaurants. And yet, despite her uniform and rank, I could still see the street-smart twelve-year-old I'd met seven years ago, wary and fierce.

"It's bullshit," she finally said. "Ban'ach interrogated me, and I don't remember a damn thing about it." Her voice cracked slightly on the last word. "How do you just... lose something like that?"

I leaned forward, resting my elbows on my knees. My own memory of encountering Ban'ach in the Syderealium was seared into my brain—the female marac Soul Ravager had been terrifying, alien, powerful. The thought of her tearing through Destiny's mind made my stomach turn.

"Soul Ravagers don't just read minds," I said quietly. "They take things. Energlyphs—pieces of your consciousness, your memories. And Ban'ach would have been looking for anything strategic—information about *Thunder*, about our capabilities, about Wolf Jaw Base."

"So I'm a security breach." Destiny's jaw tightened. "Great."

"That's not what I—"

"It's exactly what you mean." She shot to her feet, pacing the small confines of my ready room like a caged animal. "She rifled through my brain, took what she wanted, and I didn't even get the courtesy of knowing it happened."

My hands felt cold despite the temperature-controlled

environment. I had felt a similar violation when Ban'ach first connected with my mind—though that had been violent and terrifying and painful. The difference was, I remembered it.

"Des, listen." I stood, blocking her path. "There's something I can try."

She stopped, arms crossed tight across her chest, her expression a practiced mask of indifference that didn't quite hide the fear underneath. "What?"

I took a deep breath. This was risky, but I couldn't stand seeing her this way—violated and not even able to face what had happened. "I've been working on my sydereal projection skills. You know, the stuff I learned from Zeta. I received additional training in Astrithon."

"The freaky mind stuff. Yeah, I know."

"Let me help you unlock these memories," I said, my voice dropping to a near-whisper. "I think I can find what Ban'ach did to your glyphshade. Maybe even undo it."

Destiny's eyes narrowed, suspicion warring with desperate curiosity. "You want to go poking around in my head, too?"

"Not like she did," I said quickly. "I'd be helping you recover what she took. Or at least, helping you remember the experience so you're not left with this... gap."

She chewed her lower lip, a habit from childhood that emerged in moments of decision. Her shoulders remained tense, but something in her posture shifted—the slightest yielding.

"And you know how to do this?" she asked.

I hesitated. Lying to Destiny had never worked out well for me. "I've practiced. Mostly on my own glyphshade. Once with Sofia." I didn't add that the attempt with Sofia had been brief and largely unsuccessful.

"That's not exactly a ringing endorsement of your abilities, Kory."

"No, but I'm the best shot you've got at figuring this out." I reached out, not quite touching her shoulder. "Unless you want to wait until we find an igna specialist."

She sighed heavily. "Alright," she murmured, the word weighted with reluctance. "What do I need to do?"

Relief flooded through me—followed immediately by apprehension. This was uncharted territory, and if I screwed up, I could damage her glyphshade further. But the determined set of her jaw told me there was no backing out now.

"We should sit on the floor," I said, moving to clear a space. "Cross-legged is best. It helps with the mental focus."

"This better not involve chanting or incense," she muttered, but followed my lead, lowering herself to the floor with military precision.

I sat opposite her, our knees almost touching. "It'll feel strange at first," I explained, focusing on keeping my voice steady and professional. "I need to project my consciousness into the Syderealium, where I can perceive your glyphshade—that's the energy construct that represents your consciousness. If Ban'ach interfered with it, I should be able to see the damage."

"And fix it?"

I met her gaze. "I'll try. But I need you to be completely open, Des. No mental barriers. It'll be harder than it sounds."

A ghost of her usual smirk crossed her face. "I've never been accused of being an open book."

"First time for everything," I replied, mirroring her attempt at lightness. "Just focus on your breathing and try to relax. If it helps, think about something familiar.

Something safe."

"Safe," she repeated, as if testing an unfamiliar word. "Right."

We sat in silence for a moment. I watched her face—the sharp angles softened slightly as she closed her eyes. Her breathing slowed, and I matched my own to its rhythm.

I began the mental exercises I'd practiced hundreds of times since my training on Virelia. First, the visualization of my own consciousness—a gathering and concentrating of mental energy, like drawing scattered light into a focused beam. Then, the subtle shift in perception needed to sense the Syderealium—that parallel dimension of pure information that underlay all reality.

The technique wasn't easy. Most humans couldn't manage it at all. But my encounters with Zeta and other igna had triggered something in me, a latent ability that the instructors at Space Warfare School had helped me develop. Not to the level of a marac Soul Ravager or an igna specializing in sydereal arts, but enough to glimpse the Syderealium and interact with it in limited ways. I'd been told by more than one igna that I was the most powerful flairsparked seen in generations. I figured that had to count for something when it came to protecting those I cared about.

Sweat beaded on my forehead as I pushed through the resistance—the natural barrier between physical consciousness and sydereal awareness. It was like trying to peer through murky water, straining to make out shapes beneath the surface.

"Your breathing changed," Destiny murmured, her eyes still closed. "You okay?"

"Yeah," I managed. "Just concentrating. Keep your eyes closed, but try to think about Ban'ach. About any gaps in your memory. About *Thunder* and Wolf Jaw Base—the strategic information she might have been after."

A small furrow appeared between her brows. Her hand found mine, fingers gripping tightly. "I don't remember her, Kory. I just... I don't."

"I know. That's what we're going to fix."

I let my awareness expand, searching for the unique energetic signature that was Destiny's glyphshade. Every conscious being cast a reflection in the Syderealium—a pattern of interconnected energlyphs, the fundamental information units that comprised consciousness. Hers would be familiar to me after years of friendship, distinct as a fingerprint.

The ready room seemed to fade around me, the solid walls and floor becoming insubstantial. Destiny remained, but now I perceived something else superimposed over her physical form—a luminous, intricate network of light and information. Her glyphshade.

I'd attempted nothing this deep before. My heart hammered in my chest as I pushed further, extending my consciousness toward that shimmering construct.

"I'm going to try to connect now," I said, my voice sounding distant to my own ears. "You might feel... something. Just stay calm."

Destiny nodded almost imperceptibly, her grip on my hand tightening.

I reached out with my mind, crossing the final threshold between observation and interaction. The Syderealium opened to me, drawing my consciousness in like a tide pulling a swimmer from shore. I felt the momentary vertigo of transition, and then I was there—my awareness fully immersed in that strange realm of pure information, following the thread that led to Destiny's glyphshade, plunging toward the damaged places where Ban'ach had left her mark.

The last thing I heard before losing awareness of my physical surroundings was Destiny's sharp intake of breath as our minds connected.

36

The Syderealium enveloped me like a plunge into the deepest ocean trench—pressure and vastness existing simultaneously, defying physical laws. Destiny's glyphshade bloomed before my consciousness, not as the solid human form I knew, but as a constellation of pulsing, interconnected energlyphs. Beautiful in its complexity, but wounded. Fragments of her consciousness floated like debris after an explosion, severed from the luminous network that comprised her true self.

In the physical world, I'd been sitting cross-legged on the floor of my ready room. Here, concepts like "sitting" or "floor" had no meaning. I existed as pure awareness, perceiving the information landscape that was Destiny's mind. Her glyphshade shimmered with a familiar signature—quick, bright pulses that mirrored her sarcastic wit, dense clusters of steady light that represented her loyalty and resilience.

But among this familiar terrain were disturbing anomalies. Jagged tears in the network where connections should be. Distorted symbols floating untethered, like words cut from their sentences. I'd seen damage to glyphshades before—my instructors on Virelia had shown me examples during training—but never to someone I knew so well. Never to someone whose mind I'd watched develop since we were kids scraping by on the streets.

I moved deeper into the projection, a sensation like swimming through thickened air. The navigational technique I'd learned was simple in theory—focus intent, direct awareness—but far more challenging in practice. Especially here, where Ban'ach's intrusion had left such chaos.

As I approached one cluster of untethered energlyphs, they flickered rapidly, emitting information in bursts. I focused my awareness, trying to interpret the disjointed data. Blueprints. Schematics. I recognized the distinctive ellipsoid shape of *Thunder*, our ship. Systems specifications flashed by—weapons capabilities, engine outputs, crew complement. Then other information—topographical maps of the Sierra Nevada mountains, security protocols for Wolf Jaw Base, power grid layouts for the hydroelectric plant that powered Fresno County.

Strategic information. Intelligence that would be valuable to an enemy. This was what Ban'ach had been extracting when she violated Destiny's mind.

Between the floating fragments, I detected strange distortions—like ripples in the fabric of the Syderealium itself. These were traces of Ban'ach's presence, energetic signatures left behind by her invasive extraction. They pulsed with an alien rhythm, distinctly different from Destiny's natural patterns. Where Destiny's energlyphs were quick and bright, these distortions were slow and dark, leaving oily trails through the information landscape.

Sydereal fingerprints. Every being left them when they

interacted with the Sydereallium. Ban'ach's were unmistakably predatory.

Following these disturbing trails, I found myself drawn toward a particularly dense area of disruption. Here, the free flow of energlyphs was impeded by what appeared to be a massive barrier—a structure that had no business being part of Destiny's glyphshade. It emanated a low, oppressive hum that reverberated through the surrounding information field, creating dissonance in the natural harmony of her consciousness.

This had to be a sydereal lock—a construct implanted by Ban'ach to isolate and contain specific memories. Soul Ravagers used such techniques to prevent victims from realizing they'd been attacked, allowing the extraction of information without triggering defensive responses. The lock sealed away not just the memory of the interrogation, but awareness that anything had been taken at all.

I approached cautiously. The lock pulsed with malevolent energy, its structure alien to Destiny's natural patterns. It resembled a dense, twisting knot of dark fibers, each strand wrapped around captured energlyphs, binding them in place and preventing them from rejoining the whole of her glyphshade.

Disabling such a construct would require precision. During my training on Virelia, we'd practiced similar techniques, though always in controlled simulations. This was different—this was Destiny's actual consciousness, and any misstep could cause further damage.

I focused my awareness into a fine point, like concentrating light through a lens. The technique required both assertion and subtlety—too forceful an approach would trigger defensive mechanisms within the lock, too gentle would accomplish nothing. I directed my intent toward the outermost layer of the construct, identifying the pattern of its binding.

The lock resisted, its frequency changing as if sensing my attempt. I persisted, matching my approach to its new rhythm, then introducing a subtle discord—not enough to trigger defenses, but enough to begin unraveling its structure.

My consciousness brushed against one of the binding strands, and I felt a spark—not physical electricity, but a jolt of alien intent that stung my awareness. Ban'ach's lingering presence, embedded in her creation. For a moment, I sensed her—cold, calculating precision and predatory hunger. The sensation sent ripples of revulsion through my projected consciousness.

I pulled back slightly, recalibrated, and tried again. This time, I mimicked the lock's own frequency but introduced a phase shift—a technique for disrupting sydereal constructs. Gradually, almost imperceptibly, the outer layer of the lock began to vibrate out of sync with its core.

The process was exhausting, demanding a level of concentration I'd rarely sustained before. In the physical world, I knew my body would be sweating, muscles tense with effort. Here, that strain manifested as fluctuations in my own projected awareness, threatening to break my connection to the Syderealium entirely.

But I couldn't stop. Not with Destiny's memories—her sense of self-integrity—at stake.

I pressed deeper, finding the junction points where the lock attached to her natural energlyphs. These connections were the most vulnerable part of the construct, and also the most critical to disable safely. One by one, I applied focused intent, dissolving the artificial bonds without damaging the energlyphs themselves.

The lock's structure shuddered. Its resonant hum

faltered, breaking into discordant pulses. I sensed the moment when its integrity failed—a sudden release of tension in the surrounding information field. The dark fibers unraveled, dissolving into the Sydereium like smoke dissipating in clear air.

As the lock disappeared, the captive energlyphs pulsed brightly, their connections to the larger network of Destiny's glyphshade reestablishing themselves. The severed fragments I'd seen floating began to drift back toward their proper places, the tear in her consciousness gradually mending itself.

And with that reintegration came the rush of unlocked memories—not just as abstract data, but as experiential information that flowed through me as I maintained my connection to her glyphshade.

I perceived what Destiny had experienced—the sudden, invasive presence of Ban'ach in her mind during an interrogation at an HCD facility. The Soul Ravager had struck without warning, bypassing Destiny's physical senses entirely to attack directly in the Sydereium. I felt Destiny's terror and confusion as an alien consciousness ripped through her memories, extracting strategic information about *Thunder* and the base. This is how our base had been compromised. Why the Kergans had committed to such a bold attack on Wolf Jaw Base.

Ban'ach had been methodical, targeting specific intelligence—defensive capabilities, crew rotations, security protocols, power infrastructure. Information that would allow for a precise, devastating attack. And through it all, Destiny had been conscious, aware of the violation but unable to resist a being whose mastery of the Sydereium far exceeded normal human capability.

The final memory was the most disturbing—Ban'ach's cold satisfaction as she constructed the lock, sealing away

Destiny's recollection of the entire incident. "You'll never know I was here," the Soul Ravager had projected, her alien thoughts translating imperfectly into human concepts. "And when we strike, you'll never see it coming."

The implications hit me with sudden clarity—this hadn't been random. Ban'ach had been gathering intelligence for a planned attack on Wolf Jaw Base. The realization sent a surge of urgency through my projected consciousness, destabilizing my connection to the Sydarealium.

I felt the projection wavering, the immaterial realm beginning to slip away as my awareness was pulled back toward physical reality. I allowed the transition, having accomplished what I'd come to do. The disorienting sensation of return washed over me—dimensions reasserting themselves, material existence solidifying around my consciousness.

I gasped, my eyes flying open to the familiar confines of my ready room aboard Thunder. My muscles ached from prolonged stillness, my shirt soaked with sweat. Across from me, Destiny slumped against a console, her eyes wide and tremulous, her breathing shallow and rapid.

"You saw," she whispered, not a question but a realization. Her fists were clenched so tightly that her knuckles showed white against her dark skin.

I nodded, my throat too dry for immediate speech. My head throbbed with the aftereffects of the projection, vision blurring slightly at the edges.

Destiny pushed herself upright, a subtle grit in her jaw betraying her effort to maintain composure. "I remember now. All of it." Her voice was eerily steady. "She was... inside me. Taking things. And I couldn't stop her."

"Few could have," I said, finding my voice at last.

"Ban'ach is a Soul Ravager. They're trained for this—it's what maracs do."

"She knows everything, Kory." Destiny's eyes locked with mine, shock giving way to resolve. "About *Thunder*. About Wolf Jaw. About you. She said they were going to attack."

I reached for her hand, needing the physical contact to ground myself after the sydereal immersion. Our fingers met, and I felt a jolt—not from the Syderealium this time, but simple human connection, anchoring us both in the face of what we'd discovered.

"And they already did," I said. "And they failed to catch us. We're safe, now."

Destiny nodded, already pushing herself to her feet. The shock hadn't left her eyes, but something else had joined it—a fierce determination that I recognized from our years together. She'd been violated in the most intimate way possible, her very consciousness breached and manipulated, putting her friends in danger. But she was Destiny Austin, who'd survived abuse, foster homes, and the streets of San Jose. Who'd become a leader on an insurgent warship through sheer force of will.

"Kory... thank you. For finding what she took."

I stood as well, my legs unsteady beneath me. "We'll stop them, Des."

She paused at the door, her profile sharp against the light from the corridor. "Yes," she said simply. "We will."

As she left, I braced myself against my desk, still reeling from what I'd witnessed in the Syderealium. My projection skills had been enough to unlock what Ban'ach had hidden, but would they be enough to for Destiny's mind to fully heal? I didn't know. And did I fix everything that was wrong?

I took one deep breath, steadying myself, then followed her to the bridge.

37

Sofia's fingers traced along my arm like a question mark, warm and seeking. I watched her in the dim light of our quarters; her penetrating blue eyes still made my breath catch, even after all this time. The faint sound of the Pacific pushing surf onto the beach outside our tent sang to me, a distant lullaby of water and life that differed so much from the hum and vibrations of shipboard life that had become the soundtrack to our relationship—mechanical, reliable, and occasionally interrupted by moments of turbulence.

"You're staring again, Kory," she murmured, her slight German accent more pronounced in the intimacy of our shared space.

"Guilty as charged, Chief Kohl." I grinned, tugging at the hem of her standard-issue pajamas. They weren't exactly designed with seduction in mind—utilitarian gray with tiny UHC insignias patterned across them like bureaucratic confetti—but Sofia could make a hazmat suit look good. "It's not my fault the UHC assigned me their most beautiful MP."

She rolled her eyes but smiled that private smile she

reserved just for me. The one that transformed her professional demeanor into something soft and playful. "Flattery will get you everywhere, Lieutenant Commander."

"That's what I'm counting on." I leaned in, brushing my lips against her neck. The scent of her—clean soap and that indefinable something that was just Sofia—filled my senses.

Her hands moved to my chest, fingers playing with the buttons of my own equally uninspiring sleepwear. "We should sleep. Early briefing tomorrow."

"Sleep is overrated," I whispered in her ear, delighting in the small shiver that ran through her. "Besides, I've got excellent tactical training now. I can be very... efficient."

She laughed, a sound I'd once thought impossible to coax from the serious former German MP I'd first met. "Is that what they taught you at Space Warfare School? Efficiency?"

"Among other things." I shifted, moving myself over her, my lips finding hers in the semi-darkness. Her mouth was warm and responsive, and I felt that familiar surge of desire that never seemed to diminish, no matter how many times we'd been together.

Her hands slid beneath my shirt, cool against my skin, and I groaned softly. After everything we'd been through—the battle of Virelia, escaping the doomed *Inferis,* her injury and recovery—these moments felt like stolen treasures. Little pockets of normalcy in the chaos our lives had become.

I was just getting into a particularly promising rhythm, my hand sliding up Sofia's thigh, when I felt it—the sudden rigidity in her body, the way her breath caught and held. Not in pleasure, but in that now-familiar stillness that had become the bane of my existence.

"Sofia?" I pulled back, already knowing what was happening.

She didn't respond. Her blue eyes stared up at the ceiling, unfocused and distant, pupils dilated. Another flashback, courtesy of the Kergan brain implant that had saved her life but came with unwanted baggage—classified information from both HCD and Kergan databases, bursting into her consciousness at increasingly inconvenient moments.

I sighed and rolled off her, running a hand through my shaggy hair. Talk about a mood killer. The universe had a twisted sense of humor—I finally get a serious relationship, and it comes with built-in *coitus interruptus.*

"Take your time," I whispered, though I knew she probably couldn't hear me.

I stared up at the fabric ceiling of the tent, counting the rivets on the seams. Twenty-three across, seventeen down. I'd counted them many times before during these episodes. They were becoming more frequent—once every few days at first, now almost nightly. Dr. Chen had warned us this might happen as Sofia's brain integrated more of the implant's data.

The timing was becoming comedically predictable. Of course it would hit right when things were getting interesting. I might as well start a log: Day 37 of Sexual Frustration, The Sofia Kohl Edition. Entry: "Once again reached second base before neural copulatory jammer activated."

I chuckled to myself, though there wasn't much humor in it. The reality was more concerning than amusing. The implant was affecting her more, not less, as time passed. But what choice did we have? Without it, she would have died from her head injury.

Minutes ticked by in silence. I'd learned not to interrupt these episodes—the first few times I'd tried to snap her out of them had resulted in blinding headaches for her. Better to let them run their course.

"Kory," she finally whispered, still staring upward.

I propped myself up on one elbow, studying her face. "What are you seeing?"

"Hold on. I'm still... processing." Her voice was mechanical, distant.

I settled back, crossing my arms behind my head. Only Sofia could tell me to shut up and still leave me besotted. The woman had a gift. I focused on her breathing, watching the rise and fall of her chest beneath the gray pajama top. The buttons were still partially undone from our earlier activities, revealing a tantalizing triangle of skin.

Great. Now I was getting worked up again with zero chance of follow-through. The universe really was testing my self-control. I wondered if this was some cosmic punishment for past sins—perhaps for all those years living on the streets of San Jose, stealing to survive.

I tried to distract myself by mentally reviewing *Thunder*'s maintenance schedule. We needed to recalibrate the starboard vector control pods soon. And the secondary life support system had been making that funny clicking noise again...

"Ban'ach," Sofia suddenly said, the name falling from her lips like a stone.

I tensed. The name of the Soul Ravager still sent icy fingers down my spine. Our encounters with the female marac had left scars both physical and psychological. "What about her?"

"She interrogated others. Not just Destiny." Sofia's voice was stronger now, though her eyes remained unfocused. "Insurgents. People connected to the resistance."

I sat up, sleep and frustration forgotten. "Who else?"

"Many. Dozens. She was... collecting information." Sofia

blinked several times, her eyes finally focusing on me. "Project Warped Eclipse."

"What's that?" I asked, my hand finding hers and squeezing gently.

"I don't know." She frowned, the vertical line between her eyebrows deepening. "But she was very interested in it. Very... focused. It seemed important."

"Is it a weapon? A location?" I pressed.

Sofia shook her head slowly. "I don't know. The information is fragmented. But Ban'ach believed it was crucial to something bigger. Something... planned."

She sat up, pressing her fingers to her temples. "That's all I have. Just the name and Ban'ach's fixation on it."

I wrapped an arm around her shoulders, pulling her close. "It's okay. You're doing great."

We sat in silence for a moment, the implications hanging between us. If Ban'ach had been interrogating multiple insurgents about this mysterious project, it couldn't be good news.

"I should document this," Sofia said, professional instincts kicking in.

"Tomorrow," I insisted, gently easing her back down to the pillows. "You need rest."

She didn't argue, which told me how drained the flashback had left her. I pulled the covers over us both, tucking her against my side. Her head nestled into the crook of my shoulder, her breathing slowly evening out.

Sleep eluded me for hours. *Project Warped Eclipse.* The name itself sounded ominous, like something out of a bad spy drama. But if Ban'ach was involved, the reality was likely far worse than fiction.

The next morning, I gathered Destiny and Busto in my ready

room. They sat across from me, Destiny slouched in her chair with her usual defiant posture, Busto ramrod straight, with his hands resting on his knees. The contrast between my executive officer and MARDET leader couldn't have been starker.

"Sofia had another flashback last night," I said without preamble. "She picked up some interesting information about Ban'ach."

Destiny stiffened slightly at the mention of the Soul Ravager, who had held her captive and tampered with her memories. Despite her recovery, those wounds were still fresh.

"Apparently, Destiny wasn't Ban'ach's only interrogation target," I continued. "She was questioning multiple insurgents about something called Project Warped Eclipse."

"And what's that when it's at home?" Destiny asked, her dark eyes narrowing.

I spread my hands. "No idea. Sofia couldn't access any details beyond the name and the fact that Ban'ach was obsessed with it."

Destiny snorted, flicking an imaginary piece of lint from her uniform sleeve. "Well, that's helpfully vague. 'Something bad might be happening somewhere involving someone.' Should I be writing this down, Captain?"

"You're an officer now, Des. It's 'should I be writing this down, sir?'" I corrected with a wry smile.

"Sir, yes sir," she replied with an exaggerated salute. "Permission to point out this intel is about as useful as a chocolate teapot, sir?"

"Permission granted and point taken," I conceded. "But it's something to work with. We can cross-reference the name with any intelligence we gather. Maybe it'll connect to something else."

Busto, who had remained silent, cleared his throat. "Commander, may I speak freely?"

That was never a good sign. "Always, Lieutenant."

His brown eyes held mine, unflinching. "I'm concerned about Chief Kohl."

"Sofia is recovering well," I said, perhaps too quickly. "Dr. Chen says—"

"With respect, sir," Busto interrupted, "I'm not questioning her recovery. I'm questioning the reliability of information coming from a Kergan neural implant."

I felt my jaw tighten. "The implant saved her life."

"Yes, sir. And I'm grateful for that." Busto leaned forward, his voice lowered but intense. "But we have no long-term data on how these implants affect human cognitive function. Or what else they might be designed to do."

"What exactly are you suggesting?" The temperature in the room seemed to drop several degrees.

Busto didn't back down. "I'm suggesting that we exercise caution. The implant contains classified Kergan and HCD data. We have no way of knowing if it's been programmed to... influence its host in some way."

"Sofia is not 'influenced,'" I said, the words coming out harsher than intended. "She's experiencing data flashbacks, exactly as Dr. Chen predicted."

"Kory," Busto said, his voice softening slightly. "I need to ask: do you feel comfortable sleeping in the same bed with her?"

The question hit me like a physical blow. "Excuse me?"

"Kory," Destiny interjected. "He doesn't mean—"

"I know exactly what he means," I snapped, rising to my feet. "He's implying that my partner—a decorated officer who's sacrificed everything for Earth—might be some kind of Kergan sleeper agent."

Busto stood as well, not backing down. "I'm implying nothing. I'm addressing a legitimate security concern. If the chief is receiving classified data through an enemy technology implanted in her brain, we need to consider all possibilities."

"The only thing I'm considering right now is whether you're discriminating against Sofia because she has an implant," I said, my voice dangerously low.

"This isn't discrimination, Kory. It's operational security." Busto's face remained impassive, but I could see the tension in his shoulders. "We have no precedent for this situation, no long-term studies—"

"You're not a doctor, Busto," I cut him off. "So why don't you keep your naïve opinions to yourself instead of questioning the loyalty of another officer?"

We stood toe to toe; the tension crackling between us. Part of me—a part I wasn't proud of—wanted him to make a move, to give me an excuse to vent the frustration and fear that had been building for days.

"Well," Destiny drawled into the silence, "this is awkward. Should I get popcorn, or are you two planning to just glare at each other until the heat death of the universe?"

Her words broke the spell. I blinked, suddenly aware of how close I'd come to punching one of my best friends. I took a step back, rubbing a hand across my face.

"I apologize, Busto," I said stiffly. "That was unprofessional."

Busto nodded once. "Understood, sir," he said, reverting back to formality.

I sank back into my chair, suddenly exhausted. "Look, I know Chief Kohl's condition has everyone concerned. It's had me on edge too. But she's still Sofia. The implant isn't changing who she is."

Busto resumed his seat, his expression softening slightly. "I didn't mean to question your judgment, Commander. Or Chief Kohl's loyalty. I'm just doing my job—identifying potential security risks."

"I know." I extended my hand across the desk. "And I overreacted. Sofia's health issues have kept me on edge these past weeks."

He took my hand in a firm grip. "Don't worry about it, sir. I understand." He paused, then added, "I won't bring up my doubts about the chief again unless something truly alarming happens and I'm forced to."

"Fair enough," I said, relieved at the truce.

After they left, I sat alone in the ready room, staring at the sky projected onto the nearby wall display. Busto's concerns had hit closer to home than I wanted to admit. The truth was, I'd had similar thoughts myself in the dark hours of the night, watching Sofia sleep and wondering what was happening inside her brain.

And if Busto—one of the few people brave enough and close enough to voice these concerns—had doubts about Sofia, then others must, too. Many others. The thought was unsettling. This crew had followed me through hell and back, trusted me with their lives repeatedly. If they thought Sofia was compromised, what did that mean for their trust in me?

I was her partner. I shared her bed, her secrets, her life. If they doubted her judgment, her very mind, then by extension, they must doubt mine as well.

The realization sat heavy in my chest—an uncomfortable heat that I recognized as fear. Not for myself, but for what might be coming. Because if I lost the crew's trust, I might lose much more than just my command. I might lose the only family I'd ever known. At least the one I remembered.

Busto's question haunted me: Did I feel safe sleeping beside Sofia? The truth was, I didn't know anymore. And that uncertainty terrified me more than any enemy we'd faced.

38

"Got a minute?" Destiny's voice pulled me from my contemplation as I sat in my ready-room with the door open.

She stood in the doorway, her usual confident posture subtly altered by something I couldn't immediately identify. Tension, perhaps, or uncertainty—neither emotion I associated with my oldest friend.

"Always," I replied, gesturing to the vacant chair across from my desk. "What's on your mind?"

Destiny glanced around, then shut the door, ensuring no one was within earshot before leaning closer. "I remembered something," she said quietly. "From when Ban'ach had me."

My full attention snapped to her immediately. Destiny's captivity by the marac Soul Ravager had left deep scars, many of them still hidden beneath the surface of her memories.

"What did you remember?" I asked, keeping my voice neutral despite the sudden spike of concern.

"She kept asking me about something called the Noble

Phylactery," Destiny said, her brow furrowed with concentration. "Got really pissed when I couldn't tell her anything about it. I remember her talking to her subordinates about it while I was there, but..." She shook her head in frustration. "It's still mostly gibberish in my head. Fragments that don't connect."

"The Noble Phylactery," I repeated, testing the phrase. It meant nothing to me, but the fact that Ban'ach had been interested in it made it immediately significant. "Any context at all? What it might be, where it might be located?"

Destiny shrugged, the gesture tight with frustration. "Nothing clear. Just that she wanted it badly and thought I might know something about it. Which is crazy—why would I know anything about alien artifacts or whatever this thing is?"

A good question, and one without an obvious answer. "Keep working on those memories," I told her, reaching out to squeeze her shoulder gently. "If fragments are coming back, more might follow. Let me know immediately if you remember anything else, no matter how small it seems."

She nodded, some of the tension leaving her expression. "Will do, Captain." But she remained sitting across from me.

“Spit it out,” I said.

The normally sharp angles of her features seemed dulled, like a knife that had lost its edge. She rubbed her temples in slow circles, a gesture I'd seen too often since I'd restored her memories. "The headaches aren't getting better," she admitted, her voice lacking its usual sarcastic bite. "And I keep having these... moments. Like I'm not alone in my own head." A shiver ran through her slender frame, and I felt a corresponding chill crawl up my spine. Whatever I'd done to help her before, it clearly wasn't enough—or worse, I'd missed something critical.

"How long since you've slept properly?" I asked, studying the dark half-moons under her eyes. They stood out starkly against her black skin, like bruises that refused to heal.

"Define 'properly,'" she muttered, dropping her hands to her lap. "An hour here, two hours there. Nothing continuous." She looked up at me, and the vulnerability in her expression hit me harder than any physical blow. Destiny Austin didn't do vulnerable. "It feels like something's... watching me from inside my own head, Kory."

I leaned forward in my chair, the ready room's soft lighting casting gentle shadows across the small conference table between us. Outside the view display, the Pacific gleamed under sunlight, a constant reminder of our exile.

"I think I need to go back in," I said finally. "Into the Syderealium. I might have missed something when I restored your memories."

Destiny's lips thinned. "You think?"

I spread my hands. "Look, sydereal healing isn't exactly a science. It's more like performing surgery while blindfolded and wearing oven mitts."

A ghost of a smile touched her lips. "That's reassuring."

"Hey, I'm a starship captain, not a doctor," I said, rising from my chair. "But I'm also the most powerful flairsparked human we know of, so you're stuck with me."

"Lucky me," she said, but there was no heat in the words.

I moved to the small clear area of the ready room and gestured for her to join me. "We should sit."

We settled cross-legged on the floor, facing each other. Destiny's breathing had already quickened in anticipation. I reached out and took her hands in mine, her slender fingers cold against my palms.

"Try to relax," I said, closing my eyes. "This should feel like last time."

"Just... find whatever's wrong and fix it," she whispered. "Please."

I nodded and began the process of projecting into the Sydereallium, that multi-dimensional realm that existed alongside and within our physical reality. My consciousness stretched and thinned, expanding beyond the confines of my physical form. The ready room faded from my awareness as I reached out to find Destiny's glyphshade —her soul, for lack of a better term.

The transition into the Sydereallium always disoriented me. One moment I was sitting on the floor of *Thunder*'s ready room; the next, I existed in a space that defied conventional description. Here, physical laws had no meaning. Distance was measured in conceptual proximity rather than meters, and time flowed differently—sometimes faster, sometimes slower than in the physical world.

Around me, the Sydereallium pulsed with information and energy. Packets of data—energlyphs—flowed in complex networks and patterns, forming the foundation of this reality. Somewhere nearby, I sensed Destiny's glyphshade—the network of energlyphs that represented her consciousness and mind.

I moved toward her presence, navigating by intuition rather than sight. Her glyphshade appeared as a complex, beautiful constellation of interconnected points of light—millions of energlyphs forming a unique pattern that was unmistakably Destiny. The familiar sharp angles of her personality, the bright flares of her wit, the deep, steady glow of her loyalty—all represented in this intricate dance of information.

But something was wrong. Attached to her glyphshade was a diffuse ball of light that pulsed with malevolent purpose. It clung to her like a parasite, tendrils of energy worming into her network of energlyphs. The foreign presence wasn't part of her natural pattern—it was an invader.

"Ban'ach," I whispered, though I had no physical voice here. The name rippled through the Sydereailium like a stone dropped in still water.

I recognized the signature of the Soul Ravager's consciousness immediately. This wasn't Ban'ach herself—it was an ancillary glyphshade, a projection of her consciousness left behind to monitor or influence Destiny. The ancillary glyphshade looked nothing like a normal soul —instead of a network of energlyphs, it appeared as a concentrated mass of diffuse light, like a small, malevolent nebula.

How had I missed this the last time I was here? The answer came quickly: the ancillary must have hidden itself, burrowing deep into Destiny's glyphshade and only emerging after I'd completed my work. Ban'ach was nothing if not cunning.

I circled the ancillary, studying its connection to Destiny's glyphshade. The tendrils had wormed their way into her consciousness, explaining the headaches and sense of being watched. This foreign presence was literally observing her thoughts and memories—and possibly influencing them. It was spying on Destiny, and by extension, on all the rest of us.

Without hesitation, I struck at the nearest tendril, forming my own consciousness into a blade of pure will. The sydereal strike sliced through the connection, severing one of the many links between Ban'ach's ancillary and Destiny.

The reaction was immediate. The ancillary pulsed with angry light, and a tendril lashed out at me with surprising speed. I dodged, moving in the conceptual space with the ease of long practice.

"Did you think I wouldn't notice your clumsy attempt at healing?" The voice wasn't physical—it was a direct transmission of thought and intent that rippled through the Syderealium. Ban'ach's mental voice was cold and precise, tinged with arrogance. "I've been watching through this human's eyes for days."

"Get out of her head," I demanded, circling the ancillary. "She's not yours to torment."

"All lesser beings are mine to do with as I please," the ancillary replied. "Especially humans. Your species is particularly easy to manipulate."

I struck again, aiming for another connection point. This time, the ancillary was ready, deflecting my strike with a shield of concentrated will. The collision sent ripples through the Syderealium, distorting the space around us.

"You've improved since our last encounter," Ban'ach observed, her ancillary shifting and pulsing. "But you're still a child playing with forces you barely comprehend."

I said nothing, focusing instead on my next attack. In the Syderealium, combat was a matter of will and imagination as much as skill. I formed my consciousness into a spear of concentrated intent and drove it toward the center of the ancillary.

The spear struck home, penetrating the outer layers of the ancillary's defenses. Ban'ach's presence recoiled, the ball of light contracting before expanding in what I could only interpret as rage.

"Insolent creature!" The ancillary lashed out with multiple tendrils, each one a whip of pure energy aimed at different points of my consciousness.

I blocked two, dodged a third, but the fourth caught me with a glancing blow. Pain—or the sydereal equivalent—flashed through my being. In the physical world, my body might have flinched or tensed, but here, the damage was to my consciousness itself.

"Is this the best humanity has to offer?" Ban'ach taunted as her ancillary circled me. "No wonder your species fell so easily to the Kergans."

"At least we don't feed on others like parasites," I shot back, reforming my defenses. "Soul Ravager—even your title admits what you are. A thief of what you can't create yourself."

The ancillary pulsed with what might have been indignation. "I take what is rightfully mine by virtue of power. The strong consume the weak—that is the only true law of existence."

I launched another attack, this time splitting my consciousness into multiple striking points, attacking the ancillary from different angles simultaneously. Ban'ach's projection deflected most, but couldn't block them all. My will pierced her defenses at two points, and I felt a surge of satisfaction as the ancillary's light flickered momentarily.

Our battle continued, a dance of will and intent in a realm where physical limitations had no meaning. Ban'ach was powerful, but her ancillary represented only a fraction of her true consciousness. Meanwhile, I was fully present, my entire being focused on this fight.

As we clashed, I probed deeper into the ancillary, searching for information. First, I looked for any trace of my parents' memories—Ban'ach had stolen them from me during our first encounter in Arizona over a year ago.

"Looking for something?" Ban'ach's voice was smug.

"Your parents, perhaps? No, I keep those memories for myself. You'll never find them this way."

I pushed past the taunt, diving deeper into the ancillary's structure. If I couldn't find my parents, perhaps I could discover something else useful. The ancillary resisted, throwing up barriers and launching counterattacks to drive me back.

Then I found it—a cluster of information, heavily protected and carefully preserved. With a surge of effort, I broke through Ban'ach's defenses and accessed the data.

Images and concepts flooded my consciousness: an ancient artifact of alien design, glowing with power beyond comprehension. The Noble Phylactery—created by the Primordians, a long-extinct race of alien sentients. The Phylactery was no mere tool or weapon—it was a prison, designed to contain an entity of godlike power.

Nekufima. The name resonated through the Syderealium like a bell, causing ripples in the fabric of this reality. An Astral Titan, one of the oldest and most powerful glyphshades in existence, a being imprisoned within the Phylactery. And whoever bonded with the Phylactery could control Nekufima, wielding power that would make them virtually unstoppable in the physical realm.

"You weren't supposed to see that," Ban'ach hissed, her ancillary contracting with what I sensed was alarm.

"This is what you're after," I said, understanding dawning. "The Phylactery. Control of an Astral Titan."

"With Nekufima's power, I could reshape reality itself," Ban'ach confirmed, her mental voice reverberating with hunger. "The Kergans, the Collective Dominion—all would bow before me. Even your pitiful species would serve a purpose as my slaves."

"Not going to happen," I said, gathering my will for a

final assault.

The ancillary lashed out with renewed fury, tendrils of energy slashing at my consciousness from all directions. "You cannot stop what is already in motion, human. The Phylactery will be mine, and with it, dominion over all existence."

I dodged and blocked, taking hits that would have left physical bruises had we been fighting in the material world. But I had one advantage Ban'ach didn't expect—this wasn't her full consciousness, merely a projection, while I was fighting with my entire being.

In the Syderealium, imagination was power. I focused my will, visualizing something solid and inescapable. Above Ban'ach's ancillary, a massive iron anvil materialized—a construct of pure will and intent, given form by my determination.

"What—" Ban'ach began, sensing the new threat too late.

I released my hold on the anvil, letting it crash down onto the ancillary with the full force of my will behind it. The impact sent shockwaves through the Syderealium, distorting the space around us like ripples in a pond.

The ancillary's light flickered, dimmed, and then collapsed in on itself. Ban'ach's presence vanished from this part of the Syderealium with a final, outraged scream that faded into nothingness.

I waited, alert for any sign that a fragment of the ancillary had survived. Nothing. The space where Ban'ach's projection had been was empty, the tendrils that had invaded Destiny's glyphshade gone without a trace.

I turned my attention to Destiny's glyphshade, examining it carefully for any remaining damage. The network of energlyphs pulsed with renewed strength and clarity, free from the parasite that had been feeding on her consciousness. There was nothing wrong with her glyphshade now—the problem had been Ban'ach's presence all along.

That Ban'ach had been attached to her was a major problem. I had no way of knowing how much information the Soul Ravager had gained from Destiny, but it was entirely possible that Ban'ach now knew we were on this Pacific island. Even worse, she might know about our plans to establish a base on Deimos.

I ignored the anxiety for the moment, and satisfied that Destiny was now free of corrupting influences, I began the process of returning to my physical body. The Syderealium faded around me as I contracted my consciousness back into its normal boundaries, threading my awareness through the dimensional barriers until I was once again sitting cross-legged on the floor of *Thunder*'s ready room.

I opened my eyes to find Destiny already awake, blinking rapidly, as though seeing the world with new clarity. The change in her was immediately apparent—her eyes were clear, the tension gone from her shoulders.

"What just happened?" she asked, releasing my hands. "It feels like someone lifted a weight off my brain."

"Ban'ach happened," I said, rolling my neck to ease the stiffness. How long had we been sitting here? Minutes? Hours? Time moved differently in the Syderealium. "She left a piece of herself inside your head—an ancillary glyphshade. It was watching us through your eyes, probably reporting back to her somehow."

Destiny's expression darkened. "That explains the feeling of being watched." She rubbed her temples again, but this time it seemed more out of habit than pain. "Is it gone?"

"Smashed it with a giant anvil," I said with a grim smile.

"So yes, it's gone."

She raised an eyebrow. "An anvil?"

"In the Syderealium, imagination is as good a weapon as any," I explained, stretching my legs. "The point is, it worked. How's your head feeling?"

"Better." She sounded surprised. "Much better, actually. The fog is gone. The pressure is gone." She looked at me with something approaching wonder. "Thank you."

I shrugged, uncomfortable with the gratitude. "Just doing my job as your friend. And captain. And apparently, your personal exorcist."

That earned me a smile, a genuine one that reached her eyes. "Did you learn anything while you were in there? About Ban'ach, I mean."

I hesitated, the knowledge I'd gleaned from the ancillary weighing heavily on my mind. "I learned more about this Noble Phylactery you mentioned. She's looking for it. An artifact made by the Primordians—an ancient alien race everyone thought was extinct."

"And what does this Phylactery do?" Destiny asked, her tactical mind already working on the implications.

"It's a prison," I drawled, "for an Astral Titan named Nekufima. Whoever bonds with the Phylactery can control the Titan, giving them god-like powers in the physical plane."

Destiny's eyes widened. "Well, that sounds terrifying."

"Yeah." I got to my feet, offering her a hand up. "Ban'ach with that kind of power is... not a scenario I want to contemplate."

"So we need to find this Phylactery before she does," Destiny said, accepting my help.

I nodded. "If it even exists. It could be a myth, a legend. But the fact that Ban'ach believes in it enough to leave part of herself monitoring us suggests there might be something to it."

Destiny moved to the view display, looking out at our small island camp. "From hiding from the Kergans to racing against a Soul Ravager for an ancient alien artifact. Our lives just keep getting more complicated, don't they?"

I joined her at the display, watching as nanobots swarmed across the sand, working to complete *Thunder*. "At least we're headed somewhere safe. A place to regroup, plan, build our forces."

"And figure out how to find a mythical alien prison before Ban'ach does," Destiny added.

"Right. That too." I sighed, running a hand through my hair. "One catastrophe at a time, I guess."

Destiny bumped her shoulder against mine, a gesture of solidarity that spoke volumes. "We've made it this far."

I nodded, watching the stars in the sky above our little island. Somewhere out there, Ban'ach was searching for the power to enslave humanity and challenge the Collective Dominion itself. An Astral Titan, a being of godlike power, trapped in an ancient prison—it was almost too fantastic to believe.

And yet, after everything I'd seen and experienced since becoming flairsparked, I knew better than to dismiss it. If the Noble Phylactery existed, we needed to find it first. The alternative was too horrifying to contemplate.

Then another thought struck me—something that had been nagging at me ever since I realized Destiny's problems were tied to her glyphshade. I turned to her and asked, "Why didn't Nicobe help with your memory issues? Why didn't she stop the ancillary?"

Destiny shrugged. "Nicobe doesn't have much experience with the sydereal arts. She told me that while most igna are flairsparked, very few receive formal training to actually use the Syderealium."

I nodded slowly. "Makes sense. I guess that makes Zeta something of an outlier among her kind."

39

I ran my hand along *Thunder's* gleaming hull, feeling the cool metal beneath my fingertips like a reunion with an old friend who'd somehow grown taller, broader, and infinitely more dangerous. Nine days of waiting, and she was finally complete—no longer just my warship, but something evolved, something that made my chest swell with a pride I wasn't entirely sure I deserved. The tropical island breeze carried the tang of heated metal and fresh plasma conduits, the smell of a predator ready to hunt.

"Lieutenant Commander Drake appears pleased with what he sees," Queen Zeta observed from inside her floating octahedral capsule, the plasma of her true form shifting in patterns that reminded me of sunspots dancing across a stellar surface.

"Nicobe finds the human's expression most entertaining," added the crimson dodecahedron hovering beside Zeta, rotating slightly as if to better observe my reaction. "Like a juvenile being presented with an unexpectedly substantial dessert."

I pulled my hand back and straightened my uniform jacket. "She's magnificent. I hardly recognize her."

"That was rather the point," Nicobe replied, her crimson capsule pulsing slightly with what I recognized as amusement. "We have been most diligent in our work."

No longer a battle-scarred frigate, *Thunder* now stood before me, reborn and redefined—her ellipsoid hull stretched to a full 300 meters, surface gleaming with the matte black of advanced armor plating that seemed to drink in the sunlight rather than reflect it.

"Shall we proceed with the inspection of the interior?" Zeta's capsule drifted toward the main boarding ramp, which extended smoothly from *Thunder*'s lower hull as we approached.

I followed, trying to maintain the dignified pace expected of a commanding officer rather than bounding up the ramp like the excited kid I felt like. "Lead the way, Your Majesty."

The airlock cycled open with a pneumatic hiss that was both familiar and different—quieter, more efficient. The interior corridors had the same layout I remembered, but everything felt more spacious, more purposeful. The lighting had a clarity that made the old *Thunder* seem dingy by comparison.

"First, the hangar deck," Zeta announced, leading our small procession through corridors populated by busy kavreni technicians who paused their work to bow deeply as the Queen passed.

The hangar doors slid open, and my jaw nearly hit the deck plates. What had previously been a modest bay capable of housing a couple of small shuttles had been transformed into a cathedral of military aerospace engineering. The ceiling soared three decks high, with gantries and maintenance cradles suspended from reinforced tracks.

"Four Albatross assault shuttles," I whispered, taking in the sleek, predatory craft lined up in perfect formation. "That's enough to deploy a full Marine platoon simultaneously."

"A necessity for the expanded Marine complement," Nicobe confirmed, her capsule hovering near one of the shuttles. "Each Albatross carries improved armor and weapon systems compared to previous models. Nicobe believes you will find their performance most satisfactory."

I walked between the shuttles, trailing my fingers along their armored flanks. Each one was a self-contained assault platform capable of atmospheric and exoatmospheric operations. The thought of what *Thunder* could now accomplish with these assets made my pulse quicken.

"The engineering section has undergone the most substantive transformation," Zeta continued, guiding us through another set of security doors.

The moment we entered Engineering, I understood what she meant. A reactor core had been added, a gleaming cylindrical chamber encased in transparent superconducting crystal. Within, a controlled fusion reaction of helium-3 glowed with a blue-white intensity that was almost painful to look at directly.

"The He-3 fusion reactor," a familiar voice said from behind me. I turned to find Phoebe approaching, a datapad in her hand and her brunette hair pulled back in a practical bun. "It's capable of charging our chromatic batteries even during extended operations without resupply."

"Lieutenant Brooks has been assisting with integrating certain systems," Zeta explained. "Her technical expertise has proven most valuable."

Phoebe gave me a small, private smile that made my heart skip in an inappropriate manner before returning to her professional demeanor.

She's flirting with me, I realized with shock. Sofia would be furious if she found out.

Phoebe said, "The improved chromatic battery banks have a power output triple what we had before. We can run at full combat capacity for weeks without recharging."

I whistled low. "That changes everything for long-range operations."

"Indeed, it does," Phoebe agreed, falling into step beside me as we continued the tour. "No more worrying about power conservation during extended missions. We can maintain full shields, weapons, and propulsion simultaneously."

Speaking of weapons—the armory and missile batteries were next on our tour, and if the hangar had impressed me, the weapons systems left me speechless. What had been a respectable array of offensive capabilities had become an arsenal that would make any other capital ship envious.

"The missile batteries have been tripled," Nicobe announced proudly as we entered the central armory. "Vertical launch systems have been integrated throughout the hull, allowing for simultaneous deployment of anti-ship, interceptor, and GAM warheads."

I moved to the main diagnostics console, running my hands over the controls that were both familiar and enhanced. "And the railguns?"

"Upgraded to 400-gigajoule gluon-field capacitors," Phoebe replied, stepping to my side and bringing up the weapons specifications on the display. "Muzzle velocity increased by forty percent, firing a 5 kilogram tungsten penetrator at 300 kilometers-per-second. The penetration capability is... substantial."

"Substantial enough to punch through a Kergan frigate's forward armor?" I asked, studying the technical readouts.

Phoebe's eyes met mine, a hint of fierce satisfaction in them. "Like tissue paper, if you hit them right."

The tour continued through crew quarters—expanded to accommodate the larger complement—and medical facilities that would have made a small hospital jealous. Throughout it all, I tried to reconcile this new *Thunder* with the ship I'd known. She was the same at her core, but strengthened, matured, deadly.

"And now, the command deck," Zeta announced as we entered the last stretch of our inspection.

The bridge had undergone perhaps the most striking transformation of all. Gone was the cramped, utilitarian space I'd grown accustomed to. In its place stood a command center worthy of an admiral's flagship. The captain's chair—my chair—occupied a slightly raised platform in the center, surrounded by workstations arranged in a horseshoe configuration that allowed me to see every station with a simple turn of my head.

"These are the control interfaces for the enhanced propulsion systems," Nicobe explained, indicating a station to the right of the command chair. "The new tractor pods and inertial dampeners will allow Thunder to sustain accelerations of up to 25 gees for brief periods."

I let out a low whistle. "That's fighter-level maneuverability in a cruiser hull."

"Precisely," Zeta confirmed, her plasma form rippling with satisfaction. "*Thunder* is no longer an escort ship. She is a Marauder-class capital ship, designed to strike hard and fast against superior numbers."

As if summoned by the Queen's words, Destiny

sauntered onto the bridge, her dark eyes widening slightly as she took in the new command center. "Well, well," she said, approaching with her usual sardonic smile. "Looks like we got ourselves an upgrade, Captain."

I couldn't help returning her smile. "Yes, we certainly did."

"The platoon berthing is particularly impressive," Destiny continued, leaning against one of the tactical consoles. "Those Marines are going to be living better than we did in most of the places we crashed growing up."

"The ship is optimized for a complement of 150 crew members," Zeta explained, her capsule drifting to the center of the bridge. "This includes the Marine Detachment and allows for specialized personnel for each critical system."

I lowered myself into the command chair, feeling it conform perfectly to my body. The tactical displays lit up around me, showing *Thunder*'s systems at full readiness, a predator poised to strike. "I'm not sure what to say, Zeta. This is beyond anything I expected."

"The Queen expects you to use *Thunder* to her full potential in the current conflict," Zeta replied, her tone growing more formal. "Which brings us to the matter of immediate security concerns."

The moment of admiration passed, and we shifted smoothly into planning mode. Destiny took her position at the XO's station while Phoebe moved to the engineering console. Nicobe hovered near Phoebe, her crimson capsule rotating thoughtfully.

"Zeta heard about Destiny's unfortunate problem with a sydereal ancillary," the queen said.

"A problem that has been handled," I said.

"But, as you know, our intended destination, Deimos, has likely been revealed to Ban'ach."

"I'm aware of that. I planned to meet with the command team later today to discuss the problem. When can *Thunder* depart?"

"In six hours," Zeta said. "The Royal Guard frigates require additional time to complete final system checks."

I nodded, feeling the weight of command settling comfortably on my shoulders. This was what *Thunder* had been rebuilt for—to protect Zeta, to strike at our enemies, to help us reclaim what had been lost. "Let's set departure for 1800 hours. Destiny, coordinate with Lieutenant Busto for security protocols. I'll set up a meeting for the command team to discuss an alternate destination."

As the others moved to carry out their tasks, I remained in the command chair, running my hands over the controls that connected me to *Thunder*'s systems. Nine days of waiting had transformed my ship into something new, something powerful.

Now it was time to see what she could do.

40

I squinted at the logistics report on my tablet, numbers swimming before my tired eyes like minnows evading a predator. Four hours into our pre-launch preparations, and the supply manifests were still showing discrepancies that would give any commanding officer heartburn. Whoever said that war was hours of boredom punctuated by moments of terror had never dealt with the paperwork required to keep a warship operational. I rubbed my temples and reached for my coffee, now cold enough to taste like liquid regret.

"Ensign Cho counts seventeen fewer chromatic battery cells than requisitioned," I muttered to myself, scrolling through the inventory list. "And where the hell are the Mark-7 GAM warheads?"

The ready room felt too small for the mountain of administrative details, crushing my enthusiasm for *Thunder*'s rebirth. Each item on the checklist represented a potential vulnerability, a weakness that might manifest at the worst possible moment. I'd seen enough combat to know that logistics killed more effectively than enemy fire.

The shriek of the general quarters alarm nearly launched me out of my chair.

"All hands to battle stations! Commander Drake to the command deck immediately!" The voice over the PA system belonged to Destiny, her usual sarcasm replaced by the clipped precision of combat readiness.

I was moving before the announcement finished, muscle memory taking over as I dropped the tablet and sprinted for the door. The corridor outside my ready room had transformed into an organized chaos of crew members rushing to stations, the newly expanded complement of *Thunder* creating traffic patterns I wasn't yet accustomed to.

"Make a hole!" I called, and the sea of personnel parted like magic.

A young kavreni technician flattened himself against the bulkhead, his enormous eyes wide with what might have been excitement or terror. "First action, sir!" he chittered as I passed.

"You'll be fine, son," I responded, trying my best to sound unworried, though I knew the odds were now against us having a peaceful departure.

The walk to the command deck seemed to take an eternity, though my chrono showed only twelve seconds had elapsed since the alarm. When the doors slid open, the command center was already at full combat readiness, workstations manned and tactical displays glowing with threat assessments.

"Report!" I barked, striding to the command chair.

Destiny turned from the main tactical display, her face tight with concentration. "Kergan flotilla just popped up on our long-range sensors. Six frigates, heavy class, coming in low and fast from the southeast. They're running hot with active jamming and ECM."

I dropped into the command chair, bringing up the tactical overlay on my personal display. Sure enough, six red markers were approaching the island at high speed, their electronic warfare signatures unmistakable.

"How the hell did they find us?" I demanded, though the question was largely rhetorical.

"Unknown," Sofia replied from her intelligence station, her fingers dancing across the controls. I had happily added my partner to the crew roster after Chen and Kovac officially cleared her for active duty. "But their approach vector suggests they know exactly where we are. They're not searching; they're hunting."

I knew exactly how they'd found us: Ban'ach. The ancillary had tipped them off, and now that we'd uncovered and flushed the spy, the Kergans were making their move before we could vanish again. One thing was certain—Deimos was off the table as our next base. Completely burned.

Looking at a magnified view of the enemy, I recognized the ship configuration immediately—the same type of armored Kergan frigates I'd engaged in Arizona two years ago. Heavy armor, respectable armament, but limited maneuverability. In the old *Thunder*, they would have been a deadly threat. In the new *Thunder*... well, we were about to find out.

"Time to intercept?" I asked, already calculating our options.

"Seven minutes at current speed," Destiny answered. "The Royal Guard frigates are prepped for immediate launch, awaiting your orders."

I made my decision in less than a second. "All hands prepare for emergency departure. I want *Thunder* airborne in five minutes. Recall all shore parties and secure for combat launch."

The command deck erupted in controlled activity as my orders were relayed throughout the ship. Destiny leaned closer, her voice low enough that only I could hear. "We're still missing twenty percent of our crew complement, Kory. They're scattered across the island, finishing supply transfers."

"They've got five minutes to get their asses on board," I replied, though I softened it with a quick grin. "Signal the Royal Guard frigates to launch immediately and establish a screening position between us and the Kergan force. They're to delay and disrupt, not engage in sustained combat."

Destiny nodded and turned to relay the orders. On the tactical display, I watched as the two Royal Guard frigates—sleek, nimble vessels about half *Thunder*'s size—lifted from their berths and accelerated toward the approaching threat.

"Three minutes to launch," Destiny announced. "Crew recall at eighty-eight percent and climbing."

I pulled up the weapons readiness report, pleased to see that despite the logistics discrepancies, our combat systems were at full capacity. Even if *Thunder* launched with a partial crew, her teeth and claws were sharp.

"Commander," one of the sensor operators called, "the Royal Guard frigates have engaged the Kergan flotilla. Initial missile exchange in progress."

The tactical display updated to show the first salvos—streaks of light representing missiles crossing the distance between the opposing forces. The Kergan ships had spread into an attack formation, trying to envelop the two Royal Guard vessels that were executing a complex evasive pattern while firing targeted missile barrages.

"Two minutes, thirty seconds," Destiny updated. "Crew

recall at ninety-two percent."

I opened a ship-wide channel, which also reached the shore parties. "All hands, this is the commander. We are launching in two minutes, ready or not. If you're not on board by then, find something to hold on to down there. We'll come back for you when we've dealt with our visitors."

The distant thunder of detonations reached us even through *Thunder*'s thick hull—the sound of interceptor missiles meeting warheads in mid-air, a deadly ballet of explosions rippling across the sky.

"Royal Guard frigate *Tenacious* reports their missile reserves at sixty percent and dropping rapidly," Destiny relayed, her hand pressed to her comm implant. "They're requesting immediate support."

"Crew recall at ninety-eight percent," Destiny added. "Lieutenant Montana reports all essential medical personnel accounted for."

A minute later, Destiny confirmed that the last of the shore parties had boarded, with seconds to spare. I wouldn't be leaving anybody behind today.

"Helm control transferring to command chair," I announced, feeling the familiar flight controls as my seat's arm panels lit up beneath my hands. This was the moment of truth—my first time piloting *Thunder* in her new configuration.

"All stations report ready for combat," Destiny announced, sliding into her XO's chair beside me. "Weapons hot, defensive systems active."

"Launch in three...two...one..." I announced.

I engaged the main tractor pods, and *Thunder* responded with a power that took my breath away. The massive warship rose from her berth with the agility of a craft half her size, acceleration pressing me gently back into my seat despite the inertial dampeners.

Through the forward displays, I could see the battle unfolding—brief, intense flashes of light as missiles detonated in complex patterns. The Royal Guard frigates were dancing through the Kergan formation, their superior maneuverability allowing them to avoid direct hits while depleting the enemy's defensive resources.

"Taking us in," I said, feeling a grin spread across my face as *Thunder* responded to my commands with precision I'd never experienced before. The controls felt like extensions of my own body, the ship's massive power humming through the controls like a living thing eager to be unleashed.

"Recommend caution, Commander," Nicobe said from her station. "We haven't fully tested all systems under combat conditions."

I laughed, the sound surprising even me. "What better time than now?"

Thunder surged forward, acceleration pushing us to 5 gees before the inertial dampeners fully compensated. I banked the massive ship into an attack vector, targeting the center of the Kergan formation.

"Missile batteries one through six, prepare for salvo fire," I ordered. "Railgun crews, standby for point defense and opportunistic strikes."

Sofia had moved from her station to a jump seat near my command chair, her tablet still in hand as she monitored the tactical feeds. Suddenly, her eyes widened, and she looked up with an expression I'd seen before—a mixture of confusion and revelation.

"Kory, I know how to hit them," she said urgently, her voice strange. "These Kergan frigates—model KF-209—they have a design flaw in their ventral armor where the auxiliary power coupling connects to the main reactor."

I glanced at her, momentarily distracted. "How could you possibly know that?"

Sofia blinked, looking as surprised by the information as I was. "I... I think it's from the Kergan data in my implant. It just... came to me." She tapped her temple where the Kergan brain implant had been installed after her injury. "A single railgun shot at the right angle will cascade through their power distribution network."

No time to question it. "Targeting, did you get that?" I called to the weapons officer.

"Yes, sir. Calculating optimal firing solutions now."

The tactical display updated with new targeting parameters, highlighting vulnerability points on the Kergan vessels that hadn't been in our databases before.

"Royal Guard frigates report missile reserves at thirty percent," Destiny announced. "They've damaged one Kergan vessel but are being pressed hard."

"Tell them to break contact on my mark," I replied, fingers dancing across the control interface as I brought *Thunder* into an optimal firing position. "Railguns one and two, target the lead Kergan frigate, ventral section, coordinates being fed to your stations now."

Thunder shuddered slightly as the massive railguns swiveled into position. On the tactical display, I could see we were still outside optimal range, but closing fast.

"Mark!" I called. "Royal Guard frigates, break contact, vector seven-three-niner."

The two screening vessels peeled away in perfect synchronization, leaving the Kergan flotilla momentarily exposed and adjusting their targeting solutions.

"Railguns one and two, fire!"

Twin lances of hypersonic projectiles streaked from *Thunder*'s forward section, crossing the intervening space so fast it appeared instantaneous. The lead Kergan frigate had begun to turn, trying to bring its stronger dorsal armor to bear, but too late.

The first projectile struck precisely where Sofia had indicated, punching through what appeared to be reinforced plating with surprising ease. For a moment, nothing happened—then the frigate's midsection bulged outward as internal systems catastrophically failed. A heartbeat later, the vessel split cleanly in two, secondary explosions rippling along the break as its internal atmosphere burned.

"Direct hit!" the weapons officer called, unable to keep the excitement from his voice. "Target destroyed, Commander!"

"Missile batteries one through four, salvo fire on designated targets two and three," I ordered, already bringing *Thunder* into a sweeping turn that would present minimum cross-section to the remaining Kergan vessels.

The ship trembled as missiles streamed from their launch tubes, dozens of contrails stretching toward the disorganized Kergan formation. Their point defense systems engaged, intercepting many of the incoming projectiles, but the sheer volume of fire overwhelmed their defenses.

Two more Kergan frigates disappeared in expanding balls of superheated gas and debris. A third limped away, venting atmosphere and trailing thick black smoke—signs of catastrophic internal damage.

The remaining two undamaged Kergan vessels abruptly changed course, accelerating away from the battle at maximum thrust.

"They're running," Destiny announced, a satisfied smile

curving her lips. "Should we pursue?"

I considered it for a moment, watching the fleeing ships on the tactical display. "Negative. Our primary mission is to secure the Queen and establish a new base. Let them go—they'll report back that *Thunder* is not to be trifled with."

"Royal Guard frigates returning to formation," Sofia reported. "Minor damage to *Tenacious,* but all systems operational."

I leaned back in the command chair, feeling the adrenaline slowly ebbing from my system. *Thunder*'s first combat test in her new configuration had been brief but definitive.

"Get us away from Earth," I ordered. "Standard acceleration. Let's take it easy on the pods until engineering has a chance to review combat telemetry."

I signaled for Destiny, Busto, and Sofia to approach, along with Nicobe and Zeta. "We need to decide where we're going. Deimos is compromised."

Destiny's face flushed, and I knew she was feeling guilty about being the victim of Ban'ach's ancillary.

I quickly added, "It was nobody's fault. We simply learned new intelligence that suggests the Kergans may already know we intended to go to Mars. We need somewhere else."

Sofia's voice suddenly cut through the silence, her words precise and mechanical in a way that didn't belong to her. It wasn't Sofia speaking anymore; it was the thing in her head.

"HCD Surveillance Protocol 7732-A," she recited, her blue eyes fixed on nothing, "Sector 17 bypass authorization: Charlie-November-93-Echo-Tango. Designated blind spot coordinates follow: right ascension 22 hours 09 minutes 37 seconds, declination plus 30 degrees 58 minutes 44 seconds."

The command deck fell silent. Destiny spun around. I dropped my tablet and reached for Sofia.

"Sofia," I said, careful not to touch her. We'd learned that physical contact during these episodes could disorient her further. "Can you hear me?"

She continued, voice flat as a computer readout: "Orbital object designation: 1036 Ganymed. Classification: Near-Earth asteroid. Status: Surveillance exempt due to negligible strategic value. Nearest patrol route: 0.3 AU deviation."

Then she blinked, her eyes focusing again. She swayed slightly, and this time I did catch her elbow, steadying her as she came back to herself.

"What did I say?" she asked, the familiar hint of German accent returning to her voice.

Destiny was already typing the coordinates into her tablet. The woman's efficiency never ceased to amaze me.

"Coordinates," I told Sofia. "Something about an asteroid designated as a blind spot in Kergan surveillance."

Destiny's expression mixed with fascination and unease. "That's the third time this week she's gone all robot on us," she said, not unkindly. "But this time, it actually sounds useful." She gestured to her tablet. "The coordinates correlate to a known near-Earth asteroid. 1036 Ganymed. It's the largest near-Earth asteroid, approximately 32 kilometers in diameter."

I moved to the display, studying the orbital projection that appeared. "And according to Sofia—or rather, the HCD database—the Kergans are deliberately not monitoring it?"

"Surveillance exempt," Sofia repeated, now fully alert. "Due to negligible strategic value."

Destiny snorted. "A 32-kilometer rock floating in space that nobody's watching? Sounds like the perfect hiding spot to me."

I felt a surge of something I hadn't experienced in a while—genuine hope. "If this is accurate, it could be exactly what we need. A staging area beyond Earth, but close enough to maintain operations."

"If it's accurate," Busto emphasized, his voice measured. "We should consider that the implant may be providing outdated information."

Zeta's octahedral capsule hovered at the edge of the room, her plasma form pulsing with interest inside.

"The Queen wishes to know if the Chief Warrant Officer's neural interface is dangerous for her health," Zeta said. I detected genuine concern in her tone.

Sofia straightened her back, lifting her chin slightly. "The strategic value of the intelligence outweighs the personal risk."

I wanted to protest, to say that nothing outweighed the risk to her, but I knew that look. Sofia had already calculated the odds and made her decision. It was the same expression she'd likely worn when she'd volunteered for hazardous operations back in her military police days—a perfect blend of duty and stubborn determination.

"We need to verify this information," I said instead. "If Ganymed really is a blind spot in Kergan surveillance, it could be the off-world base location we've been looking for."

"Nicobe can assist with verification," came a voice from the doorway. The crimson dodecahedron of our chief engineer floated in, rotating slightly as she spoke. "*Thunder*'s new sensor arrays can be calibrated to detect Kergan patrol signatures at that distance."

Destiny clapped her hands together. "Great! So we've got a plan. Verify the asteroid intel, then figure out how to set up shop on a giant space rock. Just another day at the office."

I nodded, but my eyes were on Sofia. She met my gaze steadily, but I could see the cost of these episodes in the slight tension around her eyes, the barely perceptible tremor in her usually rock-steady hands.

"We'll continue this discussion once we've verified the information," I said. "Nicobe, work with our sensor team on the detection array. Destiny, talk to Lynda Brooks, and the two of you game out what we'd need for an asteroid-based operation."

I turned to the command deck and passed the coordinates for 1036 Ganymed to the navigation officer. "Make best speed for those coordinates," I ordered.

"Course laid in," the navigator confirmed. "ETA to Ganymed at standard acceleration: fourteen hours, twenty-two minutes."

As *Thunder* and her escort frigates climbed away from Earth, I couldn't help but feel a surge of pride. The ship had performed beyond expectations, responding to my commands with a precision and power I was still coming to terms with.

The command deck settled into the routine of normal operations, the excitement of combat giving way to the methodical tasks of damage assessment and system optimization. I used the opportunity to check in with various departments, ensuring that our hasty departure hadn't left us with critical shortfalls.

Hours later, with Earth a diminishing blue sphere on our aft sensors and *Thunder* cruising smoothly toward our destination, the command deck had quieted to a skeleton crew. I remained in the command chair, reviewing battle data and making notes for future tactical refinements.

41

I watched through *Thunder*'s main viewscreen as we approached 1036 Ganymed, a lump of rock floating in the vast emptiness that separated Earth's orbit from Mars's orbit. The asteroid tumbled slowly against the backdrop of stars, looking completely unremarkable—which made it perfect. With the Kergans occupying Earth, we needed a base they'd never think to look for, and this misshapen potato of an asteroid was our best shot.

Nicobe's research had confirmed that Ganymed was not being actively monitored or otherwise patrolled by the Kergans. That was as good as a green light as far as I was concerned. But others were not as impressed.

"Eighteen hours of flight time for this?" Destiny muttered from beside me, her fingers dancing across the navigational console. "It looks like every other space rock I've ever seen."

"That's precisely why we chose it, Destiny," I replied. "Unremarkable is exactly what we need."

The enhanced *Thunder* had cut our travel time to the asteroid dramatically. The eighteen-hour journey across 25 million kilometers would have taken the old *Thunder* days. Our two escort vessels—smaller, less powerful ships—had struggled to keep pace even after their own upgrades. Still, we'd traveled as a unit, a small fleet carrying humanity's slender hopes.

"Final approach," Destiny announced, her voice slipping back into professional mode. "Establishing parking orbit at twenty kilometers' distance."

Queen Zeta floated in her white octahedron capsule near the rear of the bridge. "The Queen appreciates Commander Drake's caution," she said.

Destiny leaned against a console, arms crossed. "Careful's all we've got left—along with bad coffee and mild paranoia.

"So the Queen has been informed," Zeta replied, the plasma within her capsule shifting in patterns that I recognized as amusement.

I ignored them both. "Prepare shuttle for surveying. I want boots on the ground within the hour."

"Technically, there's no ground to put boots on," Destiny said. "More like anchoring to the surface."

"Thank you for the pedantic correction," I said, standing from the command chair. "Prepare the survey team. Zeta, Busto, Nicobe, and the science team will accompany us. And yes, we'll use tethers and anchors."

Two hours later, I stood—or more accurately, floated while my feet rested with the weight of a feather—on the surface of Ganymed. The horizon curved away more dramatically than on larger bodies like the Moon, a constant reminder of the asteroid's modest 34-by-25 kilometer size. Behind me, Zeta's capsule hovered as her nanobots burrowed into the surface, collecting data on composition and structure.

"This asteroid contains abundant resources," Zeta announced, as her nanobots reported back. "Significant quantities of various hydrates and phyllosilicates. These will yield water, methane, ammonia—all the volatiles required for sustainable habitation. Additionally, the Queen's probes have detected significant deposits of iron, titanium, other heavy metals, and rare earth elements."

Busto, decked out in full tactical gear despite the supposedly secure location, nodded approvingly. His bulky frame looked almost comical as he gently bounced with each step, each step making him bounce half a meter in space. "Good defensible position, too. Multiple approaches means multiple avenues to monitor."

I eased forward, each step a deliberate placement of my armor's boots. The gravity here was virtually nonexistent—0.001 Earth gravity meant anything not anchored could drift away with the slightest push. I'd warned everyone extensively about maintaining tethers and anchors at all times, but warnings only went so far when dealing with scientists excited about new discoveries. A running leap could carry you 2.5 kilometers in one jump and escape velocity at the surface was just under 60 kilometers-per-hour.

"Sir, I think you should see this," Busto called, his voice crackling through my helmet comm.

I made my way toward him, careful not to move too quickly. In microgravity, a sudden acceleration meant an equally dramatic deceleration would be needed, and the last thing I wanted was to bounce off into space.

"What have you found?" I asked, coming to a stop beside him at the lip of what appeared to be a massive canyon.

"Natural formation, sir. Extends approximately four kilometers and is sheltered on both sides by solid rock walls."

I peered down into the dark gash in the asteroid's surface. Unlike the Earth, Ganymed had no atmosphere to erode sharp edges, leaving the canyon walls rough and jagged. The shadows stretched deep, untouched by sunlight despite the asteroid's slow ten hour rotation period.

"How deep?" I asked.

"Scans show about six hundred meters at its deepest point," one of the science team replied, a lanky woman whose name I should have remembered but didn't. "Solid rock throughout, with some evidence of metallic deposits."

I nodded, thinking back to our last attempt at a hidden base. "Not like *Luminara*," I said, mostly to myself.

"Sir?" Busto questioned.

"On HideyRock—*Luminara*—the rock wasn't stable. HideyRock is just a rubble pile. Nothing but a bazillion grains of gravel stuck together. We buried the ship when a section collapsed. This is different. Solid rock walls mean we can carve out spaces that won't collapse."

I made a quick decision. "This is it. The canyon gives us natural protection from observation and impacts. We'll establish the base here, with hangar bays carved into the walls and the primary facilities running along the canyon floor."

Destiny's voice came through my comm. "Taking the easy way out, huh? Just find a hole and crawl into it?"

I could hear the smile in her voice. "It's called tactical advantage, XO. Besides, I don't see you down here doing the heavy lifting."

"Someone has to keep *Thunder* from floating away," she replied. "Just make sure you don't float away, either."

By the end of our first day, the combined crews of *Thunder* and her escort ships had established a series of temporary dome habitats along the canyon floor. Each translucent structure was anchored to the surface with deep pitons and tethers, precautions against the nearly non-existent gravity.

Thunder herself rested on the canyon floor, held in place by a series of anchoring cables that made her look like a massive jellyfish with tentacles stretching down to the surface. The sight was both comical and oddly beautiful against the star-filled blackness of space. It was amazing to think that her 15,000 ton mass weighed only 15 tons under Ganymed's weak gravity.

"Environmental systems online in habitats one through four," Nicobe reported, her own crimson dodecahedron hovering near the entrance to the largest dome. "Nicobe suggests beginning crew rotations for rest cycles."

I nodded, watching as crews moved carefully between habitats. Even inside the pressurized domes, the microgravity made movement a constant challenge. Objects had to be secured, and people had to adjust to a world where dropping something meant it would bounce and float away rather than stay down.

"Habitat five having temperature regulation issues," one technician reported. "Working on it now."

I was about to respond when a shout cut through the comm channel.

"Tether failure! We have a loose crew member!"

My head snapped up to see a figure flying away from the work site—a female scientist who had been taking samples from the canyon wall. Her arms flailed uselessly as she rotated, each movement sending her tumbling in a new direction and pushing her further from the asteroid's surface.

"Name?" I demanded, already moving toward the nearest shuttle.

"Dr. Caswell," someone replied. "Her backup tether failed during a sample collection. Her borer must have hit something hard and kicked back."

I reached the shuttle, only to find Destiny already warming up its pods. "I've got this," she said, not looking up from the controls. "You keep the rest of the crew from panicking."

I hesitated, torn between going after the scientist myself and maintaining a command presence.

"Go," I said finally. "But be careful. We don't need two rescues."

Destiny grinned. "When am I not careful?"

I didn't bother answering that particular piece of self-delusion as she sealed the shuttle and pushed off from the surface.

Through my helmet display, I tracked both Destiny's shuttle and the drifting scientist. Dr. Caswell was already nearly a kilometer from the surface and picking up speed as she very probably entered an elliptical orbit around the asteroid's negligible gravity well.

"All crews maintain position and continue operations," I ordered through the general channel. "Rescue is underway. Double-check all tethers and connections."

I watched as Destiny's shuttle closed the distance to the drifting scientist. The shuttle's tractor pods emitting no flares as Destiny matched velocities with the tumbling woman. It was precision flying at its finest—too much thrust would send the shuttle past the target, too little would fail to catch up.

"Almost there," Destiny reported, her voice tight with concentration. "She's tumbling pretty badly."

"Can you compensate?" I asked.

"Please. I've caught worse things while drunk," she

replied, though the tension in her voice betrayed the difficulty of the maneuver.

The shuttle edged closer to the drifting scientist, now a full two kilometers from the asteroid's surface. Destiny fired short bursts from maneuvering thrusters, rotating the shuttle to match the scientist's random tumble.

"Got her," Destiny announced finally.

I watched as the shuttle's airlock door opened and Destiny nudged the shuttle just right so that Caswell drifted into the chamber. A moment later, the airlock door closed and Destiny reported, "Package secured. Returning to base."

A collective sigh of relief went through the command channel. I realized I'd been holding my breath and exhaled slowly.

"Well done, XO," I said. "Find out why that tether failed and how to prevent it from happening again."

"Always with the paperwork," Destiny grumbled, but I could hear the smile in her voice.

With the temporary habitats established, Zeta and Nicobe turned their attention to the genuine work of creating our new base. Using *Thunder*'s nanoforge—a miracle of technology capable of building almost anything given enough raw materials and energy—they began transforming the canyon into a hidden fortress.

I stood with Zeta at the mouth of what would become our main hangar bay, watching as billions of nanobots swarmed across the rock face, breaking down the asteroid material and reconstructing it according to the base plans.

"The nanobots are performing at optimal efficiency," Zeta said, the plasma in her capsule swirling with satisfaction. "The first phase of excavation will be complete within forty-eight Earth hours."

The nanobots worked with eerie precision, carving perfect right angles and smooth surfaces from the jagged rock. Behind them, they left reinforced walls and floors, environmental systems, and power conduits built directly into the structure.

"And the power plant?" I asked.

"Nicobe reports foundation work has begun," Zeta replied. "The fusion reactor will be operational within seven Earth days."

I nodded, impressed despite myself. The nanoforge technology of the Collective Dominion never ceased to amaze me. What would have taken human engineers months or years to build was being constructed in days.

"The base nanoforge will be our priority after the reactor," I said. "Once that's operational, we can expand rapidly."

"The Queen concurs," Zeta replied. "Self-sufficiency is essential for long-term survival."

I watched the nanobots work for a few more minutes, the tiny machines moving with purpose and coordination that made them seem like a single organism. Their work reminded me of ants building a colony, though these particular ants were constructing power systems capable of running a large metropolis.

"I'm going to check on the training exercises," I said finally. "Let me know if anything changes."

I made my way carefully back to the surface, where Busto had organized the Marines and new recruits into training groups. Despite the challenges of microgravity, he had them practicing movement techniques and weapons handling.

"Attention on deck!" Busto called as I approached.

"As you were," I said automatically. "How's it going,

Lieutenant?"

Busto's expression was as stern as ever. "Making progress, sir. The new recruits are adapting to microgravity operations. Some faster than others."

I watched as a group of Marines practiced moving with grappling guns, firing anchored lines and pulling themselves across the asteroid's surface. Others worked on target practice, compensating for the way microgravity affected ballistics.

Throughout the canyon and across the asteroid's surface, similar scenes played out. Science teams collected samples and cataloged resources. Engineering crews established monitoring stations and communication relays. Everyone moved with purpose, driven by the knowledge that our survival depended on making this rock into a defensible home.

As I stood watching our makeshift community take shape, I felt an unfamiliar sensation—something almost like hope. For months, we'd been running and hiding, struggling to survive against overwhelming odds. Now, for the first time, we were building something.

Ganymed wasn't much to look at—just a misshapen rock tumbling through space—but it was ours. And if all went according to plan, it would become the foundation for something greater: our first real stronghold in the fight to reclaim Earth.

I just hoped the Kergans would give us enough time to finish it.

42

I sipped lukewarm coffee from a squeeze bulb—the indignity of low-gravity dining—while scrolling through inventory reports on my tablet. The liquid formed a perfect sphere in my mouth before I swallowed, a sensation I doubted I'd ever get used to. Three days on this godforsaken rock, and eating still felt like a toddler's science experiment gone wrong. The construction crews promised artificial gravity "any day now," but I'd heard that particular tune enough times to compose a symphony.

Ganymed Base's main habitation dome was supposed to be our crown jewel—the first permanent human outpost hidden on an asteroid. Right now, it looked more like a half-finished warehouse with pretensions. At least the mess hall had actual tables bolted to the floor, even if everything on them had to be secured with velcro, magnets, or, in my case, embarrassing adult sippy cups.

I stabbed at the screen with my finger, scrolling through the latest munitions inventory. The numbers swam before my eyes, a bureaucratic lullaby threatening to put me to sleep despite the caffeine.

"Lieutenant Commander Drake appears to be having fun with paperwork," I muttered to myself, mimicking Zeta's royal third-person speech pattern. The self-mockery pulled a faint smile from me as I tried to spear a floating protein cube with a fork. The cube dodged my attack, demonstrating better evasive maneuvers than me at *Thunder*'s controls.

The mess hall door slid open with a pneumatic hiss. Through the opening bounded Sofia and Destiny, moving in the peculiar low-gravity lope that made everyone look like they were taking part in the moon Olympics. Their synchronized movements might have been comical if not for the identical expressions of grim determination they wore.

I knew those faces. Those weren't the faces of people about to join me for a pleasant meal of floating food cubes. Those were the faces of people bringing news that would ruin my day.

"Let me guess," I said, setting down my tablet. "The toilets are backing up again, and somehow it's the captain's problem."

Sofia didn't even crack a smile as she secured herself to the seat across from me, blonde fuzz covering her scalp. Beside her, Destiny gripped the edge of the table, her dark eyes focused and serious.

"Not the plumbing this time," Destiny said, her voice low. "Sofia had another flashback."

I felt my spine straighten, a pavlovian response to those words.

"About what?" I asked, instinctively checking to make sure we were alone in the mess hall.

Sofia leaned forward, anchoring herself with a hand on the table. "Project Warped Eclipse," she said, her slight

German accent more pronounced when she whispered. "The information connected with what we heard before."

I nodded, remembering the cryptic references we'd encountered. "Tell me everything."

Sofia's blue eyes took on that distant look they always did when she was sorting through implant-derived memories. "Project Warped Eclipse is the codename for the Kergans' program to recover the Noble Phylactery," she said. "It's not just a single operation—it's their most classified strategic initiative spanning years."

"The Noble Phylactery," I repeated, my gut sinking at the familiar name.

Sofia said, her voice steady despite the gravity of her words, "According to the memories from my implant, the Kergans believe it's the key to absolute dominance over humanity and other species. It's supposedly capable of manipulating the connection between physical beings and their glyphshades and warp space-time."

I frowned, mentally connecting dots. "So we're talking about a weapon that could control or sever the link between beings and their consciousness in the Syderealium?" The implications were staggering. Such a device might render the most powerful flairsparked completely vulnerable. People like me.

"More than that," Sofia confirmed. "The memories suggest it could potentially override or rewrite the energlyphic patterns of entire populations."

My coffee bulb hung forgotten in my hand. "Mass mind control," I translated. "Or worse."

"Exactly," Destiny interjected. "And here's where it gets personal." She glanced at Sofia, who nodded for her to continue. "Sofia's flashback shows that my escape from Ban'ach wasn't what we thought."

My stomach tightened. Ban'ach had captured and held destiny for three days. We'd only recently helped her recover some of those lost memories. The idea that there was more to the story sent a spike of protective anger through me.

"What do you mean?" I asked, dreading the answer.

Sofia reached across the table, her hand finding mine. The touch was grounding, even as her words sent my thoughts spinning. "Ban'ach let Destiny escape," she breathed. "It was calculated. She had implanted subtle compulsions in Destiny's mind to ensure she would eventually seek out information about the Phylactery."

"I was a tracking device," Destiny said, her voice flat but with an undercurrent of rage. "A bloodhound for that sydereal bitch to follow."

The realization hit me like a railgun round. "She wanted you to lead her to the Phylactery," I intoned. "But how would you—" I stopped as another piece clicked into place. "She knew we'd try to help you recover your memories."

Sofia nodded. "Ban'ach anticipated Destiny would eventually remember fragments about the Phylactery. She also calculated that we would investigate further, especially after your encounter with her in the Syderealium."

"When I banished her ancillary," I said, thinking back to that strange battle in the realm of pure consciousness. "She was hoping we'd do her dirty work—find the Phylactery for her so she could swoop in and take it."

"And my memories were the breadcrumb trail," Destiny said bitterly.

I let out a string of curses that would have made a space dock worker blush, finishing with, "Holy jumping proton balls." It wasn't my most eloquent moment, but it captured my feelings adequately.

"So we've been manipulated this entire time?" I asked, the familiar heat of anger mixing with something colder—the realization of how easily we'd been played. "All our research into Nekufima, the connections to ancient sydereal artifacts..."

"Partially," Sofia said, her calm voice a counterpoint to my rising indignation. "But Ban'ach's plan had a fatal flaw."

"Me," I said, suddenly understanding. "When I banished her ancillary glyphshade during our encounter, I broke whatever psychic leash she had on Destiny."

Sofia nodded. "The implant memories suggest Ban'ach would have maintained a subtle connection to Destiny—one that would alert her when Destiny came close to information about the Phylactery. But that connection was severed when you confronted her in the Syderealium."

Destiny's mouth curved into a fierce smile. "So the bitch's plan failed. She can't track me anymore."

I wasn't so quick to celebrate. "Maybe, but we're still operating partly on her script. We've been investigating exactly what she wanted us to investigate."

A moment of silence settled between us, broken only by the distant hum of the habitation dome's environmental systems. In the low gravity, a drop of coffee escaped from my bulb and drifted on a long parabolic trajectory between us like a tiny amber planet.

"This is too big for just the three of us to decide," Destiny finally said, swiping at the floating droplet. It broke apart into smaller spheres that clung to her hand. "The whole command team needs to know what we're dealing with."

I considered this, then nodded. "You're right. This changes our whole strategic position." I ran a hand through my hair, feeling the strands float upward in the minimal gravity. "Zeta's been intent on getting *Luminara* salvaged from HideyRock so she can return to the Collective Dominion and rally support against Arctis. But this Phylactery situation affects both our worlds."

"Zeta should have a say in what *Thunder* does next," Sofia insisted. "The Noble Phylactery could destabilize the power balance in both the Collective Dominion and throughout human space. If the Kergans obtain it, or if Ban'ach gets her hands on it..."

She didn't need to finish. We'd all seen enough of what the Soul Ravager was capable of. Giving someone like that the power to manipulate consciousness itself was like handing a pyromaniac a supernova in a bottle.

"Agreed," I said, making the decision. "I'll schedule a full command briefing on *Thunder*." I picked up my tablet and sent the notification with a few quick taps. "Two hours from now in the ship's briefing room. That should give everyone time to wrap up their current tasks."

As the confirmation pings sounded from Sofia's and Destiny's tablets, I looked at my two closest friends—my executive officer and my partner. Both had been unwilling players in larger games, both had suffered, and both had come through stronger. The thought of how they'd been used made me want to hunt Ban'ach across the stars, but for now, we had more immediate concerns.

"Until then," I said, offering them the protein cube container, "anyone want to join me in the culinary delights of asteroid base cuisine? I recommend the brown ones—they taste almost, but not entirely, unlike actual food."

Destiny snorted. "Pass. I'm holding out for gravity before my next meal."

Sofia shook her head with a small smile. "How can you joke at a time like this?"

I shrugged, watching another coffee droplet escape and

join the miniature solar system forming above our table. "Because sometimes the alternative is screaming into the void, and that tends to use up oxygen." I captured the wayward drops with a napkin. "Besides, if we're going to face cosmic horrors and mind-controlling artifacts, we might as well do it with a sense of humor."

And despite everything, they both smiled—small, worried smiles, but smiles nonetheless. In the precarious balance of our lives, sometimes that was enough to keep the darkness at bay, at least for a little while.

Two hours. Then we'd decide how to deal with artifacts of unimaginable power, soul-ravaging enemies, and an interstellar conspiracy. But first, I had to finish my floating lunch.

43

The faces around the briefing table stared at me like I was announcing the end of the world. Maybe I was. The artificial gravity tugged at my shoulders—a constant half-gee reminder we were floating in the void on nothing but metal, hope, and the collective stubbornness of *Thunder*'s crew. I cleared my throat and wondered, not for the first time, how commanding officers throughout history had delivered news this grim without their voices cracking like teenagers at a school dance.

"Let's get started," I said, tapping the console to bring up the holographic display. "What we're discussing doesn't leave this room."

The blue glow of the display illuminated the gathered faces: Destiny to my right, her expression carefully neutral but her fingers drumming silently against her thigh—a tell I'd known since we were street kids. Sofia sat beside her, back straight as a ruler, her blonde fuzz making her seem softer and more innocent. Busto's perpetually suspicious eyes scanned the room, as if expecting an ambush from behind the ventilation panels. Lynda Brooks and her daughter Phoebe sat side by side, their family resemblance striking in the artificial light. Dr. Chen's face remained an impenetrable mask of professional detachment.

Across from me, the crimson dodecahedron housing Nicobe hovered slightly above her chair, and next to her, the royal octahedral capsule containing Queen Zeta pulsed with subtle patterns of stellar plasma—like watching a star breathe.

"Project Warped Eclipse," I began, letting the words hang in the recycled air. "That's what the Kergan scientists called it. A plan to capture and control an entity of immense power."

I swiped through captured intelligence files, bringing up images of laboratories, strange containment devices, and glyphs that seemed to writhe across the display like living things.

"The Noble Phylactery is an ancient artifact, possibly predating even the Collective Dominion. From what we've pieced together, it contains—or imprisons—a being called Nekufima."

"An Astral Titan." Destiny said.

"Not exactly," I replied, leaning forward. "Something... different. From what Sofia's implant data shows, and what Destiny recovered from her memories, Nekufima is something like a cosmic wish-granter. A being of immense power that can reshape reality according to the desires of whoever controls the Phylactery."

Busto snorted. "So we're chasing a magic lamp? Should I start calling you Aladdin, Commander?"

"If it grants wishes," Destiny cut in, her voice sharp, "I'd wish for you to develop a sense of humor, Busto."

A ghost of a smile crossed his face before vanishing back

into professional stoicism.

"The Kergans believe it's genuine enough," I continued. "And they've assigned Ban'ach to retrieve it."

I saw Destiny's hand move unconsciously to her temple, where the memory blocks had been placed. Sofia's fingers twitched toward her sidearm—a reflex born of recent combat.

"We need to decide, as a command team, whether this represents a genuine threat worth pursuing, or a wild goose chase that will divert our resources from other operations."

Zeta's capsule pulsed brighter, drawing all eyes to her.

"Queen Zeta can provide illumination on this matter. The Noble Phylactery is known to the igna as the *Zha'fesii Nerithar*—the Vessel of Unbound Change. It features in the oldest of our legends, from when our ancestors first left the surfaces of stars to explore the void between."

The plasma patterns within her capsule shifted, creating what looked like ancient pictograms.

"Nekufima is not a myth. Zeta's royal lineage has passed down warnings of this entity for millennia. Unlike a normal Astral Titan, which is a creature of the Syderealium, Nekufima exists both within and without—a being that can bridge the gap between thought and reality. The Phylactery enables this capability."

Dr. Chen leaned forward, glasses catching the light. "Are we talking about a biological entity or something else entirely?"

"Neither and both," Zeta replied. "The igna have long theorized that Nekufima represents a consciousness that evolved differently than our own—not from matter organizing into life, but from the very fabric of possibility condensing into awareness."

"That explains absolutely nothing," Destiny muttered,

just loud enough to be heard.

I shot her a look, but couldn't entirely disagree. "The point is, if Ban'ach gets her hands on this thing—"

"We're cosmically screwed," Destiny finished.

"Sounds like a glorified genie in a bottle to me," she added with a dismissive wave. "Rub the lamp, get three wishes, mind the fine print."

"A genie who could grant Ban'ach's wishes would be catastrophic," I reminded her. "Imagine her with the power to reshape reality according to Kergan ambitions."

Destiny's smirk faded. She'd spent three days as Ban'ach's prisoner. The Soul Ravager had stolen her memories of that time, but we'd recovered enough for Destiny to understand the danger better than most.

"Nicobe must concur with Her Majesty's assessment," the chief engineer's crimson capsule bobbed slightly as she spoke. "Such power in Kergan hands would tip the balance not just in your human conflict, but potentially in the royal struggle against Arctis as well."

The room erupted into cross-talk. Busto argued for focusing on defending Earth rather than "chasing fairy tales across the galaxy." Dr. Chen countered that her analysis of Sofia's implant data suggested the Phylactery was more than myth. Phoebe worried about *Thunder*'s readiness for such a mission, while her mother Lynda calculated logistics for maintaining Ganymed Base in our absence.

I let them argue, watching the divisions form naturally: the ignas concerned with their Dominion civil war. The humans focused on Earth's immediate defense. Both valid perspectives, both insufficient on their own.

I caught Sofia's eye across the table. She gave me the slightest nod—we were thinking the same thing. This wasn't a matter of either/or. It was both/and.

I raised my hand, and the arguments gradually subsided.

"Queen Zeta," I said, turning to the royal capsule. "What's your assessment?"

The plasma within her geometric housing swirled contemplatively before she answered.

"The threat cannot be ignored. Neither can Zeta's duty to her people. The royalist faction requires leadership in the struggle against Arctis's forces." Her capsule dimmed slightly. "Zeta and her Royal Guard must return to Dominion space."

"You're leaving us?" Destiny asked, surprise breaking through her usual composure.

"Not abandoning, Destiny," Zeta corrected. "But diverging paths. *Thunder* and her crew must pursue this threat, while Zeta rallies the royalists. Zeta will permit Nicobe and most of the kavreni crew from *Luminara* to remain with *Thunder* to provide their expertise."

I nodded slowly. "Thank you, Zeta. We won't move until the base is complete, *Luminara* is salvaged and repaired, and you're ready to depart."

"So what I'm hearing," Busto said, leaning back in his chair with arms crossed, "is that *Thunder* is about to embark on a galactic quest to recover a magic lamp before the mean wicked witch can use it to enslave humanity. Did I miss anything?"

"Just that your sense of wonder died somewhere around your fifth deployment, Gunny," Destiny quipped. "Some of us still appreciate the occasional space adventure."

"You'll appreciate it less when we're outgunned in enemy territory," he growled, but I caught the hint of affection beneath his gruffness.

Sofia tapped her temple, where her Kergan implant

resided beneath the skin. "Both my implant and Destiny's recovered memories contain fragments of information about the Phylactery's location. We'll spend the next couple of weeks analyzing that data to determine our initial heading."

"Great," Lynda Brooks said, her lips quirking into a half-smile. "So you all get to zoom off on a grand adventure while we poor souls are left behind on this rock with no way back to Earth."

"I'll leave a shuttle," I promised. "If things get dicey, you'll have an evacuation option."

"How generous," she replied, but her tone was light. "Just try not to get yourselves killed chasing cosmic bedtime stories."

The meeting dissolved into technical discussions—supply requirements, crew rotations, weapons load outs. By the time we finished, my head was pounding with the weight of what we were undertaking.

Three weeks blurred past in a haze of activity. Ganymed Base transformed from a rough outpost to a proper installation, with defensive emplacements, living quarters, and maintenance facilities for small craft. The kavreni engineers worked alongside our human teams to salvage *Luminara*. The royal yacht, once damaged in our escape from Virelia, now gleamed under the harsh lights of our makeshift drydock.

Thunder underwent her own transformation. Every corridor and storage compartment bulged with supplies—food, ammunition, spare parts, medical supplies. We'd stripped the base of everything we could justify taking. The ship felt less like a warship and more like a hoarder's den, with crates stacked in corners and equipment lashed to walls.

"You can barely move in here," I complained to Sofia as we squeezed past a rack of pressure suits blocking half the corridor to our quarters.

"Better cramped than hungry six weeks from nowhere," she replied, practical as always. "Besides, we'll use it up faster than you think."

That night—our last before departure—I lay beside Sofia in our narrow bed, listening to her steady breathing as she slept. Sleep eluded me, my mind racing with contingencies, routes, threats. When exhaustion finally pulled me under, I expected darkness.

Instead, I found myself standing in the Syderealium.

The familiar not-space stretched around me, the indescribable colors and impossible geometries that made up this realm between realms. My glyphshade—the manifestation of my consciousness here—stood on what appeared to be a path of crystallized light stretching through the void.

"Hello?" I called out, my voice simultaneously soundless and deafening.

"Kory Drake," answered a voice that seemed to come from everywhere at once. "The human who wounded a Soul Ravager. The mortal who defied an Astral Titan."

For a moment, I thought it was Pyrakos—the Titan I'd encountered at the Astral Maul. But this voice was different—like honey poured over broken glass, sweet and dangerous, and distinctly feminine.

A shape coalesced before me, neither wholly human nor entirely alien. It shifted continuously, adopting features that seemed calculated to appeal to my aesthetic preferences, then morphing into forms that triggered primitive fear responses.

"Nekufima," I whispered, somehow certain.

"You know me," the entity purred, pleasure clear in her fluctuating form. "How delightful."

"How is this possible?" I demanded. "You're imprisoned in the Phylactery."

"Am I?" She drifted closer, and I felt an unsettling combination of attraction and revulsion. "Perhaps. Perhaps not. Perhaps I am merely reaching out through the bars of my cage to touch the mind of a fascinating creature."

Her form settled momentarily into something almost human—a figure with voluptuous female curves and facial features that reminded me simultaneously of everyone I'd ever found beautiful.

"You are extraordinary, Kory Drake. A flairsparked human with minimal training who navigates the Syderealium by instinct alone. Who defies beings that should crush him like an insect." Her voice lowered to a seductive whisper. "I have been watching you."

"Why contact me now?" I managed to ask, fighting the urge to step back.

"Because you seek me," she replied, circling me like a predator. "Because I wish to see the quality of my would-be... captor? Rescuer? Which are you, I wonder?"

"Neither," I said firmly. "I'm just trying to keep you out of dangerous hands."

Nekufima laughed, the sound rippling through the Syderealium like shattered bells. "Such nobility! Such purpose! I do so love mortals and their certainties." She leaned close, her essence brushing against my glyphshade. "I invite you, Kory Drake. Come find me. Test your will against mine. See if you are worthy of what you seek."

"This isn't a game," I growled.

"Everything is a game," she countered. "And I have been playing for epochs. But you... you might be a player worth engaging with."

Her form began to dissolve, spreading into the fabric of the Syderealium itself. "Until we meet in the flesh, brave human. I shall count the moments..."

I woke with a gasp, sitting bolt upright in bed. Sofia stirred beside me but didn't wake. My heart hammered against my ribs, and sweat cooled rapidly on my skin.

That wasn't a dream. I'd been pulled into the Syderealium while asleep—something that had never happened before. Somehow, I'd made contact with Nekufima, which should have been impossible if she was truly imprisoned.

Unless she was far more powerful than we understood. Unless the "prison" was more permeable than anyone realized.

I stared into the darkness, questioning everything. Were we chasing a genuine threat, or walking into a trap crafted by an entity playing games beyond our comprehension? Was I risking my crew on a fool's errand, or facing the greatest danger humanity had encountered since the Kergan invasion?

Dawn found me still awake, watching Sofia sleep while my mind churned. In a few hours, we'd depart—committed to a course with no guaranteed outcome and dangers I couldn't fully anticipate.

Yet for all my doubts, one certainty remained. If Ban'ach found the Phylactery first—if the Soul Ravager gained the power to reshape reality according to Kergan desires—everything and everyone I loved would be at risk.

I thought of Earth, still struggling under occupation. Of Destiny, who'd survived Ban'ach's captivity once already. Of Sofia, sleeping beside me, brilliant and fierce and determined.

I didn't know if we could find the Phylactery. I didn't know if we could contain Nekufima's power or resist its seduction. But I knew with absolute certainty that we had to try.

The universe had dealt us an impossible hand. We would play it anyway.

As the first alarms signaled the start of the day, I made my decision. *Thunder* would sail into the unknown, not because we were guaranteed victory, but because the alternative wasn't something I could live with.

Some fights you choose. Others choose you. Either way, you face them.

Ban'ach would not get the Phylactery. Not while I had breath in my body and a ship beneath my feet.

That much, at least, was certain.

The End

Please rate or review my book online! As an indie author, I *depend* on your reviews to legitimize my books in the eyes of those who have not read them.

About Joseph McRae Palmer

Joseph McRae Palmer writes speculative fiction. He is also an engineer in the telecommunications industry and holds a Ph.D. in Electrical Engineering from Brigham Young University. Joseph was born in Provo, Utah, but raised in Sitka, Alaska, and graduated from high school in 1993. Later, he served as a missionary for two years in central Mexico. He and his wife of more than two decades, Beatriz Palmer, are parents of one son and three daughters, and as of 2023 they reside in northern Utah, USA.

Joseph's fiction site: www.josephmcraepalmer.com

Printed in Dunstable, United Kingdom

67337050R00231